LORD G

Sons of the Marquess

Book 5

A Regency Romance

by Mary Kingswood

Lord Gilbert: Sons of the Marquess Book 5

Published by Sutors Publishing

ISBN: 978-1-912167-10-4 (paperback)

Cover design by: Shayne Rutherford of Darkmoon Graphics

Lord Gilbert: Sons of the Marquess Book 5

The dramatic conclusion to the series! A traditional Regency romance, drawing room rather than bedroom.

Lord Gilbert Marford is in disgrace. He joined the Hussars to stay out of trouble. Instead, he quarrelled with half his fellow officers, seduced the wives of three of them, got himself shot in a duel and sustained an injury that might end his career. Now he's being sent home like a naughty schoolboy, and he's not happy about it. So when an opportunity arises to run away, he's not about to let a little snow stop him.

Miss Genista Hamilton accepts her place as the youngest daughter of the family, staying at home to look after her father and help with his work as a country physician. She knows she'll never marry, and has never even thought of love. Until the day a young man with the face of an angel appears, unconscious, on her doorstep in the middle of a snowstorm. But how can the lowly daughter of a physician ever aspire to marry the son of a marquess? It can only lead to trouble...

Book 5 of the 5-book Sons of the Marquess series, each a complete story with a HEA.

***About Sons of the Marquess:** when the ninth Marquess of Carrbridge finds himself short of funds, his five younger brothers have to make a choice: take up a career to support their lavish lifestyle or marry an heiress. But love has a strange way of appearing when it's least expected...*

Book 0: The Earl of Deveron (a novella, free to mailing list subscribers)

Book 1: Lord Reginald

Book 2: Lord Humphrey

Book 3: Lord Augustus

Book 4: Lord Montague

Book 5: Lord Gilbert

Table of contents

Prologue

The chambers of Markham, Willerton-Forbes and Browning were enjoying their usual afternoon somnolence. Sir Rathbone Willerton-Forbes had had but one appointment at noon, after which he had dictated one letter to his clerk, Eversley, had read three letters delivered with the mid-day post, and perused the announcements of births, marriages and deaths in the newspaper. He had reached that depressing age when more of his acquaintance were to be found amongst the reports of the deceased than elsewhere. After that, exhausted by his labours, he drank one glass of port and snoozed in his comfortable chair behind the desk until such time as the clock struck the hour appointed for him to make his way home.

A sharp rap on the door announced the arrival of Eversley.

"A package just arrived for you, Sir Rathbone. Delivered by hand this moment. It being addressed to *'The Lawyer Acting for The Most Noble Marquess of Carrbridge'*, I dare presume it is for your eyes."

"Most Noble?" He sighed. "What is the world coming to when a man writes to a marquess without knowing the correct manner of address?"

Eversley had no answer to this rather sweeping question, so he bustled about tidying the discarded newspaper, arranging the pens and inkpot in their stand, straightening the sander and writing mat, placing the fire irons in a neat line.

Sir Rathbone stared at the unassuming package. Wrapped in brown paper and string, it was very light, as if there might be nothing inside it at all. He sighed. He could, of course, lock the package away in a drawer, and deal with it some other time. It was late and he wanted to go home, to enjoy his bath and the ministrations of his very efficient valet, to dress for dinner and stroll round to his club to eat. Then he would spend a quiet evening in pleasant conversation with some of his friends, just as he did every day of his life now, since his wife had inconsiderately died before him, leaving him quite alone in the world.

But duty was a difficult habit to shake off. Reaching for his pocket knife, he snipped the string, unfolded the brown paper and drew forth the single sheet of paper residing within.

"Shall I call you a hackney carriage, sir, or shall you walk home today?" Eversley said, looking up from his tidying.

Sir Rathbone gave a strangled sound.

"Sir? Is you having a seizure, sir? Shall I send for the physician?"

There was a long silence, then Sir Rathbone threw the paper forcefully to the desk. "Oh God!" he cried. "Oh, dear God!"

Eversley, having never heard his employer use such language before, was struck dumb with shock.

"This is a disaster," Sir Rathbone said. "The ramifications— No, it does not bear thinking of."

"Sir?"

"This, Eversley," said Sir Rathbone, picking up the paper and waving it under Eversley's nose, "is a special licence. It proves, beyond a shadow of doubt, that the eighth Marquess of Carrbridge was legally married to Miss Amelia Gartmore several months before he married Miss Adela March. And there was issue, Eversley. There was issue from that marriage. A son. What was the boy's name? Benjamin, I believe. Yes, Ben Gartmore is the true heir, and therefore the present Marquess of Carrbridge is not the legal heir. Is illegitimate, in point of fact. Oh, dear Lord, whatever is to be done?"

He put his head in his hands and groaned in despair.

1: A Winter Journey

Captain Lord Gilbert Marford was so angry he could barely form the words.

"Sent home like a schoolboy!" he hissed in a low voice. "It is the outside of enough! Who do they think I am, to be treated so? I joined the Hussars to fight the French, not kick my heels in Yorkshire."

"They might let you fight the French if you stopped fighting your fellow officers," Davy, his batman, said, without looking up from his task of folding shirts.

"I never minded being sent home from Eton, it was almost a point of honour to be rusticated once or twice a year, but I am an adult now! How could they do this to me?"

"Daresay you never got rusticated from Eton for bedding someone's wife," Davy said. "Pass me that coat, will you, Gil?"

"Actually, I did, once," Gil said, instantly diverted. "Did you never hear of it? Maybe it was when you were away in Harrogate. The Latin master was a dry old stick, but he had the most luscious wife imaginable whom he neglected shamefully. She had a penchant for activities that would have astonished her husband. A few of them would have astonished the Roman Emperors, I suspect. Well, *some* of the Emperors, anyway."

Davy looked up in amusement. "Did she make you dress up a toga?"

"Ha! Not quite, but she was the greatest fun imaginable, until her husband caught us in bed one afternoon."

"Really, Gil!" But Davy was laughing. Having grown up with Gil, he was quite unshockable.

"I know, and I was supposed to be in a class with Mr Cornish, the history master. Henry the Eighth. Well, he had six wives, and I never quite saw why I should not, too."

"But at least they were his own wives," Davy said, turning back to his packing.

"Well, where is the fun in that? I am the last sensible one in the family, do you realise that, Davy? All my brothers are married now, even Monty, and I never thought to see *that*. I always liked Monty. At least he never lectured me like Carrbridge does. *You are such a trial to me, Gil. Think of the family honour. Why can you not be more like Reggie... or Humphrey... or Gus... or Monty?* Bah! At least I have been out of his disapproving eye these last few months. Sometimes I wish I were not the brother of a marquess. That is the worst of this business, being sent back to Drummoor. I had rather be flogged."

"Do you have to go? Can't you just head for London and enjoy yourself until the fuss dies down?"

"If only that were possible! But no, Colonel Jefferson has written to Carrbridge and if I fail to turn up, or disappear later, he is to write at once, and I shall be cashiered and that will be the end of it. He will really do it this time, he says. It is so annoying. There is no real harm in what I do, Davy, *you* know that."

"Aye, you get bored, that's all it is, and then you get into mischief. We were as bad as each other as boys, and my father was far stuffier than yours about it. *'I'm very disappointed in you, David,'* he would say, with that awful glowering look."

He paused, and Gil clapped him on the shoulder sympathetically. "He would be more disappointed now, if he knew you had ended up as my batman. He never liked me. Thought me too ramshackle by half, and a very bad influence on you."

"Well, so you are," Davy said, grinning. "But you saved me from a worse fate after the old man lost his money. Heaven knows what I'd have done if you hadn't taken me on."

"Well, I thought you would be fun, and look how wrong I was," Gil said in aggrieved tones. "You do nothing but lecture me now, you old devil."

"I can't afford any decent entertainment any more, so I amuse myself by nagging you. And you are getting worse, you know. If it were just the gaming and an occasional scuffle with the other officers, no one would mind that. But the Major's wife, Gil! And you really should take care with that leg of yours. Every time you ride too hard or push yourself too far, you damage it. After that horse race with Captain Walters, the sawbones was threatening to cut it off."

"Stuff!" Gil said. "Nothing wrong with my leg now. Just a bit of a limp, no more than that."

"You should take care, that's all I'm saying. There, that's the last box packed. I'll get the carriage brought round."

"Carriage!" Gil said in frustration. "How humiliating to be driven about like a dowager."

"Physician's orders," Davy said firmly. "Got to look after that leg, Gil, or you won't have a leg to worry about."

~~~~~

The first flakes of snow were falling just as they turned in to the inn yard to change horses. The place was in chaos, ostlers rushing hither and thither with teams of horses, dealing with several carriages at once, to a chorus of angry shouts.

"Sorry, nothing to spare just now," a harassed ostler told them. "Everything is out, and not a pair rested enough to put to the traces. Go inside, sir, sit by the fire. Rest for an hour or two."

"Rest!" Gil expostulated, but the man had already gone. "I hardly need rest when I have been sitting on my rear for the last two hours. We will not make London today at this rate."

"It was always unlikely," Davy said. "Specially at this time of year. Look at the weather! If it settles in, we'll be lucky to make it to Sittingbourne."

"Pfft! What is a bit of snow? I have been out in worse. Surely there must be some horses for us."

He strode into the capacious stables, dodging a steaming team of bays being led to stalls. The ostler was right, there were no horses left that were fresh enough to be put to a carriage. But there was one horse...

"You there! What is your name?"

The stable boy jumped, looked around as if wondering who was being addressed, then licked his lips nervously. "Robbie, sir."

"Well, Robbie, this hack of yours... is it for hire?"

"Aye, sir, but—"

"Saddle him."

"But—"

"Just do as I say. Here—" He pulled out his purse and pushed several silver coins into the boy's hands, and had the satisfaction of
~~~~~

seeing his eyes widen. "Now saddle him, Robbie. And if you get in trouble for it, tell them that it was for Lord Gilbert Marford."

"Aye, milord. At once, milord."

It was the work of a few minutes for Robbie to prepare the horse, although the animal danced and blew and side-stepped as if, for some unfathomable reason, he was loathe to leave his warm stable to venture out into the falling snow. Gil swung himself into the saddle, and then, as pain shot through his leg, remembered why he should have used the mounting block. He grimaced, took a deep breath and fought down the nausea that assaulted him. Then he trotted into the yard, the horse dancing about the whole time.

Davy was still standing beside their carriage, chatting amicably to a couple of the tap boys. Gil would have ridden straight past his batman with a cheerful wave had Davy not grabbed the reins, causing the horse to half rear.

"What are you doing, Gil?" he cried, more fear than anger on his face.

"What does it look like? You can hardly expect me to sit here like an old woman for hours. With luck, this fellow will get me to London by nightfall."

"With luck? Gil, you're insane! It's snowing hard, you'll never make it, and think of your leg. Gil! For God's sake, Gil!"

With a quick jerk on the reins, the horse was free of Davy's restraint. With a snort, the animal bounded forward and took off through the arch, and then they were on the London road at a fast canter.

Gil laughed aloud in delight, as the snow spat freezing drops into his face. All around him, the snow fell softly, not heavy but steady now, the flakes drifting gently to earth. Already the road had a thin covering, the dark lines of coach tracks fading to invisibility.

The horse soon lost its initial enthusiasm and slowed his pace, as Gil settled down for the long ride back to London. They passed a few coaches, the drivers and outside passengers muffled up to their eyebrows, and one small town, its inns beacons of warmth in the white wasteland, but Gil was not minded to stop. That would mean admitting he was wrong to attempt the ride, and that he could never do. So he pressed on.

It was not a comfortable ride. His leg throbbed abominably, and as the snow whirled ever faster around him, it made him feel queer and dizzy. The cold seeped into his very bones. But the horse was a good one, and needed little direction, and after a while Gil stopped noticing the cold. He rode on, although the horse had slowed to a walk. And the snow fell more and more thickly. Perhaps he would stop at the next inn after all, but the thought was hazy, as if his mind were filled with treacle. But he had seen no inn for a while now, and no coaches either. Nothing to do but push on, always onwards. Sooner or later there would be an inn.

The horse stopped. Gil jerked up from his position low to the creature's neck. He had almost fallen asleep! That would never do, not in this bitter weather. He tried to kick the animal forwards but somehow his legs would not move. He flicked the reins instead, and the horse jolted into motion, almost tipping Gil off backwards.

And now that he had begun, the animal seemed to have found a sudden burst of energy for he cantered along in a manner which had Gil screaming from the pain in his leg. Where had this agony come from? And why was he so hot, with an inch of snow on his shoulders? The weather had worsened considerably, for it was almost dark. He could barely see the horse's head in front of him.

An inn… he must find an inn…

There was a light! Like a lighthouse in the gloom, ahead shone a thin golden beam. Gil pulled on the reins, but the horse tossed its head imperiously and moved even faster. Panic swept over Gil. He must stop! If he rode past the light then he might never find another one. He had to stop, at all costs!

He pulled again on the reins, heaving with every last ounce of strength remaining to him. The horse reared, and with a cry of despair, Gil slid sideways.

The ground was hard, knocking the breath out of him. For a moment he lay, too stupefied to move. The silence was absolute. Not a creature moved in this white wasteland, not an owl was abroad, nor a fox, not so much as a hedgehog rustling in the undergrowth. Was he dead? He felt neither heat nor cold, only the dull, relentless pain of his leg. He was tired, so tired. If he lay still, if he kept his eyes closed, he would drift off to sleep and he would feel better in the morning, he was sure of it. At Drummoor. He would be home soon.

No.

Something was wrong. If he slept... he must not sleep, somehow he understood that.

The light. There was a light. With a massive effort, he lifted his head. Yes! There it was, shining unwaveringly through the white shroud of the falling snow. He tried to get up, but his legs would not work. But he must reach the light, he must! His head was as thick as soup, but he knew that much. No matter how great the struggle, he must reach the light. Slowly, trembling with the strain, he raised himself a little on his arms and shifted an inch nearer to the light.

~~~~~

Genista rather enjoyed the times when her father went away. It didn't happen often, but maybe once or twice a month he would be summoned to a patient so distant that he would be required to stay overnight, and occasionally, if the patient took a long while to die or the baby was slow to be born, there would be a second night
~~~~~

away too. With the snow so thick now, surely this would be one of those occasions.

She checked the roast in the hot oven, and the vegetables in the slow oven. The soup was simmering, and the fruit pie was ready to go into the hot oven as soon as the chicken was out of it. She watched Betty lay the table in the kitchen — another treat, to eat off the plain wooden table, with no ceremony and no need to change her gown. She sighed with pleasure. She loved her father dearly, of course she did, but he did like everything just so. *'We must maintain standards, daughter,'* he always said. *'Your mother would wish it.'* And of course he was absolutely right — Father was always right — but just occasionally, it was lovely not to worry about doing things properly.

She had just closed the door of the oven when she thought she heard a noise, an odd sort of tapping sound.

"What was that? Did you hear something?"

"I didn't hear nothing, Miss Genista. Most likely it's the wind catching the—"

"Hush! There it is again. Did you hear it?"

"No, Miss."

"You don't need to be so formal, Betty. You can call me Genista when Father isn't here. Everyone else does, after all."

"That seems disrespectful— Oh! I heard it! It's at the door, Miss Genista."

"This door? Why would anyone come to the kitchen door? Oh, the light, of course. The front of the house is dark."

She went through to the scullery, where a lamp hung on a hook over the sink, shining out through the uncurtained window. There it was again, a definite tapping sound, but faint. Perhaps Betty was right, and it was just a tree or a broken branch knocking against the door. But there was no harm in checking. She slid open the bolts and opened the door.

On the doorstep, half covered in snow and just visible in the thin light of the lamp, lay a dark shape. It groaned.

"It's a man," she said. "Quick, Betty, help me get him inside. Heavens, look how wet he is, and cold! His face is frozen. Quick, we must take him through to the kitchen. Can you carry his feet? That's it. One... two... three... lift."

The man screamed, and then silence fell.

"To the rug... in front of... the range..." Genista puffed.

Half carrying and half dragging the unconscious man, they set him down as gently as they could on the rug. Genista began to unfasten his snow-covered greatcoat and loosen his cravat.

"His clothes are soaked through. We must get him out of them at once. Blankets, Betty, and towels — as many as you can carry."

Cautiously, remembering the scream when they had lifted him, she began divesting him of his sodden garments, the greatcoat first, then the top boots, then his coat. He was heavy in her arms as she raised him up, but not unmanageably so.

Betty came back in at a run, her arms full. "How did he get here, Miss Genista? There's little enough traffic on this lane, for it goes from nowhere to nowhere."

"That's a good point. He can't have walked from Eversham, for his boots aren't muddy enough. There must have been a carriage... or a horse! It will die in this weather if we can't get it into the stable. Betty, will you go and look? But don't go too far, just down the path to the lane."

With a quick nod, Betty disappeared, and Genista turned back to her unexpected guest. He lay motionless on the rug, eyes closed, his long lashes resting on his pale cheeks, his breathing rapid. He was young, very young, perhaps three or four and twenty. Tendrils of dark hair clung damply to his forehead. He was beautiful, like an angel fallen to earth, his symmetry unmarred, his nose aquiline, his lips curved. Who was he, this vision of perfection?

She touched his forehead again... cold, so cold. He was chilled to the bone. There was heat enough from the range, but the stranger's wet clothes would leach all the warmth from his body if they were not removed. Waistcoat, shirt, breeches. Then whatever lay beneath. Waistcoat, shirt, breeches. Oh Lord. If only Father were there! He would carry the man into the surgery and deal with... whatever lay beneath. But Father was not there, and if Genista did not do what was needful, then this fallen angel might well die and it would be her fault. She unfastened the waistcoat, and lifted him to slide it off. Then the shirt and undershirt, pulled off all in one movement. She paused, her eyes drawn to his bare skin, so pale in the lamplight. He'd looked so slender when they'd carried him in, but he was neither thin like a boy, nor soft like a woman. There was strength in his arms, and his chest...

A deep breath. How foolishly missish to allow herself to be distracted. She was acting as his physician now, so she must be impassive, and do what she needed to do, and quickly. Another deep breath, and then she unbuttoned the breeches, and began to wriggle them down his legs. And before she could think about it, the under trousers.

His upper left leg was an angry purple colour, the jagged scar raised and torn. Green matter oozed from one corner. With an exclamation of shock, she quickly wrapped him in blankets, then lit a candle and ran through to the mixing room for the necessary materials. Her expert hands had soon made a poultice.

Betty was in the kitchen when she returned. "No sign of horse nor carriage," she said. "I can just make out hoof marks heading towards Elversham. I guess he fell off and the beast went on by itself."

"Nothing we can do about it now," Genista said briskly. "Hold the bowl, Betty, while I apply the poultice." Lifting a small amount of blanket to reveal the injured part of the leg, she set to work.

"Shouldn't be doing that," Betty said, with a sniff of disapproval. "He's a *man*."

"He's a very sick man, who will likely die if we do nothing," she said sharply.

Betty pointed to the discarded pile of clothes, the undergarments clearly visible. "But he's *nekkid*, Miss Genista. And you a lady an' all."

"I am a physician's daughter, and my conscience won't permit me to refuse to help. Father would wish me to," she said, hoping that was true. Father could be such a stickler for propriety sometimes. Yet he had taught her everything he knew and why else but to help people, just as he did? But she felt uneasily that helping people didn't quite mean stripping handsome young men naked.

2: Lavender Cottage

With the poultice in place, and the man wrapped in several blankets and with a pillow beneath his head, the two women left him lying in front of the fire and sat down in silence to their dinner. From time to time, Genista rose to check her patient. His breathing was still ragged, but he felt warmer and the flickering flames of the fire gave his face the illusory glow of health.

When Betty went through to the scullery to wash the dishes, Genista sat herself in her mother's rocking chair. It was too dark to work without light, and she dared not waste candles on herself, so she contented herself with watching her sleeping guest. Sleeping or unconscious, it was hard to tell. From time to time he gave a low moan, then his lips moved as if he were trying to speak, but no sound emerged. Then he would thrash a little before settling again. Once a bare foot emerged from the blankets, and she carefully wrapped it up again.

"You want me to stay up with him?" Betty said when she returned. "I can call you if you're needed."

"No, I'll stay with him."

"What if he wakes up? It's not fitting, Miss Genista. Dr Hamilton wouldn't like it."

"My father is not here," she said sharply. "There's only us, and I'm the one who has helped Father over the years. I can do whatever needs to be done. Go to bed, Betty."

"You'll not get much sleep on that chair. How about we bring that sofa from the parlour?"

"Oh, the chaise longue. Good idea."

It was light enough for the two women to carry without difficulty. They set it down to one side of the fire, and Betty arranged cushions and blankets to make a bed.

"Call me if he wakes," she said, then, with a final sniff of disapproval, she took a candle and went up to bed.

On another such evening, with her father away, Genista would have gone early to bed too. Tonight she tended the fire, trimmed the lamp and wrapped herself in a blanket, then lay on her side watching this intriguing young man who sprawled uncomfortably on the rug before the range. Who was he? His clothes were of excellent quality, that much was obvious even to her untutored eye. His cravat had been intricately tied, in the manner she had seen worn by some of the gentlemen in Canterbury. And his boots! Never had she seen such fine boots, clearly polished to the highest degree before the snow had got to them.

She had torn off his clothes without much thought, but now it occurred to her that there might be some means of identification in them. Betty had rinsed out his linens and hung everything in the scullery to dry, so Genista took the lamp and went through to examine his belongings. His shirt and undergarments bore only the initials *'GM'*, and his greatcoat pockets were empty of all but a partially-eaten bun, half disintegrated by the wet snow that had seeped through it. The coat, however, yielded a pocket knife and a purse holding an astonishing number of coins. In the waistcoat pockets were a watch, stopped, and several cards, too sodden to be readable. And a locket, a tiny thing of filigree silver. A lady's locket. There was nothing else.

She returned to her post thoughtful. A rich young man, with a wife or sweetheart, perhaps. But why was he passing Lavender Cottage, alone, on horseback and in such dire weather? What crisis drove him there, far from the main roads or any town? And how did he come by that injury to his leg? She could not be sure, but it looked like it had been caused originally by a bullet.

For an hour or two she lay wakeful, her mind full of her mysterious guest. Besides, she was too used to long evenings of cribbage with her father to be tired yet. But just as sleep began to creep over her, her patient became restless. He muttered to himself, twisting this way and that, pushing away the blankets, and twice he cried out, although she could not make out the words. When she felt his forehead, he was hot, burning up with fever.

She knew what to do. Fetching water from the scullery in a basin, she began to peel away the blankets so that she might sponge him down and cool him. But then she stopped. Was it wrong of her, to look on this young man's nakedness? Yet how could it be? Surely God had directed his steps here, to the very cottage where might be found the skills to heal him, and at the precise time that her father was from home. Therefore it fell to her to do whatever she might for the poor unfortunate, thrashing restlessly in his fever.

Resolutely, she pulled back the blankets to expose his skin and began to sponge his sweating body.

~~~~~

The night passed slowly. Whether cooling his fever, or wrapping him in layers of blankets to alleviate his chills, she was kept busy. In between times, she rested on the chaise longue, watching her patient toss and turn.
~~~~~

But by the time Betty rose, and the first pale hints of dawn could be discerned, he was easier and, to Genista's eyes, seemed to be sleeping more peacefully. With Betty's help, she changed his poultice, dressed him in an old nightgown of her father's and lifted him onto the chaise longue.

"Before you make the chocolate, Betty, will you light a fire in Mama's room, and make up the bed. After breakfast we'll move our nameless gentleman to more comfortable quarters."

"Your mama's room, Miss Genista?" Her face registered shock.

"Yes. Be sure to build up a good fire, for the room will be very cold. Really, Betty, where else are we to put him? He can't stay in here, the surgery examination couch is too high, and we can't possibly get him up the stairs."

Betty grunted and went away to do as she was bid, but when she returned and began to heat the chocolate, the banging of pans suggested that she was displeased with the proposed scheme. Genista understood why. When her mother had been ill, the small downstairs room had been made into a bedroom for her, and had been her home for five years. After she had died, the room had been closed up and never again used, according to her father's wishes. Twice a year, she and Betty were permitted to go in to clean it, and otherwise it was untouched, much as it had been left. Occasionally, when her father was away, she went in to look about her and remember and play her mother's spinet, which she preferred to the pianoforte in the drawing room. She saw no need to mention that to her father. He expected the room to be left unused. Yet she had to be practical, and it was the obvious place to place her patient.

Genista spent an hour tending to the leeches, returning at regular intervals to check the young man, but he slept quietly now. His breathing was steadier, and she thought his colour was better, although that might just be her fancy. When she felt her mama's room was sufficiently warm, she and Betty rolled him onto a blanket and dragged him through, and, with some difficulty, into the bed. He stirred and mumbled a few words, but nothing intelligible. Then Genista pulled a chair nearer the bed and settled down for a long day, as the snow fell steadily outside.

~~~~~

Gil woke to the sound of harps. No, one harp, perhaps. Not a heavenly choir, exactly, but perhaps the rest of the angels were otherwise engaged today. He lay with his eyes closed, listening to the harp, wondering why he was so tired and his leg ached so abominably when he was dead, until the angel missed a note and exclaimed in vexation, in a most unangelic way. He opened his eyes in surprise.

Above him was a plain plastered ceiling, cracked and yellowed with age. Warm blankets covered him from the chin downwards, and now that the harpist had ceased playing, he could hear a fire crackling and see flickers of light on the wall from the flames. The wall itself bore a pale paper — no, not pale, faded. A pattern of roses was just distinguishable.

The harp began again… or was it a spinet? Now a voice rose in quiet song, a hymn, he thought, although she sang so low he could not quite tell. Intrigued, he turned his head.

At once the music stopped, and after a moment a face bent over him.

"You're awake! How do you feel?"

She was not an angel, that much was certain. Her simple gown of deep green worsted and the hair severely drawn back were too prosaic for any celestial being. She was just a girl, no older than he was. But her face, leaning over him with concern, was pretty enough.
~~~~~

"Are you thirsty? A sip of water?"

His mouth was dry as dust, he now realised. He nodded, and she lifted his head and held a beaker to his lips while he drank.

"There now, not too much just at first. Are you in pain?"

A hesitation before he shook his head. Not pain, exactly, but he was not comfortable.

"Your wound is troubling you, I daresay. Do you need to make water?"

Yes! Now that the idea was in his head, his urgency was great. He tried to raise himself from the bed, but she laughed.

"No, no! Don't move! You can use this. Do you understand what to do?"

She loosened the bedclothes and pushed an oddly-shaped receptacle into his hands. He got the point. She turned her back while he relieved himself, and then slid the device under the bed.

"Better now?"

He nodded, feeling no embarrassment. She was so matter-of-fact, feeling his forehead, checking the beat of his heart, then tucking the covers tightly around him again. He was warm, he was safe, he was so, so tired. He closed his eyes.

~~~~~

When he woke again, it was dark, a single lamp shedding a pool of light on the girl as she sat on a hard chair beside the bed, her head bent over some stitchery. The lamp lit her hair with a fiery glow. She wore no cap, so she was a maid, not a matron, and her clothes proclaimed her a gentlewoman, not a servant. Yet she was no simpering miss. He thought of the society ladies he knew and wondered how many of them could have dealt with him so calmly, as she had done.
~~~~~

A twinge of pain in his leg made him stir restlessly. She looked up at once.

"How are you feeling now? Better?"

"A little." His voice was so croaky, it hardly sounded like him at all. But she smiled, pleased.

"Ah, you've found your voice again. Excellent. Some water? Or a little broth?"

Broth sounded good. She bustled out of the room, returning moments later with another woman, a sour-faced servant of fifty or so, who carried a small bowl.

"Just a little of this will do you the world of good," she said. "It's chicken. Everything is chicken just now, for the fox got into the hen house a few days ago. There now, up you come."

Effortlessly she lifted him up, supporting him as she spooned broth into his mouth. It was good, warm and thick and surprisingly tasty. He drank everything she gave him, only dribbling a little down his chin. She mopped him up without comment, and then laid him down on the pillows.

"You may have a little more later, if you wish. Does your wound bother you?"

"A little."

"The inflammation is lessening, so I believe it will heal well if you stay in bed for a few days." He smiled, unable to imagine at that moment ever leaving his warm bed. "I am Genista, and the servant is Betty. What may I call you?"

He hesitated, knowing he should give her his full name, but then he would have to explain all about his family and he had no energy for it. Besides, if she knew who he was, she would call him *'my lord'* and there would be a constraint between them. He liked being anonymous, being treated as her friend, on Christian name terms. She had offered hers, after all.

"Gil."

"Is that short for anything? Gilead? Gillespie?"

"Gilbert."

"We had a pig called Gilbert once. He made very good bacon."

"You name your pigs?"

"Of course. How else might one enquire of its health? *How are you today, Gilbert? Should you like some more mash, Gilbert?* That sort of thing. The current pig is Marmaduke."

He laughed at the absurdity of it. "Where is this place?"

"Lavender Cottage, near the village of Elversham in the county of Kent."

"I have never heard of it."

"Oh, but it is quite a famous county," she said, eyes twinkling. "I had supposed that everyone had heard of Kent."

That made him laugh again. "I meant the village, as you know perfectly well. Is it near London?"

"We are sixty miles from London, but only three miles from Canterbury."

"Canterbury," he said, wonderingly. "Whatever am I doing near Canterbury?"

"Now that is a question I cannot answer," she said briskly. "You arrived on my doorstep in the snow the day before last, all in a heap, with no sign of any horse or carriage, so if *you* do not know how you came here, I am sure I do not. Are you in any pain? There is laudanum if you wish it. It might help you to sleep."

He accepted the laudanum, and when next he woke the room was filled with light so bright he could barely open his eyes. She was there at once — did she ever leave his side?

"Ah, awake at last, you sleepy creature. The snow has stopped, the sun is shining and there are diamonds all over the garden. It is quite magical. Although very bright." She drew the curtains a little way across the window, so the worst of the glare was gone. "There! Is that better?"

"Diamonds? Oh, you mean the snow is sparkling. That must be delightful."

"It is indeed, although it would be a great deal more delightful if they were real diamonds. Just think how rich I should be!"

"What would you do with your riches?" he said.

She sat down on the chair beside his bed, and tipped her head to one side. "Let me see..."

Now that he looked at her closely, he allowed her to be very pretty. Not beautiful, for her features were not quite regular enough, and not handsome, which is what one might say of a woman with more style than beauty. No, she was pretty, with softly rounded cheeks and a kissable mouth, and eyes of a deep blue quite unlike any colour he had ever seen before.

"I should like to go to the theatre," she said eventually. "And the opera, and musical recitals, and... and Bullock's Museum and the Tower of London. And Bath... oh, and Brighton. Or anywhere on the coast. I should dearly like to see the sea."

"Should you not like to live in a great house and wear silks and jewels and feathers, be waited on by servants, and live on quail's eggs and partridge and roast peacock?" he said in surprise, for most women that he knew thought of little else, and devoted their lives to obtaining such things.

"Oh no!" she cried. "That would be quite dreadful. What could be cosier than this place? We have everything we need in that way. But I have never been further abroad than to Canterbury, and I should like to see other parts of the world. Scotland is said to be very beautiful, in a wild sort of way. It is covered with mountains, which is a thing I cannot quite imagine. Have you ever seen mountains, Gil?"

"Once, when I stayed with a school friend in Wales. They are most disagreeable, mountains. Very steep, and when one reaches the top there is nothing there at all except perhaps a goat or two, and not a drop of claret to be had, and so one is obliged to descend at once. And the sea is disagreeable, too, let me tell you. It tastes appalling and if one is foolhardy enough to want to swim in it, one is liable to be hurled about a great deal. And Bath— no, you do not want to go to Bath. A very dull sort of place, full of dowagers and the sick, who somehow believe that drinking noxious waters will cure them of all ailments. But the theatre and opera are entertaining, that I will grant you."

He stopped, suddenly exhausted. To be laid so low, when he had always prided himself on his energy! It was more than a man could bear. And talking of the sea reminded him of Dover and his irate colonel who would cashier him if he failed to turn up at Drummoor.

"Is there anywhere to send a letter in... your village?"

"In Elversham? No, only from Canterbury. You wish to write to someone? Will she be worrying about you?"

She... What *she* did she mean? "Colonel Jefferson," he said. "He will think I have absconded."

"Oh dear. Army?"

"Hussars."

"Well, there is no possibility of getting through this snow until my father returns with the horse," she said. "Your colonel will understand that snow brings everything to a standstill."

"He might. Or he might not," Gil said, closing his eyes. "Why am I so tired?"

"You have been very ill. You nearly died, Gil. You need rest and sleep and plenty of chicken broth, so do not worry about letters or colonels or anything else for a while. Let me get you some more broth, and then I'll draw the curtains and you can sleep again for a while."

Having no energy for anything else, he did as he was bid.

3: Backgammon

Genista liked to watch him sleep. Gil. Gilbert Something-beginning-with-an-M. Mansfield. Manchester. No, those were places. Impossible to guess at a name. Gil the Hussar, whose colonel might cashier him if he were thought to have absconded. Gil with the light blue eyes and the impossibly long lashes. No, this was foolish. She must stop thinking of him in that way. He was a patient, just another patient.

All that day, he dozed, woke again, ate a little broth, dozed once more. Late in the afternoon, when she was sitting by the western window to get the most light to read by, he woke again and she could see by his eyes that he was more alert. Before she could take the few steps to his bedside, he had pushed his pillows up and raised himself to a half-sitting position.

"You're feeling better," she said. "Would you like to eat a proper dinner tonight?"

"Chicken?" he hazarded. She laughed, and nodded. "The roast swan is finished, then?" That made her laugh again. How long was it since she had laughed in that unforced way? "No music today? I enjoyed your playing yesterday… or whenever it was."

"Today is Sunday, so no music, but I shall play again tomorrow, if you like."

"This is an unusual bedroom," he said. "A spinet, and a backgammon table, I see."

It was a casual remark — he could not know the grief she still felt. But she answered composedly. "It was my mother's room, latterly. Her legs failed her, so Father had this room made for her, and she lived out her last few years here. The chair with wheels is hers. We took her to the dining room or into the drawing room in that, for as long as she was able. But eventually, she could not leave her bed."

"I am so sorry," he said politely. "I did not mean to stir painful memories. But I think, if I were compelled to live my life in just one room, this would be a pleasant place of confinement. There is music here and companionship, for one cannot play backgammon alone. There are windows that catch both the morning and evening sun, and from the darker patches of wallpaper, I can see that there were paintings on the walls. And there were books on these shelves once, I feel sure."

"You are correct," she said quietly. "Father sold the books, for they were frivolous types — novels and such like, not suitable for me, and he did not care for them. The paintings have gone back to her brother. They were her family's, not ours. But the spinet is still here, although I only play it when Father is away. It grieves him too much."

"Does your father leave you alone a great deal?"

"Only when his distant patients summon him, and usually he is back the next day. He is a physician, you see. The snow keeps him in Canterbury, I dare say."

~~~~~

She found that her patient healed quickly. On Sunday, he was sitting up. On Monday, he was well enough to sit in the wheeled chair and
~~~~~

be pushed through to the kitchen to eat his dinner with Genista and Betty, and after that, he persuaded her to play backgammon.

"I usually play such games for money," he said. "But I suspect that is not your usual habit."

She looked up from setting out the pieces. "No. We never place wagers. The only reward worth having is the satisfaction of the play. Shall you play red or black?"

"Black, then you may take red, which matches your gown so well."

She made no reply, for it was such a frivolous comment that she couldn't find anything sensible to say.

"If we may not stake money, let us make the play amusing in another way," Gil said. "If you throw a double, you must tell me something interesting about yourself."

She laughed, but shook her head. "That is still gambling."

"Not at all, if no money changes hands."

"Who decides if it be interesting or not?"

"That is a good point, for I can see that such discussions might become disputatious. Let us say then that whoever throws a double must tell something about himself or herself, whether it be interesting or not."

But this was not very appealing to her, for he would undoubtedly tell her something dull like the name of his horse, when really she wished to know about the lady who had given him the locket. "I have a better idea," she said. "Whoever throws a double may ask a question of the other."

"Oh, excellent idea!" he said, his face lighting up with enthusiasm. "And if the one questioned refuses to answer, the next throw is forfeit."

She laughed in delight. "Very well."

They played for some time before either of them threw a double but then a whole spate revealed that he had five brothers and a sister, that they were all older than he was, and that he lived in Yorkshire. She in her turn told him of her two brothers and two sisters, all much older than her, that she had no sweetheart or secret lover, and that she had never yet received an offer of marriage.

"What, never?" he said, then went on teasingly, "No one has lain awake at night longing to kiss that pretty mouth of yours?"

She blushed, but said, "It is to be hoped not! Indeed, why should anyone think of marrying *me*? My role as the youngest daughter is to look after Father, and help him with his work."

"And are you content with that?"

His blue eyes were fixed on her with an intensity which made her heart beat fast. He was so handsome, and when he looked at her that way, as if her answer was the most important thing in the world to him... it was flattering. She was quite unused to such attention, and lowered her eyes before answering.

"Of course. Marriage is merely to exchange one sort of servitude to a man for another, with the added burden of children."

"Not if the man should happen to be rich or titled, or preferably both. Then the children would be no burden at all. Every woman wants to marry a lord."

"Well, I do *not*!" she cried. "I can't think of anything worse! All those lords and ladies who think they're so grand and quite above the rest of the world, with their idle, selfish, immoral lives — I want nothing to do with any of them."

He seemed taken aback at her vehemence, and for a moment he made no reply.

"I beg your pardon for my intemperance," she said. "You think me irrational, perhaps, but there is... some family history on the subject. One of my sisters was betrothed to a baron, but he... he took advantage of her and then abandoned her. She was lucky to find a farmer's son to take pity on her situation and marry her. The experience has left us wary of the nobility."

"That is very bad, but not all nobles are so despicable," he said mildly.

"True, but their lives of idleness and dissipation, together with a belief in their own superiority, make them disinclined to show consideration for those of *our* kind. I could never marry such a man. I don't want to marry *anyone*, but least of all a lord."

"How curious! I never met a woman before who had no desire to marry," he said. "In my experience, it is all they think about, and very tedious it is too, trying to evade their wiles. You are an original, Genista."

She looked at him in surprise. "Hardly that! It is commonplace for a younger daughter to stay at home. Besides, my life here is all that I could wish for. Am I not well provided for, with a comfortable home and enough to eat, and my father's companionship? My work here is enjoyable and not too arduous. What more could any woman ask for? Shall you make your play?"

"I am bored with the game," he said abruptly. "Will you give me some music?"

She agreed to it, and as she settled down at the spinet, it occurred to her that such conversations were dangerously intimate, and best avoided. It was not wise to become too friendly with a man who was young and distractingly good looking and very, very charming.

~~~~~
~~~~~

Gil slept well that night, and the next morning was up and in his chair before Genista came into his room.

"Well, you're looking much brighter today."

"I feel better — up to exploring a little. Will you show me around? Pleasant as this room is, I should like to see the rest of the house."

So she wheeled him into the dining room and drawing room, silent and cold, her father's surgery, an oddly impersonal room, with its cabinets of instruments and a single shelf of medical books, and the mixing room, where the ingredients were kept for the various mixtures and lozenges and drops that her father prescribed.

"Does he remember the ingredients for each one, or does he have a book to tell him?" Gil said, gazing around in awe at the cabinets and drawers, all neatly labelled.

"There's a note book, although one gets to know the quantities for the commonest mixtures," she said. "I still look them up, though. Think how dreadful it would be to put ten times as much arsenic in a compound."

"Oh, you make them up sometimes?"

"Always, nowadays. It leaves Father free to concentrate on the important matters. Would you mind if I tend to the leeches now? I can take you back to your room if you had rather not watch."

He had no great love of leeches, but he had no objection to watching her as she checked each jar, removed one or two that looked sick to a separate container and changed the water on one jar. Then she made careful notes in a large book, while he admired the curve of her neck as she leant over to write. She hummed in a low tone as she worked, clearly happy in her employment.

She intrigued him, there was no doubt about it. He could not decide whether that resulted from his position as her virtual prisoner, or the strange intimacy into which they were thrown, or whether perhaps it was because she was so utterly different from any woman he had ever known before. There was not the least guile about her. His very mild questioning, which would have been taken as flirtation by anyone more worldly, she treated as honest enquiries, and answered with a directness that he found refreshing. And she spoke no less than the truth of her contentment with her situation. Seeing her absorbed in her work, humming almost like the purring of a cat, he could not imagine her in any other setting. Certainly her plain, high-necked gowns and the simple way she coiled her hair on her head would be outlandish in any society setting. But that hair! It looked as dull a brown as her gown that day, but when the sun caught it, it shone like spun gold — all reds and fiery ambers and gilded yellows. And so much of it. He had a yearning to unpin it, to feel it falling through his fingers like silk. He sighed in delight at the thought.

She looked up at once. "Are you tired? There! I have finished now." She set down her pen and quickly sanded the page. "Let me take you back to your room."

"Backgammon?" he said optimistically, when she wheeled him back into the bedroom.

She laughed. "Not before breakfast. I have to help Betty in the kitchen, and then there is the pig to see to. But later, perhaps, I shall have time. Shall I bring you a book to read?"

"Please. And give my regards to Marmaduke."

He read a little, walked around his chair for exercise, his bad leg stiff but free of pain, ate breakfast in the kitchen with the two women and was glowered at by Betty, then he returned to his room, read a little more, and walked all the way to the window. The sky was an angry grey, but the snow was still beautiful, even without its sun-induced diamonds. The faint scuff marks of birds and the trail of a fox were all that marred its perfection.

"Don't put too much weight on that leg of yours," she said.

He had not heard her come in, but he turned with a smile. "I feel better for being up and about. Where are my clothes?"

"In the wardrobe over there. I hope you don't object, but I went through your pockets, in an attempt to find out who you were. Your cards were unreadable, so I still don't know your surname."

"Marford," he said. "And yours is Hamilton. There was an inscription on the flyleaf of the book." He opened the door of the wardrobe and closed it again. "At least I shall be able to dress for dinner tonight." He laughed at himself, for normally dressing for dinner meant a full hour at least spent with his valet, and here it would be an accomplishment merely to set aside his nightgown. "This must be your father's nightgown I think, and I do not remember undressing at all."

"I undressed you," she said, not quite looking him in the eye. "You were soaked and frozen, and would likely have died without being wrapped up warm and dry at once. Besides, if I had not done so, I should not have known about your leg and it would have gone on festering. It was a nasty injury. How did you come by it?"

"I was shot."

"Ah. Then you have been in battle."

"Sadly not. It was a duel."

Her eyes widened but she asked nothing more. Instead she said, "Shall we play?"

"Do you not want to know? Why I was in a duel?"

She shook her head, pulling her chair resolutely to the backgammon table. With a sigh, he wheeled his chair to the other side of it, and sat down. He had already laid the pieces out, so she picked up the dice cup and threw at once. He picked up his own dice cup, then set it down again, and reached across the table to take her hand. She looked at him with wide, startled eyes.

"Thank you for saving my life, Miss Hamilton," he said quietly. Then he threw his dice and the game began.

For a while they played in silence, but then she threw a double. They had not discussed whether they would continue their game of the day before, and she had been so subdued by the mention of the duel that he had imagined she would want to know nothing further about him. However, she gazed at him, with those mesmerising dark blue eyes.

"Whose was the locket that you carry in your waistcoat pocket?"

"It was my mother's," he said at once, and found himself assailed by both grief and pleasure. When was the last time he had spoken of Mama? "The finest lady I have ever known. She always understood me, even when I misbehaved. Not that she was indulgent, or assisted me in evading punishment, but she understood the devils that drove me to mischief. That still drive me to it, if I am honest. Boredom, mostly. I always craved excitement, even as a boy. If we went to the lake to fish, I must needs jump in the water. If we went to the woods, I had to climb a tree. If nothing else offered, I would pick a fight with one of my brothers and that was doubly amusing, because they were so much older and bigger that they would often be punished rather than me. But Mama would talk to me in her quiet way, and although she never lectured me, somehow I would come to see that what I had done was wrong. But then she died..." He stopped, and now there was nothing but grief. How he missed her, even after nine years!

Into the painful silence of his thoughts, Genista's quiet voice was soothing. "How old were you then?"

"Fourteen."

"My mother died when I was eleven," she said.

"It is very hard to lose the heart of the family, is it not?" Gil said.

"Oh yes! Father has never quite got over her death."

"But what of you?" he said gently. "You must have felt it keenly. A mother is of the greatest importance to a daughter, more so than a wife is to a husband."

"Perhaps," she said, but he thought she seemed puzzled by the idea. "She was ill for so long, and faded a little more each day, so that by the time she died she was barely there. I scarcely remembered a time when she was well, whereas Father remembered her vibrant years. He was overwhelmed with grief, far more than I was, it seems to me. Besides, I had him to think of and care for, whereas he had nothing. All that he loved was taken away from him."

Her words silenced him. *'What about you?'* he wanted to cry out. *'Surely your father loved you? He had not lost you.'* But he could not speak. His own grief, and hers, rose up to choke him and render him speechless. What a strange, sad life she had led, her father so absorbed in his own affairs that his own daughter imagined herself unloved.

After that they played on in silence, and even when one or other of them threw a double, there were no more questions. It was a relief. He began to feel the danger of paying her too much attention. They had been thrown together in this intimate way, and she was very matter-of-fact about the situation, but if they were too open with each other, there was a risk of being drawn in, and she might develop expectations. He had no wish to raise hopes in her that he had no intention of fulfilling. He supposed he would marry eventually, if it became unavoidable, but not yet, and certainly not this sad little daughter of a country physician.

They had almost finished their second game when a sound was heard, distantly. Before he could begin to guess the cause, she had jumped up. "Father is home! I must light the fires."

And with that she whisked out of the room and he was left alone.

4: Roast Beef

Genista raced through to the kitchen. "Father is back!"

Betty had been sitting at the table languidly chopping carrots, but now she clucked her tongue in annoyance. "And no fish in the house, nor no beef. He'll have to have pork, and like it."

"He *won't* like it! Is there any of the pigeon pie left?"

"That soldier of yours ate most of it," Betty sniffed. "There's a bit of the veal."

"I'll make a ragout, then," Genista said. "And he's not *my* soldier. You'd better open a bottle of gooseberries for a pie. Will you start the pastry? I need to light the fires."

She lit a candle from the fire, and went off to light lamps and fires in the surgery, drawing room and dining room. By the time that was done, the gig had already rattled up the short drive and stopped outside the front door. She rushed to open it, and the familiar figure brushed past her.

"What kept you, girl? The door should be open before I get to it. After such an appalling journey, I should not have to wait to enter my own house."

"I beg your pardon, Father. Let me take your coat. How is Mr Wilkes?"

"Dead, poor soul. I could do nothing but pray for him and perform the final offices. Are there many calls awaiting my attention?"

"None at all, Father. Either everyone is perfectly well or they cannot get through the snow to request a visit. But we have one patient here."

"A patient? Here? He or she must go home, then, for there is no surgery today."

"He cannot go home, Father, for he lives in Yorkshire."

"But he must have friends in the neighbourhood, or how else would he know to come here?"

Genista stopped, realising that she would have to explain the whole story. "He became lost in the snow, and fell unconscious at the door. We took him in, or else he would have perished. His leg is injured from a bullet wound, but he is recovering now, Father."

"He is not in need of immediate attention, then?"

"No, Father."

Her father stared at her, the bushy brows so close together they looked like one. "Lost in the snow... and what day was this?"

"Friday last, Father."

There was a long silence. Genista's father had never chastised her or raised his voice to her, nor had he ever been unkind, but he had a way of looking that conveyed his displeasure all too clearly. But after a moment, his face settled back to its customary expression.

"I shall take some chocolate in the drawing room. And cake. Then you may explain his case to me in detail and I shall examine this patient of yours."

~~~~~
~~~~~

Gil listened to it all — the women, low-voiced and anxious in the kitchen, then Genista rushing about the rest of the downstairs rooms, then the creak of the front door and a deep, strong voice. Her father. He had formed a mental image of him — an elderly man, white-haired and perhaps stooped, a kindly old gentleman still grieving so deeply for his late wife that he barely noticed his daughter. He would wear black, of course, for he was still mourning. Now that he heard his harsh voice, this pleasant image crumbled. This was no kindly old man.

Doors opened and closed, and there was silence apart from the murmur of the women in the kitchen. Then footsteps in the hall again, more doors, and silence.

He had half nodded off when the door opened and a man strode in. Well, he had got the clothes right, for Genista's father was dressed entirely in black, although with Geneva bands like a clergyman. He was tall, dark-visaged and stern of countenance, and Gil could well imagine him in the pulpit denouncing sinners and preaching of eternal fires. He seemed an unlikely physician.

"You are Gilbert Marford?"

"I am, sir." Gil struggled to rise from his chair, but Dr Hamilton waved him down again.

"What is your profession?"

Gil almost laughed, and was tempted to tell him that he was the son of a marquess and had no need for a profession. But it occurred to him that Genista's hostility to the nobility had more than likely been absorbed from her father, so he held his tongue. "I am a Hussar, sir. The King's Own Regiment."

"Your rank?"

"Captain."

"And how is it you came to be on my doorstep in the snow without your horse?"

"That is a question I have wrestled with myself, sir. My wounded leg was not healing well, so I was sent home from the camp at Dover to recuperate, but somehow I ended up here, a circumstance which I am quite unable to account for. But however it came about, I am deeply grateful to Miss Hamilton for her care of me, which undoubtedly saved my life."

"Fine words. Let me have a look at you, and I'll decide how well she's cared for you."

For perhaps half an hour, Dr Hamilton was nothing but a medical man, a little brusque in manner, but both practical and thoughtful. He poked and prodded Gil, listened to his heart and lungs, unbandaged his leg, grunted over it, asked him to walk back and forth, and then pronounced himself satisfied. He arranged for the bath to be brought in, rebandaged the leg and helped Gil to dress in his own clothes again.

That afternoon, they ate dinner in the dining room, just the three of them, Dr Hamilton, Genista and Gil. Instead of the three or four dishes, there were ten, plus the soup. Genista ran back and forth to the kitchen, for she seemed to do much of the cooking. The conversation stayed with uncontroversial subjects, such as the weather, the state of the roads, news from Canterbury and a long, detailed description of the physician's various attempts to return home, thwarted until that very day by the snow.

Dr Hamilton had stopped on his way home at the butcher's shop in Eversham and picked up several joints of beef, and some game. Gil was very glad to have some red meat for a change. He had not minded chicken, but it was, to his mind, a namby-pamby sort of food, suitable only for invalids and children. There was wine, too, a jug of half-decent claret.

"Should you care for some wine, Miss Hamilton?" Gil said, when the jug passed to him, but she only shook her head, eyes lowered.

"My daughter does not indulge in wine, Captain Marford," Dr Hamilton said. "It is a drink ill-suited to the refined constitutions of women."

"Do you think so?" Gil said, trying to recall a single lady of his acquaintance who did not drink wine, or even stronger drink. "It seems a harmless enough habit to me."

"Harmless? Harmless? The woman who partakes of any wine or spirit will soon lose her lustre, Captain, and become as loose and wanton as any woman of the streets. Women have no sense of moderation or restraint, as men do. A glass of claret now will become a raging thirst for the liquid in very short order, and then all purity is lost. A man must do all in his power to protect his daughter's virtue, do you not agree?"

"Oh, indeed," Gil said, bewildered by such strength of feeling on the subject. "One can never be too careful."

There was no port offered, and all three moved through to the drawing room at the same time, Genista ringing a bell for Betty to clear the table. In contrast to the kitchen, lit in the evenings only by the fire and a couple of tallow candles, the drawing room was bright with lamps and wax candles.

"You play cribbage, Captain?"

"A little," Gil said, feeling obliged to provide the physician with male companionship, although he was light-headed from the wine and his leg was beginning to ache again.

The two settled to their game, with the bulk of the light clustered around their table. Genista worked on her sewing by the light of a single candle. Gil played poorly, and after an hour or so, the physician said, "You are correct, Captain, to say that you play but a little. You are not up to my weight."

"I beg your pardon for my ineptitude, sir. I am not at my best tonight."

"No, indeed. You have certainly been ill, of that there is no doubt. When I first heard of your presence here, I confess that I suspected some ploy to prey on my daughter, who was defenceless here. I see now that this judgement was incorrect. However you came here, you must indeed have been in desperate straits. But that is the past. What concerns me now is the future. What are your plans, Captain?"

"I confess that I have not thought much beyond the next few hours. I was glad simply to be alive. But if I must consider my plans, then so long as my health continues to improve, it should be possible for me to continue my journey north in not too many days."

The physician grunted, his head bent over the card table as he tidied away cards and pegs. "And that is all?"

Gil was bewildered. "All?"

Dr Hamilton looked up and there was fire in his eyes. "And what about my daughter, young man? What about her?"

"I have not the pleasure of understanding you, sir."

Genista was watching her father with an unreadable expression on her face, but she said nothing. She had said nothing all evening.

"Let me say this in the plainest possible terms, so that even you may understand," Dr Hamilton said coldly. "Whatever chance brought you here, and I accept that it was chance and not design, you entered my house uninvited and took advantage of my daughter's innocence in insinuating yourself under my roof — in my wife's room, sir, now desecrated by your presence. Not only have you slept under my roof while my daughter was unguarded and alone, you allowed her to tend to you with an intimacy which no maiden should ever offer to a man other than her husband. You encouraged her to spend time with you in the closest possible manner — playing backgammon, while you were unclothed! You have despoiled my innocent daughter, sir, and I ask you again — what do you plan to do about it?"

Gil's anger was so great that he jumped to his feet, despite the pain in his leg. "I am a gentleman, sir, and have not so much as touched a hair of your daughter's head. I would never harm her, and it is not my habit to seduce maidens. She has received nothing from me but my eternal gratitude for her care for me. Your daughter's innocence and reputation are unharmed."

"Not so," the physician said, looking up at him with anger flashing in his eyes. "Her innocence was lost the moment she gazed upon your naked form. She removed your wet clothes down to the last item, and now she has seen that which no maiden should ever see. You have corrupted her, sir, and she will never again be pure."

"I do not see that I can be blamed for anything that happened when I was unconscious," Gil said in indignation. "Nor can Miss Hamilton be blamed for an act which undoubtedly preserved my life."

"No one speaks of blame, for that is of no consequence. You had no say in the matter, and my daughter could not be expected to understand the consequences of her actions. Her compassion led her into error, and now her mind will be filled with lustful thoughts."

Gil's eyes shot to Genista, but she was sitting, head down, hands gripped tightly together in her lap. "This is nonsense," he said more temperately. "If a woman is pure at heart, then she cannot be corrupted in this way. Her innocence, her good intentions must protect her. There is not an ounce of corruption in Miss Hamilton, and I doubt she even understands the idea of lust, let alone is consumed with it."

"Do you presume to question my knowledge of morality, young man? Is your understanding of the world so great that you dare to argue with me on such a subject? Is it not a matter of the utmost concern to me, an object of study over many decades? Have I not devoted myself to this very subject since first I understood the unprincipled nature of most in this world? And how you have the unbridled arrogance to lecture me on the character of my own daughter, a person you met for the first time just a few days ago, is entirely beyond my comprehension."

Gil took a deep breath. His leg ached abominably, his head was spinning and all he wanted to do was to crawl into bed and sleep, yet he had to speak. He could not let this unpleasant man go unanswered.

"I beg your pardon, sir. No insult was intended. Nevertheless, I believe your fears to be unfounded. Miss Hamilton is as virtuous a young lady as it has ever been my pleasure to encounter, and I cannot stand by and allow her character to be tarnished, and by her own father, too."

"It is not I who tarnishes her character," he said in thunderous tones. "Nevertheless, however much you might protest, it *has* been tarnished, and you are the only person who can now rescue her from ruin. You must marry her at once."

"That is a ridiculous idea!" Gil said hotly. "I shall do no such thing."

"Then you are no gentleman, and I shall be obliged to write to your superiors in your regiment to inform them of this fact."

"You must do as you see fit, but I shall not be bounced into marriage for so trivial a cause."

"Oh, you consider the matter trivial, do you?"

"It *is* trivial! You make the most enormous fuss about it, but nothing at all has happened between your daughter and me, *nothing*. Even if I had set out to seduce her, I do not believe I could have succeeded, so pure of heart is she, and I am accounted an expert in that line."

"Oh, you are, are you?"

"I am!" Gil said, too angry to mind his tongue. "You malign a good woman by your insinuations, and I shall not marry her merely on that account. Some day she will find a husband worthy of her, who values her as she deserves, but it shall not be me."

He swayed a little, for the room was spinning horribly. He closed his eyes, and would have fallen except for the support that materialised under one arm.

"He is ill, Father, and needs rest. Let me take him back to his room." Her quiet voice was balm to his ruffled spirits.

"Pah! Do as you please."

With Genista's help, Gil limped back to his room and practically fell onto the bed.

"Will you be all right?" she said, her voice anxious. "Shall I bring you some laudanum?"

He shook his head, and then some mischievous devil got into him, for he said, "I shall need you to undress me."

"Hush!" she said in severe tones, but she put a hand to her mouth to hide her laughter. But then she added in an undertone, "You should leave as soon as you are able, for he will not let go of the idea while you remain here." Then, louder, "Good night, Captain Marford."

Leaving him a single candle, she whisked out of the room with the faintest hint of lavender.

5: Duty

Gil could not sleep. He managed to undress himself and crawled into bed, but sleep would not come. How had he found himself in this mess, and through no fault of his own? Or hers, come to that, for he could not find it in his heart to be censorious of Genista's actions when he would otherwise have died. Her father was a pompous, self-righteous old stick, and Gil had no intention of marrying to oblige him, and certainly not this drab, timid girl.

Yet she was not so timid with him. When her father was around, she was silent and downcast, but alone with Gil she was far more animated, with a lively sense of the absurd. Even after the heat of the argument swirling around her, she had seen the jest in his suggestion that she undress him. She was demure, however, with not the slightest degree of flirtatiousness, perfectly ladylike, yet he could never see himself marrying such a woman. When his time came to be leg-shackled, he would find himself a wife from amongst his own class, who could move in his level of society.

After an hour or two of trying in vain to sleep, he crept through to the kitchen to find himself something to drink. The room was still warm, with a homely smell of cooking and soap and cheese, so he sat at the table to drink his ale and try to work out how many days he would have to endure the physician's lecturing before he could escape.

He had thought he was very quiet, but somehow it did not surprise him when the door opened and a lamp appeared, closely followed by Genista, her hair in a plait as thick as his arm which reached all the way to her waist.

"Are you having trouble sleeping? Would you like some laudanum?"

"Thank you, it would help, I think."

She disappeared for a few minutes, returning with a small cup. "Drink it all." To his surprise she sat down opposite him.

"You should not be here alone with me, Miss Hamilton, and both of us in a state of undress."

There was that half smile again. "It hardly matters now, does it? I am corrupted and ruined beyond redemption. Such wantonness is expected of me."

"You do not believe that."

"I am as corrupt as I ever was," she said. "As a physician's daughter, it would be astonishing in me to be entirely ignorant of the male form, despite all his efforts to protect me from the evil world. You must not mind Father's ways. He will settle down and be himself again once you are gone. Any change to his routine distresses him, and all this snow makes everything ten times worse. He does not really want me to marry and go away from him. How would he manage without me? It is a foolish idea, and he will see that when he is more himself again."

Gil wondered just how true that was. The physician had seemed quite set on it, and if Gil had been less well-versed in the ways of society, perhaps he would have been cowed by all the bluster and agreed to marry the girl, and then the fellow would have been quite sunk. But he was safe enough, for neither Gil nor Genista wished to marry.

But he said no more about it, drank his laudanum, bade Genista a good night and, with a final wistful look at that wondrous hair, went back to bed.

~~~~~

Genista kept out of her father's way the next day. She went about her duties diligently, but she took care to be in a different part of the house whenever she could. Not that he behaved any differently towards her than usual, for he would never stoop to sulk or fuss, but there was that in his expression that made her quail. She took Gil his breakfast on a tray, while she and her father breakfasted in the dining room. He was just as usual, giving her his orders for the day. Gil was only mentioned once.

"Bring Captain Marford to the surgery at noon, so that I may examine him," he said. "For dinner, I should like the partridge, and some giblets in a pie. There was no veal to be had from Mr Linnet, nor venison, more's the pity. There is no flavour quite like venison. I suppose there are no beetroot left?"

"No, ours are gone. Shall I send James to the farm to beg for some?"

"It does not matter. I brought a calves' head yesterday. We had better have that today, for it will not keep."

"Yes, Father, it's already stewing, and I shall make some custards as well. You always enjoy those."

"Make some of your curry soup. And a decent cake — caraway or apple, something like that."

"Yes, Father."

"Have you been tending the leeches while I've been away?"

"Every day, Father. The record book is up to date."
~~~~~

"Hmpf. You may hang the cloths. I am minded to hold a surgery today."

"Very good, Father."

It seemed a good sign that he was willing to hold a surgery so soon after his return. He had never approved of patients simply turning up at his house for the treatment of minor ailments, so he had devised a system of brightly-coloured cloths as signals. One at Genista's window was visible from a few houses in the village, and one at the back of the house could be seen from nearby farms. From noon onwards, they would have a steady stream of injuries or requests for visits.

She busied herself with her morning chores, tended the pig and the chickens, saw to the leeches and readied the surgery. At noon, she took Gil through to be examined. He was walking much better, she noticed, and seemed brighter. How quickly he healed! And yet, he still needed to be careful, for he had faded rapidly the previous evening. It would be so easy for him to regard himself as well, and over-exert himself.

From noon, a trickle of patients began to arrive, both those with injuries or illness to be attended to, or, more frequently, those requesting medicines for others. Genista was kept busy in the mixing room. When she had a spare moment, she would dash to the kitchen to check the meat for their dinner, salt the soup or lay out the ingredients for a cake or a sauce. Betty was an adequate plain cook, if well supervised, but she had never learnt to weigh and measure, and could not be trusted with the delicate sauces the physician liked.

At five, the cloths came down from the windows and the front door was locked. Dinner was served immediately, and it always had to be a good one after the exertions of a surgery. Genista and Betty worked in silent intentness in the kitchen, filling platters and bowls and jugs, while James carried them through and laid them out on the table, where the two gentlemen already waited, making quiet conversation. Finally, Genista took off her apron, smoothed her hair and took her place at the table, and the meal began.

~~~~~

Gil kept to his room all day, apart from the half hour when he was summoned to the surgery to be tapped and prodded and bent this way and that. There was no conversation beyond the medical. Does this hurt? What about that? Any weakness, dizziness, unusual heat or chill, any bad dreams? He was able to answer every question in the negative. The physician grunted and dismissed him without another word.

It was a relief that there was no continuation of the unpleasant discussion of the day before, and Gil hoped that he had done enough to dissuade the old man from trying to marry off his daughter. Still, he would not be easy about it until he had left this place behind. He was beginning to consider the practicalities — where he might find a horse, or whether he had the nerve to ask to borrow the physician's gig. If he had a decent closed carriage, he might leave at any time, but if he had to walk to Canterbury, he would have to stay for another week, at least, and he was not sure his nerves could stand it. Genista was fine company, but the physician was not at all Gil's idea of a congenial companion.

Still, after a day alone, any company was better than none, and he was almost glad to emerge from his room for dinner, and engage the fellow in conversation. He was an intelligent man, that much was certain, for all his queer ideas of womanhood. He had originally intended a life of the cloth, and had taken holy orders as soon as he was able. However, having neither wealth nor influential acquaintance, he had been unable to find a living and could not, in the normal course of events, have afforded to marry. He had had
~~~~~

the good fortune, however, to secure the affections of a young lady whose uncle was a physician. Having no children of his own, and sympathetic to the young people's plight, he had agreed to train Mr Hamilton in his own profession, thus enabling them to marry.

All this Dr Hamilton told Gil with very little prompting. His affection for his wife and gratitude towards his benefactor were genuine, and he spoke with great feeling on the subject. At that moment, Gil almost felt that he liked the fellow. But then Genista came in.

"You have not changed your gown today, child," Dr Hamilton said, as he helped himself to soup. "I do not like to see you come to the table looking rumpled, like a servant. Your mama always changed for dinner, and you must never lower your standards below hers." His tone was not unkind, but she flushed in embarrassment.

"I beg your pardon, Father. Shall I go and change?" Her tone was low, and anger pulsed through Gil on her behalf. How dared he speak so to her! Of course she had not had time to change her dress, when she had been working every moment of the day.

"Yes, do. You will feel better for it."

"Yes, Father." She crept away, and by the time she returned in a slightly more formal gown, the choicest cuts of meat were gone.

"May I help you to some of the partridge, Miss Hamilton?" he said politely.

"Oh… thank you, but there is no need."

"But you cannot reach the dish from there. Allow me to pass it to you."

"No, no, pray do not! It is my father's favourite, and if I take a share, he will not have enough."

"Then have my portion," he said, gallantly. "I prefer the beef anyway."

"No, no, please!" she said, and he could read the alarm in her face. Was she afraid of her father? Would he punish her for eating some of his favourite dish? "I am perfectly happy with the soup and vegetables, and I shall have a custard as well as dessert. Pray do not concern yourself, Captain."

"A woman's constitution is too delicate for a great deal of red meat," the physician said. "It makes her wild and unbiddable."

"Does it?" Gil said. "I have never noticed that myself."

"That is because you have not dedicated your life to observing the human condition as I have," the physician said complacently. "Women are weak and foolish creatures, Captain, weak in body and weak in mind. They need constant guidance. That is why God ordained that men, with their superior strength and bravery and intellect, should have the ordering of the world and that women should obey them."

Gil thought of the women he knew, none of whom were weak in body or in mind, women who were every bit as brave as men, and wondered how it was that Dr Hamilton could look around him and see the world so differently. And he looked at Genista, head down, squashed so flat by her father's domineering ways that it might seem that she could never rise up again, and yet he knew there was a lively, intelligent woman behind that cowed exterior. He seethed on her behalf, but there was no point in arguing with a man so fixed in his opinions.

So he ate red meat and drank red wine, and watched Genista eat her soup and vegetables and two chicken pasties and custard, saying not a word while her father discoursed on one or two of his patients, or discussed the stocks of medicine ingredients. Occasionally, she would say, "Yes, Father," or "No, Father," but not one word beyond the minimum. His heart ached for the cheerful girl who had teased him and talked so freely about herself. That girl was locked away whenever her father was about, repressed and largely ignored, treated no better than a servant. It was heart-rending.

When James had cleared the table and Genista had fetched the dessert, her father said, "Shall you do better at the cribbage board this evening, Captain? You will want to avenge your defeat, I am sure."

He could think of little he wanted less. "Forgive me, but I am tired, and would prefer to return to my room."

"As you please. But in that case, we shall settle the matter of my daughter now."

Gil's heart sank. He had hoped it was already settled. "Sir, I—"

The physician raised an imperious hand. "No more prevarications. You have dishonoured my daughter and now you must make it right. We shall go into Canterbury tomorrow to obtain a licence, and you may marry her the day after."

"You are too hasty, sir. I have already stated that I do not recognise any offence against Miss Hamilton on my part, and have no intention of being bullied into marriage."

"Asking a man to take the honourable course is bullying, is it?"

"In this case, it certainly is. You may bully your daughter, but you will not bully me."

"Do you dare to criticise my treatment of my daughter? I, who have never had anything but her welfare in mind? I, an ordained man of God? You are insulting, young man."

"Her welfare? When she is clearly unhappy under your yoke? Look at her! She dare not lift her head in your presence, yet you claim to have her interests at heart. If you cared about her, as a father should care for his daughter, you would treat her with respect and consideration. You would consult her wishes as well as your own. Have you even asked her what her wishes are regarding this proposed marriage?"

"Of course not! How can a woman possibly judge such matters? And her happiness is of no importance. My concern is for her immortal soul, Captain."

Gil could hardly breathe at such high-handed arrogance. Her happiness of no importance? She wanted so little from life — to go to the theatre, to see mountains and the sea, such simple pleasures. Yet she was kept here as a virtual slave. At that moment, he was almost prepared to marry Genista to take her away from such stultifying confinement. Almost, but not quite. He knew perfectly well that she had no wish to marry and leave her father. He was safe, then, to ask her directly what she wished for.

He rose, and limped round to her side of the table, lowering himself gingerly to his good knee so that his eyes were level with hers, and taking her hand in his. She raised wide blue eyes to his face, but he could not read her expression.

"Miss Hamilton, your father cares nothing for your happiness, but I do. If it would make you happy, I will marry you."

Now there was definitely surprise on her face. But to his astonishment, she turned to the physician. "Father, what must I do?"

"No, no, no!" Gil cried in alarm. "I know what your father wants. Now I need to know what *you* want."

"What I *want,*" she said calmly, "is to please my father by obeying him in all things. That is my duty. If you are offering to marry me, then naturally I must ask my father for guidance on how to answer."

"But will it make you *happy?*" Gil said, in a last desperate throw of the dice.

"It always makes me happy to please my father," she said, and then he knew he had lost. After all his careful dealings with the avaricious ladies of the *ton*, he had been rolled up by a country physician. It was humiliating.

"Ha!" the physician said, a triumphant light in his eyes. "Thank the captain prettily, daughter, and accept his offer of marriage."

"Thank you for the honour you do me, Captain Marford," she said. "I accept your offer."

And Gil could only say, "The honour is entirely mine, Miss Hamilton. I shall do my very best to make you happy."

But the bleakness in her eyes dismayed him.

6: A Visit To Canterbury

A night's sleep, aided by laudanum, brought Gil back from the brink of despair. It was not what he had wanted — not what either of them had wanted — but there was no use repining over what could not be helped. He would marry the girl and settle her at Drummoor, then he could go back to Dover and, in time, the Peninsula to do his bit against Bonaparte. When he was not soldiering, he could enjoy himself just as he always had. No one expected a man to live in his wife's pocket. Perhaps he would do as most men of rank did, and set himself up a real mistress instead of playing around with other men's wives. That might work better for both of them. He would not need to see Genista more than once or twice a year, and she could live her own life in his absence. She would hardly want to make a splash in London. And when he was with her, he would be able to run his fingers through that lustrous hair of hers. No, it was not so bad.

There was another benefit to his unexpected betrothal, in that the trip to Canterbury to obtain the licence would enable him to send letters to his colonel, and also to Carrbridge, assuring them both that he had not run off, but had been kept in the wilds of Kent by the snow. He scratched a quick note to Davy, too, waiting and wondering at Marford House in London, and then, his conscience pricking him, another to the inn where he had hired the horse, explaining that he had lost the creature in the snow, but to send the bill to Marford House. He decided not to mention his marriage to anyone. It would be amusing to surprise everyone at Drummoor when he turned up with his bride.

He was uneasily aware that his brother could be quite high in the instep when it came to the family honour. Being a marquess and a peer of the realm, he was very conscious of anything that reflected badly on the Marford name, and he might well feel that bringing a physician's daughter into the family was just such a case. But then, Gil was the sixth brother, and with the eldest five all now married and breeding, only a catastrophe could raise him to the title. He was free to marry where he pleased, therefore. Or where he must, in this case. Besides, he had given his word, now, and Carrbridge would certainly not approve him crying off.

The weather was mild, the road beyond Elversham at least was tolerable, and the gig rolled along slowly enough not to cause Gil much pain in his leg. They were rather squashed at first, for the manservant, James, came with them as far as the village. After that it was just the physician and Gil, but the pleasure in being out of doors almost outweighed the physician's triumphant company. He was not so ill-mannered as to gloat openly, but there was a little smile playing on his lips.

"I do not know why there is such a rush," Gil grumbled. "Why not call the banns in the regular way?"

"Wait three weeks, when you might disappear at any moment?" the physician said. "Hardly. Now that you have finally agreed to treat my daughter honourably, I do not want to give you any opportunity to run away."

"You have a very poor opinion of me if you think I would break my word to a lady," Gil said mildly.

"Indeed," the physician said.

After that Gil lapsed into resentful silence, and the rest of the journey to Canterbury was accomplished without a word being spoken.

When they arrived at the inn where they were to leave the gig, Gil said, "This looks a likely place for me to hire a post chaise."

"For what purpose?"

"Why, to convey my bride to Yorkshire, of course."

"There is no need for that. She will stay with me. You are an army captain, you will not want her left alone while you are gadding about the Peninsula. Her home is with me."

Gil stared at him in bemusement. Gadding about on the Peninsula? Was that how he saw it? But he said only, "You have an odd idea of marriage, sir. You cannot expect me to leave the church with my wife and return her tamely to her father's house. That would look very queer."

"Hmpf. You may take her to Canterbury for a day or two. She will want to buy some new clothes, I daresay. But then you can bring her safely back to me."

"She will be safe enough in Yorkshire, with my family," Gil said.

"With strangers? She will not like that! No, she will stay in her own home, where she is comfortable and understands her place."

His expression was so complacent that Gil gave it up, for there was little point in arguing against such obduracy. But while the physician was busy making his arrangements for the gig, Gil quietly talked to the head ostler and ordered his post chaise. And there was no small satisfaction in knowing that, in the end, the physician was very much the loser from the marriage.

~~~~~
~~~~~

"You're goin' to marry him?" Betty said, her tone as incredulous as if Genista had said she were to fly to the moon. "You never are!"

"It's true," Genista said quietly, her gaze focused on the mixing bowl in her hands. "Father wishes it, and Captain Marford offered."

"Why'd he do that? He was protestin' loud enough about it the night before."

"You heard all that, then?"

"Couldn't help but hear it, they was shoutin' so loud, Dr Hamilton *and* your soldier."

Genista was about to object to the description of him as *her* soldier, when she realised that, in fact, he was exactly that, now. She would be Mrs Marford. What a strange thought. Tears pricked her eyelids again, but she blinked them away angrily, her wooden spoon flying around the bowl even faster. She would not cry about it any more. Father wanted it, and that was an end to the matter.

"But you knows nothin' about him!" Betty said. "How can Dr Hamilton marry you to a stranger like that?"

"He's a captain in the Hussars, so he has a profession. And... and he's a gentleman."

"Aye, but is he a rich gentleman or a poor gentleman?"

"I imagine Father will enquire into that." She remembered the quality of his clothes and the purse heavy with silver, and wondered.

"Yes but—"

Genista slammed the bowl down. "Betty, it does no good, all these questions. Father knows what's best for me."

"But does he know what's best for himself?" the maid said darkly. "He'll miss you when you're gone."

Genista wondered about that herself. How would he manage? Everything she now did for him in his medical work he had once done for himself, but he was not so young now, and liked to sleep late in the mornings, and have a snooze before dinner too, if it could be managed. He got muddled sometimes when prescribing medicaments, and she had to gently correct him. And there was the work she did in the kitchen, too. He would have to get another cook once she was gone, for Betty would never manage the sort of dinners he liked. It puzzled her greatly that he was so willing to see her marry and leave her home, when he depended on her so much. But no doubt he had his reasons.

James came back late in the morning with venison, veal and several brace of pigeon, as well as cheese and sugar, so she set about preparing some of her father's favourite dishes to please him after the trials of the journey to Canterbury. It was curious to think that it was all on her account, so that she might be married.

Married! She could not quite imagine it. All these years she had assumed that she would remain a spinster and look after her father, and now that life was snatched away from her. She would be a wife and, God willing, a mother. It was difficult to adjust to the dramatic change in her situation. How on earth was she to cope with it? She would have a husband. Gil would be her husband. She shivered, although whether more in pleasure or fear she could hardly say. The face of an angel and those wonderful long lashes… He was a pleasure to look at, that much was certain. But as a man? She had liked him well enough when he was just a patient. He had never given her the slightest cause for alarm through his behaviour, for he had always been perfectly gentlemanly towards her, and she had never thought of him in any other light. But now he would be her husband, and she had not the least idea what would be expected of her.

So she went about her duties with her usual efficiency, and tried very hard not to think about what was to come. She had the fires lit well before the gig returned, so when it pulled up on the drive, she had the front door already open.

Her father strode in, his face so thunderous she wondered what on earth could have happened. Usually he was tired, perhaps querulous, but never angry, like this. Behind him, Gil limped in with a face full of mischief. He winked at her as he went past. Whatever did that mean? Was the marriage to be called off after all? She felt a burst of happiness at the thought — perhaps Father had thought better of it, and would not let her go after all? Then Gil would go away and everything would be as it was before, except that she would have pleasant memories of a man with bright blue eyes and long lashes, who had gazed at her intently and wondered if any man had lain awake at night longing to kiss her.

Before her eyes, a vision appeared of the endless empty years in front of her, as her father gradually declined into old age and failing health and poverty. And what was there for her, apart from a role as nurse and then, perhaps, to be squeezed into the household of one of her brothers or sisters, the unwanted poor relation, helping in the nursery or the kitchen? And no one would ever lie awake at night longing to kiss her. No one would ever again look at her with vivid blue eyes, listening to her as if he really cared about her.

Her father retreated to the surgery and slammed the door.

"Whatever has happened?" she whispered to Gil.

But he just laughed. "You will find out soon enough."

It was not soon enough for Genista. When her father emerged from his room at dinner time, he displayed his usual composure, and talked only on indifferent matters during the meal. She could barely eat for apprehension, knowing that sooner or later the cause for his anger would be made clear. She reviewed everything she had done that day over and over, in case any misstep or omission had given rise to her father's displeasure. It was not until the dishes were cleared and only the dessert was left on the table before she discovered the problem.

"Well, daughter, it seems that Captain Marford has deceived us."

This was so unexpected that she gasped. Gil laughed again, and his amusement was so incongruous, set against her father's anger, that she rounded on him.

"Why is that funny? You should be ashamed!"

"I am ashamed of nothing," he said, his face instantly full of disdain. "It is your father who should be ashamed, for agreeing to marry you to a man of whom he knew nothing. Far from deceiving you, I have been entirely open with you, and had you ever asked me, I should have told you at once that my father was a marquess."

"What! You are a nobleman?"

"I am Captain Lord Gilbert Marford, and my eldest brother is the Marquess of Carrbridge. No one has enquired into my ability to support a wife, but you should know that I have no income other than an allowance from my brother and my army pay, in total no more than nine hundred pounds a year, and I own no property, although my brother will very likely give me a house when I marry. *If* I marry," he added, with the mischievous smile lighting up his face again. "I suspect your father is having second thoughts about that, Miss Hamilton."

Dr Hamilton emitted a low growl, and Genista looked at him in sudden terror, wondering what was to come, but he mastered whatever emotion had gripped him and lapsed into silence.

"Father?" she said tentatively.

"Nine hundred a year," he muttered. "Nine hundred a year for idle, good-for-nothing, arrogant dolts like *him*, when honest folk live on a tenth of that and work a hundred times harder. What kind of world is it that rewards the indolent and dissolute?"

"The God-given one," Gil said softly.

"You dare to speak of God?" her father said, his face darkening. "What do *you* know of matters spiritual?"

"Not much," Gil admitted. "However, is it not the case that the same God who gave men dominion over women also gave nobles dominion over commoners?"

"But God did not make them rich," her father said.

"No, the King made them rich, so that they need not till the soil or work with their hands, but might educate their minds and thereby employ their power wisely, for the good of all."

"Fine words, but how many of them bother to educate their minds or learn wisdom? They are too busy gambling and drinking and—" He stopped, with a glance at Genista. "It is of no use to argue logic with a man such as this. You cannot marry him, daughter."

"Yesterday it was imperative that I marry Gil to preserve my reputation. Today, you tell me that doesn't matter. How am I to understand you, Father?"

"Yesterday, I did not know him to be a member of the most worthless group of people in the kingdom. Would that we had dealt with our aristocracy as the French so bravely dealt with theirs! I will not have you tied to such a man, and drawn into his life of vice and depravity. Better to be ruined, for at least then you will have the opportunity to repent of your sins and pray for redemption and forgiveness."

"You are the strangest man I ever knew!" Gil cried. "You insist that Genista is ruined, and force us into a marriage that neither of us wants, even though neither she nor I can recall these sins of which you speak. You are so keen to marry her off that you make no effort to ask even the most basic question of me regarding my ability to support a wife. I could be the poorest man in England for all you know, but so long as I am willing to marry, that is all you require. Yet now, because you discover my brother is a peer, and I have more money than you, somehow I am the worst kind of reprobate, and must not come near your daughter. Half the fathers in the country would give anything to marry their daughters to someone like me, but I am not good enough for *your* daughter, seemingly."

"No, sir, you are not," he said, eyes flashing. "This engagement is at an end."

"That is for Genista to say," Gil said proudly, lifting his chin.

"Is it?" she said, turning to him in bewilderment. "Don't you have a say in the matter too?"

He turned those blue eyes on her, the eyes with the impossibly long lashes. Such a beautiful man! Almost she could wish— But that was out of the question.

"I am honour bound by my promise to you," he said, haughtily.

"You will not cry off?"

"Of course not! Despite what your father thinks, I am a gentleman and I regard myself as irrevocably pledged. But *you* still have the choice."

And there it was, the opening she needed. All she had to do was to say no, and he would go away. She would stay with her father, in the safe, comfortable world she knew. She would never have to leave her home, never marry, never *escape*.

Or she could say yes. She could have this man as her husband, and see those blue eyes every day. She could have her own house, and children, and a life beyond the orchards and fields of Kent. She could choose…

With a deep breath, she lifted her chin.

"You are mistaken. I'm every bit as honour bound as you are," she said.

Her father turned to her, his expression dark. "You cannot marry this man!"

"But I must," she said calmly. "Remember Dionisia, Father? A betrothal is *binding* and I am committed now."

He turned to Gil. "Then it is for *you* to withdraw, sir."

"That I will never do," Gil said, eyes flashing. "I will marry your daughter tomorrow, as agreed, and perhaps one day you will be glad of it."

7: London

Gil and Genista were married by the parish clergyman at Eversham, with the bride's father on hand to give her away and the two servants as witnesses. The clergyman's wife and three daughters, plus two women engaged in polishing the rood screen when they arrived were the only others present. The wedding ring was the bride's mother's, and was several sizes too large. The post chaise Gil had ordered was waiting for them as they emerged from the church, and the bride had packed a small portmanteau to accompany her on her nuptial journey. Gil had nothing to pack.

As his bride bade a tearful farewell to her father and the servants, Gil was rather complacent about the whole affair. It was true that neither of them had wanted to wed, but once it became inevitable he had seen the benefits of the scheme, and besting her father was not the least of it. The man had seen his daughter married to a hated member of the nobility, despite his wishes, and Gil was determined that he should not see her again for a long time. Then there was Genista herself, who was quite pretty enough to please him. And within hours, all that glorious mass of hair would be unpinned for him to enjoy. For the first time in his life he would have a wife in his bed who was his own, everything legal, and no risk of an irate husband turning up and causing a fuss. What a fine thing, to be sure!

The carriage lurched its way through the bogs and ruts and half-melted snow to Canterbury, as Genista watched the white fields pass by and Gil watched her pale face. They stopped briefly in Canterbury to collect a parcel from a tailor, as arranged the previous day, containing sufficient neckcloths and other necessities to last him until Gil reached London and his waiting boxes and valet. Then onwards again, as the busy streets of the town gradually gave way to open fields and woods again.

Only then did she turn to him in surprise. "Are we not stopping tonight in Canterbury?"

"No. We will spend the night in Sittingbourne and then on to London."

"Oh." Her eyes widened a little, her lips parting in the most enticing way. He was seized with the urge to press kisses onto her pretty face.

"A few days in London for you to see about some new clothes, and then we will go north to Yorkshire."

"Oh," she said again.

"I shall take you to the theatre when we are in town," he said, watching her intently. "And the opera, perhaps."

A little smile played on her lips. "I shall like that." Then, rather puzzled, "What about Father? He's expecting me home."

"You may write to him from London to tell him of our plans."

"Oh."

She made no fuss about it, for which he was heartily grateful. "How does it feel to be married, Lady Gilbert?"

"I hardly know," she said. "It has all happened so quickly, and I never expected to be married at all. This is so new that I cannot yet tell what I feel."

He slid a little nearer to her, and said teasingly, "I daresay you have never even been kissed, have you?"

"No."

At once, he wrapped one arm around her and pulled her towards him, bending his head to kiss her gently. Such sweetness in her lips! What a delightful little thing she was. She lay motionless in his arms as he pressed his lips to hers, and he broke away, laughing.

"That will never do! I can see that you have a great deal to learn of the pleasures of love, my lady, and it will be my agreeable office to teach you." He ran one finger softly down her cheek, and then across her parted lips. Her eyes were huge, fixed on his. "Here, then, is your first lesson. A kiss is not a passive business. One does not simply receive a kiss, one must give as well. Shall we try again?"

She nodded, and he leaned closer. This time he patted little kisses on her mouth until he felt her relax in his arms and her eyes closed. Only then did he pull her tightly towards him and kiss her more thoroughly. When they broke apart, she was breathing heavily.

"There! Was not that delicious?" She nodded again, her gaze never wavering. "Tonight, my little wife, I shall show you just how enjoyable kissing can be."

She smiled and snuggled closer into his arms.

~~~~~

It amused him to watch Genista's reactions to London. He was used to the noise and the busyness, the crowds and the smells, but to her it was all new and not, he surmised, very pleasant, for she displayed no animation or excitement. Several times he pointed out places
~~~~~

that he thought might interest her, but she responded to every building or park or monument with the same subdued lack of enthusiasm. "Indeed?" she would say. "I see. Is it so?"

"You are very quiet," he asked her once, puzzled. "Are you... quite well?"

"Oh yes... thank you," she said. "But it's all so... overwhelming."

"London?"

"Oh... everything!" Then she blushed and lapsed back into near-silence, and after a while, he gave it up.

They drew up outside an elegant town house just off Portman Square.

"Wait here," Gil said to her, climbing down from the carriage and limping up the steps to the front door. When it opened to reveal a stout butler, Gil marched past him. "Good day to you, Marks. And how are you keeping? Knee better?"

"Much better, my lord, thank you for enquiring. Is her ladyship expecting you?"

He pulled a wry face. "Not exactly, no. Is she entertaining?"

The butler was impassive. "Not just now, my lord. Shall I announce you?"

Gil agreed to it, and was led upstairs to the drawing room.

"Captain Lord Gilbert Marford, my lady," the butler intoned.

The lady in the room, her elegantly coiffed head bent over a fashion journal, looked up in surprise, then jumped to her feet. "Gil! Well, this is a very unexpected pleasure, but you must know..." She waited until the door closed behind Marks. "Gil, I am with Ramsey now, and he will be here this evening. I cannot—"

"Oh, no, no! Not looking for that kind of hospitality, Bella. Just a room for a night or two."

"Well, of course. Is Marford House shut up?"

"No, but I want to surprise them at Drummoor when I turn up with my wife."

"Your *wife?* Are you serious? How did I not hear about that? Not a whisper reached my ears. When did this happen? And who is the lady?"

"Oh, no one you know. Day before yesterday, and not a soul knows of it yet. You do not mind, do you, Bella? But it will be such a lark to see Carrbridge's face. Do say we may stay here, for otherwise we must find an hotel."

For a moment she was speechless, mouth round with astonishment, but she composed herself and said, "But where is she?"

"Outside, in the post chaise that brought us from Kent."

"Kent..." Bella said faintly. "Gil, you are incorrigible. Bring her inside at once."

~~~~~

Genista twisted her hands in her lap. She had no idea where she was, although the houses in the street looked very grand, several storeys high and each with an imposing portico over the front door. Within a few minutes Gil emerged, smiling, which eased her worries a little.

"Out you come," he said cheerfully, as a footman rushed down the steps to open the carriage door. Taking her hand, Gil helped her down to the pavement. She liked such little attentions, for Father had never helped her out of the gig. Tucking her hand into his arm, Gil led her up the steps and into a narrow entrance hall. Waiting for
~~~~~

them there was a very tall lady in such a flimsy gown that Genista was sure she would catch a chill from wearing it.

Gil said, "Genista, this is Lady Dryton. We will be staying with her for a few days."

She curtsied, and Lady Dryton laughed. "How well mannered! And so pretty! Although the Kent fashions will not do for London — or Drummoor, for Lady Carrbridge is fearsomely stylish."

"There has been no time to get wedding clothes," Gil said. "Bella, you will not mind taking her about a little, to arrange for gowns and so forth?"

"No time?" Lady Dryton looked from one to the other, then laughed merrily. "Well, so that is how it is! Of course, it will be a pleasure. Come, let me show you to your room. I shall have the house full tomorrow, so I can only spare you one room, but you will not mind *that*, I warrant! This way."

That evening was a strange one. After the simplicity of the inn at Sittingbourne, Lady Dryton's house was utterly different, filled with soft rugs, gilt-framed paintings and a mass of decorative furniture. There were servants everywhere, books and journals and bowls of hothouse fruits on every surface and so many candles that every room was dazzlingly bright. There were six of them at dinner, Lady Dryton and the other lady wearing such thin silk gowns, and cut so low at the neck, that Genista blushed to look at them. The men were arrayed in dark coats and waistcoats, with pale, thin knee breeches. Gil had summoned his valet from somewhere, who had spent an age fussing over him, while Genista waited patiently. She felt very rustic with her dark green worsted gown, her only concession to evening to wear a lighter fichu and add her mother's eardrops.

She could eat little of the dinner. Most of the dishes she could not identify, so refused them in case they contained red meat. She had a little of the soup and some of the veal, and there were several vegetables on offer, although most in rich sauces, or highly spiced. It was one thing, she discovered, to want to travel about and see the world, and quite another to cope with it when it happened.

Everyone else seemed to drink a great deal of wine. After dinner, the others played a card game for money while she read a book. Gil seemed to get on well with the others, laughing and joking with them, and talking about people she didn't know.

She must have nodded off, for she came to herself to find Lady Dryton bending over her. "Gil, you have worn the poor child out." For some reason, they all thought that was very funny. "Should you like to go to bed, dear?"

"Yes, if you please." So Lady Dryton summoned a footman to show her up the stairs, where she scrambled into her nightgown and was asleep almost before her head touched the pillow.

~~~~~

Gil disappeared directly after breakfast the next day, telling her that he had matters to attend to. She didn't mind that, for obviously a gentleman would have business to deal with, but she wasn't quite sure what she was supposed to do. The only other person around was one of the gentlemen from the previous night, who had spent part of the evening with Lady Dryton sitting on his lap. Gil had called him Ramsey, but whether that was his Christian or surname, she didn't know. When Gil had gone, Mr Ramsey very kindly made conversation, asking her if she had been to London before and whether she liked it or not.

"I hardly know," she said. "I haven't seen much of it yet, but it seems a very noisy place to me, Mr Ramsey."

He laughed at that. "Noisy — it is indeed, but a great deal of fun. Ah, my ham! Thank you, Marks. And more coffee."
~~~~~

"Very good, my lord."

"I beg your pardon, I didn't know you were a lord," Genista said when the butler had withdrawn.

"Not surprising," he said. "Bella is hopeless with introductions. She knows everyone herself, so she naturally assumes that everyone else does, too. I am the Marquess of Ramsey. Just a courtesy title, you know, for my father is the Duke of Camberley."

"Oh." Genista was horrified that she had been talking so freely to the son of a duke. "I beg your pardon," she said again, helplessly, not knowing what else to say.

Lord Ramsey smiled. "So who is *your* father, Lady Gil? Where is his estate?"

"He doesn't have an estate. He's a physician. Dr Hamilton of Elversham in Kent. Near Canterbury."

"Oh." He looked surprised. "A physician's daughter, eh? That is not Gil's usual style. How did you happen to meet him?"

"Gil was riding to London from Dover, and he must have become disorientated in the snow and ended up half dead on my father's doorstep."

"And your father took him in and healed him, and as he recovered from his state of being half dead in the snow, there was the pretty daughter of the house, eh?"

She blushed, but said, "No, Father was away from home. I took Gil in. And... and Father was upset when he came home, and insisted he marry me."

To her surprise, Lord Ramsey laughed uproariously at this news. "Well, well, well! Rolled up by a country physician, eh? I shall rib Gil about *that*, you may be sure!"

"I wish you will not," she said, but he only laughed the harder, and she was very glad when he went away. A long time later, when she had begun to wonder if she would be left alone all day, Lady Dryton emerged from her room, and took Genista off in her carriage to a warehouse to buy materials for gowns. They were met by a very grand gentleman in a beautiful embroidered brocade coat, who greeted Lady Dryton by name.

"Now, Dodds, this is Lady Gilbert Marford, and she is just up from Kent and wants to replenish her wardrobe."

"Her ladyship's entire wardrobe?" he said, eyes round.

"Hmm, eventually, perhaps, but just for now we will only need enough for a few gowns — morning, afternoon, walking, carriage and evening. Just two or three of each."

"And a ball gown or two, surely, my lady," he said.

"No, not at the moment. Lady Carrbridge will want to advise on that. But the usual accessories, naturally. And something for travelling."

"Of course, of course," he said, bowing so low he was in danger of falling over. "This way, my lady, my lady."

"My own woman will have something run up for you in a day or two," Lady Dryton said to Genista, "but if you are going straight to Drummoor, then you may let Lady Carrbridge take charge of your clothes, for she has excellent taste. Now, let us start with some silks for evening."

Everything Lady Dryton selected, Genista rejected as too flimsy, too diaphanous, too revealing of the female form. After an hour, Lady Dryton threw up her hands and said crossly, "You had better choose for yourself, then, but Gil will *not* be pleased, that much I can tell you. He gave me very clear instructions to rig you out in some town finery, but if you will not have it, there is nothing to be done about it. I can lend you something for tonight, but—"

"You're very kind," Genista said, "but I wouldn't be comfortable in the sort of clothes you wear."

In a very short time, she had selected several lengths of fustian, kerseymere and worsted, some of the thicker muslins and silks, and the buttons and ribbons to go with them.

"My woman will do her best, but she is not used to this sort of thing," Lady Dryton said, fingering the fustian.

"Oh, you need not trouble her," Genista said. "I always make up my own gowns."

"Make up your own—!" Lady Dryton seemed genuinely shocked. "Well, I trust Gil will put a stop to that sort of nonsense. Dodds, send the bill to Lord Gilbert Marford at Marford House, if you please. Parcel everything up and we will take it with us."

When they were in the carriage again, she said to Genista coldly, "I have no idea what Gil is thinking of, marrying someone of your ilk, but if you know what you are about, you will acquire a little town bronze before you are much older. He is not likely to find these provincial attitudes of yours amusing for long. But then, perhaps that is the point, for you will not interfere with his amusements, I daresay. He can leave you at Drummoor, while he does as he pleases. Yes, I can see how that might appeal to him."

That evening was dreadful. It started badly, with a quarrel with Gil.

"Why are you wearing that thing again?" he said, seeing her ready for dinner in her usual gown. "I told Bella very clearly to get you rigged out properly.

"I prefer this."

"Well, I do not. You look like a dowd. Good God, Genista, you might spare a thought for my feelings. Do you want everyone to know that you are a chawbacon?"

"I don't know what that is, but I'm not ashamed of who I am and I don't want to look like—"

"Like what?" he said, with a dangerous glint in his eye. "I hope you were not about to insult my friends, Lady Gilbert."

She flushed and lapsed into silence, but he patted her hand with a sigh.

"Well, never mind. It is all new and strange to you, I can see, but Connie will sort you out when we get to Drummoor. She always knows what is best to be done."

Lady Dryton threw some sort of party, so there were two dozen at dinner and any number of others arrived later in the evening, all dressed in shockingly revealing garments. Genista hardly knew where to look, and the men, in their tight trousers, were as outrageous as the women, with their low-cut and clinging gowns. Genista had never seen anything like it. The drawing room and music room beyond were filled with card tables, with more money than she had ever seen before staked on the turn of a single card or the throw of a dice. There was an intensity about their manner which she could not like. And the wine! So much wine was drunk, and she could quite see why Father had warned her so strenuously against the evils of drink, for there was no one there who was sober.

Genista was the object of much attention, finding herself examined from head to foot through quizzing glasses.

"Where did you find the chit, Gil?" one said. "Not like you to be taken in by a green girl! And really, you hardly needed to marry her. Expensive pleasure, that. You could have had the same fun for a hundred guineas."

"Less than that, surely," another said. "Not much fun to be had with *that* one, by the look of her. I would put it at no more than twenty." And they laughed heartily.

Gil threw down his cards. "I would not advise you to insult my wife, Dallen," he growled, in a tone so low and cold that Genista quaked. Even Father in his worst mood had never spoken with such suppressed anger. It was effective on Gil's friends, though, for the room fell silent and there was a tension that terrified Genista, although she couldn't have said why.

After a few moments when no one moved or spoke, one of the gentlemen said gruffly, "Beg your pardon, Marford. No insult intended. Assure you."

Another long silence. Then Gil nodded and picked up his cards, and the game and chatter resumed as if nothing had happened.

Genista shook from head to toe, wishing that the walls would open up and swallow her. What was the matter with Gil? This was not the same sweet man who had teased her over the backgammon board at Lavender Cottage, or the gentle husband who had kissed her and brought her such delight in the inn at Sittingbourne.

He had the same loud manner and oddly glittering eyes as the others, and was just as swept up in the excitement of the games. So many people! So much noise, the loud voices echoing in her head, and people pressing close, laughing, shouting, great cheers or groans as the gaming went this way or that.

She had to escape. She turned and fled, but her way out of the room was blocked by a large man with a bulbous red nose.

"Leaving already, my pretty? Stay a while, and give me a little kiss, eh? Gil will not mind. Old friends, you know."

To her horror, he clasped her firmly around the waist, pulling her tightly against him, and bent his head towards her, his wine-soaked breath disgusting. With a strength born of desperation, she pushed him away and slapped his face so hard that his head snapped back and banged into the wall. Wrenching open the door, she fled upstairs and crawled into bed, too shocked even to cry.

The noise downstairs went on for hours, but eventually she heard carriages outside and the sounds of the front door opening and closing. Then there were loud voices on the stairs, and bedroom doors slamming. She heard Gil enter the room, humming tunelessly, bumping into furniture and then giggling. She lay facing the wall, pretending to be asleep. At length the bed creaked and before long she heard the soft sounds of snoring.

And then one arm reached around her and pulled her towards him. "Ah, Bella, sweet Bella," he murmured, before lapsing back into sleep.

She tried very hard not to cry.

8: Lady Dryton

Gil woke late, with heavy eyes and aching head. He sent for Davy, bathed, dressed with town care and sauntered down to the breakfast parlour well after noon. Only Bella and Ramsey were there. Gil looked listlessly at the platters of ham and beef, covered them again without taking anything, and poured himself some chocolate.

"I suppose you have not seen my lady wife, have you?" he said.

Bella looked up from the letters she was reading in amusement. "Lost her already, have you? You should keep her in better check, Gil dear."

"Would hardly surprise me if she had gone scampering back to Kent," Ramsey said, lowering his newspaper. "Fothergill had his hands all over her last night."

"Fothergill! Still, the man may be a fool, but there is no harm in him."

"If you say so, but Lady Gil was alarmed enough to slap his face."

"Good God! Did she really?" Gil said. "There was no need for that. I would have seen the fellow off if he was bothering her."

"You think so?" Ramsey said. "When you were taking not the least notice of her?"

"She is a provincial nobody," Bella said crisply. "Why should anybody take notice of her?"

"Because she is my wife," Gil said haughtily. "Whatever she may once have been, she is a Marford now, and entitled to respect. Where is the woman anyway? Ah, Marks, there you are. This chocolate is cold. Bring some fresh. And where is Lady Gilbert this morning?"

"She went out, milord. Miss Hallows had some commissions for her ladyship, and Lady Gilbert went with her."

"Who is Miss Hallows?"

"My lady's maid," Bella said, laughing. "I suppose she did not call for the carriage, Marks? No, I thought not. Those broad country feet were made for walking."

"Really, Bella!" Gil said testily. "I will not have you expending your wit on my wife."

Ramsey snapped his newspaper shut and stood up. "You are a queer sort, Marford. What did you bring her here for anyway? You must have known she would not fit in with Bella's crowd. If you want my advice—"

"Which I do not," Gil said coldly.

"—you will take her directly to Drummoor. The poor child is not up to snuff, and she should not be under Bella's roof. It is hardly fitting."

"Ramsey, if I want your opinion—"

"Oh, stop it, you two!" Bella said. "You need not worry, Gil, for here is a letter from Bertie. He will be home today, and dragging me off to Harrogate the day after tomorrow, so we will be all respectability for a while. If you time your journey, you will have our company all the way to Drummoor."

"You are going to Harrogate?" he said, with sudden interest.

"Bertie's sister lives there, remember? She likes us to visit for Easter, and meet all the local worthies. Lord, how dull it will be! I have to be the virtuous viscountess, and you know what a strain that is for me. But after that it will be the season and all will be gaiety and dissipation."

"That is perfect," Gil said. "If you are going that way, you can take Genista with you and leave her at Drummoor. You will not mind that, will you? It will be company for you."

"Gil, you are not serious!" Then, when she saw his face, she said suspiciously, "Why? What will you be doing?"

"Lawston has this mill coming up — somewhere in Essex, I am not quite sure where. It sounds like the greatest lark, and I should hate to miss it."

Ramsey grunted, but Bella only laughed. "Gil, you are quite shameless!"

~~~~~

Genista returned from her modest expedition to purchase some necessities which she hadn't packed, thinking she would soon be home, to find that her husband had left the house, leaving only a hastily scribbled note.

'I am gone to Essex with some friends to see a mill. Bella and Bertie will take you north. Tell them at Drummoor that I will be there soon. There is money in the lowest drawer, under your handkerchiefs. Gil.'

The money turned out to be a purse with an astonishing number of coins. Genista sat on the bed, still warm where Gil had slept, trying not to panic. It was difficult enough coping with her
~~~~~

new life with Gil around, but when he was not even there... She tried not to consider the word *'abandoned'*, but it wasn't easy.

But she understood. Seeing him amongst his friends, she realised how little suited she was to him. This was his world, not hers, so how could she possibly fit in? She wasn't pretty or fashionable or clever or rich, so no wonder he was ashamed of her. And everything her father had said about the nobility, everything he had feared for her if she married Gil, had all come to pass. They were idle and spoilt and dissolute, and how she was to survive living with such people was beyond her. She could not abandon her principles and become like them. To wear such clothes, and throw away money on gambling? Never! And if Gil had seen all this, and preferred to be with his friends rather than with his staid provincial wife, she could hardly blame him.

There was a small writing desk in her room, supplied with many sheets of writing paper, all inscribed *'Clifton House, Mayfair, London'* and franked on the reverse. She had only ever seen a franked letter once before in her life, when Lucy Cornish's cousin had stayed, very briefly, with an earl, and had written to every member of her family to boast about it. The letter had been passed around the village and the frank admired with awe for months afterwards, and even years later, visiting strangers would be advised that, if they behaved themselves, they might be admitted to a sight of the famous missive. Yet here it was commonplace. Could Gil frank her letters for her? She thought not, for she felt sure it had to be a peer of the realm, but his brother the marquess could, she assumed. The Marquess of Carrbridge. Her brother-in-law. She shivered.

She sat down at the writing desk and pulled out a sheet of paper. She hadn't written to her father, telling him the change of plan. He would be expecting her home soon, and he would worry. Well, let him worry. It was his fault she was in this situation. He was the one who had pushed for this marriage, and not taken the trouble to find out who Gil was first! If he had, he would have seen how ill-suited they were, and she could have stayed quietly at home. Anger boiled up inside her. Her whole life ruined... No, she corrected herself, not ruined. That was too harsh a judgement. *Changed*, then. Her life had been changed by her father's insistence on protecting her reputation, and his haste, his foolish haste.

And then she felt guilty. Father had meant it for the best, she knew that. And, in the end, it had been her own choice to marry. She had been dazzled by blue eyes and charm, and now she was finding that everything that Father had said about the nobility was true. She had been very foolish, but it was done now, and she must make the best of it.

Dipping a pen in the ink, she wrote a careful letter on the franked paper to her sister Dionisia, whose farmer husband could least afford to pay to receive a letter.

'Dearest Di, You will find it hard to believe, I know, for I can hardly believe it myself, but I am married. It all came about very suddenly, when we were snowed up last week and Father was away.' She chewed her pen, but found herself quite unequal to the task of explaining all the details. There were not enough sheets of paper in the world to do it justice. *'I am in London just now, which is a quite horrid place, very dirty and smelly and the noise every hour of the day and night is unbearable. But soon I am to go to Yorkshire which I hope will be more pleasant.'* Here she stopped again. She ought, she knew, to say something of Gil, for Di would expect it, but again words failed her. *'My husband's name is Gilbert Marford and he is a Captain in the King's Own Regiment of Hussars. I shall write again from Yorkshire. Gen.'*

There was nothing more she could write that would not make her cry, and Father disapproved so much of females who cried at the least provocation. She was determined not to repine. However much she regretted this marriage, it was done now and crying never helped anything. She would *not* cry!

She folded and sealed the letter and took it downstairs to ask where she might post it, but the fearsome butler whisked it out of her hands.

"One of the footmen will take it at once, milady."

And she didn't like to argue with him, for a walk outside was a terrifying prospect in the frightening bustle of London. The house, with its luxury and its supercilious servants, might be oppressive, but at least it was safe.

"This package came for you, milady."

"For me?"

"I believe it contains your cards, milady."

"My cards?"

"Your new calling cards, milady. I imagine his lordship arranged for them to be printed."

Her cards. She had never in her life needed calling cards before, but now she unwrapped the small package and opened the box inside. Her cards. *'Lady Gilbert Marford'* they said, printed in a neat copperplate script. *'Lady Gilbert Marford'*, as if, somehow, by printing the name on little squares of card it would be true, and she would be transformed into a lady, and the sister-in-law of a marquess. She had never felt less like a lady in her life.

But perhaps she could look a little more ladylike. She could begin work on one of her new gowns.

"Where is Lady Dryton's sewing room, if you please?" she said.

"Her ladyship's sewing room?" the butler said.

"Yes. Where... where her ladyship does her sewing."

"That would be the drawing room, milady."

"Oh, but… there is no worktable in there. Is there anywhere with a large table, where I might spread out my fabric?"

He arched one eyebrow in haughty surprise, then gave her the smallest of bows. "I will order the dining room table made ready, milady."

It took four people to make ready the dining room table. Two footmen added and removed leaves until the size met with Genista's approval, a maid spread a felted under-cloth and then a starched linen cloth over it, and the butler supervised. Then there was a procession to Genista's room to fetch the length of fabric she required and her small work basket. She had bought a few necessities on her expedition with Miss Hallows, but she wished she had known that she was not to return home. All her favourite scissors and thimbles and spools of thread were sitting in the parlour at Lavender Cottage.

Using her travelling gown as a guide, she swiftly cut out the necessary shapes and began to pin them together. A timid knock on the door was followed by Miss Hallows' neatly coiffed head.

"Milady? Do you require any assistance? I have a pattern book— Oh, you've begun already."

"I've never used a pattern."

"Do you make all your own clothes?" The astonishment in her voice made Genista smile. "You have nimble fingers. I shouldn't have guessed your attire to be anything less than professionally created. May I sit with you while you work? I've brought my own work basket, and I'll be here if you need an extra pair of hands."

"Thank you, I'd like that."

Genista felt far more at ease with the down-to-earth Miss Hallows — Susan, she confided at an early stage — than with anyone else she had encountered in London. They talked of gowns and threads and feathers and ribbons and the difficulties of silk. Susan helped her pin the sleeves for her gown in a new shape, and Genista advised on thread colours for the flounce Susan was adding to one of Lady Dryton's gowns.

"Have you met Lady Carrbridge?" Susan said. "She's very elegant, but you'd like her way of dressing, I think. She don't wear the very light styles my lady favours. Always wears a good, solid undergown, does Lady Carrbridge, and not so low at the front."

"Oh, so not all ladies wear their gowns so...?" Genista could not think of a word that would not be derogatory. "I mean to say," she added hastily, "Lady Dryton looks lovely, but not everyone has the... the *shape* for such garments."

Susan laughed. "Oh, indeed, one needs a certain *embonpoint* to carry off such a style, as well as a certain confidence, which my lady has in abundance, don't you agree?"

And Genista could not argue the point.

They were thus happily engaged when a carriage pulled up outside the house, the front door opened and voices could be heard in the hall outside. After a moment, the door opened and an elderly gentleman with a head of white hair entered the room. Miss Hallows jumped to her feet and dropped into a deep curtsy, and Genista instinctively followed her lead.

The newcomer smiled benevolently at her. "Lady Gilbert? How delightful to find a guest in the house, and we are to have the pleasure of your company on the journey north, I understand. Allow me to introduce myself. I am Viscount Dryton."

Genista was pleased to find that this was not, after all, the home solely of Lady Dryton. Naturally there would be a man as head of the household. "Oh, then you must be Lady Dryton's father."

Lord Dryton blinked at her, and it was only the squeak of alarm from Susan that alerted Genista to her mistake.

"No," he said, with unimpaired gentleness. "I have the very good fortune to be Bella's husband."

"I beg your pardon!" Genista said, horrified, the colour rushing from her face. And then, remembering Lady Dryton sitting on Lord Ramsey's knee in the most familiar way, she said again, miserably, "I beg your pardon. I am very stupid."

"Not at all. How should you know if no one explains it to you? I have been in Bath for my health, but I do not like to drag Lady Dryton to such a stifling place, full of the sick and elderly. London is where she is at her vibrant best, and it pleases her to spend most of her time here. And naturally, it pleases me to please my wife. Husband and wife should not be in each other's pockets, should they?"

She shook her head, unable to speak.

And, still smiling genially, he went away again, and Genista sank gratefully into a chair.

"Lord, didn't you realise?" Susan said. "Your husband should have told you how it was, if you didn't guess. She couldn't be Lady Dryton if she were his daughter, would she? She'd be an honourable, and if she was the daughter of a duke or some such, she'd be Lady Arabella, not Lady Dryton... Oh dear. Don't cry. You'll get into the way of it soon enough, don't you worry, and Lord Dryton's lovely. He won't take no notice when you say things wrong. Just don't mention Lord Ramsey. The viscount don't mind what she gets up to when he's not around, but she tries not to let him know who the current one is. Better for everybody if he don't know."

That evening was quiet. There were only the three of them for dinner, Lady Dryton arrayed in a far more modest gown, to Genista's surprise, and the meal simpler and much more to her taste. Lord Dryton followed the ladies immediately to the drawing room.

"Lady Gilbert, do you play cribbage?"

"I do, my lord. My father is a keen player."

"Ah, a man after my own heart. There is nothing more entertaining than a game of cribbage, in my opinion, although my dear wife finds it rather too tame. But if you will oblige me with some cribbage, Lady Gilbert, then Bella may find some other occupation more to her liking."

Genista was very happy to oblige him, while Lady Dryton played a little, read a little, picked up her tapestry, set it down again and then walked about the room, before once more settling at the instrument. Lord Dryton was a good player, very fast but patient if she dithered, and it was perhaps the pleasantest hour she'd ever spent in that house. The only discomfort she found arose from Lord Dryton's gentle questions. He would ask about her home, her family and her journey from Kent, and would then make a seemingly innocuous jump to asking about the guests she had seen in the house on previous nights. And when she replied that there had indeed been guests, he asked her for names. She was able to answer, with tolerable composure, that she did not know who they were. Her husband knew them but she couldn't remember their names. Which was true enough.

"Ah," Lord Dryton said.

And then, after some discussion of Gil and his plans, she had mentioned that he had gone out one morning to attend to some business. "Gentlemen always have business to attend to, don't they?" she said absently, her attention caught up in the game.

"Is it business that has taken him out of town?" Lord Dryton said.

"I... suppose so. He has gone into Essex to see a mill, but I don't know whether it belongs to him. Or one of his friends, perhaps... Have I said something wrong?"

Lord Dryton's smile widened. "Ah, you come from a different world from your husband, Lady Gilbert, a world where a mill is a place for grinding corn or making things, is it not so? But to a young gentleman of the town, a mill is something else — a fight! Usually a bare-knuckle fight between two young men, with a prize purse and much gambling on the outcome. Those who enjoy such things will travel a great distance to attend."

"Oh!" She couldn't disguise her shock. "He's gone to watch a *fight?* I had no idea gentlemen did such things!"

"Indeed they do. And so you breakfasted all alone?"

"Oh no, for Lord Ramsey was—" She stopped and laid down her cards in distress. "Oh, I beg your pardon!"

He threw a quick glance at his wife, playing at the pianoforte, unheeding. Lord Dryton's eyes were filled with understanding, and he smiled in that beatific way he had. "Lord Ramsey, eh? Well, at least he is more her own age than some have been. It is your play, Lady Gilbert." But when she could not move, feeling the tears pricking her eyes, he laid one hand on hers, in a very fatherly gesture. "My dear, you are a sweet, innocent girl and your husband had no business to bring you here. But I shall take you to Drummoor, where the marquess and his wife will take better care of you, it is to be hoped."

"Thank you, my lord," she said miserably, all her pleasure in the game spoilt.

Not long after, Lord Dryton retired and Genista, finding that Lady Dryton didn't need her company, crept away to her room and climbed unhappily into the big, empty bed. Then she lay awake for hours, wondering where her husband was and when she would see him again and whether he was taking proper care of his wounded leg. But most of all, she wondered why he had brought her to Lady Dryton's house and left her there alone, and how she was to survive the long, lonely journey north to Yorkshire.

9: Drummoor

The journey to Yorkshire was a nightmare that Genista thought would never end. Having not been beyond the borders of Kent before, now towns and entire counties passed by in a whirl of noise and snorting horses and the shouts of postilions and the coachman's horns. She could not imagine why she had ever wanted to travel, for it was the most dismal affair. Quite apart from the discomfort of being jounced around for hours, she spent endless hours waiting — for meals to arrive, or rooms to be ready, or horses to be put to, or for Lady Dryton to appear, a good half hour after everyone else was ready to depart.

There were three coaches, the luxurious one that she shared with Lord and Lady Dryton, with furs and rugs and hot stones for their feet, a smaller one for the secretary, valet, lady's maid and baggage, and a third for several more servants and even more baggage. Her own belongings had grown to include a small box as well as her portmanteau, but it was only a minor part of the assemblage.

They stopped early each afternoon, and there was a great to do about luggage and rooms and parlours and meals, and a great deal of argument from Lady Dryton, for whom nothing was ever quite right.

Then, at night, Genista retreated to her own empty, silent room, with no dark-haired angel with long lashes beside her to kiss her to enchantment. She tried not to cry — she must *not* cry — but she could not force herself to sleep. She felt as though she were wound up as tight as a spring that might at any moment unravel.

In the mornings, as the carriage bounced them about, Lord Dryton would attempt to make conversation, but by noon he was tiring, and tended to fall asleep in the afternoons. Lady Dryton said nothing at all, which Genista found more restful. They spent a whole day in Grantham, since it was a Sunday, but no one seemed inclined to go to church, and Genista could only sit in the private parlour Lord Dryton had taken, reading her psalter and listening to the many church bells sounding in the distance.

She had never felt so alone, or so uncomforted by the familiar words of the litany. If she had had Gil with her, there would at least have been the memory of his stay at Lavender Cottage to connect her with the home and life she had left behind. As it was, she felt as if she had been torn up by the roots, and tossed into a rushing stream bearing her… somewhere. Drummoor, but she had no concept of the place to help her anticipate what she might find there. What if the house was empty? Perhaps the marquess had gone away, and why shouldn't he, when he wasn't expecting her? He didn't even know she existed. She would arrive on the doorstep, a stranger, yet married to his brother. What if he turned her away, or refused to believe her? How humiliating, to have to produce her marriage lines as proof. Whatever would they think of her, descending unannounced on them in this dreadful way? And yet what could she do? Gil had wanted to surprise his family, and he would certainly get his wish.

On Monday morning they set off again — more roads, more inns, more jolting about through the ever-changing scenery of farms and woodlands and villages, repeated endlessly, with only the occasional town to relieve the pattern. But gradually the neat hedges and orchards began to give way to wilder country, with glimpses of open moorland and distant hills through the rain which spattered the windows and drummed steadily on the coach roof. Genista felt sorry for the coachman, grooms and postilions, and the two footmen standing at the back of their coach ready to jump down and open doors and let down steps whenever required. They were soaked through by the bitter, stinging rain.

On Tuesday afternoon, they turned off the main turnpike onto smaller roads, rutted and puddled and very uncomfortable. Lord Dryton lay back against the squabs, eyes closed, uttering a low moan with every particularly violent lurch, and even Lady Dryton's expressionless face was set into lines of displeasure. Eventually, the carriage rolled under an arch, turreted like a castle, and the ride became smoother.

"At last!" Lady Dryton exclaimed.

"Where are we?" Genista said, although she guessed the answer.

"Drummoor. One of the finest houses in England, so they say. Henry has always wanted to see it." She cast a glance at her husband, his face pale.

"You've never been here before? But you know the Marquess of Carrbridge?"

She turned amused eyes on Genista. "My dear, *everyone* knows Lord Carrbridge. Everyone knows everyone of importance, after all. But we are not... close. And the marchioness..." She laughed. "You should get on well with the marchioness. She is a provincial little nobody, too."

"Bella!" her husband said in reproving tones, but she only laughed the more.

After a while, the coach drew up outside the house, and Genista looked up at it in shock. It was as big and as grand as a palace. Peering up through the rain, she could see battlements and masses of high chimneys. But there were lights, and footmen emerging from the front door to attend to them, so perhaps the marquess was at home after all.

As soon as the steps were let down, Lady Dryton was out of the coach, sweeping up the wide steps to the door and disappearing inside, furs trailing. Genista waited for Lord Dryton to descend, leaning heavily on the footman's arm, before scuttling into the house in his wake. The entrance hall was huge, all dark wood panelling and great, wide stairs leading up and up, with chandeliers swaying on long ropes from a ceiling far above. The stairs were guarded by a suit of armour, and swords and stags' heads jockeyed for position on the walls. One entire wall was given over to a moth-eaten tapestry of a battle. Two fires burned fitfully on either side of the hall, and beyond them, doors and passageways hinted at other parts of the house.

"We are here to see Lord Carrbridge," Lady Dryton said, tossing two cards onto a silver salver held by a bewigged and liveried butler. Or perhaps he was merely a footman. She turned to Genista. "Your card, child."

Genista scrabbled in her reticule, and produced the box of cards, fumbling with the lid. With an exclamation of annoyance, Lady Dryton grabbed the box from her and swiftly extricated a card to add to the salver. With a bow, the servant withdrew.

Lord Dryton sat heavily in a carved wooden chair beside one of the fires, his hands shaking.

"Are you all right?" Genista said, kneeling beside him. "Is there anything you need?"

He shook his head. "Just tired, my dear. Long journey."

"The squire always says that brandy is just the thing to set him up after a journey," she said, not quite sure what else to suggest.

"Ah, a wise man. I could do with a brandy." He nodded at a footman, who scampered off, returning very shortly with a glass on a silver tray. Lord Dryton reached for it, but his hands were shaking so much that Genista took it and helped him sip a little.

"Thank you. That will do for now," he said.

A commotion behind her caused Genista to turn round. Several gentlemen had emerged from some inner fastness and were gazing at her. At all three of them, but mostly at her. Not quite knowing what to do, she curtsied.

One of the gentlemen, very finely dressed, was holding the three cards in his hand, and now he gazed at them, reading the inscriptions. "Lady Dryton, Lord Dryton? Welcome to Drummoor. And..." He turned again to Genista. "Lady Gilbert?"

She curtsied again.

"Gil is married? But where is he?"

"He... he had to go to Essex, sir. My lord."

"To *Essex?* Great heavens, why?"

"To a mill."

"A mill." His voice reeked of incredulity.

She bowed her head, shivering. "Yes, sir. My lord. Oh, I beg your pardon." Her cheeks flamed with mortification. Her hands were shaking so hard that she was sure the brandy would slop over the side of the glass. Carefully she handed it back to the impassive footman, still holding the silver salver.

One of the other gentlemen coughed. "Perhaps... later, my lord? When Lady Carrbridge is home?"

"Yes, of course. Ah, Mrs Compton, there you are. We have guests. Lord and Lady Dryton have arrived. And... Lady Gilbert."

Genista curtsied again.

"Lady *Gilbert?*" Her eyes flicked to Genista, filled with astonishment, but she schooled her features at once. "I see, my lord."

"Where is it Lady Carrbridge has gone today?"

"To Tambray Hall, my lord. Lady Melthwaite..."

"Ah, yes. But... guests, you know." He seemed quite flummoxed, and Genista could hardly blame him.

"I shall myself show Lord and Lady Dryton to the willow suite, my lord. For Lady Gilbert, perhaps the jasmine room, for now? And might I suggest that Mrs Merton and Mrs Burford attend her? Since Lady Carrbridge is not here."

"Oh, yes! Yes, of course! Merton, would you...?"

Genista's head was spinning. So many names! So many people, and all so grandly dressed that she could not even work out which were the servants, and which were relations of the marquess. Had she just curtsied to a servant? She had the sinking feeling that she had.

There was a general moving about, and the Drytons were led away up the stairs, followed by a train of footmen with coats, and one carrying Lord Dryton's brandy glass on a tray. More footmen were bringing boxes and bags in from the coaches.

And then two smiling ladies stood before Genista.

"Lady Gilbert? How do you do? I am Lady Carrbridge's sister, Mrs Burford, and this is our cousin, Mrs Merton. Goodness, so much luggage! Is any of this yours?"

"That small box, and... the portmanteau over there."

Mrs Burford signalled to a couple of footmen to bring her luggage, and then the two ladies swept Genista up the stairs. "We will not put you in Gil's rooms, for he has only a bachelor's apartment here, you know. The jasmine room is very comfortable, and whenever he gets here, alternative arrangements may be made. But how unexpected! And how like Gil not to tell anyone."

"He wanted to surprise everyone," she said.

"He certainly succeeded! But Connie will be so upset that she was not here to welcome you. Have you been married long?"

"Not quite a fortnight."

The two ladies exclaimed at this, although whether in shock or pleasure she couldn't tell. She had no idea whether she was welcome here, or whether this placid reception was merely politeness hiding a seething anger. They could hardly be pleased to have her foisted on them like this, and the Drytons, too.

Within minutes of her arrival, she was ensconced in a large bedroom with a dressing room attached. Round the far corner of the bedroom was a charming little alcove with its own fireplace and sofa and writing desk, the walls circular like a medieval tower. Maids appeared to start the fires and bring a bathing tub and a heap of soft towels. Two more maids began to unpack her box and portmanteau, and ask what gown she would like readied for the evening. She pointed to her only silk gown.

"This one, milady?"

"Yes, if you please."

"I daresay you have not had time to order your wedding clothes yet," one of the two smiling ladies said. "Would you like to borrow a gown? If you wish to dress up a little."

"No, I... thank you, but... I don't think..."

"Of course, as you prefer. Well, we shall leave you to recover from your journey. Dinner is at seven. We will come back to take you to the pink drawing room at six, if that is acceptable?"

"Oh yes. Thank you," she said, curtsying from habit to their retreating backs. She had no idea who they were. One of the maids giggled and was shushed by another.

Genista would have been ready long before the appointed hour had she been left to manage her toilet alone, as usual, but it was almost six before her gown was returned to her, pressed and with fresh lace added to the sleeves. Then two maids helped her into it, primped her hair into strange shapes and offered her a range of ribbons and combs and silk flowers to decorate the arrangement. She would have liked to refuse everything, but as they were very persistent, she agreed to a single flower. The two ladies, who had arrived promptly at six, waited patiently for her, chatting comfortably about her journey north.

All in all, it was a quarter to seven when they led her through twisting passageways and several sets of stairs to the pink drawing room. It was full. At least thirty pairs of eyes turned towards her, quizzing glasses were raised and the buzz of conversation died away.

A gentleman jumped up and strode across the room towards her. "Ah, Lady Gil! There you are! I must apologise for the continued absence of Lady Carrbridge, but her aunt is very sick. However, it gives me the honour of introducing you. Do come in and meet everyone." She wondered who he might be. The Marquess of Carrbridge? Did marquesses undertake to introduce guests in such an informal way? Surely a marquess was too grand for that. She had a vision of an elderly man on a throne-like chair, perhaps seated on a dais, with acolytes around him. Nothing at all like this serious young man of not much above thirty.

He walked her around the room, tossing names around like autumn leaves. Lord This. Lady That. Mrs Someone. Mrs Someone Else. A physician — a moment of interest, but her escort passed on before she could ask anything. More lords and ladies. Lady Dryton, but not her husband. Again, she had no opportunity to ask how he was. He'd looked so old and tired when they'd arrived.

Then they went into dinner, and she was expected to sit at her host's right hand, like an honoured guest. He was very kind, offering her a little of this or that dish from the laden table, sending for lemonade when she refused the wine, and asking her gentle questions about her journey and Kent and her family, which she could barely find the words to answer coherently.

He was in mid-question, when he suddenly stopped. "Do you know, I have been terribly rude. In all the delightful surprise of your unexpected arrival, I forgot to introduce myself to you formally. I expect you have been clever enough to work out that I am Lord Carrbridge, eh? But still, it must have been very confusing for a while. How do you do, Lady Gilbert."

"How do you do, my lord," she said. She couldn't work out whether he was teasing her, or being rude in some subtle, aristocratic way.

The room pressed in on her, the noise hurt her head, and the brilliant lights dazzled her eyes. The surrounding banks of footmen in their livery seemed like an army, holding her captive. She could eat nothing, her throat too choked with misery to swallow. What was she doing there? She had no business to be in the midst of this great family, all these lords and ladies with their silks and velvets and sparkling jewels. And they thought so too, she could see it in their supercilious stares, and the unnerving way they watched her and then whispered behind their hands.

The dishes were all cleared away and another complete set appeared, even more elaborate than the last. A roast swan, a saddle of mutton and any number of smaller dishes. Oysters and crab and herrings brought all this way from the sea, and an array of larks and ducks and pigeon and pheasant. She had a little blancmange and some mushrooms, but could eat nothing else. Lord Carrbridge watched her anxiously, she thought, but gave up trying to tempt her appetite, and after a while turned to Lady Dryton on his other side for conversation.

"We are a bit much, do you not agree?" said a pleasant-faced young man on her right. "The Marfords *en masse*. You will get used to us, in time. I expect you have forgotten my name — I am Monty, one of Gil's brothers."

"Monty," she said, feeling stupid. Even so, she liked his informality, which reminded her a little of Gil. At home, she had been on Christian name terms with almost everyone she knew, and they with her.

"Lord Montague, officially, but everyone calls me Monty. Did he talk to you much about his family? No? I expect you had much more interesting things to talk about. Is he all right? Gil, I mean. Last we heard, his wounded leg was not healing well and he was to be sent home to recover. We have heard nothing since. He is all right, I take it?"

"He was when I last saw him, five... no, six days ago."

"Before he went off to Essex to watch a mill, leaving you all alone."

"Oh, I was not alone. There was Lady Dryton..."

Monty's face darkened. "And that is just like Gil, to run off and leave you with—" He stopped, glancing across the table to where Lady Dryton was in animated conversation with the marquess. Genista had seen her like that before, when her husband was not around. She leaned forward towards the marquess, one hand resting on his arm, speaking in a low, intimate tone, smiling in a teasing way. He didn't seem impressed, though. Not like Lord Ramsey had been, for he had smiled back at her, and put his arm around her waist, and later, she'd sat on his lap and he'd kissed her… and not just on the mouth.

"—very bad of him," Monty was saying in angry tones. "Carrbridge is spitting fire about it, and he will get such a roasting when he finally shows his face again. He never *thinks,* that is the trouble. He just goes ahead and does whatever he wants, and never a thought for anyone else, and it is too bad of him, it really is. This time he has gone too far."

She knew he was talking about Gil, and it was all her fault. If only she'd never married him! And that was Father's doing, mostly. Father had brought them all to this devilish coil, and now they could never escape. They were stuck with each other for ever, and obviously Gil regretted it or he would never have gone off and left her like that. And now his family regretted it too and were angry about it, angry with *her*, and everything was a hideous mess, and she had to get away from that room, from the heat and the noise, and the burning lights.

Just then, the ladies all rose. Relief! She rose too, rather shakily, and all the gentlemen stood as the ladies withdrew into the cool corridor outside, dark after the brilliance of the dining room. A couple of footmen stood by the doors, holding them open, then, as the last lady passed through, they withdrew into the dining room, closing the doors behind them, and shutting off the last of the bright light. The procession of shimmering silks and satins and waving feathers turned to the right and slowly moved off, chattering like a flock of exotic birds.

No one was taking any notice of Genista. In the other direction she caught a glimpse of the stairs. Without a second's hesitation, she turned and fled, picking up her skirts and racing on shaking legs up the stairs, round and round until she could go no further, and then following the low lamps on the walls into the shadows. She ran and ran, terrified that someone might have seen her go and come running after her. They might even drag her back into the brilliance of the drawing room, and she would have to sit with the ladies and pretend not to be terrified for another hour or two or even more. She couldn't bear it. She couldn't breathe, with so many people around her.

After a while, she thought she would try to find her room. There had been a blue and orange vase on a table outside her door, she remembered, so all she had to do was to walk about until she found it. So she walked, and she found many tables and many vases, but not the right ones. She also found odd little dead ends, and half-stairs and windows overlooking courtyards that she'd never seen before.

Eventually, she found herself in a vast gallery stretching endlessly into darkness. On the walls, the stern faces of Marford ancestors stared down at her disapprovingly. She was lost and exhausted and could go no further. She found a window seat, and curled up on it in a miserable, lonely ball. It was all too much, as the tears she'd been holding back for days finally overwhelmed her. Once she'd started, she sobbed and sobbed and sobbed.

She wished she were back with her father.

She wished she'd never met Gil.

She wished she were dead.

10: Kindly Faces

Soft voices, rustling silk, a faint waft of perfume. A murmur in her ear, and then an arm around her waist, helping her to rise, still weeping. Walking, walking, behind a flickering candle. Stairs down, more walking, a vase that looked familiar, a door opening. Willing hands helping her undress, wiping away her tears even as more fell. A nightgown slipped over her head, cool and soft, not her own. Then a warm bed. She buried her face in soft pillows, and wept on. Eventually, in blessed quietness, she fell asleep.

Every time she woke, a kindly face leaned over her. Murmured voices. The rattle of fresh coals onto the fire. Once, a male voice, but it wasn't Father. He was gone, and she would never see him again. Nor was it Gil. Perhaps she would never see him any more, either. She wept even more.

Sometimes when she woke, there was a grey light in the room, at other times there was only a lamp and the flickering light of the fire. Always, there was a kindly face bending over, smoothing her hair away from her face or wiping her forehead with sweet-smelling rose water. Sometimes, she would be lifted up and beef tea spooned into her, with words of encouragement. Sometimes, it was some sweet liquid — laudanum, she suspected — and after that she slept again. Once, her mother's perfume drifted by and she cried out, "Mama! Mama!" But it wasn't Mama, it was only another kindly face, murmuring soothing words. After that, she sobbed for a long time before sleep came again.

Eventually she woke fully. Above her, the canopy of the bed was draped in pretty muslin, the curtains pulled back on one side. There was sunshine falling onto the rug in front of the fire, but only a narrow strip, as if the window curtains were half drawn. A woman sat reading in a wing chair beside the bed. She looked up at once.

"Ah, you are awake at last! How do you feel, my dear? A little better?"

Genista nodded. "Thank you. So sorry—"

"Hush now. No need for that. I have some beef tea heating on the fire. Would you like some? Or shall I send for some proper tea? Or food — are you hungry?"

"Tea... would be lovely. Thank you. If... not too much trouble."

"My dear, it is not the least trouble. But I must tell Connie you are awake. She so longs to talk to you — we all do."

She went to the door and gave some instructions in a low voice to someone outside. Connie. The name was familiar, but Genista couldn't work it out. There had been too many names and faces and titles, and they drifted past like so much smoke.

"What time is it?" Genista said.

"Time? It is just past two in the afternoon, and it is Friday."

"Friday! But I arrived—"

"On Tuesday, yes. You have been ill for days. But Dr Hay said you were merely exhausted and I believe he was right. Ah, here is Connie now."

The door opened again, and a smiling face peeped round. "Oh, you *are* awake!" And in she came, and behind her a whole train of other smiling ladies. Some of them looked a little familiar, and she guessed these were the kindly faces who had tended her during her illness. But so many of them! A tide of panic rose inside her.

"No, no, no! Not everyone," said the lady who had been with her first. "It is too much. Remember what Dr Hay said — no more than two at a time."

With little mews of disappointment, most of them went out and the room descended into quietude again. Genista relaxed a little but she was still shaking.

"Poor thing!" the newcomer said. "You are quite done up. But you are perfectly safe now. We will take good care of you, and you need not leave this room until you are quite ready. But do you understand where you are?"

"Drummoor? And you are... Connie? But...?" She looked helplessly at the other lady.

"I am Connie, yes, the Marchioness of Carrbridge, so this is my home. And this is Belle," said Connie. "She is my sister. All my sisters are here for Easter, it is the most charming thing in the world, the first time we have all been together since Amy married. And all my sisters-in-law too, so you see, your appearing just now is the most fortuitous event. Nothing could be more delightful!"

And she smiled so widely that Genista could not for a moment doubt her sincerity. She burst into tears.

"Oh no! What have I said? Oh please, you must not cry again. Please do not."

"So sorry," she sobbed. "But I thought... you would be angry with me... turning up unannounced... so rude! And you're so kind and I don't deserve it!"

"My dear sister, how could anyone be angry with *you?* With Gil... certainly! Lord Carrbridge will likely tear him apart with his bare hands when he gets here — *if* he ever gets here! But you? No blame can possibly attach to you, my dear. What *is* your name, by the way? We cannot keep calling you *'my dear'*, like those people one meets once a year and can never remember the name of."

"My name?"

"Yes, for we tried to guess it from your things, but we did not get on very well. Your hair brushes are marked *'F H'*, you see, but the portmanteau is *'Lady Wetherbourne'*, which did not seem right, for I know the baron and there is no Lady Wetherbourne. And then your psalter has *'F D'* on the flyleaf. It was very confusing."

"I think you are a Frances," Belle said. "Or Florence? Frederica? Felicity?"

Genista laughed. "Genista."

"Oh!" they cried in unison. "Not an F at all!"

"That was my mother. Flora Draper before she married, and Flora Hamilton later. And Lady Wetherbourne..." She stopped, the ever-present tears rising to the surface again. But that was old history. "My sister nearly married a baron, but he cried off at the last minute."

"Oh!" they said again. "What a wicked thing to do!"

"Yes, because he left her with child and ruined, and she had to marry a farmer and it was all horrible and Father was so *angry* about it, and I think that was why he was so determined that I should marry Gil, in case I got *spoilt* like Di." And then the whole story tumbled out and they listened with such sympathy that she felt, for the first time, that someone understood.

"You poor dear!" Connie said, wiping away tears of her own. "I do feel for you most sincerely. Marriage is not an easy business even when one loves one's husband very deeply, and I cannot imagine enduring all that has happened to you without going mad, or wanting to kill someone. Probably Gil, to be truthful. That is where the blame lies. He is a sweet boy in many ways, but never a thought in his head beyond the moment."

"Marriage will settle him, when he comes round to the idea," Belle said. "It is difficult to find oneself responsible for a wife and children without growing up just a little. He is very young, still."

"But do you like him, Genista?" Connie said. "He can be very charming, when he sets his mind to it."

And Genista blushed and said yes, she had noticed that. Charming and with the face of an angel, although she didn't mention that, naturally. The two ladies smiled, and exchanged glances. But her feelings were never the issue. Gil was handsome, worldly and rich, and when he turned his attention on her, he made her feel as if she were drowning in those blue eyes with the impossibly long lashes. Naturally she was drawn to him, as she had been from the first moment she had met him. It could not be otherwise, and with the least effort he could surely make her head over heels in love with him. Indeed, she was already most of the way there.

But she was everything he was not — plain, rustic and poor, with nothing at all to attract him. He would never love her as she loved him, that was clear to see. He would always want more, and so he would always look elsewhere for affection. There would always be someone to draw him away — someone beautiful and worldly and enticing like Lady Dryton. She understood that. However despondent it made her feel, she understood it and accepted it. That was how the world was. Not everyone could have the good fortune to marry for love. But it made her sad, all the same.

~~~~~

Gil ached all over, and his leg felt as if it were burning up. When he slithered in unusually ungainly fashion from his horse in the inn
~~~~~

yard, Davy said, "Right, that settles it. We'll go the rest of the way by post chaise." Gil was too weak to argue. He left Davy to arrange their accommodation, content merely to collapse into a chair beside the fire as soon as their parlour was readied for them.

"Now don't be angry, Gil, but I've sent for the local physician," Davy said diffidently. "Someone has to take a look at that leg, and I don't want to answer to his lordship if it has to come off in the end, when it might've been prevented."

"I wish Genista were here," Gil said fretfully, shivering over the fire.

"Lord, Gil, you're not in any fit state to be thinking about that sort of thing. You need to take things easy for a while."

Gil managed half a smile. "No, not in that way. She put some foul poultice on my leg down in Kent, but it was damned effective."

"Of course. She was the physician's daughter. I suppose she knows all sorts of remedies."

"She remedied *me* well enough. I was sick as a horse when I arrived on her doorstep, and frankly I would not have wagered a farthing on my chances, but she had me in plump currant in very short order. Clever little thing, my wife. I hope she got to Drummoor safe and sound. God, it is hot in here. Are you hot, or is it just me?"

"It's just you, Gil. You're burning up with fever. How about we stay here for a couple of nights, get that leg properly rested?"

Gil shook his head violently. "Got to get to Drummoor. Genista will straighten me out. Is there any brandy? Or a decent claret?""

The physician came, tutted over Gil's leg, cleaned, poulticed and bound it, and went away ten guineas richer.

"Lord, you must be ill," Davy said, grinning. "Never known you pay the sawbones without making a fuss before."

"Leg feels better," Gil said, half asleep beside the fire, brandy glass in hand. "Happy to pay for that."

"Do you want some of this mutton?" Davy said. "There's a decent pigeon pie, too."

"Think I might go to bed."

He slept tolerably well, ate a modest breakfast and made no protest when Davy pushed him into a post chaise. The weather had turned, and there was a certain satisfaction in sitting, dry and warm, in comfort while the rain cascaded down outside. He was still tired enough to doze, off and on. When they next stopped, he himself suggested sending for a physician.

Davy threw him an anxious look. "You must be bad."

"Just... feeling foolish. Should never have gone to Essex. Not even an interesting mill, in the end, and all that riding... damned leg! But I do *not* want to lose it. I need to be sensible, for once in my life."

"Aye, well, it would be a first, true enough," Davy said, grinning.

"Be home tomorrow," Gil said. "Then I shall be fine. Be glad to be back at Drummoor, although I suppose Connie will have the place full to the rafters. Be lovely to see Genista again, and hear all about her adventures."

Another good night's sleep, aided by some medicament from the physician, saw Gil in a happier frame of mind the next day. His leg was much better, and his fears of losing it were receding. Besides, every mile northwards saw them a mile closer to Drummoor and home. By the time they pulled up outside the front door, he was filled with happy anticipation.

It was only when Crabbe and his troop of footmen came slowly down the steps and made no effort to unload the luggage that Gil began to wonder.

"Good day to you, Crabbe! How are you?"

"Very well, thank you, my lord, but pray tell your man not to unload anything. You will not be stopping."

"Not be stopping? Whatever do you mean?"

"I have orders not to admit you to the house, my lord."

"Not—? What, is there measles about, or some such? I am sure I have had everything of that kind."

"Nothing of that nature, my lord, but I have very explicit orders from his lordship not to admit you to the house."

"What nonsense!" Gil said, but uncertainly, having no notion what to make of his sudden prohibition. "Why?"

"I couldn't say, my lord, but my orders are very clear. If you would get back into the carriage—"

"I shall do no such thing! What a ridiculous idea, to turn me away from my own home like this. Where is Carrbridge? Let me talk to him, and see if he can make sense of it. Carrbridge! *Carrbridge!*"

"My lord—" the butler said, reaching out a restraining hand.

As soon as Crabbe laid a hand on him, Gil flew into a rage. "How dare you! Get away from me!" And giving the butler a sharp push, he ran for the doors. The footmen all raced to intercept him, but he shoved one aside, and the others were too slow to intervene. Ignoring the screaming pain in his leg, Gil tore up the steps and through the door into the entrance hall.

"Carrbridge! *Carrbridge!* Come here and talk to me like a man, not a worm! Where are you, you cowardly dog? What is going on here? *Carrbridge!*"

And there Carrbridge was, his face suffused with anger, Merton trotting along in his wake. And Monty, looking anxious. Monty always looked anxious when there was trouble.

"What the *devil* is going on?" Gil yelled. "Crabbe seems to think—"

"Get out of here!" Carrbridge yelled back. "Go on, go away! You are not welcome here, you despicable piece of pond slime! Go away!"

"What is the *matter* with you? This is my *home!"*

"Not any more. This is *my* home, Gil, and you were only ever here on sufferance, because you never gave us anything but trouble, your whole life. Well, this time you have gone too far. You are a total disgrace to the family, and I will not have you here any longer, you hear?"

"What am I supposed to have done?" Gil said, but he had a premonition of what was to come.

"What kind of man would marry a sweet, innocent young lady, and then *abandon* her, leaving her all alone—"

"She was not alone!"

"—with only your *mistress* to look after her? For God's sake, Gil! What were you thinking? But you never do think, do you? Did you ever once consider her feelings rather than your own? She came all this way to meet your family, and you could not even bother to accompany her, to explain anything she might need to know, to help her over the difficulties. She was very distressed when she arrived, I can tell you, very distressed indeed, and who can blame her? She is under *my* care now, and you are not to come near her, you hear?"

"But she is my *wife*, Carrbridge! A man is entitled to see his wife, surely?"

"You forfeited any entitlement when you abandoned her. You may do as you please, Gil, as you always have, but while I have breath in my body you will not mistreat a lady. No gentleman would ever do such a thing, and I will not have it, you hear? You are a disgrace to the Marford name, and you are no gentleman and no brother of mine. Now get out. I never want to see you again."

Gil's blood ran cold at the implacable hostility in his brother. He had never seen him like this before.

"But where am I to go?" he whispered. "The nearest decent inn is at Sagborough."

"You may rot in a ditch for all I care," Carrbridge said.

Merton coughed. "Perhaps Lord Gilbert would not mind staying at Lake Cottage? Mrs Merton would be happy to have a guest for a night or two — until something more permanent can be arranged."

"I would not inflict him on anyone civilised," Carrbridge said disdainfully.

"Thank you, that is very kind," Gil said quickly. "I should be happy to accept."

Carrbridge grunted and folded his arms, his mouth set into a thin line.

Monty crossed the hall in three quick strides. "Are you able to walk through the park? It is so much quicker… but the carriage might be best," he added hastily.

Gil felt himself sway, the room spinning around him. Damn it, he would not faint, not in front of his brother. He would not give him the satisfaction. Slowly he turned and, with as much dignity as he could muster, walked back outside to the waiting post chaise. Monty matched him step by step on one side, and Merton on the other, and although he felt their sympathy, it still felt as though he were being escorted away from the house. His home. Or perhaps not, any longer.

He climbed wearily into the chaise.

"I shall get my coat and run down to the house," Merton said. "I shall be there before you, so that Mrs Merton can make all ready for you. I am afraid you must take your pot luck tonight. Our dinners tend to be simple."

"Doubt he'll eat more than soup," Davy muttered. "Look at him! Quite knocked up, he is."

"So he is," Merton said. "I shall ask Dr Hay to look in. There you are, my lord. I shall await you at Lake Cottage. Drive on!"

The chaise lurched into motion, as Gil leaned back against the squabs, eyes closed.

Now what was he to do?

11: News

Dr Hay came within the hour, poked and prodded Gil thoroughly, and then tutted over his leg. He was a dapper man, younger than Gil had expected and so frail he looked as though the least breeze would push him over.

"The bones are sound, which is the main thing, but infection is the greatest risk," he said. "You must rest it, my lord."

"I know, I know," Gil said testily. "You can fix it, though, I daresay? Stop it hurting all the time?"

"I shall do what I can. A new poultice—"

"My wife's poultice was the best. Got me right in no time."

"Lady Gilbert physicked you?"

"Her father is a physician. She knows what she is about."

"Ah. Then I shall ask her what she used."

"Have you seen her?" Gil said, sitting up abruptly from the chaise longue where he had been stretched out. "How is she? Carrbridge said she was distressed."

"She has been quite ill—"

"Ill? She has been ill? And he will not let me see her! It is abominable! But is she better now?"

Dr Hay looked up from his bandaging, his hands stilling. "She is a great deal better, certainly. Her illness was no more than exhaustion from the journey, and then finding herself amongst so many people. Your wife has led a quiet life, I think, Lord Gilbert. She is not accustomed to society — balls, dinners, the theatre, that sort of thing."

Gil gave an exclamation of annoyance. "I was going to take her to the theatre. She said she had always wanted to go."

"She would have found the crowds troublesome," Dr Hay said. "What she needs most is quiet, and gentleness, and to be sheltered from company as much as possible. Lady Carrbridge is taking good care of her, I believe. But Lady Gilbert is anxious about *you*, my lord. She will be happy to know that you have arrived safely. In a day or two, I hope to be able to give her a good report of this leg of yours, too."

"Will you see her soon? Will you give her a message from me? If I write something?"

"I should not like to go against Lord Carrbridge's instructions," Dr Hay said quietly. "However, I shall represent to him that it would settle Lady Gilbert's anxieties if she were to see you for herself. She frets about you rather."

"Does she? Poor Genista!" he said, lying back dispiritedly. "Two weeks married, and already she is fretting about me. I imagined she would be enjoying herself. I never thought..."

And he remembered Carrbridge's words... *'You never do think, do you?'*

Gil sat through the Mertons' dinner, and discovered that Merton was right, it was very simple, no more than five or six dishes, not including the soup. He ate a little, without enthusiasm, while Merton and his wife carried the conversation between them. At first, they enquired about his journey and his time at the army camp at Dover, but when his answers grew monosyllabic, they talked together on domestic matters and left him to his thoughts.

Later, Dr Hay returned, armed with Genista's poultice, made with her own hands, and the news that she was very glad to hear that he was safe and well, and would be happy to see him whenever it suited. That just made Gil angry all over again. Carrbridge was so high-handed these days, and far too sensitive about the family honour. He had no business to keep a man from his wife, it was despicable. And probably illegal, although he was no lawyer.

But when he said as much to Merton over a final brandy, after Mrs Merton had retired for the night, Merton had set his brandy glass down and steepled his hands.

"Maybe it is not my place to tell you this, my lord, but Lord Carrbridge is, if I may be so presumptuous as to comment, not quite his usual even-tempered self at the moment. He has his own difficulties to contend with which make him perhaps unwilling to be as tolerant as he has been in the past."

"Difficulties?"

"I am not sure I should say..."

"Damnation, man, you cannot say so much and then not tell me all. Is it the money? Are we still in the suds?"

"No, no! His lordship's estates and holdings are in much better order now."

"Then it must be Connie... or one of the children. Nothing else would give him any real anxiety. I know he nearly lost Connie with this last baby, so—"

"It is nothing of that nature," Merton said. "That was a bad time, but in the past, thank God."

"Ah! So... Sharp, perhaps? Is the man still giving trouble?"

"No, he has gone to ground, taking a goodly portion of Lord Carrbridge's fortune with him, one must suppose. If he has been careful with money, he may have fifty thousand pounds to call upon, enough to live a life of ease, if not quite in the style he assumed previously. His wife, or whatever she was, is in prison in Northumberland, so that is something, but there were two sons... Well, I dare say we have seen the last of him."

"It is concerning, though. A land agent is in a position of great trust, and if he chooses to betray that trust, the consequences can be appalling. But most of the money has been recovered?"

"A great deal, certainly, and most of the property — everything we know about, at any rate."

"So if it is not Sharp... I have exhausted all the possibilities that spring to mind," Gil said.

"Do you remember Ben Gartmore?" Merton said.

"Gartmore? One of Father's little by-blows? What of him? Is he causing trouble?"

"No, he himself is no trouble. He was with Mr Gaffney, the gamekeeper, for a while, but now he is working for Lord Montague over at Kirby Grosswick. Gardening, tending the coverts, chopping wood — that sort of thing. He recently married a tightrope walker."

"A tightrope walker! Good grief!"

"A very pleasant woman, by all accounts, and very useful when the river flooded the village and she was able to get ropes here and there to rescue people. But that is by the by. There was some suspicion that there might have been a legal marriage between the eighth marquess and Miss Amelia Gartmore more than thirty years ago, making Ben a legitimate son of the marquess, but there was no evidence for it. But now..."

"A *legal* marriage!" Gil said, feeling the blood drain from his face.

"There was a special licence, and it is just possible that the marriage in fact took place."

"If so, then this Ben Gartmore is the marquess and Carrbridge... Good God!"

"If the first marriage took place and is proved legal, then the second marriage, between your father and mother, must have been illegal."

"So we are all bastards. Dear Lord, no wonder Carrbridge is so testy. All this could be snatched away. But what happens now?"

"We are awaiting the lawyers from London. They will bring the special licence which has now so conveniently appeared, and will advise on the circumstances and recommend what needs to be done. That is why Lord Augustus is here, for all of you are affected. And Lady Carrbridge's sisters all descended to give her their support. A letter was sent to you at Dover, but I daresay you had left before it reached there, with all this bad weather."

"Poor Carrbridge!" Gil said. "I was spitting fire about his high-handedness, but, my God, he has trouble enough on his plate. He could lose everything — the title, the fortune, the house! We could even lose Drummoor!"

"Let us hope it will not come to that," Merton said.

Gil shivered. Losing Drummoor was unthinkable.

~~~~~

Genista had lost weight, for her gown hung loose on her. She would have to take the new one in even before she had worn it. She stared at herself in the mirror, noting the pallor of her skin and the way her shoulder bones protruded so unbecomingly. She adjusted the fichu a little to hide them. Father had always hated her to reveal any bare
~~~~~

skin, even in the evenings. "That is how your sister's downfall began," he'd always said. "Showing herself in that indecent way — no wonder she disgraced herself. You must do better, daughter." And yet Di had gone off to Canterbury with the squire's daughter and a dress cut lower than usual, and hadn't she come back betrothed to a baron? And it hadn't been her fault that he'd turned out to be a dishonourable snake.

"How about this, my lady?" Holland said, holding out a strip of frothy lace. "A little more elegant than the fichu, yet just as decorous."

Obediently, she tried it, but she could still see the flesh beneath. "I beg your pardon, but... I don't think..."

"Very well, my lady. Just as you please, but perhaps this fichu might work a little better with the colour of this gown. Let me try. There now, that looks very well on you."

She had to agree that it did. It was lighter and paler than her usual choice, but it still managed to conceal everything. She smiled, and Holland nodded in acknowledgement. A small victory in the daily war between the maid's sense of fashion and the mistress's sense of propriety.

Holland had been Connie's idea. "You must have a maid, naturally, and generally one would take one of the more promising chamber maids or house maids and train her up, but you will not want to do that, I daresay. What you need is a proper lady's maid, one used to the upper echelons of society, who knows all the tricks and the latest styles, and she will be able to advise you. You need not follow her advice, naturally, for you must always do what makes you comfortable and one should never let one's maid bully one. But when the time comes, as it will, that you go into society, she will be able to tell you what the other ladies will be wearing, and so you will at least know. Then you may decide what makes you the least uncomfortable — being the same as everyone else, or being different."

"I do not mind being different," Genista had told her. "I have no desire to be fashionable, if it means wearing clothes which are too thin for modesty, or too tight to move in, or too over-decorated for practicality. And so many different clothes, for walking in or driving or visiting... Forgive me, but it seems a shocking waste of money."

"I daresay it does," Connie had said, not offended. "I thought so too, at first. I was never used to spend so much money on myself! But I found that if I looked fashionably dressed, it reflected well on my husband. If I did well in my sphere as a society hostess, then it enhanced his standing too, in some unfathomable way. And if I buy a great number of gowns for myself, then I can give them away after a season or two to all the poor relations, of which there are a great many, and that makes me feel that I am doing some good with all this money I spend. And perhaps we shall all be poor relations before too long, and the question will be whether we can even afford to eat, never mind about new gowns."

"Surely it won't come to that?" Genista had said, shocked.

"Who knows?" Connie had said, with a sad little smile. "I shall not mind it, if it happens, for I grew up making do, but Lord Carrbridge will feel it, and the children... But there is nothing to be done except wait and see how things turn out."

Once Holland had dressed her to the satisfaction of both, Genista settled herself in her little sitting room to work on her new gowns. It was Belle who had suggested finding a proper worktable for her, and with a little rearrangement of the furniture, it fitted well and she could sit and be employed without ever venturing out into the world beyond her room. Once or twice, Connie had offered to take her for a walk around, to look down into a different part of the gardens, or to the minstrels' gallery above the great hall, where she could observe, quite unseen, the servants setting places for a grand dinner that evening. But she had not wanted to. She need never do anything or go anywhere that distressed her, Connie had said, and so she did not. She sat in her room, with its tiny circular sitting room, and tried to forget where she was and who she was, and concentrated on her sewing.

Now that she knew that Gil was there, somewhere, and his leg was improving, she was almost contented. She would like to see him, of course, but she wasn't surprised that he hadn't come to see her. Naturally he didn't want to. He regretted his marriage, she knew that, and would want nothing more to do with her. That was only to be expected.

She missed him, but she was not lonely. She always had company. Even at night, one or other of the kindly ladies would stay with her, in shifts of a few hours at a time. During the day, two or three of them would sit with her, working on their own stitchery, and talking companionably to each other, and not expecting her to talk to them at all. It was very restful.

Genista thought she liked Grace best. She had only been at Drummoor for two days, but already she had broken a cup, spilt her wine and knocked over the suit of armour at the bottom of the stairs. She told these tales against herself very freely, laughing at her own clumsiness. She always had a tear in her gown somewhere, and she herself readily admitted that it was hard to imagine that one day, when her husband inherited his title, she would be Lady Graham, the wife of a baronet.

It was Grace who had brought the blackboard through from the schoolroom, and carefully inscribed the names of all the Marford brothers, and their wives, and the various aunts and uncles presently in residence, of which there seemed to be a great number.

And when Genista asked, she added all Connie's sisters, too, and their various husbands, so that Genista might learn who everyone was.

"For it is so confusing," Grace said. "I declare that I got all the names muddled when first I visited Drummoor. In the end, I found it easiest just to call everyone *'my lord'* or *'my lady'*, because most of them are, after all. I do not wonder that you found it all overwhelming and ran away, Genista. But how lucky someone found you when you were lost."

"That was Monty," Connie said. "He noticed you were missing after dinner, and sent someone to check that you had reached your room safely. And when it was found that you had not, he set every servant in the house looking for you. Monty is a kind soul."

Genista nodded, and checked the blackboard to remind herself — the fifth brother, married to Melissa. "The clergyman?" she said, and Connie smiled and nodded.

"There is another letter from Kent for you," Grace said one day. "That is the fourth. Will you not read them?"

"No, for they are from my father," Genista said. "I don't want to read anything he says."

"You look so fierce when you talk about him," Grace said. "Are you so angry with him?"

"Grace, dear..." Connie said. "Perhaps Genista does not wish to speak of such things."

"I beg your pardon!" Grace said cheerfully. "I am always saying the wrong thing. It makes my mama-in-law quite despair of me, I assure you. *'Grace, my dear, that is not a very ladylike turn of phrase'* she keeps saying, or *'A lady does not notice such things, still less comment upon them'*, but then I remind her that I have given her two grandchildren and she forgives me everything."

Genista laughed with the others, and wondered what it must be like to say whatever came into your head without the stomach-churning fear that always gripped her. Even now, she felt that if she made one false step that these fine ladies would turn and look at her, horror upon their faces, and never want anything more to do with her. They were so kind to her, when they were so grand and clever and knowledgeable about how the world worked, and she was just an ignorant country girl. How they must secretly despise her! They hid it well, but she must never, ever do anything that reminded them of it.

"Have you written to your father?" Connie said gently. "He must be worried about you, having no word."

"He knows she is safe at Drummoor, I daresay," Grace said.

"Even so, a brief note to let him know you have arrived safely..." Connie said. "Will you not read his letters, dear? Surely you want to hear the news from home?"

Home. But it wasn't her home any more, was it? "I'm not sure..."

"But it might be bad news, and then you would want to know, wouldn't you?" Grace said. "If he were ill, or something."

"Father is never ill."

"But do you not want to hear how he goes on without you?"

And there was some attraction in that. How *would* he manage without her? So she agreed that Grace might read the letters out loud, and then, perhaps, help her write a reply.

'Daughter,' Grace read. *'I suppose your plans have changed. Please let me know when we might expect you home. We are all well. Father.'*

In silence she opened the second letter. *'Daughter, Pray let me know where you are and how long you are to stay there. Also, I cannot find the key to the small medicine cupboard, and I need to get the arsenic. Where do you order mercury from these days for Kepler says he does not stock it any more? Where are you, daughter? It is too bad of you not to let me know. I expected you home long since, and now I am left to wonder and not even the courtesy of a letter to tell me your direction. I am writing to Marford House because the squire believes it to be your husband's family home, but in truth I have not the least idea where you have gone to and it is very awkward when people ask. Write at once. Father.'*

Without a word, Grace broke the seal on the third letter. *'Dear daughter, Where are you? I am prey to all sorts of fears for your safely. I entrusted you to a stranger and now I am well rewarded for my foolishness, for all manner of ill may have befallen you. If you are safe, please, please write to me at once. I found the key at last, but I am having trouble with the leeches. Do write to advise me on your methods. I have tried to work it out from your notes, but it is confusing, and I think I got the jars muddled up. Are you all right? Please write to let me know. Your sister gave me an address where you are staying in London, so I shall send this there in the hope that it reaches you. Please let me know that you are quite well, and that your husband is treating you properly, for I cannot rest until I am certain of your wellbeing. Father.'*

"The fourth letter is in a different hand," Grace said. "Shall I read it?"

When Genista said nothing, she broke the seal and read, *'Dearest Gen, Your letter was the most tremendous shock! I got Harry to take me over to Elversham in the dog cart as soon as the lane was fit to get through, and found Father in a dreadful taking. He expected you to come home in a day or two, and is worried sick about you. I gave him the address in London from your letter, and he is determined to go there and find you, and if you are not there he will go to this Marford House the squire mentioned, and to Yorkshire, too, if need be. Yorkshire! But he is quite prepared to go even so far. He said he will go to the ends of the earth to find you and bring you home. Hide well, little sister! Do not let him find you, for you have escaped him now and I wish you joy of your freedom. My own escape was more clumsily managed, but I am free and happy now, and with all my heart I wish the same for you, dearest Gen. Your loving sister, Di.'*

"Do not let him find me!" Genista cried, jumping up. "He must not find me!"

"Let him come," Grace said stoutly. "We shall protect you, never fear." And she wrapped her arms around Genista in such a fierce hug that she was almost bowled over.

12: A Large Family Dinner

Gil tried his best to behave. He sat quietly in Mrs Merton's drawing room reading the newspaper or a book, resting his leg, trying not to fret about Genista or think too much about this business with Ben Gartmore, but it was very difficult. The physician came twice a day to attend to his leg, and brought reports of Genista, too.

"She is beginning to eat a little now—"

"Eat a little!" Gil said. "You mean she has *not* been eating?"

"Not a great deal, no. At first she slept a great deal. Now I see signs that her appetite is returning. In view of her continuing progress, I have represented to Lord Carrbridge that it would be good for the two of you to meet, and spend a little time together. Perhaps, in a few days, you might be permitted a half hour..."

"A half hour!" Gil said. "Damnation and hellfire, Hay, am I supposed to sit tamely by while you all conspire to keep me away from my wife? It is not right, not right at all!"

Hay was silent for a moment, repacking his medical case and closing the catch with a snick. Then he looked up at Gil. "May I speak frankly, my lord? I believe Lord Carrbridge is concerned that you might allow some... intemperance, shall we say, to affect your behaviour at such a meeting. Lady Gilbert requires tranquillity above all else, and must not be distressed."

"I have never been intemperate with—" He stopped, remembering certain moments in London when he had been impatient with her, and the times when he had not given much thought to her at all. He had not been kind to her, but then she had shown no signs of distress, not then. How could he have known that she was so miserable when she did not tell him so? He could not read her mind, after all, and he had never meant to make her unhappy. But he should have treated her more gently, he knew that. In the end, he said in quiet tones, "I should very much like to see her again, if I may."

The physician grunted, and went away.

Later that morning, Carrbridge came to Lake Cottage to see him, together with Monty and Gus. Monty looked anxious and Gus was serious, but those were their habitual expressions, so there was nothing to be read from them. Carrbridge looked harassed, that was the only word Gil could find to describe it.

"Well, Gil, so you are better?" Carrbridge said. "Hay said your leg is on the mend, and as long as you are careful, you will not lose it, is that so?"

"That is what he told me," Gil said. "I am trying to be sensible. Carrbridge, about the regiment—"

"I have written to Colonel Jefferson to tell him that you are here and recovering. The delays are easily accounted for by the weather."

"No one is mentioning Essex," Gus said with a twinkle of amusement. "Or mills or anything of that nature."

Gil gave a lop-sided smile. "Oh. Thank you, Carrbridge, you are very good."

"But whatever possessed you?" Gus said. "Taking off like that, and leaving poor Lady Gil to a woman like Bella Dryton. No, Carrbridge, getting angry again is no help. We said no more shouting, remember? I should just like to know what was in his mind, to make him do such a thing."

"I cannot say," Gil said, hands spread wide. "I just felt... stifled, somehow. In need of excitement. It is like a madness that comes over me, the way some men need to gamble, and some need to tame brutish horses, like you do, Gus."

"Yes, but... how could you just leave her, like that? Barely married, uprooted from everything she knew, and—"

"I can see that *now!*" Gil said, jumping to his feet and then, wincing, sitting down again. "*Damn* this leg! Honestly Gus, there is no need to go on about it. I can see now that it was not at all the thing, but... I did not know what to do with her. Never been married before, and it was all a bit... sudden. I thought she would just... fit in. But she did not fit in at all, and I had no idea how to manage."

"But surely—" Gus began, but Monty waved him to silence.

"It is not easy, marrying in that hasty way," Monty said in his quiet voice, "knowing nothing of one's wife and tiptoeing around, trying to find out how to go on together. Gil and Lady Gil are not the only ones to be hurtled into matrimony. Being married is a very grown-up state, I have found, and sometimes it seems to me that I am not sufficiently grown-up for it. I was very willing to marry Melissa, even knowing nothing about her, but I will confess that it has not been easy for me. Consider how much worse it must be for Gil, when he was *forced* into marriage, and with someone very ill-prepared for the position she is expected to occupy. Think how much easier it would have been with someone from our own level of society, who would know how to go on. And very likely, when Gil proposed taking off to Essex, she would simply have given him a piece of her mind over it."

"And quite right too," Carrbridge muttered. "Monty, you are too generous. You always see the best of everyone, even Gil. Abandoning a lady in that way is not the work of a gentleman, and that is an end to it. But she is a generous soul, and is willing to see you. Come for dinner tonight, Gil, and then you may see Lady Gil for a short time afterwards. But do not distress her, mind! Treat her very gently, for God's sake."

"I will, and thank you, Carrbridge. I cannot express my gratitude—"

"Yes, yes, but there is no need. Thank Dr Hay, if you must thank anyone, for this is due to his intercession. Tomorrow, I must trouble you to come up to Drummoor again, for we have our first meeting with the lawyers at noon to discuss the Ben Gartmore business."

"This is really happening, then? You will truly lose everything?" Gil said, horrified.

"Tomorrow is just about explaining the implications, and the possible next steps," Carrbridge said. "Who knows what will happen thereafter? But Merton has been advising me. Lady Carrbridge's settlement is secure, and you are all safe, financially, so that is a weight off my mind. Harriet has her own house and income, so she is safe too, and I have made over the full value of Dr Hay's hospital into a secure fund, so that may go ahead whatever happens."

Gil's spirits plummeted. "Then you believe you will lose it all?" he whispered.

Carrbridge sighed. "We must be prepared for the worst, I fear," he said bleakly.

~~~~~
~~~~~

The Mertons were also dining at Drummoor, and since their carriage was to be called out anyway, Gil felt no shame in riding with them. It was no more than a ten minute walk from Lake Cottage to Drummoor, but he virtuously rested his leg for the almost half hour journey by road. He put on his uniform for the first time since leaving Dover.

"How very dashing you look, Captain Marford," Mrs Merton said, smiling at him.

He did not feel dashing. He felt like a naughty schoolboy summoned by the headmaster to be reprimanded. But Carrbridge had finished scolding him, and greeted him with apparent pleasure.

"Do not stand about, if your leg bothers you," he said to Gil. "Sit, and let everyone come to you for once."

"I am not quite that much of an invalid."

"No, but... do not overtire yourself. Lady Carrbridge is worried about you."

"Connie is all goodness," Gil said. "Pray reassure her that I am being very sensible, for a change."

And Carrbridge laughed, leaving Gil with the pleasant feeling that he had been, if not forgiven, then at least allowed to let his transgressions fade into the past. The drawing room was full to overflowing, although it was mostly family, gathering protectively around the marquess in his hour of trouble. In one corner, a cluster of unfamiliar faces — the lawyers from London, there for the meeting the following day. And one familiar face — Gil was not pleased to find Bella still in residence.

"What are you doing here still?" he murmured, as he bent over her hand. "And where is Bertie?"

She rolled her eyes in a most unladylike manner. "Eating calves' head broth in his room. Almost before we arrived, he was struck by an inflammation of the lungs, and has kept to his chambers ever since. I do not believe we will make it to Harrogate at all now."

"How unfortunate," Gil said.

"Oh, not for me!" she said, laughing. "Drummoor is *far* more entertaining than Harrogate would have been. I have been very well taken care of, I do assure you."

Gil could see at once, by the number of young men clustered around Bella, how that might be. Connie liked to fill the house with guests, and there were numerous cousins, the Whittletons and Marfords, Brants and Marches, for whom Bella Dryton in all her glory was as irresistible as a flower to a bee. And she was very much in all her glory here, her London gowns clinging and cut low, her perfume exotic and her swaying, provocative movements designed to inflame every man who saw them.

For the first time, Gil was shocked by her. In London, in her own saloon and the ballrooms of the *ton*, she was nothing of note, just one of many women married to an older man and enjoying a certain freedom on the fringes of good society. But here he saw her as she truly was, a corruption amongst the solid goodness at the heart of his family. He disliked it intensely.

He had not seen his family for almost a year, and a great deal had happened in that time. When they had all last met, Reggie was on the point of betrothal, but since then Humphrey, Gus and Monty had all fallen in love and married. Well, in Monty's case it had been the other way round, for he had married first in an outbreak of generosity and only then, in Monty's easy-going way, had he fallen in love. Humphrey's gaming house in York would be opening soon, Gus was running a stud in the north and Monty was a clergyman and had his own living. They were all settled, all happy, and looking to the future with their wives.

And what had Gil done with himself in the past year? He had quarrelled with half his fellow officers, seduced the wives of three of them, got himself shot in a duel and sustained an injury that might end his career as a Hussar before it had properly begun. And if he, too, had married, it was not for love or generosity or even duty, but because he had been pressed into it against his will. There was no happiness to be found there. Somehow, he felt he deserved no better. He had been every kind of fool, and had pushed his luck once too often, and if he was now to be denied his chance of marital happiness, there was a perverse kind of rightness to that.

So he bore patiently with the aunts and uncles, and answered their questions uncomplainingly, as far as he was able, and whenever they became too shrill in their condemnation of his behaviour, one or other of his brothers materialised at his shoulder and bore him away to some other part of the drawing room. When they went in to dinner, he found himself claimed by Lady Humphrey.

"Forgive my presumption, but I have been longing to get to know you properly. It is not often I meet someone who is almost as disreputable as I am."

That made him laugh. "I have heard one or two tales of you, it must be confessed, but if you hope to best me in outrageousness, I fear you will be disappointed."

"Oh, we shall see about that," she said breezily, and he had to admit that she was entertaining company. On his other side, he had one of Connie's sisters, who began the meal by spilling her soup, and then, hearing Lady Humphrey's tales of tigers and elephants, contributed an escapade of her own, when she briefly became a highwayman.

When the ladies had withdrawn, Humphrey slipped into the chair beside him. "Well? What do you think of my delightful wife? Is she not an original?"

"Oh, very, but how much of that is true?"

"All of it, dear brother, every last bit of it."

"Even the tigers? And the other lady — who does she belong to?"

"Grace? She is Mrs George Graham. Another original, although... I say, Graham, did your wife really hold up a coach and steal the ladies' jewellery?"

The young man so addressed laughed, and said, "My lips are sealed, my lord. Although... I do not say that it *did* happen, for it might not have done, you understand, but if it *did* happen, it was my cousin's carriage, and she had herself stolen the jewellery from my mother."

"What adventurous wives you have, gentlemen," Gil said.

"Whereas Lady Reggie and Lady Gus are perfect ladies in every respect," Humphrey said.

"How very dull," Gil said. "What about Lady Monty?"

"Ah, now, Lady Monty travelled by stagecoach from Hampshire in order to honour a betrothal to the Earl of Deveron," Humphrey said.

"The Earl of Deveron? Who is a mere three? Four?"

"You exaggerate. He is a well-grown five now. It was a short-lived betrothal, as you may imagine, for all parties agreed they would not suit. And then Lady Monty caught a burglar, which was very pleasing. See how much you have missed, going off into the army, brother dear. And what about Lady Gil, eh? Is she going to be an original or a perfect lady?"

"Hard to say," Gil said, with perfect truthfulness.

Not long after the gentlemen rejoined the ladies, Connie came to find Gil. "Genista is waiting for you in the morning room."

He stood up, rather more circumspectly than usual, for his leg was aching, and followed her in silence through the darkened corridors. Now that the moment had come, he was not at all sure what he felt. Oddly nervous, for him, and with the dreadful thought in his head that he might not even recognise her after so long. He had an image of dark blue eyes, and a mass of hair gleaming with gold and copper, but he could not call to mind whether she was short or tall, or the shape of her face, or the way she talked. And beneath it all, he still burned with anger. She was his wife, after all, and it was not right to keep him from her. A man was entitled to be with his wife, surely.

As soon as he saw her, his heart turned over in pity. She was so pale, so thin! Surely she had not looked so... so *ill* before? She hung her head as he entered the room, and then, with a quick look at him under her lashes, she bobbed him a curtsy before the head dipped again.

"Ten minutes, Gil," Connie said. "And if Genista becomes distressed, you must leave at once. Belle will stay with you."

Belle. One of Connie's endless array of sisters.

"So I am to be chaperoned with my own wife, am I?"

"She has been ill, Gil. I shall be back soon."

And with a snick of the door, she left and the room settled into silence. The low-burning fire and a few lamps scattered about brought little light to the room. Beneath a candelabra near the fire, Belle settled down with her stitchery, her back to them. In the centre of the room, the worktable was covered with a velvet cloth, with dishes of sweetmeats, a bottle of Madeira and two glasses, and a small candelabra. Two chairs were conveniently placed, but Genista stood behind her chair, head down, looking miserable.

"My lady? Will you sit?"

A quick look at him, then she nodded and quickly sat down. He took his own chair, wondering what on earth they were to say to each other. It was the strangest situation he had ever been in. He had never been tongue-tied with a lady before, but now, with his own wife, he could think of nothing to say.

He licked his lips. "Do you want some wine?" She shook her head, just as he remembered that she never drank red wine. "Some champagne? Lemonade?"

"No, thank you." The head drooped again.

"How are you?"

"Better, thank you. Much better." Her voice was a mere thread. A long pause, then, "Your leg?"

"Better too," he said, with a half smile. "Dr Hay has been using your kind of poultice, and that did the trick."

"I'm glad. I'm very glad."

A long pause, then he said, "You have gone very thin."

She looked up at him suddenly with wide eyes. "I beg your pardon."

"It was not a criticism," he said quickly. "Is that a new gown?"

That brought a flash of a smile. "Yes. I bought fabric in London. With Lady Dryton."

Ah, yes, the visit to the warehouse with Bella. He had forgotten that. "It is a very pretty colour. It suits you."

"Thank you, my lord."

And then he ran out of conversation altogether. How stupid it was to sit here with his wife, engaged in meaningless chatter about subjects that neither of them cared about. He wanted to share a meal with her, to dally over a game of backgammon, to joke about Marmaduke the pig and watch her tend the leeches and admire the shape of her neck as she bent over the desk, writing her notes. He ached to touch her smooth skin, to unwind that wondrous hair and watch it fall right down her back and run his fingers through it. And her lips — so soft and luscious and enticing. He yearned to lift her into his arms and kiss her and kiss her, until she forgot what a miserable specimen of humanity he was and *smiled* at him. How he longed to make her smile again. It was almost more than he could bear to sit still, and make mindless conversation and not touch her.

He practically jumped out of his skin when the door opened and Connie appeared.

"That was never ten minutes!" he cried in frustration, jumping to his feet.

"No, it was nearer fifteen. You can see Genista again tomorrow, perhaps."

Then she led Genista away, with Belle following, and he was left alone. He collapsed back onto his chair, and, with a groan of despair, buried his head in his hands.

13: A Meeting With The Lawyers

Gil had no idea how long he sat, alone, in the morning room, as the fire died down, and, one by one, the candles guttered out. It seemed an apt metaphor for his life, every possibility snuffed out one by one. His schooling interrupted so many times by rustication for some misdemeanour. His time at Oxford abruptly cut short after that incident with the Chancellor's daughters. His career... what a mess he had made of *that!* And now Genista, dragged away from her home and dumped here, amongst strangers. She was so unhappy, he could see that. And it was all his fault. If he had only stayed with her—

The door creaked open, followed by a wavering candle. "Gil? Are you all right?"

Carrbridge. Followed by Monty, with another candle.

"Connie said it went well?" Carrbridge said, making it a question more than a statement. Carefully he set the candle down on the table.

"Did she?"

"Is she wrong about that? Here, have a drink." He pushed a glass of Madeira across the table. "You look as if you need it."

Gil stared unseeingly at the glass, shaking his head. "I cannot say. We sat, we talked, we said nothing of any note. We were strangers. Dear God, Carrbridge, what have I done? I have ruined her life! I have torn her away from everything safe and familiar, and... and I was so pleased about it. Do you know, when I first knew her, she was mistress of her father's house. Energetic, competent, composed... nothing upset her. She healed me, she tended the leeches and looked after the surgery, she did the cooking, too, and played the spinet and... we played backgammon, and talked about all manner of things in the easiest way imaginable, and she had the most enchanting sense of humour. I could have stayed there for ever, quite content.

"And then her father came back and she curled up into a little ball like a hedgehog. She said nothing, offered no opinions, became a timid little mouse, while he expounded on the weaknesses of women, both physical and mental. How they should never drink red wine or eat red meat, for it would inflame them to uncontrollable lust, and suchlike nonsense. And she sat there, head bowed, and ran round after him and said nothing at all. And in all the idiocy of our marriage, that was the one good thing, I believed — that I was taking her away from *him* and his malign influence. Finally, she could blossom and be the wonderful person I knew her to be.

"But tonight — God, Carrbridge, she is like that with *me* now! She sits with her head down, saying nothing, terrified of me. I cannot *reach* her! She is trapped inside somewhere, and I want to get her out, to help her fly away like a butterfly, and I have not the least idea how to do it. I thought I was saving her and I have *ruined* her. Whatever am I to do?"

"Oh Gil, you poor boy!" Carrbridge said. "Surely she will come round in time? She has been ill—"

"Everyone says that! She has been ill, she has been ill! As if that accounts for everything. But this... this way she is with me, it owes nothing to her illness. That is how she is. She was that way with her father, and now she is like it with me."

"You have taken the place of her father in her mind, I daresay," Monty said.

"I am *nothing* like her father!" Gil cried, running his hands through his hair. "She is not stupid, she knows the difference between a father and a husband."

"I mean only that you are the man who controls her life," Monty said. "When you were just a patient, she could be her normal self, but now you are the man who rules her life. She feels she must be subservient to you."

"But I do not want a slave for a wife, I want an equal," Gil said. "I want her to argue with me, to tell me I am wrong. Because I usually am, God knows."

Monty laughed. "You are learning humility, as we have all had to."

"Not you, Monty. You were always humble."

"Oh no, I was horribly self-satisfied and smug, always quoting the Bible at people. Marriage has knocked *that* out of me, at least."

"And I was so arrogant I assumed my dear Connie would marry me without the least effort on my part," Carrbridge said, with a wry smile. "She brought me down to earth with a bump."

The two men smiled fondly as they thought of their wives, and Gil wished with all his heart that he could feel the same affection for Genista, instead of this terrible confusion that tore him apart.

"I should be very glad to be humble if I could also be as happy as you two are," Gil said bleakly. "All of you — it is a wonderful thing, to see you all so much in love, and I wish... I wish..." He rubbed his face tiredly.

"Do you know, Gil," Carrbridge said gently, "you remind me of myself when I was your age, drifting about like a rudderless ship. Not knowing what to do or how to go on. Not in society, I mean, but in life. Everyone needs a purpose, like Monty wanting to be a clergyman. A direction, if you will. For me, it came when I married Connie. I decided there and then that nothing in my life was so important as making her happy, so I have devoted myself to that end ever since. I find it answers very well."

"And that is perfect for you," Gil said. "And Monty has his living, and Gus has his horses, and you all have wives you adore, and that makes everything easy. I do not know what *my* direction is, for the army has not worked out as well as I had hoped, and that is all my own fault, I know that, so you need not tell me so. And now I am married to a woman I barely know, and I have not the least idea how to make her happy. Not the least idea."

"But you like Lady Gil very well, I think," Monty said gently. "You respect her, and there can be no better foundation for marriage."

"Oh, yes! She is all that is admirable. Far more admirable than I will ever be. She has strong principles, not like so many of the women one meets in London. Like Bella — ha! There is a woman with no principles at all. It is hard to imagine now what I ever found attractive about her. I am so very sorry I inflicted her on you all. She was supposed to deposit Genista and then go off somewhere else... Harrogate or some such place. But Bertie is sick, and now you are stuck with her, it seems."

"She seduced the chaplain, you know," Carrbridge said, with a sudden smile. "Poor Mr Bridlington! He was so mortified."

"Good Lord, how dreadful!" Gil said. "I had no idea you even had a chaplain, not since poor Mr Penicuik." He wondered how much other family news had escaped his notice. Connie wrote diligently and at great length, but he never read her missives with much attention. He had missed a great deal while he had been away.

"We found it so comfortable when Monty was here all the time and holding services in the chapel, so we took on a chaplain. Only a few weeks ago, so no wonder you knew nothing of it. It is very pleasant not to have to leave the house on a Sunday. Such a devout and *worthy* young man, and within two days, your Bella had him in her bed."

"Good Lord," Gil said again.

"You must not worry about Lady Gil," Carrbridge said. "She will get used to us eventually, and be herself again. You just need to give her a little time."

"And talk to her," Monty said. "You will not go down to London for the season, I daresay, but once Carrbridge has gone the house will be quieter and you will be able to spend more time together. Or you could come and stay with us at the parsonage."

"Or with Humphrey," Carrbridge added. "He and Lady H. are staying, too. Reggie is going south, of course, and Gus, too, as soon as these lawyers have had their say."

"Carrbridge, I am such a selfish creature," Gil cried. "Here I am heaping all my woes on your head, and you have far more serious matters to weigh you down. You must be feeling desperate tonight."

"Not in the least," Carrbridge said, with a hint of a smile. "Whatever happens with the lawyers is of no importance. No, truly!

Do not look so disbelieving. The title, the money, even the house — none of that matters very much. It can all go, as far as I am concerned, for I have the one and only thing that matters to me."

"Connie," Gil said, in sudden understanding.

"Yes. Connie. The children, too, of course, but mostly Connie. Three months ago, I nearly lost her. That was my darkest hour, Gil, the moment when I stood on the brink of utter despair. I cannot imagine what I would have done if..." He paused, taking a ragged breath. "But Monty prayed for a miracle, and a miracle there was, for Dr Hay saved her, and I thank God for it every day. Nothing else is of the slightest importance," he ended simply. "So take your time with Lady Gil until you know what will make her happy and then... then you devote the rest of your life to providing it, whatever it is."

Gil nodded, and, for the first time in a long time, he smiled. "That sounds like an admirable plan."

~~~~~

They met the lawyers in the ship room, so called because of the numerous naval paintings on the walls. It was both office and retreat to the marquess, but today it had the air of a courtroom, and one, moreover, where the judge might be expected to reach for his black cap. The judge, in this case, was Sir Rathbone Willerton-Forbes, and he was supported by Sir Lester Markham, and another, younger, Willerton-Forbes, all lawyers from his chambers, together with another lawyer, Lord Hillingyre, representing the Master of the Rolls, who maintained the official list of peers. In addition, an earl and a viscount were in attendance as representatives of His Majesty, to observe proceedings. These six sat in a row, like so many ravens in their dark coats, behind the desk.

On the other side of the desk, a rather larger number of chairs stood in neat rows. All six of the Marford brothers were present, together with several of the uncles, and Mr Merton, taking notes.
~~~~~

Huddled miserably near the door, as if he wished to escape the ordeal, was Ben Gartmore, dressed up for the occasion in his Sunday suit. Monty sat beside him, and Gil, being one of the last into the room, pitied him and went to sit on Ben's other side.

"My lords, gentlemen," Carrbridge said, "we all know why we are here. Pray begin, Sir Rathbone." He sounded remarkably calm, considering the nature of the meeting and its possible devastating consequences.

The elderly lawyer nodded, and held out his hand. The younger Willerton-Forbes placed a paper into it. "This, my noble lords, gentlemen, is the cause of the difficulty. This paper was delivered to my chambers several weeks ago now, hand delivered, by a junior lawyer from a nearby chambers who was paid the sum of five guineas to do so, although no enquiries have elicited the identity of the man who paid for this service. This is a special licence, a genuine one, for we have verified it with the Archbishop of Canterbury's office, permitting the marriage between Mr Charles Marford and Miss Amelia Gartmore. Mr Charles Marford, I need not remind anyone, later became the eighth Marquess of Carrbridge. Now this, in itself, does not mean anything, for a special licence need not be used. However, this note in the margin here, states that the marriage did, in fact take place, and gives the date and location. And I must tell you all that I have written to the parish of Garthorpe, and received confirmation that there is indeed an entry in the parish register recording the marriage. Here, my lord, pray examine the special licence and the letter from the clergyman at Garthorpe."

He passed the papers across the desk to the marquess, who gave them a cursory glance before passing them on. When they reached Merton, he began copying the details with swift movements of his pen. Sir Rathbone, meanwhile, rested his hands on his ample stomach, and watched the marquess.

"But what does it mean?" Carrbridge said. "Are we... illegitimate?"

"Oh, *no*, my lord. No, no, no. Nothing of the sort. The marriage of your parents is recognised as valid in law."

"Then... the title must be surrendered?"

"Oh, indeed not, my lord. Such a thing is impossible. You have quite properly claimed the honours of your father, and His Majesty has graciously seen fit to grant the claim. You are indubitably the true and legal Marquess of Carrbridge at this moment, that cannot be denied, and the title cannot be surrendered."

"Then... I do not quite see..."

Sir Rathbone smiled and steepled his pudgy fingers. "Ah, but it is a most interesting case, is it not? Here we have the suggestion of a marriage... a *secret* marriage, my lord. Secret, because, even if it took place exactly as described, it was not made public by way of the reading of the banns or by a notice in the usual newspapers or by any introduction by the gentleman of his supposed wife into society. Indeed, not only was this marriage not made public, but *another marriage*, taking place just a few months later, between Mr Charles Marford, or Lord Charles, as he was by then, to Miss Adela March, *was* made public. *That* marriage was undertaken in the conventional way, by a reading of the banns and notices in the newspapers, in the presence of many witnesses, some of whom are, I believe, in this room as we speak." Two or three of the uncles nodded in acknowledgement. "Subsequently, Lord and Lady Charles took their places in society as a married couple, their children were acknowledged as true heirs, Lord Charles claimed the marquessate in due course and all is as clear as it could possibly be."

"But then...?"

"Let us suppose, however, that the earlier, secret marriage did indeed take place and that there was issue. As there was — a son, in fact, of that supposed marriage, who is in this room now. Mr Benjamin Gartmore. That son might, if he were so minded and being the *eldest* living son, feel that *he* were the true heir of Mr Charles Marford, later Lord Charles, and eventually the eighth Marquess of Carrbridge. And if he were so minded, he might then lodge a claim in the usual way, by petition to His Majesty, to be given the honours he feels are his by right. And then — and *only* then, my lord — does there arise any question of legitimacy. Or otherwise."

Every eye in the room turned on Ben Gartmore, who went beetroot red. He got slowly to his feet. "My lords, I don't intend to make any claim of any kind. I want no title and I certainly don't want to do anything which would hurt his lordship and her ladyship, who've been very kind to me."

"So is that the end of it?" Carrbridge said. "Ben will make no claim, so we are safe?"

"Not quite," the lawyer said. "Mr Gartmore may feel now that he has no desire to claim the marquessate for himself, and that is his right, of course. But he may change his mind at any time, and that too is his right."

"I shan't!" Ben said fiercely. "I'll never make this claim."

"Never…" the lawyer said musingly. "One should never say never, because who knows how circumstances may change? But there is another consideration. Mr Gartmore may father a child of his own. A son, perhaps, and that son also has the right to claim the title. And his son after him, in perpetuity, unless the male line dies out. Do you have a son, Mr Gartmore? Or the expectation of one?"

"I… have a wife, and… and the expectation, yes," Ben said. "But… can't I… I don't know, swear that I won't make a claim and my heirs won't either? Can I do that?"

"Renounce the right to claim? Not officially, no. Your heirs will always have the right, even if you choose not to exercise the right yourself."

Merton coughed discreetly. "But a son could not claim during his father's lifetime, is that not so?"

"That is true. If Mr Gartmore lives a long life, then his lordship and his heirs will be free of any threat of a claim for many years."

"But there will always be a threat?" Carrbridge said. "We must live with this possibility forever hanging over us?"

Sir Rathbone gestured to the man sitting beside him. "Lord Hillingyre is an expert on peerage law. Let him give you his opinion, my lord."

"Lord Carrbridge, may I reassure you at once that a claim of this nature is excessively difficult to prove. One must demonstrate not only that the marriage took place, that every legal requirement was complied with and that the people married are those named, and that the claimant is indeed the heir of the person named, but one must overcome the obstacle of secrecy. Secret marriages are the very devil, and the entire purpose of the Marriage Act of 1753 was to eliminate as far as is humanly possible anything of a clandestine nature. All marriages must be made public, in the interests of ease of inheritance. So there is a great resistance to recognising the legitimacy of a secret marriage, and in this case, where there was no public acknowledgement, and in fact a later, very public, marriage, one would have to suspect it either never took place at all, or was not valid in some way."

"Is there nothing we can do, except to sit and wait?" Carrbridge said.

"In this case, sitting and waiting is exactly what I would recommend," Lord Hillingyre said.

"I do not understand," Carrbridge said.

"Consider," the lawyer said, smiling. "This marriage, if it occurred, took place more than thirty years ago. Mr Charles Marford is dead. Miss Amelia Gartmore is dead. The two witnesses, who were housekeeper and coachman to the officiating clergyman, are both dead. The officiating clergyman is the only remaining witness to the marriage, he is eighty eight years old and in frail health. Yes, indeed you should sit and wait, for in a very few years the last witness to this marriage will be in the churchyard, and then there will be no possibility of proving the validity of the marriage. At that point you would certainly be safe, my lord."

"And yet, I might not be entitled to my honours," Carrbridge said with quiet dignity. "I should not wish to profit from that which is not lawfully mine. Even if Ben has no wish to make a claim, his son might, and it would be dishonourable in me to obstruct the possible success of such a claim. Besides, the uncertainty is... corroding to everyone's peace of mind. I should like to know the truth of the matter, one way or the other."

"My lord, in law there is no *truth*. There is only interpretation. There is only one way to determine the validity of this supposed marriage, and that is for Mr Gartmore or his heir to press a claim. That claim would then be judged in the usual way and a ruling arrived at and a recommendation made to His Majesty. Then it would be a matter for His Majesty to determine, and one must not presume to know the King's mind in such a case."

"No, no, of course not."

"Even if the law were to be satisfied as to the legality of the marriage, His Majesty may still, for his own ineffable reasons, choose to deny the claim and leave matters as they stand, and that is entirely for him to decide."

"Of course."

"So you see, there is nothing to be done, nothing at all. The situation is... noted, but unless and until a claim is made, no further action is possible. It is unsettling, of course, but one must not allow the uncertainty to affect one."

"I suppose not," Carrbridge said, but he sounded subdued.

Gil and Monty exchanged glances. It was all most unsatisfactory.

14: The Long Gallery

The lawyers disappeared, the uncles drifted away in a muttering group and Ben Gartmore scuttled away to the stable court, where he was staying.

"Well, that is not so bad as I feared," Humphrey said.

"Not so bad?" Reggie said. "When we have this hanging over our heads indefinitely?"

"Every great family has a situation like this somewhere in its history," Humphrey said with a shrug. "We are getting off lightly, I think, for Ben will never pursue a claim, and if he has a son, that will be many years away."

"Who did he marry?" Gus said. "If his wife is ambitious—"

"She is, or *was*, a tightrope walker in a circus," Monty said. "She is one of Harriet's lame ducks. You know, this group of fallen women she is helping."

"A tightrope walker and a fallen woman? She has a child already, then?" Gil said.

"She does," Monty said. "It seemed a good match when she caught Ben's eye, but if he ever becomes a marquess—"

"We must just hope that never happens," Reggie said gloomily. "Lord, what a mess! Well, I must get home to Robinia and tell her all about it."

"I shall ride with you," Gus said. "A gallop will clear my head of all this lawyer-talk. Gil, are you riding again yet? Want to come along?"

For an instant, Gil had a vision of the open moors and a fast horse under him. How he longed to! Gus was a hard rider, and it would be a challenge to match his pace. Just a few weeks ago, he would have accepted like a shot, with silver on the outcome. Today, his mind was elsewhere.

"Thank you, but I am going to play backgammon with Lady Gil, if she is willing."

"Ah well, far be it for me to come between a man and his wife," Gus said, grinning.

The brothers drifted out of the room and dispersed, leaving Merton still busily making notes.

Gil collected a backgammon set and made his way to Genista's room. As he knocked on the door, he was unaccountably nervous. No matter how many times he told himself that she was his wife, and he was perfectly entitled to spend time with her if he wished it, he was not sure he wanted to face the humiliation of being turned away by one of Connie's many sisters.

It was Lady Humphrey who open the door, however. She smiled, and stood aside for him to enter.

"Lord Gilbert. What a pleasant surprise."

He stepped into the room, feeling a little like an intruder, for it was very much a lady's bedchamber, with flowery wallpaper and delicate furnishings, the bed curtains drawn back to reveal the neatly turned sheets and soft pillows. He was assailed with a longing to slide between those sheets with Genista, to wrap his arms around her and sleep with that glorious mass of hair tickling his nose. As he was fully entitled to do, he thought indignantly. But there was no use in strutting around like a farmyard cockerel, talking about entitlement. He must do whatever Genista wanted now.

"I thought Lady Gil might like to play backgammon," he said, gesturing at the box.

"I see." Then she leaned closer, eyes twinkling, and said in a conspiratorial whisper, "Has Lord Carrbridge approved your visit?"

Gil's anger at his brother was not far below the surface, but luckily he recognised the bantering tone and answered just as lightly. "Do you know, I find I do not much care any more whether Carrbridge approves or not."

"Good for you!" Lady Humphrey said, laughing. "I confess, I think he has been too hard on you. It is not good for brothers to quarrel."

"I hate being at outs with him, but undoubtedly he is right, for my behaviour has been abominable. I do not want to cross him, but I should very much like to see my wife, if she is willing."

"Shall we find out? Genista! Here is Lord Gilbert to see you."

And there was her face peeping round from some inner fastness. She was so pale, her eyes huge and wary, that he softened at once, all his residual anger against Carrbridge draining away. Today she wore one of her old gowns that he recognised from Lavender Cottage, dark and plain, yet it enhanced her ethereal beauty. It seemed appropriate, too, if they were to play backgammon, just as they had done when he was ill and in her care.

He rattled the box. "I brought a backgammon set, if you would like to play a little."

"With you?"

"Certainly with me. If you wish to. But if you are busy—"

"Oh, no, no. Just... sewing. Thank you! I didn't expect..." She trailed off, leaving him wondering what it was that she did not expect. To see him again so soon? "That would be pleasant. Thank you."

Lady Humphrey found a small table to take the playing board, and directed Gil to carry it to a corner where spring sunshine flooded through the latticed windows, and a bowl of flowers nearby gave off a pleasant perfume. He set a pair of chairs either side of the table.

"There!" Lady Humphrey said, as Genista began to lay out the pieces. "You will not miss me for an hour or so, will you? I should like to find Humphrey and hear all about this meeting with the lawyers."

"Of course. Do go," Genista said. Her voice was not much more than a whisper.

"Just scream if Lord Gilbert misbehaves, and one of the footmen will rescue you."

"Oh, I am sure he would not—"

Lady Humphrey laughed. "I am teasing you, Genista. You are perfectly safe with Lord Gilbert. He is your husband, after all." And so saying, she whisked out of the room.

"I am gratified that someone trusts you to me, at any event," Gil said lightly, throwing his dice. "A six and a three... There. Your turn."

Her head had dropped, and for several moves she said nothing, throwing and moving without even looking at him. He watched her, his heart aching for this strange girl-woman who was his wife and yet was an utter mystery to him. How could he reach her? Dare he ask her directly, or was it better to pretend everything was normal? He had not the least idea.

But then she threw a double. Her head shot up, her eyes — those wonderful deep blue eyes — gazing at him, their expression unreadable. He had to guess her meaning.

"Do you want to ask a question?" A quick nod. "Go ahead then." She licked her lips, took a breath, released it. Still she gazed at him. "Genista, you may ask me anything at all, just as you did at Lavender Cottage."

"Are you angry with me?" she said quickly.

"Angry? With you? Not in the slightest. Whatever made you think I might be?" The head dropped again, two spots of pink on her cheeks. "Because I went off to Essex and left you behind, is that it?"

The head lifted again. "Oh no! No, that was perfectly understandable. I know I'm very boring to be with, so when something more exciting offered—"

"You are not boring at all," he said, puzzled.

"Oh." For the first time, she looked at him fully. "But...?" She trailed off, looking confused.

"I went to Essex because I was drunk and restless and foolish. If I was bored at all, it was with London and Bella and the crowd she runs with. And they taunted me, you know."

"Because of me?"

"No. Well, a little, but that never bothered me much. Because of my leg. They were talking about this mill in Essex and someone — and I cannot even remember who it was, now — said, *'You will not be up to it, Gil, not with your bad leg.'* So of course I was wild to go, just to show them that I was perfectly well able to. I could never resist a challenge. Ever since my first day at Eton, when some insufferable older boy, a great tall fellow — a marquess, I think —

looked me up and down in a supercilious way and said, *'Ah, the Marford runt.'"*

"How horrid!" she said.

"Boys are rather horrid when they get together, I think. That is the trouble with being the youngest, and small for my age, too. Too many comparisons. Carrbridge got through school pretty lightly, being an earl by then, and Reggie was too polite even to notice insults. Humphrey and Gus were big, bruising fellows, so no one tangled with *them*. As for Monty — he is too good-natured for this world, so he always believed the best of everyone. He was just taken advantage of. But I... I did *not* like being put down, so I learnt to fight, and to earn the respect of my fellows by being outrageous, and always rising to the challenge. But it is a foolish way of going on, as I discovered in Essex. My leg gave me trouble almost from the start, and then I wished I had stayed with you, because you make me feel better. And I never even took you to the theatre."

"Oh, *that* does not matter."

"But it does. I promised you," he said simply. "I am *supposed* to be a gentleman, and a gentleman always keeps his word, especially to a lady."

"But I'm not a lady!" she said, smiling at him, and something inside him twisted and melted and warmed his heart. If only she would always smile at him in that way! But he had no idea how to make that happen.

"Yes, you are!" he said fiercely, wishing that he dared to kiss her, or just take her hand, but he was terrified of bringing back the fearful Genista with the lowered head. She blushed, and he went on quickly, "So if it was not the going to Essex, what was it that made you think I would be angry with you?"

"You didn't come to see me," she said, tipping her head to one side, eyes wide, so that his heart jumped again. She was so innocent and defenceless, and he so badly wanted to protect her from the harshness of the world, as he should have done right from the start. "When you arrived here. And I thought... you were angry... or ashamed of me... because I ran away."

"You ran away?"

"The first evening I was here. So many people! I have never in my life—! And all the footmen... and the ladies all dressed up, and the gentlemen too... everyone so grand and so *many* of them... I felt I was suffocating. So I ran away and I got lost and... and I was upset."

"Oh, Gen, I had no idea! I... what is it?"

She giggled, hand over her mouth. "You called me Gen."

"I beg your pardon, I—"

"No, no! It is quite all right. My sisters call me that. I like it. Father never calls me anything but *'Daughter'*. He never calls me by name," she ended sadly.

"Gen..." And this time he reached across the table and took her hand, for he could not resist. "Will you come for a walk with me?"

The fearful look returned instantly. "Where to? Will there be other people?"

"No, no. Just around the upper corridors. I want to show you something."

With a quick nod, she rose and followed him to the door. He wondered for an instant what Carrbridge would say if he knew of the venture, but then dismissed it from his mind. He was not to be kept from his wife by Carrbridge or anyone else. So long as she were willing, what right had Carrbridge to object? And he was determined to deal gently with her. Indeed, he could do no other, for all the charms and subtle flirtations he normally used with a lady were impotent against Genista. She had no more idea how to flirt than a child, and she was too straightforward and honest for him to wish to spin webs around her. There was something about her innocence that he responded to in the same open way. He wanted to sit beside her and pour out his heart to her, knowing that she would listen gravely, those big eyes fixed on his. She was so different from any other woman he had known, and yet she was utterly beguiling. She made his head spin.

He showed her first the secret gallery above the chapel, where anyone who was sick could still attend the services without appearing in public. Then, through the minstrels' gallery above the great hall, empty and echoing today.

"There will be a ball here in two days' time," he said. "The final grand event before everyone goes down to London for the season."

"Will you go to London?"

"Only if *you* wish to go," he said, smiling and tucking her arm into his. "But if you do not, we shall stay here. Or not necessarily here at Drummoor. We could go and annoy Monty, if we wish, or Humphrey. Or we could take a wedding tour, if you like the idea. Whatever would please you. Now down there is the kitchen court. There were chickens there when I was little, but one of the aunts complained about the cockerel waking the whole house at dawn, so they were banished to the gamekeeper's garden. Let us go into the long gallery. This way."

She walked meekly beside him, but her head was down again.

"Gen, the only reason I did not come to see you as soon as I arrived was because my brother refused me."

Her head shot up. "Lord Carrbridge? He wouldn't let you see me?"

"Exactly so. He would not even let me into the house. Banished me. I am living in exile with Mr Merton, the secretary, who luckily has a house in the village. Last night was the first time I was even allowed to cross the threshold."

"Oh!" She stopped abruptly, turning to face him. "You wanted to? See me, I mean?"

"Well, of course! But Carrbridge was adamant. We had the most appalling row about it in the entrance hall. I am astonished you did not hear us yelling at each other."

"I knew nothing of it. The ladies... they're so... so *protective*, but I wish I'd known. Why was he so angry with you?"

"Because I had neglected you shamefully, and abandoned you to Bella, who is *not* an appropriate companion for you. He was quite right to berate me, you know, so you must not look so... outraged."

"I beg your pardon," she said, in subdued tones, and her head dipped down again.

"I intended no criticism," he said, stroking her hand, where it still rested trustingly on his arm. "Shall we go on? The long gallery is just around this corner."

Their feet echoed hollowly as they entered the gallery, pools of sunshine casting golden rectangles on the wooden floor. A few chairs scattered about and some urns on plinths were the only furnishings.

"Oh, I remember this place," she said, gazing around her at the line of portraits stretching away into the distance. "This was where I ended up, when I ran away. I was trying to find my room, but I got horribly lost."

"Everyone does," he said lightly. "A veritable rabbit warren, Drummoor. It used to be just the great hall and the chapel court and stable court, and that part of the house is big enough, but it got extended here, there and everywhere. This is the new part, being not much more than a hundred and fifty years old. Now this fine fellow is the first Earl of Deveron. Not that it was painted in his day, of course. Not sure there even were portraits in those days. There were barons before that — Baron Wolfstone — but the viscountcy came at the same time as the earldom. Viscount Mishcombe. The second earl, the third — that one is so bad it might be a true portrait. They could not get the perspective right in those days. The fourth... and the fifth is missing. Bit of a black sheep, the fifth earl. Everyone pretends he did not exist. And that one is the sixth earl, and the first Marquess of Carrbridge. That was painted in 1647. You can see the Marford nose very clearly there. The second marquess... and the third... and the fourth, the first Francis. After that, the eldest son was always Francis. Even the younger sons, sometimes, followed the tradition and named the first son Francis, just in case they came to inherit. Are you tired? Forgive me, I am boring you with family history."

"Oh no, it is fascinating! To see the images of your forefathers in this way — it is wonderful! Mama had a cameo of her mother, which she wore for special occasions, but nothing like this. Your leg is hurting you, I think."

"A little. Shall we sit down for a while?" He led her to the window seat opposite the portrait of the eighth marquess, and she studied it fixedly.

"That is your father, then? He has a very *strong* face, doesn't he? Very stern looking. And the nose is quite distinctive. You have it too."

He laughed, then winced as he stretched out his aching leg. "We all do, except Reggie. Even the bastards have it. But you see before you all the weight of Marford family history. Sometimes it presses down on me dreadfully, and I feel I should like to have been plain Mr Smith of Nowhere-in-Particular. And sometimes — quite often, truth be told — I run away too, when the drawing room is overfull of elderly aunts and uncles and cousins, and all of them eyeing me disapprovingly."

"Do you really run away?" Those big eyes turned to him, with a shy smile.

"Indeed I do. I have nothing against Connie, but she will stuff the place to the roof, and it gets a bit much sometimes. But now I have you, so we can run away together."

For a while they lapsed into silence, as she gazed at the portraits, and he gazed at her. She wore no matron's cap yet, so her hair was coiled smoothly on top of her head, just as it had been in Kent. The afternoon light caught it and lit it up with the colours of fire — gold and orange and red. It was better at night, when the flickering candlelight brought her whole head to shimmering life, but it still enchanted him. He wished he could reach out and stroke it, but he was terrified of driving her back to timidity. How ironic that he, who had always prided himself on his ability to win over any woman he set his mind to, found himself incapable of charming his own wife. And the reason hit him with the force of a thunderbolt — it was because she *mattered* to him, in a way that none of his many lovers and mistresses ever had. He cared about her. Perhaps he was even half way to being in love with her.

He smiled at the thought, and immediately her attention was caught. "I... I beg your pardon, my lord."

"Now, what is that about? Why should you beg my pardon?"

"You're staring at me, so I thought..." The eyes dropped, and her cheeks reddened.

A thousand frivolous answers rose to his lips, but she deserved his honesty. "I am looking at you because you are beautiful."

Her lips parted in astonishment, and the urge to kiss them, to sweep her into his arms, was so overwhelming that he shifted restlessly. She flushed even more, but before she could answer him, a commotion was heard from somewhere below them. Even as they strained to listen, one irate voice rose above the hubbub.

"Where is my daughter? I want to see my daughter, *right now*!"

"Father," she whispered, her face chalk-white. "He is here."

15: A Visitor

Genista jumped up, panic threatening to overwhelm her. "What am I to do? What does he want? Gil, what should I do?"

He stood too, and she caught the slight wince. Poor Gil! His leg was still bothering him. She should look at it... but no, he had Dr Hay to attend to him now. He didn't need her help any more.

"Do you want to see him? You can go back to your room if you want, and let me deal with him."

The voice floated up the stairs. "Certainly not! I shall not stir until I have seen my daughter, sir!"

"Perhaps it would be better for me to see him, but..." She trembled from head to toe at the prospect. As if it helped, him coming all this way to find her! What could he mean by it? Such a foolish thing, for he had no claim on her now. And yet... there he was, somewhere down below, shouting at the servants. "I don't know what he wants of me, but I *must* see him, I think."

"Just remember that he cannot make you do anything you do not wish to do, not any more. He has no power over you, and there is nothing to be afraid of. I will protect you."

"You will not let him take me away?"

"Absolutely not! He cannot do that, and he will have me to deal with if he tries it. Shall we go down?"

He sounded so fierce! Could he really protect her, even from Father? It was hard to believe. He had tried to stand up to Father before, but that hadn't worked. He offered her his arm, but still she hesitated.

"Gen, you are in *my* care now. You are my wife, and I will not allow *anyone* to hurt or distress you. If you want your father thrown out of the house, then out he will go."

Her eyes widened. "You could do that?"

"Of course. At least — it would be more dignified to get the footmen to throw him out, but I shall haul him outside myself if it pleases you."

She giggled nervously, covering her mouth with her hand.

"Gen, do you trust me?"

"Oh yes!"

"Then let us go downstairs and talk to your father."

She nodded, resting her hand gently on the proffered arm. There were stairs through an archway, and they descended slowly, as the shouting from below grew closer. Then there was a corridor, with windows on one side overlooking a courtyard with a fountain in it, and they emerged into the entrance hall at the foot of the main stairs.

Quite a crowd had gathered — the butler and a gaggle of footmen to one side, awaiting orders, and little clusters of people, the women whispering behind their fans, the men with forbidding faces, one or two remonstrating with the cause of the trouble. Father. Red-faced, shouting, in the centre of the hall.

"Where is she? I want to see my daughter! Don't think you can hide her from me!"

Genista shook from head to toe, hanging her head, but Gil rested his hand over hers, holding her firmly to him.

"Good afternoon, Dr Hamilton. What an unexpected pleasure to see you here," he said calmly.

The hubbub died away.

"You!" Father said, turning to Gil. Then he spotted Genista. "Daughter! There you are. I was worried about you when I received no letter. Hurry now, go and pack your things. I have a post chaise waiting."

Anger boiled over inside her, and she clutched at Gil with both hands. There was so much she wanted to say, but the words wouldn't come. Except for one. "No," she said.

"Now, now, don't be a silly goose. Father knows best, daughter."

Gil held her hands tightly, and she straightened her spine. "No." More strongly this time.

"Lady Gilbert is not going anywhere with you," Gil said, in the same calm tones.

"She is my daughter!"

"And she is my wife, and there is an end to the matter."

"You were to bring her back to me! You promised! Two or three days, perhaps, to buy wedding clothes, and then she was to come home."

"No." His tone was implacable. "Her home is beside her husband. She will never again live at Lavender Cottage, never, do you understand?"

And Father seemed to collapse into himself, like a balloon losing air.

Through the crowd came a small figure in pale figured muslin. "Why, how delightful this is! You are Lady Gilbert's father, I understand? I am the Marchioness of Carrbridge. How do you do! Welcome to Drummoor. And you have come all the way from Kent to visit us. How charming."

Father's mouth opened once or twice, but no sound came out.

"Mrs Compton, pray prepare the mulberry room for Dr Hamilton. Crabbe, pay off the post chaise, if you please. Fitch, see to the gentleman's luggage. Do come this way, Dr Hamilton. How fortunate that we have another physician staying with us just now, a Dr Hay. I am sure you will have a great deal in common. Was your journey a good one? The roads have been so bad this winter, but I am persuaded there has been much improvement over the last week or so, and I fancy we have seen the last of the snow."

This deluge of polite charm was so effective, that Father meekly followed her up the stairs and disappeared round the curve, although Lady Carrbridge's voice could be heard for quite some time.

Gil burst out laughing. "Carrbridge, your wife is incomparable."

"She is indeed," one of the onlookers said. "I thought Gil would come to blows with the fellow."

"I am very sorry to disappoint you, Uncle Joshua," Gil said.

Genista felt weak enough to faint, but Gil still had his strong hand firmly over hers, warm and reassuring, so she took a deep breath and tried to be calm despite the crowd of people around her. Some were drifting away, but the rest pressed close.

"Well, at least we avoided a mill in the entrance hall," someone said — was it Lord Carrbridge? She thought it was. "But I was not aware you planned to see Lady Gilbert today, Gil."

Gil went very still. "I do not need your permission to see my own wife, Carrbridge."

There was a sudden tense silence.

Someone — was it Lord Montague? — said softly, "Lady Gil seems perfectly happy with the arrangement, Carrbridge."

Lord Carrbridge looked at Genista, and then at Gil again, but his mouth was set in a harsh line.

She had to speak! For if she did not, maybe Gil would be banished again, and she could not bear it. She lifted her chin. "I'm always happy to see Gil," she said with dignity. Then, anxiously, "Please don't send him away!"

Lord Carrbridge's face softened into a smile, and there was a ripple of laughter amongst those still gathered around them.

"Typical Gil!" someone said. "Always did have a way with the ladies."

"Ah, he could charm honey from the bees," someone else said, to more laughter. "Enjoy your honey, Gil!"

"Ignore them," Gil said quietly, smiling down at Genista in a way that made her stomach flutter oddly. "Shall we get away from this crush?"

And he led her firmly out of the circle of onlookers and down a quiet corridor. She followed meekly, for he still held her tightly, although she had no desire at all for him to loosen his grip on her. It was so reassuring, being able to hold onto him in that way. Even Father could not terrify her when Gil was by her side.

Did Father terrify her? She'd never thought of it in that way before. It had just seemed like the natural order of the world, that when Father was there, she was subdued, every faculty bent on not displeasing him. When he was away, she felt as free as air. But it *was* fear, there was no doubt about it. And now she was not afraid.

Father could not order her life for her any more. Now it was for Gil to tell her what to do.

He closed a door and she found that he'd led her into a darkened room. "Now, I am just going to open the shutters," he said. "Do not run away, will you?"

"Oh no, I shan't," she said, timidly.

He let go of her, laughing. "I am teasing you, Gen."

"Oh."

He moved about in the darkness, and then there was light, and more light, as he threw open shutters and whisked aside the curtains. "There," he said at last. "Sorry about all the dust. This room is hardly ever used. But look, I remembered this."

He took her hand, and led her through the mote-filled sunbeams to the far wall. A spinet!

"Oh!" she breathed. "Just like Mama's."

"Yes," he said, smiling. "When I saw your room, I realised what it was missing. Would you like to try it? I daresay it is horribly out of tune."

It was, but it hardly mattered. Oh, the joy of music again! She played piece after piece from memory, her fingers flying over the keys. She didn't sing, for her voice was not fully under her control yet, but the music alone was enough, for now. Gil said nothing, sitting on a sofa listening. Whenever she looked at him, he was watching her with an intensity which mystified her.

The snick of the door opening made her jump.

"Ah, here you are," Lady Carrbridge said. "I have been looking for you, dear."

Genista jumped up so fast she almost knocked over the stool. "I beg your pardon. I didn't know..."

"How should you, indeed? But Gil is looking after you, so I was not in the least concerned. Now, dear, your father is settled, but I do not think he will like to eat with the family any more than you did. We are only thirty five for dinner tonight, but even so... And besides, you will want to catch up on family news. I thought you could have a quiet dinner elsewhere, in—"

"Not alone with him!" Genista cried. "I could not!"

"No, no! Gil will be there, of course, but who else? Perhaps Dr Hay and his sister, if you think your father might wish to talk to another medical man. Or there is Monty and Melissa — a clergyman, you know, most unexceptionable. Even your father could not object, for all Monty is the son of a marquess."

"Has he been holding forth about the iniquities of the nobility?" Gil said, laughing.

Lady Carrbridge went rather pink. "He has some very decided opinions, it is true. And perhaps he was not quite aware of who I was, or he would surely not have spoken so of my husband. Or of you, Gil. He does not like you at all, which is very strange considering he insisted you marry his daughter. Perhaps the Hays would be best, then."

"And how about the chaplain?" Gil said.

"Oh, yes! Poor Mr Bridlington! He has been taking a bowl of broth in his room, but that is just because... well, I am sure he will be very happy to... and that would make six. You would not mind a dinner for six, Genista? Perhaps at five o'clock? In the willow room, Gil."

She bustled out of the room in a flurry of pale skirts.

When Genista looked up, she saw Gil watching her, a little smile playing on his lips. If only she knew what he was thinking! With Father, she had had years to learn his ways, and she understood the subtlest change in his mood, but Gil was a mystery to her, like her father's Greek texts, where she could see the words very clearly but not understand the meaning. With Gil she could see emotions cross his face, and sometimes hear tones in his voice, but what did they mean? She had not the least idea. She blushed and lowered her head beneath his gaze.

"No, do not do that," he said, and she could hear the gentleness in his voice. "What makes you look down like that?"

She gave him a quick glance. "I... it seems as if I have done something wrong. When you look at me that way."

"I have told you, I look at you because the sight of you gives me great pleasure. But when you look down like that, it makes me feel as if I have offended you in some way."

"Oh, no, no! Nothing of the sort." She looked up at him, but he was smiling at her in such a way—! She looked down at once, flustered. "But I do not know..." She tried another glance. He looked more serious now. "I should like to know... how I may please you."

"You please me very well just as you are."

"Oh." She blushed even more fiercely. "But... I am not like the other ladies here. Do you wish me to dress like them?"

"Not unless you wish to." Again he smiled at her, in that heart-stopping way of his. "If you would like to be a lady of fashion, then Connie will be delighted to help you."

"Is that what *you* want?"

"Oh, I see. Did your father tell you what to wear, and how to behave? Well, I shall not do so."

"You said I looked like a dowd. When we were in London. Oh, I beg your pardon..." His face changed and a bolt of fear shot through her.

"Lord, did I? What a churl I was. That seems like a lifetime ago, before—" He stopped, his eyes not meeting hers.

There was a long silence. Eventually she said, "So you do not mind? What I wear?"

"You must dress as you feel appropriate, my love. You know yourself best."

My love. If only he meant that! But it was too much to hope for.

Gil took her back to her room, but she had not been there half an hour when there was a knock at the door, followed by Gil's smiling face peeping in.

"Only me again. Where would you like this?"

He opened the door a little wider to reveal two footmen carrying the spinet. Then there was the pleasure of finding a good place for it. The little sitting room would have been ideal, except for the oddly curved walls, and it was already crammed with furniture. Instead, she found a place in the main part of the bedroom by moving aside a large chest of drawers.

"I forgot to bring the stool for it," Gil said, as soon as the spinet was in position.

"There is a footstool round the corner that will be just right," she said. And so it proved. "Will you stay while I play?"

And she thought there was genuine regret on his face. "Much as I should like to, I had better not. Besides, I have to get back to Merton's house to change for dinner. We are eating early tonight."

"Oh, yes. Five o'clock, just as Father likes. I don't know where the willow room is."

"I shall collect you… shall we say half past four? Very well, I shall see you then."

So it was that when Lady Humphrey returned, she found Genista alone, playing the spinet contentedly.

Not long after that, Holland arrived to bathe her and dress her for dinner.

"Your usual gown, my lady?"

"Holland, what would you suggest? I don't want to feel half-naked, but I don't want to look like a dowd, either."

The maid's face lit up in delight. "Oh my lady, if I might make so bold... Lady Carrbridge has an evening gown that would suit you to perfection, a dark blue merino wool that she wears occasionally for a family dinner, which is the exact colour of your eyes. May I fetch it?"

Genista had to agree that it was perfect. With a few quick stitches, Holland fitted it more closely to her form. The bodice was lower than she liked, but a frothy piece of lace made a perfect fichu, and although the sleeves were short, a pair of soft evening gloves reaching above the elbow covered almost all her bare skin.

"How shall I dress your hair, my lady?" Holland said. "You have such lovely hair, it seems such a shame to wind it so tightly around your head. May I leave a little of it loose, like this? And I brought a few ornaments... although something simple like this silver circlet might suit you best."

Genista allowed her to do as she pleased. The arrangement was simple enough, and far more so than the elaborate confections she had seen in London on Lady Dryton and her friends, yet it made her feel decadently stylish.

When Gil arrived to collect her, his face lit up with a degree of admiration there was no mistaking. "How beautiful you look, Lady Gilbert," he said, bowing formally to her. "I like your hair that way." One hand reached out to touch the loose strands, but he pulled back quickly. "And I have brought you something... if you would like it..."

The something was a delicate cameo.

"Your mother?" she said as he carefully fastened it around her neck.

"No. For some reason there is no likeness of my mother in existence. This was hers, however. It is her sister as a girl... Aunt Jane March. There! Do you like it?"

"Oh yes! Thank you. How kind you are."

"It is only a trinket, really. Maybe if Connie has an hour to spare, we can go through the rest of Mama's jewellery, and you can pick out a few pieces you like. Sapphires would suit your eyes best."

"Sapphires! I should never dare to wear anything so—"

"So vulgar? You are quite right. Diamonds are the most elegant jewels, are they not?"

For a moment she was shocked, but then she caught the twinkle in his eyes. "Oh, you are teasing me again."

"I am, rather. I beg your pardon. Are you ready, Lady Gilbert? Shall we go down and brave the lion in his den? Or at least, your father in the willow room."

She nodded, and he offered his arm with a warm smile. His light-heartedness lifted her spirits. The evening promised to be a difficult one, but she couldn't be downcast when Gil was beside her. With an answering smile she took his arm.

16: A Small Family Dinner

Until she saw her father awaiting her in the willow room, Genista hadn't realised how much she had changed already, whereas he was exactly as he always was. He had put off his daytime coat and waistcoat, and donned his Sunday version, but that was his only concession to the grandeur of Drummoor. Whereas Gil had bathed and changed into knee breeches and a coat that had clearly been fashioned by a London tailor. He looked resplendent, while her father looked tired and slightly shabby, like the provincial physician that he was.

He sneered when he saw her. "Ha! All dressed up like these empty-headed London women, are you? You look like a—"

"Lady," Gil said sharply. "Your daughter looks like the lady she is, Dr Hamilton."

Genista said nothing, but she was not ashamed of her attire. Her gown was modest, and her hair was dressed very simply. It was pleasant to bathe and then change into a clean chemise, and put on a pretty gown for the evening, instead of racing through to the table, hot from the kitchen. On Gil's arm, she felt very much like a lady. Holland had given her a fan to carry, although she had no idea how to use it. Mama had used one occasionally, she remembered, and Di had taken it with her on her ill-fated trip to Canterbury. Perhaps she still had it.

Gil escorted her to a seat near the fire, and fussed about with screens, to ensure that she was neither scorched by the flames nor feeling a draught from the windows. How kind he was! Meanwhile, her father skulked back and forth, looking ill-tempered.

The other guests arrived. Dr Hay she already knew, since he had been to see her several times during her illness. Miss Hay was very like him, thin and pale, and dressed in the sort of flimsy silk gown that all the ladies wore, although not so revealing as Lady Dryton's.

"How lovely to see you looking so well, Lady Gilbert!" she cried, almost before she was properly in the room. "I declare, I was so worried about you that first night, for you looked pale enough to faint at any moment." She plumped herself down beside Genista. "But Perry has got you in health and looks again. Or is that Lord Gilbert's influence?" she added, in a whisper. "See how he watches you! He is quite in love, I can see."

Genista blushed, finding herself entirely unequal to answering this onslaught. But when she dared to look, he *was* watching her, and with that little smile on his lips that made her heart beat a little faster. Oh, if only he were to fall in love with her! How happy she should be. But that was just Miss Hay's fancy. She knew where Gil's tastes lay, and it was not with a dowdy nobody like her.

Dr Hay engaged her father in conversation, and the final guest slunk quietly into the room. Mr Bridlington was a young man of no more than twenty-five, his hair already beginning to recede. Gil chatted to him, but he seemed unwilling to respond. It was, perhaps, a relief to everyone when the footmen arrived and began laying out the first course.

The willow room was a long rectangle with a high ceiling decorated with cherubs half hidden by foliage and exotic birds. The wallpaper reflected the same penchant for birds, although this time set amidst the willows that gave the room its name. Around the walls, gilt-painted urns and classical statuary alternated with glass cabinets housing arrays of stuffed birds. One end of the long room was arranged as a sitting room and the other was fitted with a small, round dining table.

Once the dishes were in place, one of the footmen announced dinner, and Gil led Genista on his arm towards the dining table, ushering her to a seat and himself taking the seat beside her. He waved Miss Hay to the seat on the other side of him, but the others were left to sit however they would. It didn't surprise Genista when her father sat next to her, glowering at her bare arms as she removed her gloves preparatory to eating.

It wasn't as intimidating a meal as she had feared. Dr Hay dominated the conversation, talking at length about the new hospital which was being built to his design in Sagborough, and that was a neutral enough topic to avoid any dissent. Gil helped her to the various dishes, and Father didn't notice when she accepted some of the beef, and then a little pheasant. She even sipped the red wine that the footman poured for her.

It was only when the first course had been removed, and everyone was losing interest in the second that matters became contentious. Father mentioned leeches, and Dr Hay immediately said, "Ah, I no longer leech or bleed any of my patients, Dr Hamilton. I have observed how much the loss of blood may weaken even the strongest constitution."

"Then how do you remove the foul humours from the body, Dr Hay? If you allow such to fester within, the patient cannot possibly improve."

"I feed the body stronger blood, in order to fight the pestilent blood of the patient. Ox-blood, or red meat, or blood pudding... any of those will do. Even beef tea, if the patient is too weak for anything else."

"Beef tea!" Father muttered. "What nonsense!"

"A friend told me of a case he had a few years ago of two sisters," Dr Hay said. "Both succumbed to the same putrid fever, but only one agreed to be bled. The one who was not bled recovered well, but her sister weakened and would have died except that my friend decided to stop all blood-letting. Thereupon she eventually recovered."

"There are always exceptions," Father said, "but for almost all cases, removing the internal malaise with cupping or leeches is to be preferred. I myself always insist upon leeches, unless the patient absolutely refuses. It is wilful negligence in any medical man not to do so."

"Negligence?" Dr Hay said. "That is a strong word to use. There is much we do not understand in the body's workings, and to my mind it is better to observe and learn and try different treatments, always taking the constitution of the patient into account."

"A little more wine, gentlemen?" Gil said.

Father tossed his napkin onto the table with a huff of annoyance.

"Or shall we withdraw?" Gil went on smoothly. "There is perhaps no purpose in the ladies withdrawing alone to the other side of the room, but we may still enjoy the port, or brandy if you prefer. And perhaps some cards? Cribbage, Dr Hamilton?"

"Do not look to me for a partner," Father said gruffly. "I already know your incompetence, Captain Marford."

"You may try me, if you wish," said Dr Hay mildly. "And Mr Bridlington is a rare one for cribbage, if that is your game, sir."

Father stood. "I did not come to this God-forsaken place for entertainment. Look at it!" He waved an arm vaguely about, to encompass the room. "Nakedness even on the ceiling, and the statues wearing nothing but a strip of cloth. Such decadence! It is no wonder these people are nothing but idle rakes and Paphians. Noble? Pah! And their clothes! Look at him," he cried, pointing at Gil. "Nothing but a dandy, and as for the women, showing everything they possess? It is disgusting. Look what a few days in their company have done to my daughter, who was a chaste and modest girl when she was in my care. I came here to rescue her from degeneracy, but I am too late, far too late. I am ashamed of you, daughter."

All the anger roiling inside Genista boiled to the surface, and she jumped up too. "And *I* am ashamed of *you*, Father. You are impolite to speak so of people who have taken you into their home as a guest, who have offered you nothing but kindness and civility. You have been impolite to Gil, and impolite to Dr Hay, and you have *never* been polite to me. You are no gentleman, sir!"

He straightened his back, and looked down on her from his greater height. "I suppose you imagine yourself a lady now, do you, daughter? But a fancy title doesn't mean anything. It doesn't give you the right to pass judgement on your betters. All it does is make you as idle and useless as the rest of them."

She was shaking like a leaf, so weak she felt she might faint, but she would not back down, she would not! And although she hadn't seen him move, suddenly Gil was at her side, his arm sliding around her waist and holding her fast in his warm grip.

"Pah!" her father said. "I wish you joy of this evil family, daughter. You will see the corruption in them, in time, but it will be too late to save you."

And with one withering glance around the shocked company, he stalked out of the room.

There was a roaring in her ears and her knees gave way, but Gil caught her as she fell, scooping her up and striding across the room to lay her gently on the sofa. "A little brandy, Hay, if you would be so good. There, my love, he has gone. You are quite safe now."

"I beg your pardon..." she whispered.

He smiled and stroked her forehead. "Hush now. Ah, thank you, Hay. Here, Gen, drink a little of this. It will make you feel better."

She sipped, and the brandy burned its way down her throat, but it did indeed make her feel better. Before long she was able to sit up again, although she made no protest at all about Gil's arm which was securely around her, so that she could lean back comfortably against him.

"Well, what a disagreeable man!" Miss Hay said. "I am very sorry to say it of your father, Lady Gilbert, but he is not at all the thing, even though he is a physician."

"He expresses his opinions most forcefully," Dr Hay said. "What does he have against the nobility, I wonder?"

"There is some family history," Gil said. "We need not speak of it now, however."

"But he is wrong, and I will speak of it, if you will not," Genista said. "He blames the entire nobility for the wickedness of one man. Baron Wetherbourne deceived my sister and abandoned her when she was with child."

"Good Lord, I know him well," Gil said. "I had not realised he was the one of whom you spoke."

"Baron Wetherbourne?" Dr Hay said. "I have seen him, when I attended Lady Melthwaite at Tambray Hall. He is staying there — some distant relative, as I understand it. And he dishonoured your sister, and then abandoned her? And did he acknowledge the child?"

"No, nothing of the sort. They were betrothed, but he changed his mind. *He* is all that Father says. But it is not right to condemn all nobles on that account. What wrong has Lord Carrbridge ever done, or Lady Carrbridge? Or Gil, for that matter?"

Gil smiled ruefully. "You may think Carrbridge and Lady Carrbridge paragons of virtue if you choose, and I will not quarrel with you on that score. But for myself, your father's accusations are a truer hit. My brothers would say there is not paper enough to list of all my iniquities over the years. I have been selfish and degenerate and idle — everything your father accuses me of. But the past is gone, over and done with. Nothing can remedy my past sins, or amend the harm I have done to those who trusted me. I may have committed no crimes and broken no laws, but I have given great pain to friends, and to my family too. And to you, Gen. I abandoned you to strangers, and that was a dreadful thing to do to an innocent like you."

His blue eyes were fixed on her with such intensity that she couldn't move, could barely breathe. He still had one arm around her, and his free hand held hers tightly, squeezing it with each word. She gazed up at him, mesmerised.

"But a man may change," he went on. "Whatever wickedness I succumbed to before, I can choose to follow a different path. None of us is defined by one mistake, or even a succession of mistakes. Is it not so, Mr Bridlington?" But the chaplain seemed incapable of speech. "God will judge me by my *whole* life, not just the early part of it, and if I can do better… I *will* do better, Gen, I swear it, and I have the best reason in the world for it now, for I have *you*."

His intensity swept her away on a tide of overwhelming emotion. Genista turned her face into his coat, and wept.

There was a heavy sigh, then Miss Hay said, "Oh, that was *so* romantic! You are so *lucky*, Lady Gilbert."

Through her tears, Genista wondered. It was a powerful speech, but it was far from a declaration of love. But she was held tight in his arms and, for the moment, that was enough.

~~~~~

Gil summoned the carriage to convey him back to the Mertons' house, for his leg ached and his head, too. It had been a long day, with the meeting with the lawyers, his afternoon with Gen and the arrival of her father, and then a somewhat fraught dinner. The Mertons were still at table, so he went through to the drawing room to await them. He had not been there long when the housekeeper came to find him.

"Mr Merton begs the favour of your company in the dining room, my lord. He would be obliged if you would take a glass of port with him."

When he entered the dining room, Mrs Merton rose at once to withdraw, leaving the two men together.

"How did your family dinner go, my lord?" Merton said, pouring port into a glass and sliding it down the table.

"It could have been worse, I suppose," Gil said, with a rueful laugh. "Not a great deal worse, however. But there was one great triumph — Lady Gilbert dared to defy her father, which I never thought I should see. She told him he was not a gentleman, and I was so inspired by her bravery that I swore to live a life of perfect
~~~~~

rectitude from now on. Do you think I shall manage such a feat? It is ambitious when I begin from such a low point."

Merton laughed. "None of us is perfect, my lord, with the exception of my wife, who is an angel."

"You come damned close, Merton. You do not gamble or drink to excess or keep a mistress. Even your manner of dress is sober."

"Every man has his weakness, even if he hides it well," Merton said. "Mine is money. As the youngest of five boys, there was never much to spare. My schooling was paid for, but that was all. I never had coins in my pockets like so many boys did. But then I met Osborne — Sir Osborne Hardy — and he was positively dripping with money. He was a timid soul, so he used to send me out to buy things for him, and... and I am ashamed to say that I often returned fewer coins to him afterwards than I should have. A florin here, a crown there... it was riches to me, and he never noticed. Fortunately for me, when I left school he offered me a position as his secretary. He intended it as a sinecure, but I was so grateful to have money of my own that I made it my business to repay him a thousand fold for all my thievery over the years. I gradually reduced his expenses and improved his investments until he was a great deal richer than he had started out."

"As you are, too," Gil said lightly, waving an arm to encompass the house. "You have done well for a secretary."

"I have," Merton said. "But it is all honest, in case you had any doubts. I invested the bulk of my salary, and then Osborne was generous enough to leave me a bequest when he died, enough to enable me to marry. Once I had an income of my own, I never took so much as a penny piece extra. So do not despair, my lord. It is very possible to fall into wickedness and yet to leave it behind. But there has to be change. One cannot live the same life and expect not to fall into the same errors."

"I do not know how I can change my life," Gil said. "But I have had my Epiphany, Merton. Or rather, two Epiphanies. I have come close to losing this leg of mine through my own recklessness, and I do *not* want to, not if it can be avoided, so I am being very careful. And I have had the very good fortune to meet a woman who is everything that is good and estimable and honourable. I am not worthy of her, yet I am determined to be, in time. I want her to be proud to be my wife, but I am not sure I shall ever be able to achieve such an aim. I have been a worthless human being all my life, and it will be a challenge to alter that."

Merton smiled. "You have never shied away from a challenge, my lord."

"True. But this one might be beyond me."

"But worth the effort," Merton said. "What finer objective could there be for any man than to be deserving of a lady's regard?"

Gil laughed, and agreed to it. But it would be difficult, all the same.

17: A Grand Ball

There were fewer grand balls at Drummoor than in times past, for Connie liked to do most of her entertaining in London during the season. Two or three times a year, however, the great hall was cleared of extraneous suits of armour and odd items of furniture awaiting a new home, and given over to dancing for a few hours.

Gil tracked down Connie in a side room, giving orders to the flower arrangers.

"Gil! Are you coming tonight?" she said, a large urn in her hands. "I suppose Genista will not wish to."

"I imagine not, but you may depend upon my attendance. Connie, is Lord Wetherbourne to be here?"

"Aunt Emma's second cousin? He is invited, certainly, and I am fairly certain I have received an acceptance from him."

"Then I give you fair warning that I shall do something this evening that will embarrass you. I intend to give him the cut direct."

"Oh!" She almost dropped the urn in shock. Grabbing Gil's arm she led him out of the room, away from the interested ears of the servants. "But why? Is it something to do with Genista? Oh, her sister! I remember now. Well, at least you are giving notice of your scandals this time. It *will* be a scandal, you do realise that? Lord Wetherbourne is received everywhere."

"Then he should not be," Gil said firmly. "He is a loose fish, who should not be allowed to mix in good society. I am no paragon of virtue, God knows, but I would never abandon a lady under those circumstances. No gentleman would."

"And is it quite certain that this happened so? He was betrothed to the elder Miss Hamilton, he took her virtue and then left her ruined?"

Gil nodded.

"Then you must cut him, beyond all question. But must it happen in the great hall?" she said nervously. "Perhaps if it were to happen in one of the card rooms..."

"Which would materially reduce the effect, do you not agree? No, it must be done, Connie, and it must be in as public a place as possible. I accounted him a friend, you know, and I cannot possibly keep up the acquaintance under such circumstances."

"No. No, I do see that, dear. I wonder if—" She stopped, frowning. "There was a young lady last season, a Miss Hyde, who was supposedly on the brink of a betrothal to Lord Wetherbourne. It never seemed very likely to me, since she had neither connections nor fortune, and one felt that that he was hanging out for a rich wife, but so it was rumoured. And then she disappeared, and I heard she was married very quietly to a cousin not long after. Oh dear! I wonder if Miss Hamilton is not the only unfortunate young lady to fall victim to the baron. How dreadful! But I am very glad you have told me of your plans, Gil, for there is nothing more fatal to a successful event than a *surprise*."

~~~~~
~~~~~

Gil spent the afternoon with Genista, playing backgammon and, when they tired of that, listening to her play the spinet. Once or twice, one of Connie's sisters looked in on them, but finding their company was unneeded, they went away again.

They went for a walk around the upper corridors, and Gil took her to the minstrels' gallery so that she could see the bustle going on down below, with the wooden floor being polished, potted plants and chairs arranged, and the musicians' dais being erected.

"They do not play here in the gallery?" she said in surprise.

"For grand dinners they do, for there is no room for them down below, but when they play for dancing, it is better if they can see the dancers. This gallery will be empty tonight. Do you wish to attend the ball?" he said, suddenly anxious, for if she decided she would like to, it would greatly interfere with his plans.

"Oh, no! Not in the least!" she said.

"Do you wish me to keep you company tonight? I can bring you here to watch, if you like."

"No. You go and dance and enjoy yourself."

"I shall not dance much, not with this leg," he said, with a rueful grin. "And... I daresay I shall not enjoy myself much. Someone I dislike will be there, a man I once called a friend."

"How unpleasant! And you will not be able to avoid him, I suppose."

"I do not wish to avoid him, for I plan to give him the cut direct. Do you know what that is?"

"It's when you refuse to acknowledge someone. That's a very serious matter, isn't it? He must have done something terrible."

"He has. It is Lord Wetherbourne."

She gazed up at him, shocked, and he lifted her hand to his lips and kissed it. "I do this for Dionisia," he said. "And for you."

~~~~~

Gil dressed with unusual care that evening, appraising his uniform for the smallest deficiency. Normally such attention was due to a lady, but tonight was different. He had never before given the cut direct, or received it, either, which was something of a surprise considering his past behaviour. But then his own misdemeanours were those expected in his level of society — gambling, pranks, affairs with married women and quarrels with their husbands.

Wetherbourne's actions were different — a gentleman who compromised a lady's honour, even inadvertently, was obligated to marry her. One might perhaps play games with the parlour maid, but not with the respectable daughter of a professional man. It was ironic to consider his own situation, married even though both sides were innocent of any wrongdoing, whereas Wetherbourne, who was not innocent in the least, had walked away. And perhaps his cut direct would have no effect and Wetherbourne would sail blithely on in society. But still, it would be noted and talked about and questions would be asked, and Gil was very happy to answer them.

He drove to Drummoor with the Mertons in their carriage, sat in near silence through dinner, and then made his way through to the great hall for the opening of the ball. Carrbridge and Connie stood just inside the door to receive their visitors. The first guests arrived, the musicians struck up and the dancing began. Gil ambled about here and there, talking to acquaintances and trying to keep a smile on his face as he was asked again and again about his sudden marriage.

He saw Dr Hamilton standing a little apart, watching the dancing with a scowl on his face. With his new-found wish to be respectable uppermost in his mind, he made his way across the room to the physician's side.

"Good evening, Dr Hamilton," he began.
~~~~~

The physician huffed, muttered, "Popinjays!" and stalked off.

"A cheery soul, your papa-in-law," said a voice in his ear. Humphrey.

Gil laughed. "He is out of his milieu."

"Lady Gil safe in her room, is she?"

"I hope so."

"Ah, here comes your mark," Humphrey said. Gil was not surprised. Naturally his brothers would know all about it, and perhaps Connie had primed them.

At the entrance to the great hall, Gil recognised Connie's maternal uncle, Lord Melthwaite, with a gaggle of his brothers. Beside them, his chest puffed out self-importantly, was Lord Wetherbourne.

Crabbe banged his staff, and intoned, "The Right Honourable the Viscount Melthwaite, the Right Honourable Lord Wetherbourne, Mr and Mrs Gerard Heatherington, Mr and Mrs Herbert Heatherington, Mr Jerome and Lady Annabel Heatherington, Mr Peter Heatherington."

Gil took up his position, well inside the room, and just in front of the sofas set out for the titled dowagers. Humphrey was still beside him, and Reggie, Gus and Monty materialised out of the throng, forming a solid cluster of Marfords. Lord Melthwaite and his party moved slowly into the room through the crowds.

Uncle Lucius appeared at Gil's elbow. "Let the fun begin," he murmured. "Never liked his father, either."

Step by step, the group drew nearer. Uncle Lucius and Uncle Joshua deftly drew Lord Melthwaite and his brothers aside, and suddenly, as if somehow they knew, the crowds parted and Wetherbourne was staring directly at Gil.

He smirked, and Gil knew exactly what he was thinking. "Gil, my old friend! How are you? I am to wish you joy, I understand." And he laughed, the insufferable knowing laugh that, in a previous time, Gil would have dealt with using his fists.

Instead, Gil looked Wetherbourne in the eye and then, very slowly, let his gaze drift away. Then, as a shocked silence fell, he turned his back and walked away from him. He did not walk alone, for all four of his brothers were with him, passing the raised quizzing glasses of the dowagers with their heads up, making their way in stately fashion to the far corner of the room, beside the benches for the wallflowers.

Humphrey slapped him on the back. "There, all over now. How about some cards? Or dice?"

"Later, perhaps," Gil said.

"Oh, you are in so much trouble," Monty said. "Look."

From the far side of the room, Carrbridge and Connie could be seen weaving their way through the crowds towards them.

"Connie knew all about it," Gil murmured.

And indeed she was smiling. They were *both* smiling. Carrbridge slapped him on the arm, and then, as if that was not enough to display his brotherly approval, put an arm around his shoulders.

"Nicely done, Gil," he murmured. "Never liked the fellow myself. Only put up with him because he was a friend of yours. Drink? There is some of Grandfather's brandy in the tapestry room. It must be older than I am."

"I have no intention of hiding away just yet. First, I am going to dance. Connie, who would you like me to dance with?"

"Are you serious? Well, then, Miss Princeton over there. Pretty little thing from Sagborough, and sharp as a needle. Her father has not a feather to fly with, but I should so much like her to be *noticed.*"

"Introduce me, then, and I shall limp through the cotillion with her."

And so Miss Princeton, just seventeen years old and attending her first ever ball, was the unlikely recipient of Gil's practised charm, as he demonstrated to the whispering onlookers that he had not a care in the world beyond entertaining his partner. He had the amusement of seeing that Wetherbourne was standing somewhat solitary, glowering at everyone who came near, before stalking off in high dudgeon.

After that, since his leg was aching abominably, he let Humphrey steer him to the card tables, where he answered a great many curious questions about Wetherbourne while he won fifty pounds at vingt-et-un, lost a hundred at whist and finally won two hundred at faro. And then, despite an urge to see out the night in the same way, and probably plunge to the tune of a thousand or two, he virtuously scooped up his winnings and took himself off to the supper room. There, at Connie's behest, he sat with a group of worthies from Sagborough, listening with seeming interest to a long discussion on the merits of some new-fangled agricultural practice.

By this time, he was tiring, and his leg was aching horribly. The Mertons were still dancing energetically, so, after telling them that he would make his own way back to their house, he limped out into the hall to wait for a carriage heading through the village. There was no one about except the two footmen in charge of cloaks and canes, so he retreated into the darkness down the corridor to look for a seat.

He had not gone ten paces when he heard a familiar voice from behind him.

"There you are, Gil! Just the man I want. Where have you been hiding?"

"Evening, Bella. Not hiding at all. Are you following me?"

She gave him an enquiring look. "A little touchy tonight, are we not? But where is your lady wife? Alone in her bed, by all I hear, as she has been since London. Have you bedded her at all, Gil?"

"Really, Bella, that is hardly your concern. Or anyone's, I should think."

"But indeed it is my concern, for if your wife is not attending to your needs…" She took his hand and pulled him behind a nearby pillar. "…then who is, I should like to know? And since my husband is not attending to *mine*—"

"Stop it, Bella!"

"Ooh, I like a man who puts up a bit of a fight," she murmured, pushing him against the pillar and holding him there with her voluptuous body.

Even though Gil could not but be aware of her womanly charms, resting, as they were, directly against him, yet he was not tempted in the slightest. He took her arms and pushed her away, not roughly but firmly.

"That is all over, Bella. You really are a trollop, you know. Do try for a little decorum when you are among decent people. Could you not have left the chaplain to himself, for one?"

"I gave him a night he will never forget," she said defiantly.

"True enough. He thinks he is damned for all eternity, poor man. Go back to London, Bella, where you belong, for there is not a shred of virtue in you."

"You have gone very righteous since you married, Gil Marford, but you have no cause. You can snub Wetherbourne all you like, but that sister of your wife's was no better than she should be, so I hear, and I daresay it runs in the family. You will find out what your wife is like soon enough."

He grabbed hold of one wrist and pulled her so close that her nose was an inch from his own. "She is worth ten thousand painted, empty harlots like you, Bella Dryton. You disgust me!"

"Good God, Gil, I do believe you are in love with the chit! Whoever would have thought it?"

He only laughed. "Maybe I am, at that!"

Releasing her abruptly he strode off, forgetting that he was waiting for a carriage. He headed for the main stairs, taking the first few steps two at a time, until his leg screamed in protest. After that, he proceeded more circumspectly. He had no very clear idea where he was going, but his feet found their way without direction to his old room. It was in darkness, so he lit a candle from the lamp in the passageway outside, went in and shut the door.

It smelt fusty and unused, as if the windows had not been opened for a long time, but the bed was made up and there was a fire burning low, as if he was expected. Connie's doing, he supposed. He lit a couple more candles and then walked around, touching the familiar furnishings. This room had been his since the age of seven, when he had accidentally set the nursery on fire. Candles were devilish dangerous things, especially to a boy who always wanted to know what would happen if... Well, he had found the answer to the question of what would happen if he placed a candle behind velvet curtains. There would be a very pretty pink glow for about five seconds, followed by a whump of flames and a rather spectacular fire. After that, he had moved to this room, and been forbidden access to all naked flames for several years.

He set the candles down on his small writing desk. This was where he had composed crude acrostics when confined to his room for some misdemeanour or other. It was also where he had written his first very bad love poem, and penned secret missives to certain married women, using a code so that their husbands would be unsuspicious if the letters were intercepted.

He was almost light-headed with relief. His meeting with Wetherbourne had gone better than he had dared to hope, he had resisted the charms of both Bella and the gaming tables, and he had even done his duty socially. He had been extraordinarily well behaved. His heart quailed at the prospect of maintaining this level of respectability indefinitely, but for one night he had done well.

Laughing for sheer joy, he paced up and down the room, and for an instant considered going to Genista's room to tell her all about his triumph. He dismissed the idea almost at once. It was gone midnight, and she would surely be asleep long since. A vision rose unbidden in his mind of her head on the pillow, her glorious hair spread out behind her and he was assailed by a longing so profound he was almost swept off his feet. Maybe he truly *was* in love with her. Was it love, this burning need for her? Not just the physical need to touch her and kiss her and hold her in his arms, but the need for her approval. More than anything in the world, he wanted her to esteem and respect him. Perhaps, if he behaved himself, she would even like him?

But love? He did not dare to hope for that.

Tossing aside all clothes except his shirt, he climbed into the familiar bed and was asleep within moments.

18: An Evening At Silsby Vale House

The Drummoor guests and most of the family began to depart for London, but Gil, for once, was not going with them. He was to stay quietly in Yorkshire to allow his leg to heal fully. Humphrey was also staying in the north, preparing to open his gaming house in York and awaiting Lady Humphrey's confinement. Monty had his parish to nurture, and Merton, rather harassed, was also to stay behind.

"I hope to take Mrs Merton to London for a few weeks later in the season," he told Gil, "but there is too much to do just now, what with Lady Day falling so close to Easter this year, and there have been so many changes to the tenancies... It would be better if we had a proper land agent again. I must be the only person here who actually misses Mr Sharp."

"We are still better off without him, I should say," Gil said, amused. "How much did he steal from Carrbridge over the years?"

"It must be two hundred thousand pounds, and a substantial amount of it not recovered," Merton said gloomily. "But at least he dealt with the tenants and properties, after a fashion. Now that he is gone, it all falls to me, and, frankly, it is too big a job. There is a property of his lordship's whose tenants reported a leaky roof. I paid a man fifty pounds to fix it, and now the roof is leaking again. It needs me to go over there and look at it, and supervise the work, but I cannot spare the time."

"You are more of a desk man anyway, I should have said."

"True enough. Clambering about on roofs is not my strong suit. I must see about getting another agent, I suppose — when I have time."

Gil and Genista left Drummoor in an ancient travelling coach, their boxes piles up at the back, and, rather precariously balanced, and copiously wrapped in sacking, the spinet. Gil sat decorously beside Genista in the coach, with Holland opposite, while Davy rode behind, leading Gil's horse. He wondered how long it would be before he dared risk riding again.

"That is a new pelisse, I think," he said to Genista.

She flushed. "It is. You told me to buy material in London, if you remember. This is one of the lengths I bought." Her voice was anxious and she gazed at him as if expecting a chastisement.

"Did you make it yourself? You are clever with a needle," he said. "It suits you very well." And there was no lie to the compliment, for the ruby colour enhanced her complexion. She had trimmed a bonnet to match, he noticed. It was all rather plain by *ton* standards, but for Genista it was as radical as drinking red wine and eating beef.

This time she blushed with pleasure. "Holland helped me with the trimming. Frog... something."

"Frogging, my lady," Holland said. "Very fashionable in London."

"And in the army," Gil said with a smile. "Ah, we are just coming into Sagborough now. We are going to stop here for an hour or so for a spot of shopping," he said.

"Shall we wait in the coach for you?" Genista said.

"No, for it will be you doing the shopping. And Holland, of course." He pulled a small velvet bag from a pocket. "I had some luck at the card tables, so you may buy yourself whatever takes your fancy. There is a jeweller's shop in Sagborough, and a milliner, and a haberdasher. Oh, and a boot-maker. The circulating library sells a great many trinkets that might catch your eye. Holland will advise you. There is one hundred and fifty pounds there."

"Oh!" Her mouth went round in surprise. "How much may I spend?"

"Well, all of it, if you wish," he said, smiling. "This is by way of a marriage gift. You will have your regular allowance just as soon as I can arrange it."

"Allowance..." she said faintly.

"I am not sure quite how much I can afford, but we can start with two hundred a year and see how you manage on that."

"Two hundred a *year!* Why, that's almost half of Father's income! I can't possibly spend so much on clothes and... and trinkets."

"You do not need to spend it all. You can send some of it to your father, if you wish. Or to your sister, perhaps."

"Oh, *yes!* I should like to do that! Even a pound or two would make all the difference to her. Thank you, Gil!"

And she smiled at him so warmly that his heart twisted painfully. If only Holland were not there, watching them with interested eyes. He remembered their first carriage ride, just after they had married, when he had swept her into his arms and kissed her for his own amusement, careless of her wishes or feelings on the matter. And now, when he desperately wanted to share a kiss, a gentle, tender kiss, he dared not touch her in case her head dropped and she curled up into a hedgehog-like ball of fear again.

So he answered her smile with one of his own, and tried to enter into her happiness. But he felt lost and rather alone. It reminded him of when his mother had died, and he had realised that something he had never greatly valued as he should had been taken from him, leaving him bereft.

Sagborough was a success. Gil lounged in a parlour in the inn, drinking coffee and writing a letter to Colonel Jefferson to tell him of his progress and his new direction. Then he ordered a cold collation to be prepared, and settled down to await his wife's return.

It was a little more than an hour, but when she came, she had a smile of such delight on her face, and a great mountain of small packages in Holland's arms, that he was thrilled with the effectiveness of his little scheme.

"I spent *twenty pounds!*" she confided, in hushed tones. "Father would think me so wicked!"

"Your father spends what is appropriate for his station in life, and you must do the same," Gil said.

"That's what Holland has been saying to me," she said. "I should like to send some money to Di. How may I do that?"

So he explained about putting a coin under the seal, or, if she wished to send as much as five pounds, the note should be cut in half and sent in two separate letters. Then she wrote a letter to her sister, and he helped her to seal it with a guinea concealed, and himself took it to the post office across the road while the two ladies enjoyed the cold collation. After that, they drove on to Humphrey's house in great contentment.

Silsby Vale House was as different from Drummoor as it was possible to be. It was modestly sized, a pretty house surrounded by neat gardens, the rooms filled with old-fashioned furniture that Lady Humphrey confessed she had not quite got round to replacing.

"We have concentrated on the nursery rather," she said with a laugh. "And frankly, so long as there are beds and chairs and tables enough, I have no great interest in furnishings. We have added a couple of card tables, but that is about the extent of it. Now this is the morning room, where your spinet will fit very well, Genista. And this is Maria, Mrs Cecil Andrews, my companion. She is a widow of many years' standing."

Maria was a well-rounded lady of middle years, who appraised Gil with such a knowing eye that he guessed that she had not suffered a lonely widowhood. He thought it an odd arrangement, but then Lady Humphrey was herself an oddity, having spent much of her life in India, where her father had made his fortune. But she and Humphrey seemed well-matched.

Upstairs, they were shown to a light, pleasant bedroom overlooking a lawn surrounded by banks of towering shrubs. Leaving Holland and Genista excitedly unwrapping packages, Lady Humphrey showed Gil through another door.

"That was a happy thought, to take her shopping. Now this is the dressing room. You will not mind sharing a room, will you? I have no other room suitable just now, and we are not accustomed to visitors."

The dressing room was all dark wood panels, with a couple of wardrobes and a dresser, a tall looking glass and not much else.

"Can you have a bed put in here?" he said.

She gave him a searching look, but answered, "Of course. I shall give the orders. Tea in the drawing room in half an hour."

The rest of the day passed off pleasantly. Lady Humphrey was not a person to stand on ceremony, and Mrs Andrews was an amiable and maternal creature who took Genista under her wing, so the three ladies fell into instant friendship, disappearing for a long spell to some upper fastness currently under preparation for the coming baby.

Humphrey and Gil, meanwhile, settled down to play piquet for fish. Gil knew Humphrey's skill with the cards well enough not to waste good coin on a game.

"She is a pleasant little thing, Lady Gil," Humphrey said, as he expertly shuffled the cards. "She will suit you very well, I think. It is surprising how these matters turn out for the best. I thought I was destined for some vacuous society lady, but I ended up with Hortensia, and I could not be happier about it."

"One assumes one will end up with a vacuous society lady because one never meets any other type, except by accident," Gil said, taking the dealt cards.

"By accident — that is so true," Humphrey said. "You and me, Gus and Monty… even Carrbridge, if you consider the matter, for Connie, for all her charm, was not bred to the *ton*. Reggie is perhaps the only one of us— but no, for Robinia is not exactly all the crack. Very straight-laced, but terribly provincial."

"Not as provincial as Gen," Gil said. "A physician's daughter. Father would not have approved. Lord, Humphrey, I hope you deal me better cards when I visit this gaming house of yours. If you treat all your patrons so shabbily when you are an ivory-turner, you will be as rich as Croesus."

"I shall never be an ivory-turner," Humphrey said huffily. "My establishment will be a place where a man may play high or low, as he pleases, and without any fear of being fleeced, I assure you. Are you playing or shall we have a look at the stables? I acquired a few of Gus's horses when he decided to sell, so I am very well set up now."

But the stable yard brought a surprise — several of the grooms were gathered about a mud-bespattered and ill-favoured horse that had clearly just arrived after a long journey. Its rider, a roughly dressed young man, looked tired.

"There 'e is," one of the grooms said, pointing at Gil. "That's Lord Gilbert."

The rider turned to Gil, his face brightening. "Milord! I've brought your 'orse."

"My horse? This is not— Wait, where have I seen you before?"

"Blue Parrot, Bishopsbourne, milord." Then, seeing Gil's mystified expression, he added helpfully, "Kent, milord. You 'ired an 'orse, an' it got lost in the snow so you paid for 'im. Paid 'andsome, too. And then 'e turned up in some farmer's barn, right as ninepence. But 'e's yours, milord, so Mr Caton tol' me to bring 'im to you. Went to Lunnon, you wasn't there. Then to that place like a palace. You wasn't there. Tol' me you was 'ere, and 'ere you are, milord."

"Good God," Gil said. "I never thought to see that horse again. Or you, either. Let me see... Robbie, I think."

"'S'right, milord," he said, with a pleased smile. "Fancy you rememb'ring."

"Well, thank you very much, Robbie. I shall write directly to Mr... erm, Caton to thank him for his honesty. You will have five guineas for your trouble, and the fee for the mail coach back to... somewhere in Kent. But first, I expect Lord Humphrey's men can find you some ale to drink, and a hot meal."

They agreed to it cheerfully, and Humphrey, with no more than half a dozen sighs and a barely suppressed shudder, agreed to allow the rundown hired hack to be stabled alongside his own prime horseflesh.

~~~~~

Dinner was rather more haphazard than Gil was used to. There were two courses, although he suspected that some dishes from the first course had been sent out again to serve duty on the second course.

"Do not expect such a sumptuous repast every night," Lady Humphrey said. "Kennet is a bit scatter-brained, so one does not quite like to push her to her limits."

"So long as there is a good joint of meat and some soup, I do not much care about the rest," Humphrey said. "But you may tell Kennet, if you please, that turnips are not comestibles, no matter how fancy the sauce, and she may leave off serving them. And those fruit tartlet things. Quite disgusting. Some more game would be pleasant."

"I shall try for game," Lady Humphrey said, "but Ben Gartmore is still at Drummoor. If you see Monty, Humphrey, let him know that we should like some more pheasant or pigeon or partridge, whatever may be had, just as soon as Ben is back. That is the only disadvantage of this house — we do not have our own coverts. The farmers round about are very generous, but one cannot send a man out with a gun. Instead, one must smile sweetly and express one's gratitude for yet another gift of rabbits. I hope the servants like to eat rabbit, for I am sure I do not."

"Why is Ben still at Drummoor?" Gil said.

"One of the lawyers is staying on to talk to him," Humphrey said. "They want his life history, and whatever he can remember of his mother."

"I thought we were not pursuing the matter?" Gil said sharply. "We do not want them persuading him to claim the title."
~~~~~

"No, no, the fellow has a very clear brief not to offer any advice on that subject. This is just precautionary — looking for any holes in the story that might break it right away. Gus vouched for the lawyer — he knew him in Northumberland, that business with the duke. Willerton-Forbes, his name is. And he is to take Lady Gil's father south with him when he goes. Dr Hamilton seemed reluctant to travel with anyone with a title." Humphrey smiled at Genista. "Your father is quite a character, Lady Gilbert. We are surrounded by sycophants, so it is salutary to have a man of strong principles around to induce a little humility in us."

Genista looked up from her soup, but she said nothing to this well-intentioned speech and her head soon lowered again. She ate from most dishes, drank a little wine and answered any questions that were asked of her very readily, but she volunteered nothing. It was Humphrey, Lady Humphrey and Mrs Andrews who carried most of the conversation, with the ease of familiarity. Gil joined in when he could, but mostly he was content to listen and to be with Genista.

He watched her avidly. She wore the same blue gown as for the dinner with her father, although tonight her hair was piled on top of her head in its usual plain style, and she wore no jewellery. Such simplicity only served to emphasise her delicate beauty, and the rippling candlelight set her hair aflame. He was entranced.

When the ladies withdrew, and the port had been poured, Humphrey said with a teasing smile, "Sleeping in the dressing room, Gil? You are swift enough to slip between the sheets with other men's wives. I would not have expected you to be so reticent with your own wife."

Gil laughed, not offended. "Ah, but other men's wives know exactly what they are doing. They give me signals in a language I understand very well. Genista and I are in very different country, with no language in common. We cannot understand each other. We started well, but I made a mull of it in London and now it will take time for us to reach an accommodation. I intend to take it very slowly, very gently, and wait until she is quite ready."

"How will you know when she is ready?"

"She will tell me."

"You could just ask her," Humphrey said. "She seems like a sensible little thing."

"That is just what I cannot do," Gil said. "She would give me whatever answer she thinks I want, just as she did with her father. I had no idea of it at first. When she nursed me back to health, she was everything that was open and amiable and charming. Her father's presence subdued her, but once she was away from him, I imagined she would be herself again. But she is not, and she is such a sweet creature, that I cannot bear to see her *cowed* like that, Humphrey! Above all else, I want her to be happy, and not afraid of me, and I will wait as long as it takes before thinking of my own happiness."

"Well, she has wrought a great change in you, and that is commendable," Humphrey said. "But do consider, Gil, whether perhaps her happiness may already be interwoven with yours."

"You think...?" But he could not say the words.

"I do indeed think that your wife may be more than half in love with you, so perhaps you need not be so hesitant. Shall we rejoin the ladies?"

Lady Humphrey was playing the pianoforte when they returned to the drawing room, while Mrs Andrews and Genista were hard at work on their sewing. After a couple more songs, Humphrey, Lady Humphrey, Mrs Andrews and Gil formed a four for whist.

Genista sat on by the fire, her needlework on her lap, her head bent over it, and the needle flying back and forth. Sometimes, when he could spare his attention from the game, Gil looked across at her purely for the pleasure of seeing her there in the room, admiring the curve of her neck and the ever-changing colours in her hair. And once or twice, his eye caught hers. Then she would blush and look quickly down at her stitchery, and he could not tell whether she was embarrassed to be caught watching him or angry with him for looking at her. Her face told him nothing. He wished he knew. Was it possible that Humphrey was right, and she was in love with him? All he knew was that he had never in his life been so drawn to a woman as he was to Genista.

After a few rubbers, Lady Humphrey declared her intention of going to bed. One by one they all drifted away. Humphrey offered to play on with Gil, but he made his leg the excuse and Humphrey made no demur.

Davy was waiting in the dressing room, and undressed him wordlessly, for which Gil was grateful. His mind and his heart were too full for casual conversation with his valet. When Davy had gone, he sat on the edge of the low bed that had been brought in for him, and wondered how he was ever going to get through the night, with his head so full of Genista.

As Davy had left, the draft from the door to the corridor had pulled the connecting door half open. Gil could hear the two female voices from the bedroom, Genista's, light and soft, almost inaudible, and Holland's deeper, more strident. She said something and Genista giggled, making him smile. What a charming laugh she had! If only he could make her laugh so.

He got up and carefully stepped nearer to the door, hoping to hear her laugh again. But then he stopped, mesmerised. Through the open door he could see Genista sitting at her dressing table in her nightgown and robe, and her hair, that wondrous mass of hair, was uncoiled and hung all the way to her waist. Holland, on her knees, was engaged in brushing it vigorously.

The lure was irresistible. One step, two, then a third. He pulled the door further open, and she must have seen the movement in the looking glass on the table in front of her.

"Gil?" she said, without turning, watching him in the mirror.

"May I... do that?" he said, his voice oddly hoarse. "I have always wanted to."

"If you wish," she breathed.

Holland rose to her feet, and silently handed him the brushes. Her face was inscrutable. "Do you require me to stay, my lady?"

"Oh... no, thank you, Holland. Good night."

"Good night, my lady." With a curtsy, she silently withdrew.

Gil knelt down, with only a slight wince as his leg protested. Then, hesitantly, he began to brush. It was so soft under his fingers, so soft and fine, and yet so much of it! And it was surprisingly hard to pass the brush through.

She giggled. "You need to work the brushes really hard. It's so thick, you won't get through it otherwise."

"Ah... I see." He tried again, a bit harder. That was better. He laughed. "You have the most amazing hair, have I ever told you that?"

She shook her head, her eyes wide. "Do you really enjoy brushing it?"

"I do. Shall I plait it for you? That is how you like it when you sleep, is it not?"

A nod. "Do you know how to plait hair?"

"I have plaited many a horse's tail, and this is much the same."

That made her giggle, and he gloried in that simple little sound. Such a small thing, but it pleased him beyond all reason to hear her happiness. So he brushed until the hair was smooth as silk, and then he deftly plaited it and tied the end with a ribbon. And then, with a heart so heavy he could barely move, he kissed her bare neck and bade her goodnight and made his way back to the dressing room.

He shrugged off his robe, blew out the candle and sat on the edge of the bed, willing his rapidly-beating heart to still. That glorious hair! He had never encountered its like before, nor had the delight of touching it, letting it ripple through his fingers. Even when he had shared Genista's bed in Sittingbourne and in London, it had been chastely plaited, and he had not liked to ask her to loose it for him, not then. One day, he would. One day, when she invited him back to her bed, then perhaps he might ask her for that pleasure. But for now it was enough to have seen it loose, and brushed it, and plaited it. He smiled as he remembered, and climbed into bed.

Through the gap under the connecting door, he saw Genista's candle move as she made her way from the dressing table to her bed, then he heard the slight creak as she sat on the edge. He waited for her to blow out the candle. The thin line under the door shone on. Perhaps she liked to sleep with a candle burning? Perhaps she disliked the dark? Another thing to discover about her. He knew so little about his own wife. He closed his eyes, ready for sleep.

A sound. It was very slight, just on the edge of his hearing. There it was again. His eyes shot open. She was crying.

He was out of bed in a moment, feeling his way across the room to the connecting door, guided by that thin strip of candle light. Then he hesitated, but only for a moment. He could not leave her alone and miserable. Swiftly, before he changed his mind, he turned the knob and opened the door.

She was sitting in her nightgown on the edge of the bed, the flood of tears on her cheeks glittering in the flickering light of the candle.

"Gen? What is it?" He crossed the room to sit beside her, arms around her. There was no conscious thought to it at all, but he could no more stop himself than he could cease breathing. "Gen, darling, whatever is the matter?"

With a sob, she threw herself into his arms, buried her face in his chest and reached one arm to grab hold of his shirt.

"Hush now," he murmured, into her hair, her soft, sweet-smelling hair. "Tell me what troubles you. Hush now, my love."

She turned her face up towards him and he could not help himself, for she was quite irresistible. He planted little kisses all over her tear-stained face, her forehead, her cheeks, her nose, and finally her mouth... Her warm, sweet mouth... so soft, so yielding. He was aflame for her, and it took all his self-control to be gentle with her and restrain his passion.

And she kissed him back with a fervour that took him wholly by surprise. He pulled away, just an inch, looking at her. And she gazed back at him and then, quite deliberately, stretched nearer and kissed him again, gently at first and then even more passionately than before. He wanted her so much... but he dared not assume.

Again he pulled away. "Is this what you want?" he whispered, his throat so tight he could barely speak.

For answer she kissed him again, and for a long time they clung together, unwilling to break apart. Every part of him pulsed with joy at the hot touch of her lips.

Even then, doubt remained, and he had to be certain. With a little groan of sorrow he pulled back. "Do you want me to stay with you?"

"Yes!" she said fiercely. And then, so intensely that he could not possibly misunderstand, *"Please!"*

A bubble of pure happiness rose in him. "Thank you, darling Gen," he murmured.

19: A Perfect Day

Genista woke the next morning to the clatter of the fire irons. No matter how carefully the chambermaid crept into the room to relay the fire, Genista was so unused to a servant in the room that she invariably woke. Today she didn't mind. As soon as the chambermaid had gone, she slipped out of bed, put on her nightgown and robe, and then pulled a chair nearer to the bed so she could admire the countenance of her sleeping husband.

At last he was back in her bed, and it hadn't seemed at all the dutiful attention of an unenthusiastic husband. She smiled at the thought of it, watching his face as he slept. The face of an angel, with those blue eyes and the impossibly long lashes, resting now on his cheeks. And he was *her* angel. The thought gave her such a rush of pleasure that she almost giggled from sheer joy. Dear Gil! He'd been difficult to know with his London friends, but since her illness he'd been nothing but solicitous of her wellbeing.

He stirred, half woke, rolled over and went back to sleep again. Now she could admire the back of his head, his dark hair, his strong arms and broad shoulders. There was a small scar on his back, rather ragged — not a sword or knife cut. Perhaps a fight with his brothers when he was a boy? Or had he fallen out of a tree once? He'd always been up to some mischief or other, she knew that, and his carefulness now was only a temporary respite. She was not stupid. She knew she was too uninteresting to keep a man like that at her heels for long. He would go back to London, take another mistress, get into fights again, she understood how it would be. But for now, for this short time, he was hers and he was truly an angel.

She'd seen him give the cut direct to Lord Wetherbourne. Creeping through the dark upper corridors to the minstrels' gallery, and finding it empty, she'd stayed there, wrapped in a shawl, watching the colour and movement of the dance below. She'd seen Gil at once, resplendent in his uniform, and then his brothers, and although she hadn't heard any of what was said, she'd realised what was happening, and had gloried in it. The baron had stood there, quite still, for some time, then he'd marched away and she'd lost him in the crowds.

She had no trouble seeing Gil. He'd danced for a while with a young lady in pink silk, and her heart ached to see him limping through the steps. He must have been in such pain, yet he hadn't shown it. Then she'd wondered what it would be like to dance with him, to hold his hand and twirl and jump about like that. The young lady had seemed quite at her ease, chattering away, and Gil had talked to her, too, but Genista couldn't imagine dancing in that public way, in front of so many people. After that, Gil had disappeared with his brothers, and she hadn't seen him again. Eventually, she'd crept back to her room and gone to bed, but for a long time she'd lain awake, hearing the faint pulse of music in the distance and wondering what Gil was doing.

He turned over in bed again, and this time those blue eyes flickered open. He smiled. "Good morning, wife."

"Good morning, husband. I'm afraid the chocolate isn't here yet."

"Who needs chocolate, when I have you?" He lifted himself up so that he was leaning against the backboard, his chest exposed. "Will you come back to bed for a little while? I should like to talk to you."

Blushing a little, she climbed in beside him, and he wrapped an arm around her in the most comfortable way imaginable. She sighed with pleasure, resting her head against his shoulder.

"Thank you for letting me stay with you last night," he said quietly.

She shifted position so that she could look up at him, and to her delight he was gazing down at her with that little smile, the intimate little smile that she loved so much. He was very confusing, sometimes. "That is your right," she said, puzzled.

"True, but that does not mean that I need not regard your wishes in the matter. Our marriage has had rather a difficult start, but I mean to do better. You did not marry me from choice, and the life I lead is not one that comes naturally to you, nevertheless it is my intent to do all in my power to make you happy. Whatever you want, you may ask of me and I will provide it if I possibly can. But you must *ask*... I will not give... or take... of my own volition, or ask for anything myself. Do you understand?"

"I think so. But why will you not ask for what *you* want?"

"Because I think your father trained you to instant obedience to male demands, and I never, *ever* want you to be sad and downcast, as you were with him. I could not bear to hear you say *'Yes, Gil'* and *'No, Gil'* the way you did with your father. One day, I hope to see again the lively and delightful Miss Hamilton who nursed a poor, sick soldier back to health, so you may ask for anything, and if it is within my power I will provide it."

"Yes, Gil," she said. Then, horrified, "Oh, I beg your pardon!"

But he burst out laughing, and then she laughed too. She didn't understand him at all, but she loved him so much she ached inside.

~~~~~

Humphrey was the only one in the breakfast parlour when Gil reached it. He poured himself coffee and sat down.

With a wink, Humphrey said, "Sleep well?"

Gil laughed. "Small house."

"And a chatterbox of a chambermaid. I do not imagine that even the scullery maid is unaware that the guest who asked for a bed in the dressing room in fact spent the night in bed with his wife. And why not? I was right, was I not? She is in love with you?"

"I cannot answer *that*," Gil said, "but *I* am entirely besotted with *her*."

Humphrey laughed. "It rather seemed to me that you might be, for you could not take your eyes off her last night. How amusing for my urbane little brother to fall for the physician's daughter. She is not at all your usual sort."

"No, but I have decided that my usual sort is not so enticing these days."

"Expensive, too, I should think."

"Not when they are married," Gil said, grinning. "Lord, I was a dreadful rake, was I not?"

"Was?" Humphrey said, pausing from spreading preserve on his bread. "You have given all that up for good, then?"

"I should like to think so. It was so *tedious*, in some ways, all that sneaking around and always trying to avoid irate husbands, not always successfully. One chased me all the way to Drummoor, remember, with his sword ready sharpened. He would have had my head on a platter if Merton and Reggie had not fended him off. And the other night, at the ball — I was quite proud of myself, giving
~~~~~

Wetherbourne the cut direct, and then *not* celebrating by losing a couple of thousand on the bones or bedding Bella. Who offered, I might add."

Humphrey spluttered over his chocolate. "Did she really? She also had a try for Monty and Reggie, who were too polite to avoid her, unlike me, and I saw her consoling Wetherbourne enthusiastically in one of the card rooms later. She is quite incorrigible. And she leaves her sick husband to the Drummoor servants."

"Well, to be fair to Bella, she is not well suited to the sick room," Gil said with a raised eyebrow. "She is a drawing room butterfly. Ah, Lady Gil." The two men rose politely, and Gil held the chair for her. "What will you have? Coffee or chocolate?"

"Chocolate, but— Oh, thank you!"

"There are some hot rolls here... or do you prefer the cold? Or there is cold beef."

"A hot roll... thank you. You are very good."

He sat down, pleased with his efforts, trying to ignore the amusement in Humphrey's face. Mrs Andrews bustled in just then, and sat down beside Genista.

"And what would you like to do today, my dear? The weather is fine, so we could order the carriage and go out somewhere. Or we could rest comfortably beside the fire in the morning room. What do you say?"

Genista looked helplessly at Gil.

"It is for you to decide," he said, smiling at her. "What would you like to do?"

"Oh... then if I may choose... I should rather like to go back to Sagborough."

"More shopping?" he said teasingly.

"If you please. There are some warehouses, Holland says, and I should like to buy some new shoes."

"What an excellent idea," Mrs Andrews said. "Let us both go. It is too tame an expedition to tempt dear Lady Humphrey, I am sure, but there is nothing I like better than to walk around the town from shop to shop, doing just as I please."

"May I come, too?" Gil said. "I should like to take you to the jeweller's shop." She turned huge eyes on him. "Your wedding ring is too large for your finger. I should like to buy you one that fits better, or else arrange for that one to be adjusted, if you prefer."

"Oh. Thank you!"

She beamed at him, and Gil smiled happily back at her.

With the addition of Holland, the Humphreys' carriage was full for the journey to Sagborough. Gil found that his wife was a decisive shopper — "Father so hated to be kept waiting," she explained — and in under an hour had acquired several lengths of material, and an array of threads, pins, buttons, ribbons and lace, as well as a sizable work basket, complete with scissors, thimbles and needles, her own having been left behind in Kent. Another hour saw her possessed of new boots, two pairs of shoes and some soft indoor slippers, as well as two bonnets. After the rapid purchase of a new wedding ring, so that her mother's ring might be returned to her father, they all repaired to the inn where the carriage had been left, and enjoyed a light luncheon. On the return journey, they called on Monty and Lady Monty, admired the church and took tea and cake in the parsonage.

In the evening, Monty and Melissa came for dinner, and Mrs Andrews played dance tunes while the others danced. Gil taught Genista the steps to some reels, the cotillion and the quadrille, and was thrilled to see her smiles of delight when she got the movements right. One day, perhaps not too far off, he would be able to take her into a ballroom and dance with her in proper form.

And then, as the perfect end to a perfect day, he went into her bedroom to wish her a good night, and, blushing rather, she invited him to stay. He thought he had never been happier in his life.

The next day was wet. Genista settled down contentedly with her sewing — she truly enjoyed such tasks, to Gil's astonishment — but Gil wondered what on earth he was to do with himself.

"Are you up to riding?" Humphrey said. "I thought I would go over to Drummoor and chase up Ben Gartmore. He might have been out with the dogs over there, or there might be something already in the game room that would not be missed. It is not so far over the moors."

Genista's head came up, as she listened with interest.

"Will you be all right here if I go?" Gil said to her. "For if you prefer me to stay—?"

"Oh no, do go. I am perfectly well occupied here, as you see, and I have Mrs Andrews to bear me company. But... it is not too arduous a ride? I should not wish you to inflame your wound again."

"How long does it take, Humphrey?"

"I can do it in not much more than an hour, but even at the steadiest pace, it cannot be more than two hours."

Gil chewed his lip thoughtfully. "I should enjoy the ride of all things, I confess. But if I find my leg pains me by the time Drummoor is reached, then I shall summon a carriage to bring me home. Will that satisfy you, Lady Gilbert?"

She smiled, and agreed to it.

Despite the rain, the sort of incessant drizzle that looked like nothing more than mist but gave anyone venturing out a thorough soaking, Gil enjoyed himself. Humphrey was normally a bruising rider, who thought anything less than a gallop was tediously dawdling, but in deference to Gil's leg they jogged along at a very steady speed, and Gil dismounted in the Drummoor stable court with no more than a twinge of discomfort.

Ben Gartmore, they were told, was inside the house. "With that lawyer from London," Lester, the head groom, told them. "Not good news, I'd say, milords."

"What does that mean, Lester?" Humphrey said. "Come on, man, out with it."

"It's that Dr Hamilton, milord. He's been spending a lot of time with Ben, and I don't like it, not at all. He's got some funny ideas, that man, and begging your lordship's pardon," he said to Gil, "for all he's your father in law, he's an odd fish."

"I cannot disagree with you," Gil said. "But there is no harm in him befriending Ben, and the lawyer has permission to talk to him, after all. There is nothing in that."

But Lester looked disbelieving.

"Still, I cannot like it," Humphrey said, as they made their way through the echoing corridors of the house. Already it had the silent and closed-up air of an empty house, most of the rooms draped in holland covers, its few remaining occupants living in just a few rooms. Only the oldest and youngest Marfords remained — a handful of aunts and uncles, too frail to brave the season, and the three children in the nursery, who were to travel south later with the Mertons. And the Drytons, Gil reminded himself. And Dr Hamilton.

They found Ben and the lawyer in the writing room, once the eighth marquess's private room, and now the office of Daniel Merton, the secretary. Ben, standing before the desk like a naughty schoolboy, hat in hand, was surprisingly attired in his Sunday best. The lawyer, a rather ostentatious little man dressed in flamboyant

London style, sat behind Merton's desk. Merton, in his usual sombre but stylish black, stood behind him. And at Ben's shoulder, the familiar drab black of Dr Hamilton.

As Humphrey and Gil entered, Merton looked across at them, relief plainly etched on his face. "Ah, my lords! Your arrival is… timely."

The two brothers made their bows and greetings. Then Humphrey said, "Now, Merton, what is all this about?"

Merton waved a hand helplessly towards Ben.

"Ben?" Humphrey said.

Ben turned the hat in his hands and gazed at him with terrified eyes. "I… the thing is, my lord… you see…"

"Yes, do tell us what the thing is," Humphrey said testily. "*Someone* explain what is going on here."

The lawyer said smoothly, "Mr Gartmore is reconsidering his decision not to claim the title."

"What?" Gil said. "Why, you two-faced little—"

Humphrey laid a restraining hand on his arm. "Not helpful, Gil. So you want to be a marquess, do you, Ben?"

"*No!* But I'm not sure it's right for anyone else to be one, either. I mean, it's not right for some people to own everything, just because of some twist of history."

"So you have been listening to Dr Hamilton," Gil said bitterly, "and now you disapprove of the entire peerage, and probably the monarchy too. That is all well and good. I disapprove of some parts of it myself. But how does it help for you to claim the marquessate? If you succeed, you become a peer yourself."

"Yes, but that's just a title, and I wouldn't have to use it," Ben said. "But if I had all the money that goes with it, I could give it to those that need it, and everyone would be better off."

"Except us, of course," Humphrey said. "Except the Marford family. You would be happy to see Lord Carrbridge forced to chop wood and plough fields to prevent his wife from starving, I suppose. Or perhaps Lady Carrbridge might take in washing, eh?"

Ben flushed unhappily. "I'd see them right, of course. I wouldn't let her ladyship suffer."

"Oh, very generous," Gil said. "How kind! How considerate of Lady Carrbridge's welfare, to throw her out of her home, and take all her money and then give her a few coins here and there to buy bacon. I am sure she will be deeply grateful to you."

This time Humphrey made no move to silence his wrath. "Can he do this, Willerton-Forbes? Can he take everything?"

The lawyer sat back in his chair, regarding his thoughtfully. "It is an interesting question. The title — that is a matter for the House of Lords, and will be determined by them and by His Majesty. But his lordship's fortune — the estates and holdings, the tenancies and tithes, Drummoor itself and Marford House — these are inherited in the usual way, as determined by law, and therefore it would depend upon the late marquess's will and the exact wording therein. If it was left to the present marquess by name—"

"It was not," Merton said. "I have seen all the late marquess's legal papers, and everything is entailed to the legitimate heir in the male line."

"That is the common way," the lawyer said. "But in that case, to answer your question, my lord, if Mr Gartmore can succeed in wresting the marquessate from the present holder of that honour, then he will indeed take everything."

20: A Change Of Plan

"We cannot sit here tamely and allow that little runt to take everything we have!" Gil said. Ben and Dr Hamilton had left, and Gil, Humphrey, Merton and the lawyer remained in the writing room.

"The law must take its course," the lawyer said. "I will write to my chambers for advice, but if he insists on pursuing this, we cannot prevent him."

"You are *our* lawyers," Humphrey said. "You will not help him, surely?"

"We are the lawyers of anyone prepared to pay our fees," Willerton-Forbes said sharply. "Besides, we work for the whole Marford family, and he is indubitably a part of that, no one denies it. But no, I do not imagine *we* would act for him, not against Lord Carrbridge's interests. We shall help him find a lawyer to act for him, that is all."

"Well, I shall write to Carrbridge in London," Humphrey said. "He may come back here, and Reggie and Gus too, to talk some sense into Ben. I have to say, Gil, you have the most unspeakable father-in-law. I thought Connie's father was the worst, but Dr Hamilton is positively evil."

"This is like some nightmare story from the nursery," Gil said. "Do you remember that nursery maid who used to tell us bedtime stories about hobgoblins and wicked witches? There was one, I recall, where the evil father had done some deal with the devil, and could only be killed by being skewered to a tree in the middle of the forest. Do you want me to skewer Dr Hamilton to a tree, and leave him to die? Because I am very much inclined that way at the moment."

"I will hold him, while you skewer him," Humphrey said. "Lord, what a mess! Willerton-Forbes, how would you estimate his chances of success?"

"You heard Lord Hillingyre's thoughts on the matter — he regarded it as a very difficult case to prove. Even if the marriage took place, the fact that the eighth marquess never once acknowledged the lady as his wife means that—"

Merton coughed.

"Forgive me for interrupting, but in a sense he *did* acknowledge the marriage, although not in public. When Ben was first discovered, there were a great many letters written from the eighth marquess to Ben's mother — to Miss Amelia Gartmore. They were brought here, and sorted into date order and filed away, in case any of the family should wish to read them."

"You did not read them yourself?" Willerton-Forbes said.

"No, for I felt it inappropriate. But... one cannot help noticing certain distinctive words and phrases. Every letter that I saw opened with the words *'My dearest wife'*. So you see, in private, he admitted that she was his wife."

There was a long silence.

Gil, scuffing one foot in some embarrassment, said, "It might be... and this does happen occasionally... that a fellow might address his mistress in such terms. If she liked him to do so, I mean."

Humphrey chuckled, but Merton answered in his usual serious tones. "That is an interesting point. It might have been no more than a term of endearment. After all, he obtained the special licence, so he *intended* to marry the lady. If, in the end, he felt obliged to cry off, he might have addressed her in those terms. Would such a thing be regarded as evidence of the marriage, Mr Willerton-Forbes?"

"It might be. It would depend what else the letters say. If they go on to say, *'If only you were truly my wife'* or *'If I only I could acknowledge you publicly as my true wife'*... either would make a difference. But one would have to read them all to know for sure."

"And that we must not do," Humphrey said. "Lord Hillingyre's advice was very clear — do nothing, allow as much time to pass as possible, wait until a claim is made. Ben may still decide not to do it. I suppose we cannot simply burn the letters?"

"That is for Lord Carrbridge to say," Merton said. "However, he has a very delicate sense of honour, and would probably not permit it. I agree that the best course of action is to do nothing at all, and so I shall advise Lord Carrbridge."

"And I," said Willerton-Forbes.

"So we sit here tamely, and wait for the sky to fall on our heads?" Gil cried in frustration. "*My* advice would be quite different."

"Let us hear it, my lord," Willerton-Forbes said politely.

"It seems to me that we are remiss in not conducting our own investigation into this marriage. The lawyers have made written enquiries, but have not examined the church register where this supposed marriage took place, nor talked to the clergyman who supposedly solemnised the marriage. We might be able to prove at once that there was some irregularity about it."

"Or you might prove that it was perfectly valid," Humphrey said. "What then?"

"Why, then it would still be a matter for His Majesty to decide at his pleasure," Gil said. "But would it not be better to *know*, once and for all?"

"But this clergyman, Gil!" Humphrey said. "He is the only surviving witness, and if we wait, he may die and then there is no possibility of proving the case. If we talk to him now, and he confirms the validity of the marriage—"

"But you do not believe that, surely?" Gil said. "Father had his faults, the Good Lord knows, but a bigamous marriage? Would he really have married this Amelia Gartmore, and then, just a few months later, entered into a second marriage? It is inconceivable!"

Humphrey pressed his fingers to his lips, lost in thought.

"That is a good point," he said slowly. "Father was always so conscious of his honour. Imagine the scandal if it should have come out! As it would be now… but we can perhaps hold Ben at bay by telling him we are investigating ourselves. It is a terrible risk, for you might end up proving exactly the point you wish to disprove, but… it should be attempted, I think. But I cannot go anywhere just now. I must be in York all next week, preparing for the opening of my gaming house. Merton? Can you go?"

"To Garthorpe? Mrs Merton will be very cross to be left behind. I have been promising her a trip to that part of the county ever since we married. Still, I daresay I can manage a few days away. There is a house near there with a leaky roof that needs my attention too, so I have a good excuse."

"Willerton-Forbes?"

"Ah, no. My brief is very clear, to stay here until recalled."

"Then it will be just you and me, Merton," Gil said, grinning. "An expedition — such fun! I particularly look forward to the leaky roof."

While Humphrey galloped off to tell Monty of developments, and Merton took up his pen to write to Carrbridge, Gil went to the coach house, and organised a carriage for the journey. There were few options, all the better travelling coaches having been called upon for the journey to London. Nor were there any curricles available.

"It's either the old luggage coach or Lady Georgiana's carriage, milord," Lester told him.

Gil looked from one to the other. "Lady Georgiana? You mean Grandmama? Good grief. Which one is older?"

"Hard to say, milord. They're probably as old as each other."

"And Grandmama's was probably built for her marriage, so that must be... let me see... sixty years ago?"

"Maybe a bit more'n that, milord. But in full working order. Nothing unsafe about either of them, and perfectly adequate for two gentlemen and not much luggage."

"Well, it had better be Grandmama's, then. Have we anyone left here who can drive the thing?"

"I'll drive you myself, milord."

"Excellent. You will need to collect Mr Merton tomorrow morning at eight, he will breakfast with me at Silsby Vale at ten and then we shall go on from there."

~~~~~
~~~~~

Genista had passed a pleasant morning. The three ladies had designated it a sewing day, so while Lady Humphrey and Mrs Andrews steadily produced tiny baby garments, she worked on her wedding wardrobe. With Mrs Andrews' enthusiastic help, she had finished a new day gown, and begun work on an evening gown. The material was a pale blue silk shot through with darker threads which gave it an unusual textured appearance. She'd rarely worked with silk before, but this was a thicker type which, with a proper petticoat, would not cling too much. She'd just begun stitching the bodice together when Gil arrived in a haze of excitement.

"Ah, there you all are. There is uproar at Drummoor. Ben Gartmore is minded to make a claim against the title after all, so Merton and I are off north for a few days to look into this supposed marriage. With luck we can scotch the whole idea. We shall be off tomorrow morning. Just going to pack." He disappeared through the door again, bobbing back almost immediately. "Merton will be here for breakfast, Lady H. I hope that is all right?"

And without waiting for an answer, he disappeared again, and his feet could be heard thumping up the stairs.

"Oh dear," said Mrs Andrews. "That is very bad news. Poor Lord and Lady Carrbridge! What a dreadful thing! But it may come to nothing, I dare say."

"It may," Lady Humphrey said. "We can only hope that Ben thinks better of it, or that the claim is rejected. I suppose the lawyers will have to come back again. How vexatious! Maria, do you suppose..."

Genista hardly took in a word of it. Only one thought was in her head — Gil was leaving her. And he seemed very pleased about it, too. She could not recall seeing him so excited before.

She laid down her sewing carefully, and then sat, considering. Just as in London, he was going away, leaving her behind again.

When it had happened before, she hadn't known him at all, and would never have dared to say a word. But now... Surely she knew him well enough now? In sudden determination, she rose, left the room and went upstairs.

He was in the dressing room, pulling shirts and neckcloths out of drawers, tossing them onto the bed. Davy, on his knees, was folding them, laying them in a travel box. A box... that meant a carriage. At least he was not planning to ride. That was something.

"Lady Gilbert," Davy said, with a bow. "I'll just fetch your other coat from below stairs, Gil."

"Good idea." Gil half turned, smiled at her, then turned back to the drawers.

"How long will you be gone?" she said.

"A few days, I expect. Four... five. Oh, if we are delayed, there will be Sunday to consider, so it could be more than a week."

She hesitated. It was so hard to find the right words. But she must speak, before her courage deserted her. "Did you mean what you said?" she blurted. "About... me asking, and you would do it?"

"Yes, of course," he said absently.

"Then may I come with you?"

"You would not enjoy it," he said, without looking up. "Bad roads, worse inns, a lot of sitting about with nothing to do. Much better to stay here."

"Then you didn't mean it," she said, hanging her head. Her disappointment was a physical pain that shot through her insides horribly. She had believed him! What a fool she was.

For the first time, he spun round to look at her fully. "I *did* mean it," he said in injured tones, "but why would you want to come along, when you can stay here? Good food, servants, every comfort provided, and friends to gossip with. Do you not like Lady Humphrey and Mrs Andrews?"

"Oh yes, they are everything that is amiable!" she cried. "But they are strangers."

"Well, *I* am a stranger, if it comes to that," he said, coming nearer, so that she could see the bewilderment on his face.

"But you are *my* stranger," she said softly. "I don't want to be left behind like a parcel to be collected later. I'd be no trouble, truly. I'll be as quiet as a mouse, and keep out of your way."

He gazed at her, head tipped on one side, as if he'd never looked at her properly before. "You would really enjoy such a trip? Better than being comfortable here? You truly want this?"

"Oh yes! Please, Gil. I'd rather be with you than anywhere else in the world." She hadn't meant to say that, but somehow the words had just risen straight from her heart and flown out of her mouth.

And he wasn't angry. He smiled, and cupped her face in his hands. "Then let it be so, and you shall enjoy exactly the same discomforts of travel and indifferent inns that I do."

She laughed at that. "I don't mind! I'm more at home in an inn than a big house like this."

"We shall need to take Holland..."

"I can manage perfectly well without a maid," she said.

"True, and I can brush your hair, after all..." He stopped, with a sigh that she could interpret very well. "But there may be times when Merton and I will need to go off together and leave you at the inn, and I should not like to leave you alone. Oh, but perhaps Mrs Merton would like to come along? She has a great desire to see that part of the county apparently. Would that be acceptable to you?"

"Oh yes, of course."

He smiled, and kissed her gently on the lips, and that kiss turned into a much longer and more ardent kiss, and they only sprang apart, rather flushed, when Davy returned.

~~~~~

They travelled slowly, for every few miles there was another hill, another precipitous valley, another vista to be enjoyed. Mrs Merton had a guidebook to the area, and so they were constantly on the lookout for an oddly-shaped stone, or a fork in the road, or a clump of trees which marked the next spot to be exclaimed over and delighted in. The carriage would come to a halt and they would all climb down and conjure up a new set of effusions over the beauties before them.

To Genista, whose whole life until a matter of weeks ago had consisted of some nine or ten square miles of Kentish countryside, every hour was a delight, and one she felt free to enjoy because she had Gil by her side and no unexpected arrival before an astonished marquess to anticipate with dread.

Sometimes she sat beside Mrs Merton, but the best times were when she could sit beside Gil, and slip her hand through his arm and rest her cheek on his broad shoulder. It astonished her now to recall his arrival on her doorstep, almost dead from the cold and his festering wound, yet now he was her husband, her delight, her love. She knew he was no angel, but when he was by her side, nothing could dismay her.

They stopped early, since Gil knew of a particularly good inn, where they had the snuggest private parlour Genista had ever seen, with a roaring fire, a big dining table, a sofa and several very comfortable chairs. There they passed a pleasant evening with a good dinner, several rubbers of whist without a single coin changing hands and not the least formality.
~~~~~

The next morning saw them on the road shortly after eight o'clock, and heading into even wilder country. A little after noon, they came to a place where their road, high upon the moors, looked down into a broad valley. Some distance along it was a neat little village, its church, cottages and grazing lands clearly visible.

Mr Merton did not need the guide book to identify it. "High Berenholme village, and just beyond it you might make out the chimneys of High Berenholme itself."

"Where Amelia Gartmore came from?" Gil said, in surprise.

"The very same. The property with the leaky roof is probably the house hidden by the trees just there."

"But it is next door to High Berenholme!" Gil exclaimed. "That is... a curious coincidence."

"Not really," Mr Merton said. "Watersmeet, the house with the leaky roof, is the property made over to Lady Hester for her lifetime. I could wish the seventh marquess had not been so generous, but there we are. Any number of these small estates were given to various Marford ladies to enable them to live independently, if they chose not to marry or in widowhood. This one was much used when Lady Hester was younger, by all I have heard, for she was quite a gay lady and liked a party. I imagine that in Amelia Gartmore's time, it was a convenient hiding place for the young men of the family wishing to escape the constraints of Drummoor or Marford House. Naturally, since Lady Hester moved to Drummoor permanently, it has been leased out."

"So my father came here and visited the neighbours at High Berenholme and thus met Miss Amelia Gartmore," Gil said.

"That would be my guess," Mr Merton said. "Lord Reginald came here last year and talked to old Mr Kiddleston at High Berenholme, who remembered your father well. The Gartmore sisters were poor relations of the Kiddlestons."

"I remember now," Gil said. "No one ever heard what happened to the younger sister... what was her name?"

"Annie. She was friendly with Sharp. He was your father's batman and valet in those days, so he went everywhere with him. It was only later he became the agent."

Gil frowned. "So Amelia paired up with Father, and this Annie paired up with Sharp? And Amelia may or may not have married Father, but Annie and Sharp...?"

"We know what happened to *him* — he became the Marford land agent," Mr Merton said. "But Annie disappeared. No one knows where she went."

"We can guess, though," Gil said in sudden excitement. "Sharp had that cosy little arrangement up in Northumberland, where Gus is. The mill town..."

"Drifford. Oh, you mean...?"

"The woman there... the one who gave him so much trouble... I will wager any money you like that was Annie Gartmore."

"Mrs Ballard," Mr Merton whispered. "Oh, that makes so much sense. We suspected that Charles Ballard was Sharp, and yes, of course Mrs Ballard was Annie Gartmore. So he whisked her away from High Berenholme, settled her at Drifford and let her run the place while he was fleecing Lord Carrbridge in his role as agent. Good grief! I have even met her!"

"But she, at least, is under lock and key," Gil said in satisfaction. "She was caught trying to burgle Reggie's house, and was sent north to answer for her crimes there, was she not?"

"She *was*," Mr Merton said sadly. "Unfortunately, she escaped from gaol a few weeks ago. Lord Augustus brought us word when he was here."

"So she and Sharp are both running loose?" Gil said in disgusted tones. "And they still have thousands of Carrbridge's money to enable them to live like lords. There is no justice in this world, none at all."

21: Garthorpe

Garthorpe was as different from the little village of High Berenholme as it was possible to get. Not quite a town, yet too big to be called a village, it sprawled in ungainly fashion along the road, lined on both sides by large warehouses and manufactories. One or two boasted tall chimneys belching black smoke, so that the air was choked with it. After driving for a mile or so with no change, they eventually crossed a busy turnpike road, and beyond that lay the more respectable, older part of Garthorpe, with a fine church, some shops and a few better houses arranged around a square. Mrs Merton's guidebook led them to a quiet inn on a side road — *'catering for the gentry and all those of a sober and peaceable nature, where accommodation guaranteed to please the most fastidious may be had for a very modest sum'*.

Genista had already discovered that Mr Merton was as fastidious as anyone she had ever met, liking everything to be just a certain way, but even he declared himself not displeased with their bedrooms and the substantial parlour they had secured.

"What, no bed bugs to be detected?" Gil said teasingly.

Merton raised a wintry smile. "There are always bed bugs in an inn bed, my lord. It is as inevitable as Easter following Lent. But I take my own sheets and pillow when I travel, so I am tolerably optimistic that I shall survive."

Mrs Merton laughed. "So long as he has a good dinner and plenty of claret, he will not regard the bed bugs, I am sure."

And Merton laughed amiably and patted his wife on the cheek. "I dare say I shall not, and if I do, I shall not complain about them above twenty times. Ladies, my lord — the church is very close. Shall we walk down there before dinner?"

They all agreed to it, and, apart from the smoke, it was a pleasant enough place for a walk, and the people respectable and well-mannered. One or two doffed hats or curtsied as the group passed by, recognising by their clothes that they were persons of consequence. Genista had not had occasion before to walk about in company with anyone other than her father, and she was acutely aware of the difference. Gil had a certain air about him that commanded immediate attention. It was not arrogance, exactly, so much as an expectation that he would be looked at, an awareness that he was of interest to persons beneath him on the social scale.

Indubitably he looked very much the lord. His well-fitting coat, his carelessly arranged hair that she knew took considerable time to achieve each morning, the immaculate neckcloth with its elaborate folds and the highly polished boots — all proclaimed him a man of fashion and substance, even when the title was not known. Mr Merton, by contrast, wore garments which proclaimed him to be a gentleman, wealthy but without the slightest ostentation. Mrs Merton was dressed with great elegance, yet without any undue flamboyance.

Genista had never been more conscious of her own dowdy appearance. Even her new pelisse with its little bit of frogging seemed very plain and ordinary beside the others. For the first time, Genista realised that she owed it to her husband to dress well, for her garments reflected his status. She would study Mrs Merton's gowns, she decided, for they had a pleasing simplicity which, if she could contrive something similar, would not make her feel too grand. Father had always had a horror of what he described as *'jumped-up shopkeepers'*, and Genista could not be comfortable in the sort of frivolous fashions that Lady Dryton wore, or even Lady Carrbridge. But she could afford the finest fabrics now, and she need not worry about the practicality of her clothes any more. She could wear higher waists and tighter sleeves and paler colours, and she might dare to add a feather or two to her hats. The idea pleased her so much that when Gil asked her in the most solicitous tones if she were enjoying herself, she beamed happily at him and told him in all sincerity that she had never enjoyed herself so much in her life.

He laughed at that. "I am glad of it, for you have had little enough pleasure in your life, I think. This was a happy thought of yours, Gen, to accompany me, for it delights both of us."

She had a sudden urge to cry, and was too gratified by his words to make any further response.

The church being deserted, they went instead to the parsonage next door, and were received with delight and many bows by Mr Kilroy, and deep curtsies from his wife and sister-in-law. They had the sort of threadbare gentility typical of many clerical families, the same serviceable and well-worn clothes that Genista was used to in her own family, and had seen much of in the more respectable families of Elversham. She felt she could estimate Mr Kilroy's income very well — perhaps one hundred pounds a year from the tithe, and each Sunday would necessitate an anxious examination of the offerings box, the farthings and pennies carefully added up. Would there be enough to order more coal, or buy another box of candles or a new pair of boots?

But they greeted their unexpected guests with pleasure, and much gratitude for the condescension shown to them. In honour of the occasion, tea and cake were brought out, and even Madeira offered. Gil accepted a glass, but the others refused, and Genista thought she detected relief in Mrs Kilroy's face. A bottle of Madeira would be hard to replace when every ounce of tea and piece of meat must be carefully considered before the expense could be justified.

It was not long before Gil came to the point of the visit.

"Oh, indeed, we remember the letter from Sir Rathbone Willerton-Forbes," Mr Kilroy said. "Is it not so, my dear?" The two ladies nodded their agreement. "Such an exciting day for us! We rarely have any letters from London, so it was quite an event to receive such an *important* communication. Why, we have it here, and a copy of our reply." The ladies rose as one, and together fetched the two papers from a drawer. They were so conveniently located, that Genista suspected them to be prizes which were often brought out to be shown to their acquaintance.

Gil gave both pages a cursory glance, then passed them at once to Mr Merton, who studied them for several minutes. "You have the register to hand, Mr Kilroy?"

"Oh yes, indeed we do. Is it not so, my dears?" Again the two ladies rose and went out of the room together. "Since learning of the significance of this particular entry in the register, we have kept it under lock and key here in the house, as you may imagine, my lord. It is even more secure than the law requires. We should not wish anything untoward to happen to it. Think of the possible consequences! How dreadful it would be if it should be required as evidence by the House of Lords! If, perhaps, His Gracious Majesty should require sight of it and it could not be produced... How catastrophic! We could not assuage our guilt if such an eventuality should occur."

"Your letter appears to be an exact copy of the register entry, Mr Kilroy," Mr Merton said. "In addition, it matches the special licence in every particular. The register entry is not the only record of this marriage, so you need not worry unduly about its safety."

"Oh!" Mr Kilroy looked very startled. "Even so, sir, it is very important evidence, is it not? One must do one's utmost to keep such records safe, surely? It would be unforgivable to fail in such an endeavour, for safeguarding such evidence is a matter of sacred duty, imposed on us by the highest in the land. Are we mistaken in supposing so?"

"I believe Merton is saying that it will not be a treasonable offence if the mice should get to it," Gil said.

It was fortunate that the two ladies returned at that moment, for Mr Kilroy seemed about to take offence at the very thought that he might tolerate mice anywhere in the vicinity of the precious book. However, in the act of laying it with all due ceremony on the table, and carefully turning the pages to the correct place, his ire was dissipated, and nothing further was said of mice.

Mr Merton then produced a small writing box and proceeded to make his own copy of the entry. Returning the precious book and the two letters to Mr Kilroy, whose two ladies replaced them in their homes, the party turned back to the rather good cherry cake.

"The clergyman who performed the marriage ceremony does not live in the town any longer?" Gil said, between sips of Madeira.

"Mr Culpepper? No, oh no. As I explained to Sir Rathbone Willerton-Forbes, when Mr Culpepper became too elderly to undertake his duties here, he engaged me as curate and went to live with his daughter, at Haddlewick. That is quite some distance from here, on the Scarborough road. He is a very elderly man, very elderly indeed. We do not know whether any communication was received by him from Sir Rathbone Willerton-Forbes."

"We plan to visit Mr Culpepper," Mr Merton said. "The two named witnesses are both dead, I believe? Mr James Granger and Mrs Winifred Caulsby. They were employed here, it seems."

"Oh yes. Mrs Caulsby was the housekeeper here, and Mr Granger was the coachman. Long dead, sadly."

Mrs Kilroy coughed.

"Yes, my dear?"

She leaned forward and practically whispered in his ear. "Meg Caulsby is cook at Holly House, and Jack Granger is head groom there. Perhaps...?"

"Oh, indeed. Meg is Mrs Caulsby's daughter and Jack is... um...?"

"Mr Granger's nephew," she said, in a mouse-like voice.

"Should you like to talk to them?" Mr Kilroy said. "We can fetch them here in a moment."

And without waiting for a reply, the two ladies jumped up and shot out of the room again.

"How obliging," Gil murmured.

Mr Kilroy was so affected by this innocuous remark that he must leap to his feet and bow deferentially. "Your lordship is most condescending. So gracious. Such an honour."

Silence now fell upon the room, which Mrs Merton broke by making some complimentary remarks about the church, and from there, with the aid of Mr Merton, the conversation flowed readily onto the subject of Garthorpe itself, its streets, buildings, shops and inhabitants all coming in for their share of the praise. All of this, Mr Kilroy responded to with bows and expressions of gratitude.

Eventually, when even the civility of the Mertons was wearing thin, Mrs Kilroy and her sister returned with Meg Caulsby and Jack Granger. The latter was dispensed with almost at once, since he had no memory at all of the marriage or his uncle's role in it. The cook, however, remembered it well.

"Oh, yes, milud, it were right here in this room it happened, so my ma said. I must 'a bin about ten or thereabouts at the time, but she talked about it after. She was allus talkin' 'bout it! Special licence an' all — even Mr Culpepper were excited 'bout *that*."

"And did you see the couple that were married?" Mr Merton asked.

"Oh no, no one did, 'cept Mr Culpepper and my ma and James Coachman. My ma let them in the front door, they came straight into this room, then out the front door after. Everyone wanted to see them, but no one did."

"Did no one happen to look out of the window?" Mrs Merton said in amusement. "There is always so much interest in a bride that I should be surprised if no one peeked."

"Oh, but it were night," the cook said brightly. "Dark night, nothin' to be seen at all."

Mr Merton questioned her diligently, but there was nothing else of interest to be learnt from her.

The four walked back to the inn in silence, and it was only sometime later, when their dinner had been laid out in the parlour and the servants had withdrawn, that Mr Merton exclaimed, "At night! That is very odd."

"May I ask a question?" Genista said timidly.

"Of course, Lady Gilbert," Mr Merton said politely. He was so unfailingly polite.

"I don't understand why they didn't just marry in the church. It's right next door to the parsonage, after all. I wouldn't want to get married in that shabby little parlour instead of the church."

"It is a good point," Gil said. "Why marry in Garthorpe at all? They both came from High Berenholme, where there is a perfectly good church, or, if they preferred it, a parsonage with a parlour just as shabby as Mr Kilroy's."

Mrs Merton laughed. "I must take issue with you about the shabbiness of the parlour, Lord Gilbert."

"You astonish me, Mrs Merton. I thought it an excessively shabby parlour myself."

"Oh, certainly it is now, but it surely was not so at the time of this marriage," Mrs Merton said. "Remember that Mr Culpepper was wealthy enough to keep a carriage and employ a housekeeper. Mr Kilroy is only the curate, and lives very impecuniously, that much is clear. What is also clear is that the late marquess wished to keep this marriage very secret. The special licence, the marriage in a different town altogether where neither party was known, even marrying at night — they did not wish to be seen, or have the marriage known about."

"But why marry at all, in that case?" Gil said impatiently, setting his knife down with a clatter. "Why go to all the trouble of obtaining a special licence, which is a great deal of bother when one lives so far from London, and then marry in this havey-cavey way, and not tell a soul? And look at the date — Grandfather was already the seventh marquess by the time Father married Amelia Gartmore, so Father was Lord Charles by then, and there is no mention of *that*. Even if the special licence was in the old name, he should have married under his new title. And then less than a year later, he married Mama! That makes no sense to me, and I do not understand any of it."

For a while they all ate and drank in silence. The bowls and platters gradually emptied, and the jugs of wine and ale, and eventually the servants cleared away the dishes, and replenished the jugs, and placed small dishes of nuts and sweetmeats on the table.

Mr Merton raised his glass to his lips, took a small sip and then set the glass down, smoothing the cloth around it. "There is a possible explanation that springs to mind, my lord." He sounded almost apologetic.

"Let us hear it, Merton," Gil said. "I am willing to listen to anything plausible at this stage."

"Suppose that Mr Charles Marford, as he was then, found himself in difficulties with Miss Gartmore. They were unofficially betrothed, let us say, and he had no reason to suppose there would be any objection to his marrying the lady. He was very far from the succession at that point. So, finding the matter urgent, he rushed down to London to obtain a special licence—"

"But why?" Mrs Merton said. "The banns would be almost as quick."

"When Lord Reginald visited Mr Kiddleston at High Berenholme," Mr Merton said, "the old gentleman said that his wife was very sick at the time, and the special licence would allow them to be married at the house, so that she could attend."

"So the intention to marry was public knowledge?" Gil said in surprise.

"It was," Mr Merton said. "Clearly, the special licence was obtained, but that was at precisely the moment when news of the death of the sixth marquess and his heir would have reached London. At that point, your grandfather became the seventh marquess, and your father became of great importance to the family. His oldest brother was sick, and his second brother had only daughters and was not likely to have a son. There would have been pressure on him to make a society marriage and set about securing the succession. So, instead of the public marriage, he married Amelia Gartmore in great secrecy and established her in such a way that she could have her child without public censure and live a quiet, but respectable life thereafter. And then he married a viscount's daughter, Miss Adela March, in a fanfare of publicity, and no one ever knew about his previous secret marriage. Until now."

There was silence, apart from the coals shifting on the fire, sending sparks up the chimney.

"Well, my lord?" Mr Merton said.

"It is very ingenious," Gil said. "It is almost plausible."

"Almost? You see deficiencies in my explanation?"

"Several," Gil said. "For one thing, Father may have been the most likely person to inherit the title in the end, but he also had two younger brothers, one of whom already had sons, so the succession was secure and the pressure to marry would not have been so great. Secondly, Miss Amelia Gartmore was at least a lady, unlike Great-Uncle Francis's wife who was a bootmaker's daughter. From bootmaker's daughter to marchioness would have been a great leap. Although it was undoubtedly something of a scandal at the time, no one stopped him marrying her and she was accepted into society without any difficulty as soon as she had produced a couple of lusty sons. It was not her fault that they were later carried off by putrid fevers. She was a redoubtable old lady who lived to be almost a hundred."

"You think there would have been no objection to your father marrying Miss Gartmore?" Mr Merton said.

"There would have been objections, but I cannot imagine Father giving them a moment's thought. He never cared two straws about the opinions of others. But the greatest deficiency in your theory, Merton, lies not with Miss Gartmore at all. My father was a reprehensible human being in many ways, and makes me look like a saint, but he was very, very careful to keep his activities to the sort of gentlemanly racketing that society and the law can both ignore."

"Ah, I see your point," Mr Merton said.

"It is to be hoped that you do, for to my mind it informs every part of this strange business. However wild he may have been, my father would never, *ever* have married one lady and then later bigamously married another. It is utterly impossible. Whatever happened all those years ago, there is another explanation for it."

22: A Leaky Roof

The party left Garthorpe the following morning, but not for Haddlewick and the elderly Mr Culpepper. They were to visit the village of High Berenholme and investigate the leaky roof of Watersmeet. Gil was not averse to investigating roofs, leaky or otherwise, having spent a good part of his boyhood clambering amongst the Drummoor chimneys, and moreover he had had plenty of time to grow bored with their journey. There was a certain pleasure in ambling about the countryside with a pretty wife at his side, but he was unused to sitting idly in a carriage and was growing restless. He missed his horses, and the possibility of a fast ride across the open countryside to blow away his fidgets. He wished he had his curricle with him, but he had gambled it away months ago and had not yet had an opportunity to replace it.

Having bespoken rooms at the inn, the four set out to walk the short distance to the house. The tenants, Mr Barton and his wife Lady Anne, received them gratefully. The house was not large, but pleasingly proportioned.

Before they could discuss the business which had brought them there, it was necessary to sit in the drawing room drinking tea, eating cake and fruit, and making boringly civil conversation. Gil wanted only to look at the roof and be off to Haddlewick, but nothing could be done in a hurry. He tapped his foot impatiently as Lady Anne talked about their children, and their convoluted and uninteresting reasons for leaving their previous home and moving to High Berenholme, which involved pigs in some unfathomable way.

"Are you aware, my lord, of the dangerous nature of pigs?" Lady Anne said.

"Oh, indeed," Gil said. "That reminds me of poor Mr Penicuik, our former chaplain who once..." He gazed around at the expectant faces watching him. "But it is of no consequence."

Merton leaned forward. "Oh, do tell us about poor Mr Penicuik."

"Is it an amusing story, my lord?" Lady Anne said.

How to answer such a question? It was amusing, in a way, but also not. "It was too dreadful for words, and we never speak of it. I should not have mentioned the subject."

To turn the conversation into a different channel, he asked about the Bartons' neighbour in the great house.

"Mr Kiddleston lives alone, I gather?" he said.

"Oh dear, did you not know?" Lady Anne said. "Old Mr Kiddleston died last year, and the sons had a very good offer for the estate, so they sold out. They live in York now, and spend part of each year in London, I believe. Yes, we have new neighbours now. The Prestwicks. An elderly couple and several grown children. Two surviving sons, for one died tragically, we are given to understand. Four daughters, which is another kind of tragedy. Well, the daughters are not properly out, I believe, although what *that* means I cannot say."

"You have not met them, my lady?" Merton said.

She pursed her lips. "Mr Barton called upon Mr Prestwick, Mr Richard Prestwick and Mr Harold Prestwick," she said. "Mrs

Prestwick has been in Bath for her health until very recently, and so I have not yet made my first visit. It must be done soon, I suppose." There was just a hint of superciliousness in her manner that Gil could recognise.

"Trade?" he said.

"Wool," Lady Anne said, with an almost visible shudder. "They have sold out now and live quite as gentry, so one is obliged to recognise them, or at least Mrs Prestwick and Mrs Richard Prestwick, not to mention however many of the daughters are out. Still, it is disconcerting to have neighbours with whom one has no acquaintance in common. No one has ever heard of the Prestwicks of Oldham. And they got rid of Mrs Huddleston, too. One does not turn off a housekeeper in such a manner, on a whim, and without even meeting her. The cook, too. They asked for a list of servants and struck out a great many, some of whom had been there for years, to be given immediate notice. What sort of people are they, to act so?"

"You are too fastidious, my dear," Mr Barton said, smiling. "No doubt they wanted a fresh start. Mr Prestwick is not, perhaps, from the top drawer, but there is nothing in his behaviour to disgust anyone, and the sons might move in any society. The young ladies are each to be given a season in London. A chaperon has been engaged, since Mrs Prestwick's health does not permit her to undertake the task herself. Miss Prestwick is already on her way south."

"I am sure I wish her good fortune there," Lady Anne said, sniffing. "No doubt the objective is to buy a titled husband for her, and then she may bring the others out, but I cannot like it. Such people should stay in the sphere to which they belong."

"We all started with nothing and climbed upwards," her husband said mildly. "Your distant ancestor was nothing but a lowly member of the King's army before he was noticed and ennobled, and I am sure Lord Gilbert's family has a similar history."

Gil was bored by so much talk about people he did not know and long forgotten family history, so he took the first opportunity to turn the conversation to the matter of the leaky roof. The Bartons took up the subject with enthusiasm.

"It is the night nursery which is the worst afflicted," Lady Anne told them. "It is most inconvenient, as you may imagine, for the children must now sleep on the same side of the house as we do ourselves."

"They are directly above us," her husband said, with a rueful grin. "You may guess how much sleep we are able to obtain in such circumstances. A man came and inspected the roof, and that gave us some relief for a while, but now the case is as bad as it has ever been, and we dare not use the room for fear of the ceiling collapsing. I do not understand it at all, for the entire roof was retiled and releaded only five years ago. There should be no question of a leak."

They were shown upstairs, past a cloud of giggling children, and into the affected rooms, with their many buckets and bowls collecting drips, and an ominous bulge in the corner of the ceiling in one room.

"This is very bad," Mr Merton said. "We must attend to it at once. How does one access the roof?"

"There is no door from inside the house," Mr Barton said. "We have been all over the attic rooms, but no way to access the roof can be found. It can only be done by ladders from outside."

They all repaired downstairs again, past the children, who shrieked and ran away, and outside to the lawn at the side of the house, where a couple of gardeners stopped raking to stand and watch with interest. Mr Barton shooed them away, and they downed tools and disappeared.

They all gazed up at the windows of the affected rooms. The central part of the roof was pitched, but around the edge was a strip that was flat.

"There is the reason for your difficulty," Gil said.

The others stared at him, bemused.

"Do explain, Lord Gilbert," Mr Barton said.

"There is a blockage in that rainwater pipe there, behind the tree. Probably it is choked with leaves or some such."

Merton looked at him quizzically. "How can you tell that, my lord?"

"It is not raining, so all the other pipes are dry," Gil said. "That one, however, is still seeping water at the bottom. There is probably quite a puddle up on the roof above the trap. I daresay the fellow who looked at it cleared away a few leaves at the top, but left the pipe still partially blocked. Do you have ladders?"

"Nothing long enough, my lord, but—"

"No matter, that tree looks stout enough. Merton, hold my coat."

"My lord, I must advise against this," Merton said. "Now that we suspect the problem—"

"But that ceiling could come down at any moment! Besides, this will be amusing."

"Gil, no!" Genista cried. "Think of your leg — you could do untold damage—"

"Nonsense! You worry too much." Now that the idea had occurred to him, he was boiling with excitement. A tree to climb! He had not done such a thing for years, and the last two or three times had concerned a lady and were therefore a little nefarious, whereas this was a matter of rescuing two people from sleepless nights and saving the cost of replacing a ceiling. Such fun!

Tossing his coat to Merton he strode off towards the house. The gardeners had left a rake behind, which he grabbed as he made his way to the base of the tree.

A small figure arrived in a flurry of skirts and grabbed his arm. "Gil, don't do this, *please!* You said you would do what I wanted, so I'm begging you, *please*, leave this to someone else. You mustn't risk damaging your leg again."

Angrily, he shook her off, too energised to listen. "Never tell me what I *must* do," he said coldly. "Now leave me be. It is only a tree, after all. I have done this a thousand times."

"Gil, please!"

Tears coursed down her face but he took no notice of them, his attention fixed on the problem at hand. Besides, how could he back down, just because his wife asked him to? It would make him the worst kind of coward. And he *wanted* to do this. There was not the least harm in it, and very little risk, so why should he not?

"Oh, stop fussing, Gen, for God's sake!"

Turning his back on her, he set his hands to the tree and began the slow climb. It was a good solid tree, with plenty of side branches convenient for hands and feet. Had he not had the rake, he would have shinned up in no time, but he would need it at the top, so he climbed slowly and carefully, juggling the rake from hand to hand, careful not to drop it.

There was only one sticky moment, where there seemed to be no convenient hand holds at all, and his bad leg somehow would not stay on its branch. He clung there for some time before he realised that if he went down a little, he could shuffle across to the balustrade of a balcony and use that as a perch before going on upwards.

Before too long, he had gained the topmost branches and could haul himself over the balustrade onto the roof. He fell with a splosh into a deep puddle that spread halfway along the house. But the blocked corner was clearly visible. He waded ankle-deep to the corner, and examined the outlet to the rainwater pipe. There was no blockage there, so, as he had suspected, the problem lay within the pipe itself. Now he had to try to clear the pipe using only the five foot handle of the rake. It was not easy, for it required him to reach through the balustrade and that meant kneeling in the water. But he was already soaking wet, so what did a bit more water matter?

It took some careful manoeuvring to get himself and the rake in the correct positions, and then it was awkward to get any force behind his proddings, but eventually he managed it, wiggled the rake handle vigorously and was rewarded with a gurgle and the sight of the puddle draining slowly away. A cheer from below told him that his success had been noticed.

He stood up gingerly, gave them a cheerful wave and then looked about him. There was a fine view over the Watersmeet gardens, a part of the High Berenholme parkland next door and most of the village, the chimneys quietly smoking below him. But he was not there to admire the view, he was looking for a door from below. There had to be one, he was sure of it. Every attic at Drummoor, and he had explored them all rather thoroughly, had a door out onto that part of the roof, and he could not imagine any house being built without such a thing. Every roof needed maintenance, after all.

He prowled around the flat perimeter of the roof, examining the ridged central part carefully. There, if anywhere, was where the door would be. But there was no sign of one. He took a second circuit, this time looking at the leaded flat roof. The leading was in good repair, as expected when it had all been replaced recently, and he was about to give it up as a lost cause when he noticed something odd — a metal hook on a chain, bolted to the inside of the parapet. It looked exactly like the type of hook which would be used to prop open a door. Except that there was no door. Unless...

He groaned. A trapdoor! Somewhere under that fine new lead sheeting was a trapdoor that led to some inner fastness of the house. But he could not uncover it himself, so he noted the position of the hook and went back to his tree to begin the descent. He still had the rake in his hand, but there was no need to climb down with it in his hands. He lobbed it over the edge into a flower bed.

It should have been much easier to descend without the rake, but somehow it was not. First was the awkwardness of clambering over the balustrade. He was soaked through, and his leg would not do what he wanted it to, so it took some experimentation to get himself onto the tree. Then it seemed to be far more difficult going down. He had forgotten how precarious it was to feel about for a branch with a foot, quite unable to see it, and trust his weight to it without being entirely sure it would hold. Twice he had to draw back sharply when a branch broke under his foot, and once he slithered downwards and had to grab at anything to stop himself falling.

By now his leg hurt appallingly, and he could not concentrate for the pain. In the end, he slipped and skidded the last few feet and ended in an agonised heap on the ground.

Genista was there at once. "Are you all right?" Her voice was shrill, her face blotched with tears.

"Of course I am all right!" he spat, in too much pain to mind his language. "Help me up, will you, and stop asking foolish questions."

At once she put his arm about her shoulders and heaved him to his feet with surprising strength. He staggered on his bad leg, then caught himself before he toppled over ignominiously. "See? I am perfectly fine."

To his surprise, she pummelled his chest with her fists, almost knocking him over again. "No, you're *not!* You could have killed yourself! What were you thinking? And heaven only knows what damage you might have done to that leg. You stupid, *stupid* man! Why would you do anything so blockheaded?"

Rage rose up in him like a tide, all his pride in his achievement swept away by his utter fury. What right did she have to speak so to him? Who was she anyway? Nobody! Some lower class nobody, until he had married her, and what was she doing ranting at him like a washerwoman?

He grabbed her wrists so hard she squeaked in surprise. "Shut *up!* Stop that screeching, woman, and go away."

"But you could have fallen!" she screamed. "You might have *died!"*

"Shut up! Stop it this instant! Never, *ever* speak to me in this manner again, do you hear me? Go away. Get out of my sight. *Now!"*

Her face froze into shocked terror, and she leaned away from him. Realising he still held her fast, with a cry of despair he flung her from him and she turned and fled.

Some distance away across the lawn, Merton, Barton and their wives still stood, studiously not watching the altercation. He took an unsteady breath, then another. With a huge effort, he willed his legs to move and walked off, limping heavily, across the lawn.

~~~~~
~~~~~

Every jolt of the carriage shot pain through him until he was almost screaming. It took every last ounce of his strength to keep his face bland, to keep his legs from restlessly shifting position, to keep his fists from clenching. But he would not — *would not* — admit how much he hurt. That would be to admit that he had been wrong to climb the tree and that he would never, ever do.

At Gil's side, Genista sat, head down, sniffling occasionally. She had not stopped weeping the whole time. How many hours was it now? Two? Three? And still she wept. Dear God, how could she cry so much? And it was all his fault. A part of him wanted to sweep her into his arms and bury his face in her glorious hair, and tell her how sorry he was, that he was a worm and he would listen to her in future, and would never, ever make her cry again.

And then there was the other part of him, the rigid shell he had built around himself as a protection against the hurts of the world. That part could never apologise, could never *grovel*. He had his pride, and as long as he maintained his anger he would never have to admit to being wrong.

So his emotions warred within him, and kept his anger burning bright. And still Genista wept on, and he could not bring himself to offer her any comfort. Damnation! Being married was so difficult.

Opposite them, the Mertons sat with their faces frozen into studied composure. Merton had argued, of course. He should rest his leg, take time to recover, they could stay another day at High Berenholme, or two maybe. The Bartons invited them to stay, or at least to come for dinner. But Gil was not in the mood for staying. He would move on, and Merton had no choice but to accept his authority. He would not be gainsaid.

So they drove on and on, and the ride became smoother as they picked up the York road.

"Would you consider an overnight stop in York, my lord?" Merton said in his quiet way. "There are some excellent inns and hotels there, and it has been a long day for the ladies."

Gil would have liked to refuse, to press on for another two or more hours for Haddlewick, but the shreds of good sense that he still retained, not to mention the violent pains in his leg, were becoming insistent. The prospect of a hot bath and a bottle of claret was too appealing to be denied. He could yield a little, but not the whole way.

"Very well. You may choose the place, Merton, but there must be three bedrooms. I shall want my own room tonight."

The slightest hesitation. "As you wish, my lord. Shall I ask the innkeeper to send for a physician to examine your leg?"

"Certainly not!"

"As you wish," he said again. "If it troubles you, Lady Gilbert is very well able to attend to it."

His tone was level and perfectly affable, but his words put Gil into such a rage that he would have sworn that Merton was trying to provoke him. As soon as the rooms were secured at the discreet inn Merton had chosen, Gil stormed upstairs while a little flock of servants streamed up and down with ewers of hot water for his bath.

Once he was immersed, he felt better. The damp had seeped into his bones, but with heat around him, he gradually relaxed and began to feel more himself. So it was a shock when he found he was unable to lift himself out of the tub. His arms had the strength, but somehow his recalcitrant leg would not obey his commands. After three attempts he sat back, exhausted, and waited for another servant to appear and haul him unceremoniously onto the rug.

It shook him rather. But once he was dressed again, his hair properly disordered and his cravat very orderly indeed, he felt more like himself and ready to face the evening.

He found Merton and Mrs Merton in deep conversation. They sprang apart when he entered.

"Are we to have the pleasure of Lady Gilbert's company this evening?" he said, trying not to sound disgruntled at finding her not present.

"She is almost ready," Mrs Merton said. "She will be here in a moment, I am sure of it."

"We shall not wait for her. Merton, tell them we are ready for our dinner."

But Genista crept in, white-faced, while Merton was outside giving the orders.

Dinner was not a comfortable affair. None of them ate much, and Genista nothing at all, crying silently the whole time. She went to her room straight after, and Mrs Merton with her. Gil was in the mood to become thoroughly drunk, so having consumed a quantity of wine with the meal, he now began on a bottle of port, drinking steadily as he and Merton played piquet for guineas.

Having lost all the coins in his pockets, Gil rose, swaying slightly. "Shall go to bed now."

"My lord," Merton began, and even in his inebriated state, Gil recognised the solemn expression on his face. "I have no right to advise you—"

"Indeed you do not," Gil said, glowering at him, but Merton was never a man to be deterred from what he saw as his duty.

"No. But nevertheless, however unwelcome, it must be attempted."

"Oh, do not feel obliged, Merton. I shall not be disappointed if you keep silence on any matter where your advice would be regarded as unwarranted interference." He stumbled somewhat over one or two of the words, but he cared not.

"My lord, I answer to Lord Carrbridge in all things, and I feel that he would wish me to speak to you now, since he cannot."

He paused, but Gil, seeing that he could only postpone the lecture by retiring to his room, resigned himself to the inevitable. With a dramatic sigh, he sat down, poured himself another glass of port and prepared to be scolded.

"My lord, Lady Gilbert is very young and very… inexperienced in the ways of the world. She has not learnt the fashionable art of concealing her feelings. When she saw you undertake a seemingly risky action, she was, not surprisingly, distraught. Mrs Merton would be just as distraught, I believe, were I to attempt anything so dangerous."

"But she would not scream at you like a fishwife, would she?" Gil said. "Mrs Merton would never be anything other than ladylike."

"Lady Gilbert is very innocent of the ways of the world," Merton said again, not looking at him. "She has come from a very humble life to her present elevated position, and it is not surprising if she finds the adjustment trying. As you must do, also. Everything in her life has changed very quickly, and she is… not her usual self at the moment. She has shown herself to be a steadfast and restrained person, so it must take some unusually heightened sensitivity for her to address you in such strong terms. I would ask you to bear in mind all the changes that she must be experiencing just now, and be sensitive to her circumstances. God willing, your marriage will last for many years, my lord, so I would advise you to consider the future." He lifted his head to look directly at Gil. "That is what is important now — the future."

He fell silent, gazing steadfastly at Gil as if he were waiting for something.

Gil drained his glass and waved the half-empty bottle. "My future is in here, Merton. At this moment, it is the only one I want."

And so saying he swayed out of the room, bottle in hand, and up the stairs to bed.

23: Memories

Genista sent Mrs Merton away as soon as she could. What was the point? It was not female comfort she needed, but male. One male in particular, and since that was most unlikely to happen, she needed to accustom herself to being alone.

She was soon undressed and ready for bed. She scrubbed her face repeatedly, but no soap could eradicate the puffy eyes and blotched cheeks. Even now tears trickled from her eyes, and she was helpless to stop them. She knelt beside the bed and said her prayers, a rather longer business than usual, for she had great sins to be confessed and forgiveness to be sought from One who might, she hoped, be more forgiving than Gil. She had tried to apologise to her husband, but he had said, "It is of no consequence," in such a cold manner, that she was cast lower than she had ever been in her life before.

When she had run out of supplications and impassioned pleas to God, she rose and went to the window. Her room overlooked the street, and although it was not one of the main streets, there was still plenty of bustle and many comings and goings, even so late at night. Carriages rattled over the cobbles, one or two sedan chairs were carried past in near silence, and any number of people on foot. Couples, so many couples. There were a few men on their own, but many a gentleman had a lady on his arm, and they passed by, all smiles and laughing conversation, so gay and companionable. It made her feel so lonely.

Still, there was a familiarity to being in town. Her two or three trips to Canterbury each year with her father were always a pleasure. Visits to the shops and warehouses, calls on acquaintance or professional visits, walking the busy streets and being part of the life of the town before returning to their tiny rooms at the inn, all of it was a delight to her country-weary eyes. Then the excitement of returning home with the gig laden with oddly-shaped packages, and the thrill of making new sheets or bonnets, using the new pot for the kitchen, and seeing the mixing room shelves restocked.

She liked towns, she decided. Not London, which was unbearably big and noisy and busy, but small towns like Canterbury and York. It was the same with houses. The palatial Drummoor oppressed her, and even somewhere like Silsby Vale House felt too grand and formal, but a small cottage was just the right size. Where would she live when Gil went back to his army camp at Dover? She could only hope it would be somewhere small, but at the back of her mind was the gnawing terror that he would leave her behind again, that she would have to survive, somehow, in the overwhelming grandeur of Drummoor.

Every time she thought of Gil, the tears flowed a little harder. Dear Gil! He could be so gentle and kind and even affectionate when he was in the mood, but when he wasn't… Another tear trickled down her face and dripped off her chin. Angrily she brushed the back of her hand across her face. She must stop crying. It did no good at all, and Gil would not think the better of her for it. How he must despise her!

She mustn't give way in this weak manner. She had to be strong now, and think of the future. She had her secret, and that was all that mattered, not her own feelings or what Gil thought of her. She hadn't told him yet, and she couldn't, not until he'd calmed down a little. Mrs Merton had guessed, and would no doubt tell Mr Merton, but not Gil. Would he be pleased? She could only hope he would. It was what every man wanted, wasn't it? A child of his own, a miniature version of himself, a son to follow in his father's footsteps. In Gil's case, someone to be taught to ride and shoot and hunt and dance with grace, someone who would be able to move with practised ease through the saloons and country estates of society. Unlike her.

She climbed into bed, trying not to think how empty it was without Gil, and closed her eyes, hoping for the welcome oblivion of sleep. Perhaps she even dozed a little. But then a noise woke her, the door opening and closing, and the sounds of a man, a rather inebriated man, bumping into furniture and giggling. Gil. He must have forgotten he'd taken a separate room. Once, he must have banged his bad leg, for there was a sharp intake of breath, a muttered oath and then complete silence for a while, as he stood waiting for the pain to ease. That worried her, but she was lying on her side facing the wall, and she dared not roll over to look at him, in case he realised he had a room next door and went away again.

Eventually, he started moving about again, more circumspectly by the sound of it, and the bed shifted as he climbed into it. He lay still for a while, and she was equally immobile, listening to every breath of his. Then he rolled towards her, wrapped a careless arm around her waist and buried his face in her hair.

"Ah, Gen," he murmured. "Sweet, darling Gen."

Then he slept.

Genista cried a little, smiling through her tears. The warmth of his body against her back was such a comfort after the trials of the day. In time, she too slept.

~~~~~

Genista was used to small villages, but Haddlewick was as nondescript a place as she had ever seen. There was a large and busy coaching inn on the main road, with the date *'1562'* engraved on the lintel. A few cottages straggled on either side of the road, and the village itself was tucked down a side road, consisting only of a church and parsonage, together with another handful of cottages, and no manor or property of any merit to be seen. The inn looked respectable, and Gil told them that Gus had patronised it, so the stables at least would be acceptable. It looked respectable enough to Genista.

Having secured their three bedrooms and a parlour, and discovered that Mr Culpepper lived at the parsonage, they made their way there at once. It was still early, but if the old gentleman was a late riser, then they could return later that day to talk to him. They were admitted by a smartly dressed housekeeper, and shown into a small parlour and left there. It was expensively furnished, but with the slightly chilled and fusty air of a room that is only used occasionally, perhaps for unexpected guests while it was decided what to do with them. The fire was laid, but not yet lit.

Genista sat patiently with the others, watching Gil prowl restlessly about the room. He'd been cross all morning, grumbling about the noise outside, but that was unavoidable in a town inn. There was always something going on. Most likely it was the after-effects of his drinking the night before. She could tell that his leg was hurting him, but he wouldn't sit down and she dared not say a word, for fear of being on the receiving end of his wrath again. She had to bite her lip and try not to look at the set expression on his face, or the awkward way he stood, trying to relieve the pain. Such a stubborn man. Would it be so difficult to admit to a weakness now and again?
~~~~~

The door opened, and a woman of middle years entered. "Good day, my lord," she said, unerringly detecting Gil as the nobleman of the group. "I am Mrs Harvey, Mr Culpepper's daughter. I understand you wish to see my father?"

"If it is possible," Gil said politely.

"My lord, my father is eighty-eight years of age," she said. "He is very frail and tires easily, so you will not object if I stay and watch over him? If I grow concerned, I shall have to ask you to leave."

Gil agreed to it, and she led them to the rear of the house, into a pleasant room with a roaring fire, one wall filled with bookcases, the others hung with so many portrait paintings crammed together that not an inch of uncovered wallpaper remained. Scattered about on various tables were books which proclaimed themselves to be from a circulating library. Clearly, Mr Culpepper was not a clergyman who confined his readings to doctrinal tomes.

As his daughter had said, Mr Culpepper was indeed frail, so thin and wizened that he looked likely to fall over at any moment, his breathing laboured. He was immaculately dressed, however, a wig covering what hair remained to him, and stood to make a very deferential bow to Gil. He, too, picked him out of the group at once as the lord.

He professed himself delighted to have visitors. "No one comes to see me any more," he said with a chuckle, and a distinct wheezing in his chest. "Parish enquiries go to Hobbs, my curate here, and there are some who call upon Violet. My daughter, you know. And the farrier's boy hangs about the kitchen for the scullery maid." He laughed, the wheezing more pronounced. "But who is interested in an old man like me? I have never been further afield than Yorkshire, have never been to war or to sea, have no tales of derring-do to report. Do sit down, my lord, my lady. And Mr and Mrs Merton, too." He scanned their cards a second time. "Marford, eh. I can guess your business, my lord. My curate at Garthorpe sent me word that there was some interest in a marriage I conducted involving a Marford. He was a relative of yours, I presume."

"My father," Gil said. "You remember the occasion, sir?"

"Oh, indeed, my lord. I remember it well. I was ordained at the age of twenty-five, so, as you may imagine, I have conducted a great many marriages in my time. Most of them were routine, three readings of the banns and then off to church. A few were by common licence — no banns, but everything else the same." He paused to catch his breath. Genista noted the blue tinge to his lips — a bad sign, she knew. "But only twice, just twice in almost sixty years, have I conducted a marriage by special licence, my lord. One was for the daughter of Sir Henderson Forley down in London. He was dying, he had no son and only the one daughter, and he promised to leave everything to whoever married her. Got a special licence so they could be married right there in his bedchamber, and the lawyer there too, so he could change his will at once, and the poor man went to his maker the very next day. That was one special licence." Another pause. Wheeze in. Wheeze out. And again. "The other was your father, my lord. Although he was not enobled then. Plain Mr Charles Marford, as I recall."

"Your memory is excellent, sir," Mr Merton said.

"There is nothing at all amiss with Father's mind," Mrs Harvey said, with a smile. "He always was sharp as a needle, and is so to this day. He plays chess with Mr Hobbs every night and always wins."

"Well, well, not *always*, my dear," the old gentleman demurred. "But I remember my two special licence marriages very well."

"Did Mr Marford give any reason for wishing to be married by special licence?" Mr Merton said.

"No, not to me," Mr Culpepper said. "The reasons are immaterial. If His Grace the Archbishop of Canterbury sees fit to issue a special licence, it is not for a humble cleric like myself to question the matter."

"No, indeed," Mr Merton said. "But naturally you satisfied yourself as to the legality of the marriage."

"I questioned both the lady and the gentleman very thoroughly. It is a very particular requirement with a marriage by licence, for without the publication of the banns, one has no other means of discovering possible impediments. Both parties were asked about their ages, any previous marriages, consanguinity and if they be fully willing to take the solemn step before them." He paused again. "Forgive me... trouble breathing..." A longer pause, with loud wheezing. Mrs Harvey shifted to the edge of her seat, ready to intervene but the old gentleman waved her back. "Fine now, my dear. All their responses were perfectly satisfactory. I should perhaps add that, by the time of which we speak, I had been exposed to such an array of humanity in all its manifold varieties, that I was quite comfortable in declaring them to be both sincere and honest in their answers. There was no deception in either of them."

"And did you also ascertain that they were the persons named on the special licence?" Mr Merton said. "Miss Amelia Gartmore and Mr Charles Marford?"

"Indeed I did. They both provided evidence." More wheezing, sounding loud in the otherwise silent room. "The lady showed me some letters addressed to herself, and her handkerchiefs embroidered with her initials. The gentleman showed me letters also, and a pocket watch with his name engraved upon the back."

Gil shifted restlessly in his chair. Genista watched him anxiously. This was not going as well as he had expected, she guessed. It might be assumed that a man of eighty-eight would, at the least, be hazy about details and might even have forgotten some aspects altogether. But this pin-sharp old man was calmly proving the impossible — that Gil's father, so conscious of his own honour, had married bigamously.

"But what did they look like, these people?" Gil said testily.

"Mr Marford was tall, very handsome, and exceedingly well-dressed — like yourself, my lord." He took several laboured breaths. "The lady was handsome, too, rather shy, as brides tend to be."

"What colour hair did they have?" Mr Merton said.

"Impossible to say, sir. They both wore wigs. Everyone did in those days."

"And did my father look anything like me?" Gil burst out.

Mr Culpepper considered the question carefully. Then he said slowly, "That is a hard question to answer after all these years, my lord. One sees a face, and remembers it. I shall remember yours, my lord, just as I remember your father's, and if I had them side by side, I could certainly compare them. But to compare a living face with a memory... that is more difficult."

"But would you recognise my father's face if you saw it again?" Gil said eagerly. "His portrait, for example?"

"I believe I should, my lord, if it be a good likeness."

"Then you must come to Drummoor and look at my father's portrait there."

"Impossible," Mrs Harvey said at once. "My father is too frail to travel anywhere. Look how his hands shake from the effort of talking to you, and he can barely breathe. He will only leave this house once more, my lord, for his journey to the churchyard next door."

"Then I shall just have to bring the portrait here," Gil said stubbornly.

"I shall be happy to look at it," Mr Culpepper said with greater strength, "if it will convince you that I am telling the truth." He'd gone rather red in the face, and he put a hand to his heart as if he was in pain.

"Oh, there is no question of *your* dishonesty," Gil said at once. "Pray be easy on that score."

"You believe, then, that it was *not* your father who was married that day?" Mr Culpepper said. "That it was some other man masquerading as him?"

"It could not possibly have been my father," Gil said, raising his chin defiantly. "My father did many foolish or even outrageous things, but he never acted dishonourably or outside the law. Yet you would have me believe that he married Amelia Gartmore, and just months later bigamously married my mother? No! It is impossible."

"But if it is as you say," Mr Culpepper wheezed, "and some other person pretended to be Mr Charles Marford, the question arises — why? Why would anyone do such a thing? What could possibly be gained by it?

That, of course, was the heart of the matter, but no one could answer him.

As soon as they returned to the inn, before they had even gone through the door, Mr Merton said, "I shall go and alert the ostlers that we will need the carriage within the hour. I take it you will wish to leave for Drummoor immediately, my lord?"

"Yes, but not by carriage. I shall ride."

Genista's heart almost stopped beating. She wanted to cling to him, to cry out, to tell him that he mustn't... but she dared not. She pressed her hands to her mouth, as if to stop the words that rose up from spilling out. It was Mr Merton who protested.

"My lord, I—"

"Think about it, Merton," Gil said. "Today is Friday, and we cannot possibly get to Drummoor today by carriage. We shall have to overnight in York again, and reach Drummoor tomorrow. But the day after is Sunday, so we cannot leave before Monday, at the earliest, and perhaps the journey back will again take two days. Five days away! That old man could be dead by then, and I want this thing settled, once and for all. Whoever he married that night so many years ago, it was *not* my father, and I want that proved beyond all doubt. I want Culpepper to look at that portrait and say, *'No, that is not the man I married.'* Culpepper is as honest and astute a witness as I ever saw, and he will speak truly. Then we can be *done* with this whole business. I shall go to the stables to bespeak a fast horse."

"My lord, let *me* go!" Merton cried, grabbing his arm in desperation. "I can ride fast, you know I can, and—"

Gil looked disdainfully at the hand clutching his sleeve, and Merton withdrew it at once, hands raised in apology. "Your pardon, my lord. That was unforgivable of me."

He bowed deeply and Gil gave a curt nod of acknowledgement. "Merton, you have been in Yorkshire a year, or not much more. Most of that time has been spent chained to your desk. You may know the ways around Drummoor, but you do not know the country this side of York, not as I do. I can reach Drummoor tonight with ease by riding cross-country, and if I leave by carriage with the portrait at first light tomorrow, I shall be here before dark."

Genista gave a squeak of terror, but Gil didn't so much as glance her way. He had that excited glitter in his eyes which she recognised all too well now. She felt hot and dizzy, and somehow she couldn't breathe.

"I must advise against it, my lord," Merton said in some agitation.

"Advice noted. Take the ladies indoors, Merton."

And he strode off, as fast as his limp allowed, towards the stable yard.

Merton turned helplessly to Genista. "I am sorry, my lady, but there is no gainsaying him when he is in this mood."

"I know," Genista whispered.

"Can you not go with him?" Mrs Merton said quietly.

"And leave you here alone? I think not. I will try to persuade him to take a groom, but most likely he will refuse. Beyond that there is nothing more to be done."

"Except to worry about him," Genista said, her voice sounding oddly far away.

And then everything blurred and went black.

24: Hero

Gil had not been riding for more than an hour before he realised his error. Riding hard was the worst possible thing for his injured leg, and every motion of the horse shot unbearable pain through him. But he would not surrender! If he went crawling back now, the day would be lost and it would take even longer to get the portrait to Haddlewick, and Mr Culpepper could be struck down at any moment. He was impelled by a terrible sense of urgency. Culpepper was the only man who could now save the marquessate, and if he died before seeing the portrait, then Carrbridge would lose everything and it would all be Gil's fault for interfering in the first place.

But he had never thought that Culpepper would be so lucid, or have so much calamitous evidence. Clear as a bell in his mind, he heard his brother's voice — *'That is the trouble with you, Gil, you never do think.'* Damnation! What a mess he had made of it! But he had a chance — this one chance — to make everything right, and he must not fail. So he pushed on, trying not to scream.

He made a small detour through a larger village which he knew had an apothecary, and purchased a quantity of laudanum. After that, he got on much better, and reached Drummoor, muddy and exhausted, shortly before nightfall, limping through the house barking orders at the astonished junior footmen and housemaids, all that remained of the usual staff. Mrs Compton, the housekeeper, was still there, however, and she efficiently organised a bath, a temporary valet, a half-decent dinner and several gardeners to manhandle the portrait.

While he was soaking in the bath, Gil bethought him of a new scheme — if he took a selection of portraits, there could be no possibility of Culpepper making a mistake. There was another one of Father at a much younger age, almost the age he would have been when he married, although not so good a likeness, and there were portraits of the long-dead Uncle Reginald and Uncle Francis. There was one of Uncle Lucius, too, who was not even a Marford, which would be a good way to confuse the old man, if he were at all susceptible to being confused. He gave the orders as soon as he was dressed again, and Mrs Compton said, "Yes, my lord. I'll see to it, my lord," without the least hint of argument. It was very soothing to have people about one who made no protest, no matter how inconvenient the request. He was so very tired of argument.

Dinner was a tray in his room, and what with another dose of laudanum and several glasses of claret, he was feeling much mellower. He did not particularly relish the early start and long day tomorrow, and he would have to drive himself for there was no one left in the stables who could handle the reins, but at least he would be moving, and he had the laudanum to keep the pain at bay. He would take a groom to deal with the horses. It was a pity that the only usable conveyance was the old luggage coach, for it was a lumbering beast, and even with four horses, their progress would be slow.

He was sitting over a final glass of claret, and mulling over whether he should go to bed at once, when there was a tap on the door. Without waiting for a reply, it opened and Bella's head peered round.

"Ah, so the rumour is true. And is it also true that you are packing all the ancestors off for a holiday?"

Gil laughed at this description. "Something like that."

She ambled into the room uninvited, but Gil was not averse to a little company. She had brought her own wine glass, so they sat having a comfortable coze, in the way of old friends, and finishing the claret, after which they began on the port. Gil told her his travails at Garthorpe and Haddlewick, and how the portraits were to be a last attempt to settle the matter satisfactorily. She was a receptive listener, and when he had told all, she brought him up to date on all the latest *on dits* from town in the most amusing manner. He relaxed in her undemanding company, and felt he had not been so well entertained for weeks.

So when, by some means he could not quite account for, he found her sitting on his lap, it seemed the most natural thing in the world and he made no protest. And before long, somehow or other, they were kissing and he found himself enjoying it very much.

"Now this is more like your old self," she murmured, between kisses. "I have been so worried about you, Gil dear. You have been so moped lately, not at all like you. Is this not the most pleasant way to pass the evening? And look, your bed is so conveniently to hand, is it not?"

He had no intention of going that far, but a cuddle was very pleasant. He had had a difficult time of it, and surely he deserved a little respite from it all? How delightful to be with a woman who was soft and yielding and did not stare at him with those mesmerising blue eyes... No, he was not going to think about that. Think about Bella instead, who perhaps was not as pretty or sweet or enticing as

Gen, but at least she never shouted at him. And she was here, in his arms and that was what mattered, surely.

"I shall get rid of Ramsey, I think," Bella mused. "I am tired of him. A married man is preferable for my needs. A bachelor is always thinking of his reputation, because he will want to marry some day. But a married man need not care. He has done his duty, and may leave his wife to bloom without further attention. Your little nonentity will be blooming soon, I daresay. Perhaps she already is."

It was a casual remark, but it hit Gil with the force of a blow, knocking all the breath out of him. Blooming? His Gen? Was it possible? Was that why she was so pale in the mornings, and so uninterested in food? Maybe that was why she had been so upset — a woman in that delicate condition was far more sensitive, or so he understood. And Merton had tried to tell him! *'Not her usual self... unusually heightened sensitivity... be sensitive to her circumstances... consider the future.'* Dear God, and he had railed at Gen and made her weep for *days*. His poor Gen... he must go to her at once. *At once!*

What on earth was he doing with Bella on his knee? "Get off me, Bella," he said harshly. "Go away."

"What! But we are having such an agreeable time, and it was about to get a great deal more agreeable, I had hoped."

He pushed her off his knee. "Go and find your amusement elsewhere. I am a married man now."

"It is a little late to think of that," she said huffily. "Come on, do not play games with me, Gil. Come to bed, just like the old days."

She began to tow him towards the bed, but he pulled himself free and marched, a trifle unsteadily, to the door, hauling it open.

"Out!"

"Really, Gil, you are no fun any more."

But, to his infinite relief, she went, swaying provocatively past him, her eyes tilted flirtatiously. He slammed the door shut, and then leaned against it from sheer weakness, eyes closed. He had come so close, but he must not, he *would* not betray Gen like that.

His mind conjured up her face, smiling in that way she had, her eyes shining up at him, and he groaned in anguish. He should never have left her side, he knew that now. He should have listened to her, and not let the madness overtake him. Darling Gen, his own sweet love, who cared so much about him that she had screamed at him, trying to make him listen. And he had ignored her. Even after he had promised her that he would always abide by her wishes. He groaned again, balling his hands and beating futilely against the door in his frustration.

Carrbridge was right about him — he was nothing but pond slime. How could he ever make things right?

~~~~~

The next day it rained. It seemed as though even the heavens were pouring disapproval on Gil's behaviour, so he accepted it as no more than his due, a small part of the punishment for his appalling behaviour.

The four horses, a motley collection drawn from the remnants of the stables, blew and snuffled in the early morning light. The groom, aged about fourteen, had borrowed a greatcoat from someone considerably larger, making him look shrunken and even younger. The coach was as shabby as anything Gil had ever been in before, and he could hardly believe he had to drive the disreputable old thing. The full-length portrait of his father, wrapped in multiple layers of sacking and oilcloths, was secured into the large hold beneath the body, and the four smaller portraits wedged into the body of the coach, between the wooden seats.
~~~~~

Mrs Compton was in the stable court to see him off. "Will this be the end of it, my lord?" she said. "This difficulty with Ben Gartmore is... very trying for the family."

"Indeed it is," Gil said quietly. "It is the greatest pity that Dr Hamilton has seen fit to propagate his ideas, and that Ben is so receptive to them, but with luck I shall be able to prove that Ben's claim is unfounded."

"You are a hero, Lord Gilbert," Mrs Compton said fervently.

Gil felt so unlike a hero that he could not begin to formulate a response to this remark, so he merely smiled a little and climbed, with a grimace of pain, onto the driver's seat. The groom hopped up beside him, Gil coaxed the horses into movement and the elderly coach lumbered under the arch and out of the stable court.

It was a long, dreary day. The rain fell steadily and seeped all the way through Gil's greatcoat and then, with mindless disregard for his comfort, through every other layer, too. Even with laudanum, he could not mask the relentless throbbing in his leg, and he began to wonder how he could possibly endure the distance to Haddlewick. Every milestone passed was a small victory, another mile nearer the end of the journey. Whenever he flagged, which was almost constantly, he reminded himself that Gen was waiting for him at his destination, and tried not to wonder what on earth he was to say to her.

Then he had a piece of luck. To protect his leg from the worst jolts and ruts, he chose to stay on the better roads, which led him through York. Almost the first person he saw was Humphrey crossing the street in front of him.

"Lord, Gil, whatever are you doing driving this old wreck?" Humphrey said cheerfully.

But when Gil explained, he frowned.

"Haddlewick? You will not be there before dark, and you look done up. Are there no coachmen at Drummoor? No, I suppose not. Everyone is in London. But you cannot do this by yourself. Where are you changing horses?"

"The Lion and Lamb."

"Wait for me there, and I shall drive you myself. You can ride in the back, and rest that leg of yours."

Gil laughed. "Humphrey, you are the best of brothers! I should be very grateful."

"You are in worse case than I suspected if you are not making even a token protest. Completely done up. I shall not be above half an hour."

At the inn, Gil dosed himself with laudanum again, and equipped with a bottle of brandy and a couple of rugs, squeezed past the wrapped paintings onto the hard wooden bench inside the coach, and slept away the afternoon. Occasionally he woke to find the coach in comforting motion, so he drank some more brandy and slept again. Once, the coach was stopped with some kind of altercation going on between Humphrey and another man, but they soon rumbled off again. Gil turned over and closed his eyes.

The next time he woke, the coach was stationary, and it was dark outside. He could hear voices in the distance. After a while, the coach door opened and a lamp dazzled him momentarily.

"My lord, I am very pleased to see you." Merton, smiling broadly for once. "Are you quite rested?"

"Of course he is rested," Humphrey said heartily. "He has been asleep for hours, the lazy good-for-nothing. Out you get, Gil. We have arrived."

He scrambled out past the paintings, and almost toppled over when he tried to put weight on his bad leg, which seemed to have seized solid. Humphrey caught him in time to save him from an ignominious tumble.

"Up you come! No sitting down just yet, for we have to get all these monstrosities inside."

They were outside the parsonage, Humphrey, the Mertons, Culpepper's daughter and a couple of servants with lamps. But one face was missing. There was no sign of Gen.

"Do come inside, Lord Gilbert," Mrs Harvey said. "You must be exhausted. Come and sit by the fire. I have some hot broth waiting for you."

He was too weak to argue. Meekly, he allowed Humphrey to take his arm and help him inside. He was taken to the back of the house first, to wash and relieve himself, and then back to the little parlour they had been shown into when they had first arrived — was it only yesterday? It seemed like a lifetime ago. There was a good fire burning this time, and he was wrapped in warm blankets and given a bowl of broth to drink.

"Chicken broth," he said, bemused, feeling that in some unfathomable way, he had slipped back in time and was still at Lavender Cottage. At any moment, Gen would come in and feel his forehead for fever. "Where is Lady Gilbert?"

"I believe she is at the church," Mrs Merton said.

Gil set down his bowl and pushed back the blankets. "I must talk to her."

"There will be plenty of time for that later," Mrs Merton said.

"The portraits are the most important consideration now," Merton said. "Mr Culpepper was most unwell yesterday. He is a little better today, but still... we should not delay in putting them before him."

Gil nodded. “Humphrey can take charge of the paintings now. Get them unwrapped and show them to Mr Culpepper. I am going to find my wife.”

He rose unsteadily, but although willing hands reached out to help him, he walked out of the room unaided. Outside, he realised that he had left his greatcoat and hat inside. By the time he had walked the short distance to the church, the rain had soaked him all over again. The church door was ajar, with a space narrow enough for a slender lady to slip through. Gil was too large to fit through the gap and the door was stiff, so he had to heave it open, creaking and protesting.

Inside, a cluster of candles in a niche were the only lighting. The draught made the flames jump about, making shadows that danced like giant marionettes about the body of the church. She was sitting in a pew near the back, her head down, her face shaded by the side of her bonnet. He limped in, his footsteps echoing on the tiled floor, but she made no movement when he eased himself into the pew beside her.

He sat in silence, not knowing how to begin. What could he possibly say to her? What words could adequately convey all that was in his heart? He had always prided himself on his ability to sweet-talk a lady, to flirt, to make the sort of light-hearted conversation that suited the drawing room or ballroom. Or the bedroom, perhaps. But to sit in church beside the woman who meant more to him than anything else in the world—

And how had he come to *that* point? He had married her because he had been forced to, this little dab of a girl — a physician’s daughter, no one he would ever have looked at in the normal course of events. But somehow she had wormed her way into his heart, and taken it captive. He *loved* her, not in the light way of his flirts and mistresses, but in a deep, world-changing way that shook him to his core. He wanted, more than he could say, to be worthy of her, to earn her regard, or at least her respect. Yet he had failed, utterly.

He cleared his throat, and the sound ricocheted shockingly about the emptiness. Gen's head jerked up, and she threw him a quick glance, then she looked down at her lap again. Her hands were so still, one gloved hand resting on the other. So neat, so demure. So *good.* Gen was goodness itself, and he was beneath contempt.

He had to say something, but what? How could he find the words? All his eloquence failed him. The only way was raw honesty.

"I am not sure what to say to you," he said, leaning forward so that his head nearly touched the back of the pew in front, his breath ragged. "I want to tell you how sorry I am, to beg your forgiveness. I want to promise never to treat you so appallingly again." He leaned back and ran his hands through his hair. "But how can I? I said all that before, and meant it too, and that did not keep me from this... this *madness*." He wrapped himself in his arms, rocking slightly in his anguish. "Whatever I say to you now, whatever promises I make, no matter how great my sincerity, there is no certainty that it will not happen again. I have no idea how to make myself behave well. I have always been wild, and everyone remonstrated with me — my father, Mama, my schoolmasters, my tutors at Oxford, Carrbridge, my colonel — and it never made the slightest difference. I would be wild, because that was who I was. *Oh, Gil Marford, he is such a rogue, did you hear what he has done now?* I was wild and proud to be so. Nothing could induce me to change, and it never mattered because who was hurt by it except myself? Or so I thought." He closed his eyes, one hand to his mouth, but the flood of words was unstoppable. "Until I met you. I never *wanted* to change until I met you, and now I do and I have not the least idea how to go about it.

Help me, Gen, please. *Please*." A half sob escaped him. "Tell me what I must do, because I cannot see any hope for me."

All the time he was speaking, she had not looked at him, but when, finally, he had run out of words, she lifted her head and turned her great blue eyes on him. Those eyes! Ah, the pain in them, and it was all his fault. He almost broke down and wept at that point.

"I can't help you," she said, and her words had the finality of a death knell. "When you go crazy like that, I can't reach you, so how can I possibly help you? If you won't listen to me, or to anyone, then the only person who can make you change is *you*. No one else can do it."

"Then what am I to do?" he whispered.

"You are in church," she said softly. "You could try praying. Perhaps God will help you, if no one else can."

25: A Bath Before Dinner

For a long time, he sat, head bowed in despair. He tried praying, but it seemed selfish to pray for his own better behaviour, something which ought, after all, to be under his control. Mama had always taught him to pray for others, so he prayed for Gen to have a better, kinder husband and to be happy, and then he prayed for Carrbridge to be spared the annoyance of his wastrel of a brother, and then, because he could not help longing for it, he prayed for Gen to feel *some* affection for him, even if he had lost all hope of ever winning her love. And perhaps at that point there was a tear or two which escaped.

"How is your leg?"

He jumped, so lost in his own thoughts that he had half-forgotten that he was not alone. "Fine," he said instinctively.

"Truly?"

"Actually, not fine. I found an apothecary yesterday and acquired some laudanum. That has helped. And brandy. But... it still hurts. It hurts all the time, Gen."

"You're not feverish, which is a good sign."

"How can you tell? You are supposed to put your hand on my forehead," he said indignantly. "Although I have already had my chicken broth, so perhaps I am better already."

She smiled, unbuttoning her glove. "I suggested the chicken broth to Mrs Harvey, for you would be sure to need it, after driving all this way in the rain." She placed the back of her hand on his forehead. "There. No fever, you see?"

He clasped her hand, and held it to his cheek, eyes closed for a moment. "Thank you! Oh, thank you!"

"Whatever for? The chicken broth?"

"For smiling," he said. "For treating me like a normal human being, and not the worthless piece of scum I really am."

"You're not worthless!" she said fiercely. "Don't say that! You brought the portrait, didn't you? That was a heroic thing to do, so don't ever call yourself worthless again. You're just… a bit lost, that's all. You'll find your way again, I know you will."

He could not answer her. Happiness welled up inside him like a spring. She believed in him! It was the second time that day he had been called a hero, and although he felt like the least heroic man ever, especially as he had spent the afternoon sleeping with the aid of laudanum and brandy while Humphrey drove through the rain, it could not but lift his spirits a little.

He gave her a somewhat wobbly smile, not letting go of her hand. In some unfathomable way, that little touch between them comforted him more than anything else. He wanted to wrap her in his arms and never, ever let go of her, but he dared not, not until he was surer of where he stood with her. Until then, holding her hand would have to be enough.

Miraculously, she responded to his smile with another of her own. “Have you shown Mr Culpepper the portrait? What did he say?”

“Several portraits, and I left Humphrey to unwrap them.”

“Lord Humphrey is here?”

“We met in York by chance, and he drove the rest of the way here, while your heroic husband slept in the coach.”

“That was a very good idea,” she said solemnly. “Shall we go and find out what is happening?”

He nodded, and, hand in hand, they went back to the house.

Mr Culpepper was excited. When Gil and Genista reached his room, he was pacing up and down in front of the five paintings which had been propped up in front of the bookcase.

“Ah, Lord Gilbert! And dear Lady Gilbert. I was just saying to Lord Humphrey and Mr and Mrs Merton that this portrait of the eighth Marquess of Carrbridge in his robes of state is a splendid piece of work. Portraits are something of an interest of mine, as you may observe from my walls, and there are more in my bedchamber, but I have nothing so fine as this. And a splendid figure of a man, so dignified in his ermine. One may sleep easy at night, knowing that the realm is in the hands of such men as this. His speeches were so finely wrought. I have several that I kept when they were printed in the newspaper, so that I might read them again and again. His demise was a great loss to our nation. But your brother is to make a speech soon, as I understand it, Lord Gilbert?”

“Father, do not tire yourself,” Mrs Harvey said. “Will you not sit?”

“I shall sit when I feel tired, my dear, but my breathing is so much better after the steam bath that Lady Gilbert so kindly suggested, that you need not be concerned. Your wife is a treasure, Lord Gilbert."

"I know it, sir." He squeezed her hand, as she blushed and hung her head.

"But you may be easy, my lord. This is most assuredly *not* the man I saw married all those years ago."

"Ah..." Gil let out a long breath. Finally! It was as he suspected, and here was the proof at last.

"Who are these other gentlemen?" Mr Culpepper asked, pointing to the other portraits.

"Those two are my father's older brothers, Francis and Reginald, long dead. The other is Uncle Lucius March, Mama's brother."

"And this one, the young man with his first stag is your father again, I presume? Much younger than the imposing peer of the realm over here. But side by side, despite the inadequacies of the artist, one sees the likeness. And who are these other men?"

"Just the servants of the day," Gil said. "Dead, by now, most of them, I should imagine."

"Not necessarily," Humphrey said, kneeling down to look more closely. "That one there is Crabbe, look. He is our butler now, Mr Culpepper, and a very grand fellow. Gaffney, the gamekeeper. Elkham, who was probably just a footman then, but ended up as Father's valet. Lester, who is head groom now. That one I do not remember, nor that. Village men, perhaps. Oh, there is Sharp, our land agent. Ha! He is not dead, regrettably, but has gone very much to the bad. The Fitch brothers, and Harper — whatever happened to him? And the boy in front must be Harris, who became head gardener."

"How interesting," Mr Culpepper said. "A fascinating glimpse into the household of the day. It is not a good likeness of your father, but what about the rest? Good enough for you to recognise them all, Lord Humphrey, eh?"

"Actually, they *are* good likenesses. I daresay the servants were more willing to sit for the painter."

"That is probably it," Mr Culpepper said. "But you did not bring this painting all the way from Drummoor on account of the servants, Lord Gilbert?"

"It is the only likeness of Father at about the age he would have been at the time of this marriage, sir."

"Indeed. Nevertheless, it is a very fortunate circumstance that you thought to bring it. It makes me even more sure that your father had no part in the marriage I performed. Because this man here, standing beside your father — I am reasonably confident, my lords, that this is the man who stood before me all those years ago, and married Miss Gartmore."

"Sharp?" Humphrey and Gil exclaimed in unison.

"Impossible," Gil whispered.

It was Merton who voiced the crucial question. "But why?"

~~~~~

The inn was full that night, and Humphrey was obliged to take Gil's room.

"You will not mind bunking with Lady Gilbert for a couple of nights, will you?" Humphrey said with a wink.

Gil smiled a little. Naturally everyone assumed that all was well again between him and Gen, since they had arrived hand in hand. He was not at all sure what had been in Gen's mind at the time, but to him it had felt more like a drowning man clinging to any piece of wreckage that might save him. Could Gen save him? And even if she
~~~~~

could, would she want to? She had said he was not worthless, but that did not mean she was happy to be married to him, or would want him cluttering up her bed again. That thought made him entirely miserable.

When they went upstairs to change before dinner, there was one bath in front of the fire, filled with steaming water.

"I shall wait downstairs for half an hour," he said.

"Don't be silly. We're married, aren't we? We've both seen everything there is to see. I undressed you before I even knew your name, remember? Get your clothes off and get in that water before it gets cold. I'll lay out clean clothes for you. Humphrey brought everything through all higgledy-piggledy, so it will take some sorting out first. Take your time and have a good soak. If I slide this screen round like so, you won't feel a draft."

And rather cleverly, she had contrived to give him some privacy. Sheltered by the screen, he undressed and stepped into the blessed warmth of the bath water. Somewhere out of sight she was humming softly to herself, and, presumably, laying neckcloths and shirts into neat piles. He smiled to hear her, for she sounded happy, impossible as it was to believe.

"Dark breeches or light?" she called out.

"Dark. The light ones are only for day wear."

"Oh." A long pause. "You usually wear light breeches in the evenings."

"When they are silk or some such. The ones I brought with me are buckskins. For riding, or day wear, but never in the evenings."

"Ah, I understand. I'd make a terrible valet. Do you want me to scrub your back?"

Oh, the temptation! But he dared not. He could not trust himself to behave properly. "Thank you, but I can manage. I have almost finished and then you may have a turn in the water."

Stepping out of the bath, he dried himself and pulled on the shirt she had left draped over the screen for him. He found her kneeling before a capacious chest of drawers, carefully putting the neatly folded linens away. On a chair, his clothes were laid out ready for him. His shaving water and razors, strop and brushes awaited him on the wash stand. A swivelling looking glass was adjusted to the right position for him to shave and tie his neckcloth.

"I think you make a rather good valet," he said.

She smiled, but demurred. "Just don't ask me to tie your cravat. Do you want me to look at your leg?"

"If you would be so good."

"No point being married to a physician's daughter if you don't make use of me. Lie down, then."

She ran cool, dry hands over his leg, looking at it with concentration. To him, it looked like an angry, misshapen mess, still oddly coloured. But she nodded as if satisfied.

"How much laudanum have you been taking?"

"Just what the apothecary told me to take. The bottle is in my coat pocket."

She brought the bottle out, read the label and sniffed the contents. "It's a weak dose, which was a good choice when the apothecary didn't know the circumstances, but you'll need something stronger for a day or two. That way you won't need the brandy. There is no visible infection, and the wound itself has healed well. It feels a little hot, but it's not at all as bad as I feared, after all that climbing about on trees and then riding at speed. Gil..." She lifted her head and looked him straight in the eye. "I'm so very sorry

I shouted at you at High Berenholme, but I was so terrified…" She closed her eyes, and he had the feeling that she could not bear to talk about it.

"That I would fall?" he said gently.

"No…" She opened her eyes and sighed. "Well, partly, of course. But mostly I was afraid you would damage your leg beyond repair. I know how you like to be active, and if it had gone wrong… being crippled and not able to do anything would drive you insane." She paused, but he had nothing to say to this nightmarish vision of his future, described in such a matter-of-fact way. "I shall have my bath," she said, moving away from him and disappearing behind the screen.

He shaved, then dressed slowly, listening to her humming in the bath. She sounded so *happy*, yet he could scarcely believe it. How could it be possible? When she emerged from behind the screen, he was engaged in the tricky business of arranging his neckcloth. Some men were perfectionists, and would throw away a slightly misaligned effort and begin again. Gil prided himself on achieving the desired effect at the first attempt, but it took time and the greatest care. His chin was high in the air as he adjusted the folds, but he was aware of Gen sitting quietly on the bed in her shift, watching him.

"If you hope to see me fail, Lady Gilbert, you will be disappointed, I vow."

She gave a low gurgle of merriment. "I like to watch. It fascinates me, the way you create those intricate folds and knots. It is a work of art. Whereas Father's Geneva bands are the simplest arrangement imaginable."

Gil had to concentrate after that, so silence fell, but he was very conscious of her nearness, and her attention fixed on him. She sat so still, all in white like a marble statue. Yet she was not cold and unfeeling like marble, for had she not been so fearful for him that she had screamed and pleaded with him? And she had told him he was not worthless — he clung to that thought.

Eventually, the neckcloth was satisfactory. He turned and smiled at her. "There. Do I meet with your approval, my lady?"

"You always do, my lord," she said. She had never acquired the knack of paying compliments, so such a statement must be entirely honest, and it quite took his breath away. Something inside him shifted at her words. Was it possible that she cared for him, just a little?

Before he could frame a sensible reply, she had turned to her own clothes, neatly set out at the foot of the bed, and he sat to savour the pleasure of watching her dress. It was the stockings that mesmerised him, always. The careful rolling up the leg, very gingerly so as not to spoil them, and the prospect of later seeing them being just as carefully unrolled — it was entrancing. Her innocence was utterly beguiling. When Bella dressed, she was very aware of her audience and would smooth each stocking seductively, and throw flirtatious glances at him. Gen, his sweet Gen, was incapable of such stratagems. She dressed, as she did everything, with total concentration, but humming gently.

"I like to hear you humming like that. It makes you sound happy," he said in wonder.

She looked up at him, smiling. "Of course I am happy! You came back to me, and all in one piece, God be praised."

"You dislike being left behind, I know, but I could not have taken you with me this time."

"I *hate* being left behind, but so long as you come back to me, I am happy. Will you help me with my stays, if you please? I don't want to have to summon a servant."

His fingers fumbled with the laces, but that was more from her nearness than unfamiliarity with the garment. He could feel the warmth of her body under his hands, and there was a hint of lavender about her from the soap. A few damp tendrils of hair clung to her neck. His heart beat so fast and loud it was a wonder he could hear his own thoughts. When the laces were tied, he gently wrapped his arms around her waist and kissed the back of her neck very softly. He felt, rather than heard, her rumble of laughter.

"Later," she whispered. *"Please."*

~~~~~

There was an air of celebration about the party that evening. Humphrey had acquired a bottle of champagne from somewhere, and was already in high spirits by the time Gil and Genista arrived at the parlour.

"Ah, here is the hero of the hour," Humphrey boomed across the room. "Let us drink a toast to Gil's dashing ride through the rain to prove the case for Carrbridge's honours."

"That is the third time today I have been likened to a hero," Gil said. "Never was an epithet less deserved."

"Nonsense!" Humphrey said. "Who knows when the portrait might have been got here, without your efforts. As it is, Merton has in his pocket a written statement confirming that Father was not the man who was married that day, and Culpepper may go off to meet his maker whenever he chooses now, although, God knows, I wish him a long and contented life."

"He looked a great deal better today, I thought," Gil said. "Lady Gil's remedies have wrought a wondrous improvement."

"It's an illusion," she said. "The steam bath helps him to breathe more easily, but his heart is still weak, and may give out on him at any moment."
~~~~~

"You see?" Humphrey said. "Had you dallied, all might have been in vain. Victory is ours, brother, and all thanks to you."

"But I still do not quite see why Sharp married Amelia Gartmore," Gil said plaintively.

"Ah, Merton has a theory about that," Humphrey said.

The servants entered in procession just then, bearing an array of dishes for their dinner, and for some time the only topic of conversation concerned mutton and partridge and carrots and claret. Gil watched Genista carefully, and was pleased to see that she ate a little of everything that was offered to her. She never asked for a dish, but if he brought one to her, she would accept with a shy smile, and she drank a little of the claret, too.

Eventually, with only the dessert and wine left on the table, Merton elaborated on his theory.

"I cannot believe that Amelia Gartmore would marry Sharp. All the signs are that she was betrothed to your father. No, I would wager that Sharp's bride that day was *Annie* Gartmore. But the question of why is more problematic. The marriage is almost certainly not valid, since the participants were acting under false names, and quite intentionally so. They both produced letters, for instance, and Sharp had a pocket watch engraved with your father's name."

"A family tradition," Humphrey said. "We were each given one when we went up to Oxford. I gambled mine away in about five minutes, I regret to say."

"As did I," Gil said. "Perhaps Father did the same, and lost it to Sharp. But I see no purpose to the marriage. They could never use the names they had assumed, so what was the point?"

"Perhaps we may never know the reason," Merton said.

"Monty and I have been working through Father's letters to Amelia Gartmore," Humphrey said. "Some more information may yet arise from that source. Would it be worth the effort to go to High Berenholme, and make more enquiries there? Some of the Kiddlestons might remember that year, and be able to shed some light on what Sharp was up to."

"The Kiddlestons have gone," Gil said. "Old Mr Kiddleston died and the two sons sold the place."

"Oh. Well, the servants, then. I am sure Reggie mentioned the housekeeper who was very helpful."

"All gone," Merton said. "The new family, the Prestwicks, cleared out all the long-standing... all the long-standing..." He stopped, his expression shifting to puzzlement, and then slowly dawning comprehension. "Oh, what a fool I am! And Mrs Prestwick has been in Bath for her health. Ha! *Not* Bath, I wager. Four daughters and two surviving sons, and Mr Richard Prestwick is married."

"Merton, are you quite well?" Humphrey said. "Is it a riddle? Must we guess your meaning? Perhaps you would care to turn it into an acrostic, while you are about it?"

"Do you not see?" Merton cried, jumping to his feet in his agitation. "High Berenholme! Where she came from, where she was nothing but the poor relation, little regarded and probably treated not much better than a servant. Then along comes Sharp to take her away from it all. And now, when there is plenty of money, finally she can return in triumph, no longer the poor relation, but the mistress of the house. No wonder they turned off the oldest servants, who might have recognised her. Mrs Prestwick, you see, is *Annie Gartmore*, also known as Mrs Charles Ballard, and Mr Prestwick is Sharp himself. They are living at High Berenholme, practically under our noses!"

26: A Walk In The Woods

Genista rose early enough to attend Matins with Mr and Mrs Merton, and was sitting down to breakfast when Gil drifted downstairs, still yawning. He leaned over her, and kissed her on the forehead, putting her to the blush.

"Why did you not wake me?" he said. "I suppose you have already been to church?"

"You were sleeping so peacefully," she said. "The rest will have done you good, and you may attend the Eucharist later if you wish to improve your spiritual wellbeing also. The rain has stopped, and it is a beautiful spring day outside."

She went again to church, for the pleasure of being with him, watching him covertly as he made the responses. He looked so serious, and yet somehow very young. He was so experienced in the ways of the world that it was easy to forget how young he was. She was a year older than he was, yet she had done nothing and travelled nowhere by comparison. She had had no education except from her mama's teaching and books, and he had been to the best school, the best university. She knew nothing, and he knew so much. Yet he was the one who was lost, and struggling to find his way in the world. She had long ago realised where her path to happiness lay. Now she could only sit and watch and hope that, when he finally understood his own future, it would have a place for her.

After the service, instead of turning up the lane to return to the inn, he looked in the opposite direction and said, "Shall we walk for a while? It is so pleasant after the rain."

She was happy to agree, taking his arm, walking down the lane past a few straggling cottages, and then they were beyond the village. They went slowly, although his limp was less pronounced than it had been, and he seemed to be in less pain. Even so, she watched him carefully, and suggested a rest as soon as he seemed to be tiring.

"I thought we should talk," he said diffidently, as they sat on a broad stile. "About... what we both want, for the future."

She went cold. Was this the point where he told her that he was leaving her behind for good? That he was going to London to join his family, and she must stay at Drummoor. Bowing her head, she determined that she would *not* cry!

"Gen?"

Taking a deep breath, she said, "It's for you to say. You're my husband, you say what happens."

To her surprise, he laughed. "Oh, the way Carrbridge tells Connie what is to happen, you mean? Or Humphrey lays down the law to Lady H? That is not how marriages work in my family. I never knew Mama when she was well, but from her bedchamber she managed the whole household. Everyone danced to her tune. She spoke so softly, but no one ever gainsaid her. I would not want anything different. So tell me what *you* want."

Without hesitation, she said, "I want to fulfil my duties as your wife, and be wherever you are, making your life comfortable."

"Is that how you see it? As nought but a duty?"

"Not all of it. Some is... great pleasure." She blushed as she spoke, and he gave a low chuckle. "But some aspects would be... more troublesome to me. If you wished me to accompany you to London and go to balls and so on, I should find that... difficult."

"I can see that it would trouble you now, but you might, in the future, feel differently. In Kent, you were barely out in society at all. Once you have grown accustomed to dining in company and have mastered all the dance steps, you may wish to experience the full glory of the *ton* — Almack's, Vauxhall Gardens, Carlton House. Should you not like to meet the Prince?"

"Perhaps, just once," she said shyly.

"Once is certainly enough of His Royal Highness, I would agree. The Tower of London, perhaps — you said that you would like to go there. And Scotland. We can go and plague Connie's relations up there any time you like. You might even see mountains, if it is not raining, although I have heard that it usually is. Or snowing, for variety. But you would not want to live in Scotland, or in London, I believe. Where *would* you like to live, if you had a free choice? Drummoor? Or a little house in the country, like Lavender Cottage, so that you could keep a pig called Marmaduke?"

That made her laugh a little, but she could not answer the question. "I'll be happy to live anywhere that you live."

He swept one of her gloved hand to his lips and kissed it. "Ah, that is just what I love about you, my sweet wife, your devotion to duty. But I want you to be happy, my darling, so will you answer me honestly? What sort of house would make you happiest, if you could choose to live anywhere?"

She had trouble catching her breath. *'...just what I love about you... my darling... love..."* Did he mean it, or was it just words to him? Oh, if only it were true! But of course it was impossible. He was such an accomplished flirt, he could make even his dowdy nobody of a wife feel cherished. So she tried to answer him composedly. “Honestly? Then I should like to live in a town.”

“Truly? With all that bustle?”

“I don’t mind bustle on the streets, for then I can stay inside if I wish. I always loved going to Canterbury, and York is the same. Or Sagborough. They are not overwhelming, as London was, but so convenient. Just imagine the pleasure in being able to dash out before breakfast to buy buttons!”

“Oh, shopping,” he said, nodding understandingly.

“Exactly! A little house in town would be just the thing, then I could shop every day, if I wished, or go to the circulating library. It was so difficult being out in the countryside, and having to eke everything out until the next trip to Canterbury, and not always succeeding. One time we ran out of tea, and Father was so cross, you cannot imagine. Well, you have met him, so perhaps you can! I should so like never to run out of anything ever again.”

“You like spending money, then, Lady Gilbert,” he said teasingly, and her insides flip-flopped alarmingly as his blue eyes twinkled at her.

“No… well, yes, I suppose I do,” she said, trying to hide her confusion. “But I still have one hundred and twelve pounds six and fourpence in my reticule.”

He laughed out loud. “How precise you are! Very well, then, a house in town it shall be. You may choose the town.”

“Don’t you have to go back to Dover, some time?” she said gently. “To your regiment?”

He sighed. “Gen, will you give me your truthful opinion? Do you think this leg of mine will ever be right?”

She took a long time to find the right words. “I don’t think it will ever be as good as it once was, and perhaps you will always have a slight limp, but if you are careful and rest it as much as you can, it will serve you well enough for you to be a soldier again. If that's what you want."

"That is the real question, is it not? The idea of resigning my commission has begun to appeal to me rather. My colonel would certainly not be sorry to see me go. I have wanted to be a Hussar for so many years that it had never occurred to me to wonder whether it would suit me. If I could have gone straight to the Peninsula and pointed my sabre at the French, all would have been well. Instead, there was endless training and then kicking our heels in camp at Dover, waiting for orders. And a military camp is full of men, which is no surprise, but a large body of men becomes quarrelsome. Or at least, I do, for I do not like men half so well as I like women. So I ended up fighting my fellow officers and seducing their wives, and it is not conducive to discipline. Now why do you laugh, my lady? You should be shocked and mortified to hear your husband speaking so to a delicately brought-up young lady."

"I'd much rather you were open with me, and not mealy-mouthed. I know about your seductions, remember? You took me to stay with one of your mistresses. I know it's normal in your world. Although perhaps ill-advised, sometimes. Not conducive to discipline, indeed! No wonder someone shot you. An irate husband, no doubt."

"Oh, yes. Very irate. Called me out and then actually shot me, and he was trying to kill me, too, which is very bad form. He was only a lieutenant, and it is really not done to kill a superior officer. Lucky for me he was not a very good shot."

"I suppose he had some cause to be angry," she said.

"He had better have saved his anger for his wife, for she was the one who moved on *me*. I have never seduced a wife who was not already well on the way to being unfaithful. It just so happens that I have encountered quite a few of them. They seem to be drawn to me, somehow."

"Well, of course!" she said, smiling up at him. "Who would not be drawn to you, so beautiful as you are."

"Are you drawn to me?" he whispered, gazing at her with an intensity that made her heart pound.

"Oh, Gil!" she said, running one finger down his cheek. How else could she answer, except with the absolute truth? "The first time I saw you, lying on my doorstep in the snow, I thought you were an angel fallen to earth. Such blue eyes, such impossibly long lashes. I had never seen anyone so... so *mesmerising.*" She sighed. "I think I fell in love with you on the spot."

His face registered his astonishment, and for a moment he said nothing, staring at her, his lips slightly parted. Such shapely lips, that made her think of kissing and other things besides.

"But now you know I am no angel," he said, his voice husky and trembling. "So you cannot still feel that way... can you?"

"I can. I do. I always will."

He uttered a sound more like a sob than anything else, then pulled her tightly into his arms, pressing her close against his chest. "Oh, Gen!" he muttered, into the collar of her pelisse. "My darling, darling Gen. I love you so much. You bring me such contentment, and yet I thought I had lost you for ever with my stupidity."

She was rocked with such joy that she hardly knew what she was doing. She clung to him, held firmly in his strong embrace, letting the tears fall. Her world had tilted under her feet, but it was all right, everything was all right and nothing need ever trouble her again, for Gil loved her and she was safe.

"Can you ever forgive me?" he whispered, pulling away from her abruptly, his eyes filled with anxiety.

"It's not for me to forgive you," she said quietly. "You must learn to forgive yourself."

Then she raised her lips to his, and they didn't talk for a long, long time.

After a while, when his bad leg was protesting at the inactivity, they walked on a little way and turned into the woods that bordered the lane.

"You would not mind, then, if I were to resign my commission?" he said.

"That is for you to decide."

"That little house in town sounds perfect. Where shall it be? I do not mind where we live, for I shall have you and the perfect joy that results from that, but it would be pleasant not to be too far from family. Yours or mine. Should you like to live near your sister?"

"No, for that would be too close to Father. Perhaps we might visit Di sometimes, and my other sister, and my two brothers. They all live near Canterbury, so we may see them all on one visit. Let us live near your family, instead, for I like Yorkshire very much. Sagborough would suit me very well."

"Then Sagborough it shall be, my lady, and you may want to take an interest in Dr Hay's new hospital, if you are minded for some activity outside the domestic sphere. Not tending the leeches or making lozenges, perhaps, but the patronage of Lady Gilbert Marford would be valuable. Miss Hay would be a friend to you, too. Although I shall have to have something to do, too, or I shall go mad, and start doing foolish things again, and I do not think I would be of much help to a physician."

"You like clambering about on roofs, I think?" she said tentatively.

"Oh yes! Buildings are so interesting, do you not find? No? Well, I love exploring houses, and discovering how they fit together and how everything works. I am not fond of the crowds at Drummoor, for the aunts and uncles are so disapproving and that is very lowering, I find, but the building itself is quite marvellous. It is not just one house, but many different houses all joined together, so there are passages that go nowhere, and secret rooms and stairs, and windows that look into blank walls. I used to spend half my time on the roof, as a boy, even sleeping up there. We re-enacted the Wars of the Roses on the roof one summer, every single battle. I wanted to do the Civil War the following year, but Mama said we had not enough bandages for it. Roofs, gutters, drainpipes, chimneys... once, when I was quite small, I attached myself to the chimney sweep, and wherever his boy went, I went, too. Up one of the library chimneys, and all over the house, emerging finally in the ship room. We had meant to come out in the pink dining room, but we got a bit lost. Such fun! Chimneys are amazing places, you know. One just has to watch for lit fires. But Father disapproved. In fact, he railed at me so much, he went quite purple in the face. Fighting or gambling or wenching he never minded, but heaven forbid that a son of his should scramble around inside the chimneys."

She laughed. "I can see his point. But if you want something to do, Lord Carrbridge needs an agent."

He stopped dead, and since she was holding his arm, she was obliged to stop too.

"Then I could run around on roofs all day," he said, his face alive with excitement. "But... might you worry about me? I should not like you to have a moment's anxiety on my account. I have given you more than enough fraught moments as it is."

"Roofs do not bother me," she said. "Trees bother me a little, when they are very high, but roofs not at all. It was only the possible damage to your leg that distressed me. And you were very quick to recognise the problem of the leaky roof. I suspect you would make an excellent agent."

"Then I shall talk to Merton about it," he said happily. But then his face fell. "But Gen, however am I to stop myself from going crazy and doing something foolish again? You said it is up to me, and you are quite right, but I have not the least idea how to go about it, and I am terrified of it happening again."

He was limping more noticeably, so she directed him to a fallen tree trunk for a rest, which gave her time to consider her answer.

"When Mama was alive," she said slowly, "we used to have visits from her cousin occasionally. It was always a fraught event, for Cousin Deirdre was something quite grand. She had married the Duke of Purbeck's great-nephew who lived in a park — Duckbury Park, in Wiltshire. We had to get out the very best china for the occasion, and there had to be three kinds of cake, at least, and fruit, but not the common varieties. Oh no, Cousin Deirdre had to have the hothouse type, which she probably saw every day but which we could ill afford. I never understood why she could not have eaten strawberries or pears, which we had in the garden, but Mama was adamant. And since our cousin handed out half crowns when she came, I suppose it was worth while. But we all had to be on our best behaviour. Duckbury Park manners, Mama called it, and whenever one or other of us misbehaved, even on other occasions, Mama would say, *'Duckbury Park manners, if you please.'* And then we would remember. Perhaps... perhaps we could try something like that when you show signs of... of doing something you might regret later? A word or two to remind you of the need for calm. What do you think? Would that work?"

"It might," he said. "How clever you are! That is ingenious, my love. So when I rush off to climb a tree, you could say... what? Not

Duckbury Park. Watersmeet, perhaps, to remind me of my foolishness there. Or Haddlewick, because it was here that I came back to you, and you smiled at me, and I knew that you would take me back."

"I will always take you back, Gil," she said seriously. "Whatever you do, however many times you go away and leave me behind, I shall always be waiting for you."

"Because it is your wifely duty?" he said.

She smiled and shook her head. "Because I love you, and because everyone is entitled to put their mistakes behind them and try to do better in the future."

"Even when one does something unforgivable?"

"Nothing is unforgivable, if you truly repent."

"I have repented often," he said sadly. "Yet I still make the same mistakes again and again."

"Everyone makes mistakes, Gil. No one is perfect. Whatever you do, just be sure to come back to me and start afresh."

"Is that truly possible? Can one ever leave the past behind and begin anew?"

"Look around you," she said, waving a hand around the clearing where they sat. "What do you see?"

"Trees? Brambles? Fallen leaves?"

"Over there, do you see? The first bluebells are just coming into flower. No matter how hard the winter, eventually the snow melts and there are the bluebells turning the woodland floor blue. It happens every year. They always get their fresh start, and so can you."

He sighed, and squeezed her hand. "Is there hope for me, then, my darling Gen? Is it possible that one day I might make a halfway decent man? I should rather like to be boringly respectable, to have people say of me when I die, *'He was a good man, a good friend and brother, a good husband.'*"

"And a good father," she said quietly.

The anxiety on his face melted away into something else. Hope, perhaps. He kissed her softly on the lips, and held her very tight for a long time.

27: High Berenholme

Gil and Genista, together with Humphrey and the Mertons, returned to Drummoor, to send word to Lord Carrbridge of the satisfactory conclusion to the affair. Carrbridge, Reggie and Gus returned from London within days. Behind them, travelling a little more decorously, were the lawyers from London, to examine the sworn statement from Mr Culpepper and see the portraits for themselves. Ben Gartmore was sent for, and the situation explained to him. Although bewildered, he confessed himself relieved not to have the threat of a title hanging over him.

"I really didn't want to, my lord," he told Carrbridge. "It was just that Dr Hamilton made it seem like it was my duty. I'm glad it's all over."

That was a sentiment they could all agree with.

"You can go back to your regular work now, Ben," Carrbridge said.

"You're not going to turn me off?"

"Of course not. You were led astray, that is all, and thanks to Lord Gilbert's determination to resolve the issue, everything is settled satisfactorily. I remain in the role I was trained for from birth, and you remain in the station you believed yourself born to.

Everything is as it should be, would you not agree? So you may return to your position with Lord Montague."

"And if we could have some partridge or pheasant, that would be most welcome," Humphrey said.

"Yes, my lord, I'll see to it."

There had been departures from Drummoor, too. Lord Dryton was finally well enough to travel again, but instead of returning to London, he was to go on to Harrogate to stay with his sister and take the waters there. Bella, however, was not minded for Harrogate and had set off back to London, where she felt most at home. Dr Hamilton had also departed for the south in the company of the lawyer, Mr Willerton-Forbes. No one had pointed out to the physician that Willerton-Forbes was, in fact, the son of an earl and therefore an honourable.

There remained the matter of Sharp to be resolved. Despite Merton's confidence in his own deductive powers, and the conviction of all the brothers that Mr Prestwick must indeed be Sharp, there was still the possibility of error, and no arrest was possible until the identity was assured.

Gil and his brothers, together with Merton, met in the ship room to discuss the question.

"I suppose we cannot leave him be?" Monty said sadly. "He is a good age, after all, and may not have many years left to him. His wife has been ill, also. I should not be comfortable hounding a sick lady."

"Monty, you are very naive sometimes," Gil said. "The story has been put about that Mrs Prestwick was in Bath for her health, but if she is indeed Mrs Ballard from Drifford, then she has in fact been in prison in Northumberland."

"Remember, too, that Sharp has defrauded me of two hundred thousand pounds over the years, by Merton's estimate," Carrbridge said. "I am not minded to be lenient. Sharp must receive the penalty due to him."

"He should hang for his crimes," Humphrey said grimly.

"The lady also, for attempted murder," Gus said. "God may forgive her for that, but I cannot, and please do not lecture me about Christian charity, Monty. This is my step-son we are talking about. The event is still too raw for me to be merciful."

"That is understandable," Monty said quietly. "But how are we to be sure that the Prestwicks are indeed Sharp and Mrs Ballard?"

"We must go there and see them for ourselves, of course," Gil said.

"How are we to do that?" Carrbridge said. "We cannot simply walk in, even if they would admit us to the house."

"We shall have to be sneakier than that," Gil said, with a frisson of excitement. "I suggest that we get into the grounds at night, and look in through the windows."

"And if we are caught?" Monty said. "How would we explain our presence there?"

"No need to explain," Gil said, laughing. "We run away! Or fight — there are six of us, after all."

"Seven," Merton said in injured tones. "You will not keep me away from this without tying me up. Besides, I can also identify Mr Richard Prestwick and his wife."

"As can I," Gus said. "So how soon may we go to High Berenholme?"

"As soon as we have planned the sortie thoroughly," Gil said firmly. "The last thing we want to do is to alert Sharp to our knowledge of his whereabouts and have him take off again. So we need to identify him and his wife, and immediately arrest him, while ensuring that there is no possibility of escape. That means securing all the exits from the grounds beforehand. We shall have to do some reconnoitring before anything else."

"Ah, the military mind at work," Humphrey said, with a smile. "Plan your campaign, Captain Lord Gilbert Marford, then give us our orders."

~~~~~

It was more than a week before Gil had everything in place. The Bartons of Watersmeet were very helpful, and invited Gil to stay for as long as was necessary.

"We can accommodate your brothers, too, if need be, but it would be rather a squash," Lady Anne said. "Not at all what I would wish for a marquess."

"For the moment, it will only be me," Gil said. "And my wife, if it is not too much trouble."

"No, indeed, we should be delighted to have Lady Gilbert as our guest," she said, with apparent sincerity.

Gil was not sure he trusted her, however. "Is she being kind to you?" he asked Gen as they retired to bed on their first night there. "She is terribly superior, and might feel that you were not quite up to the mark."

"Oh, no, she is perfectly amiable, I assure you. Holland says that all the servants have been told to treat us well, because you are the son of a marquess. I suppose the title makes me socially acceptable in her eyes. Besides, my father is a professional man, and my mother is distantly related to the Duke of Purbeck. She was impressed by that when I told her of it, did you notice?"

"Or perhaps she just likes you, for who could not, after all?" he said, making her blush. He loved to see her confusion. One day,
~~~~~

perhaps, she would be so accustomed to her new life that she would accept compliments as no more than her due. She might even learn to flirt a little. But for now, her innocence and openness were entrancing.

Apart from the Bartons' hospitality, Watersmeet was important in another way, for the property adjoined High Berenholme. There was even a gate in the wall between the two properties, testament to the close association between the families living there in earlier times. With a little oiling and the removal of a padlock, the gate would give the brothers access to High Berenholme at the required time.

The trapdoor to the roof had now been uncovered, and the inside access found, so now Gil need only climb the servants' stairs to reach it, rather than a tree. From the roof, he had a clear view over the trees into the grounds of High Berenhome. He spent hours up there with a telescope, waiting patiently for signs of the family. He saw men riding, far away in the furthest reaches of the park, but he could make out nothing about them. Three young ladies, accompanied by a woman in the drab attire of a governess or maid, made a decorous walk about the shrubbery and round the lake each morning at eleven o'clock precisely.

On the fourth day, two ladies, one older, wearing black, and one younger, in vivid purple, emerged from a room bordering the terrace and sat for some time on chairs in the sunshine. Gil had never seen Mrs Ballard, but the older of the two women was matched the description he had been given. The younger woman he presumed to be Mrs Richard Prestwick.

And then, on the fifth day, the whole family emerged onto the terrace. The three young ladies and their governess. Mr and Mrs Richard Prestwick. Mr Harold Prestwick. Mrs Prestwick.

And Mr Prestwick. He was, quite unmistakably, Sharp.

Gil sent for the constables.

~~~~~

It was another week before the constables from Northumberland and York had all arrived, and they could make their move. The plan was a simple one — two constables would go into the house and attempt to arrest both Sharp and his wife. If, as was expected, they were denied, they would leave quietly, with the promise to return the following day with reinforcements.

Sharp and his wife would almost certainly then attempt to escape. The role of the Marford brothers was to ensure they did not, by securing the main gate. When Sharp's carriage was forced to stop, the constables would emerge to arrest him and his wife.

"Now, you all know what you have to do?" Gil asked his little army as it assembled in the stable yard at Watersmeet. It was a rather larger army than he had planned for, since a number of Drummoor servants had offered their services. Mr Barton was keen to do his part, too, and accordingly had volunteered several of his grooms and gardeners to join in, who had armed themselves with scythes and pitchforks in readiness to defend the honour of Watersmeet.

"You may leave all the ironmongery behind," Gil said firmly. "Several of us will have pistols, just in case we should be shot at, but otherwise fists will be enough, and even that will be a last resort."

It was worrying, having an untrained mob on the loose. Not that Gil was much more trained himself. On the basis of six months causing havoc in an army camp, and a summer spent enthusiastically commanding the Lancastrian forces on the roof of Drummoor at the age of twelve, he was deemed competent to lead his motley collection of soldiers.

"We take control of the lodge first, then we keep out of sight," he told them. "The Northumberland constables will play their part,
~~~~~

and leave. Then, we wait for the approach of a carriage. Only then do we emerge to block the gates, understood? When the carriage stops, our Yorkshire constables will make the arrests. No one else is to go near the carriage or attempt to intervene. We are only here to make a show of strength and help out if it comes to fisticuffs. If shots are fired, drop to the ground and try to get behind something solid. There is a risk, so if any of you wish to stand aside at this point, no one will think the worse of you."

One or two of the men exchanged glances at this, and shuffled their feet awkwardly. "I've a wife an' bairn back home," one said.

"Then you should certainly not risk your life," Gil said resolutely, trying very hard not to think of his own wife and coming child.

Two or three men turned and crept away. The rest drew closer to hear their final instructions, and there was a sparkle in their eyes that Gil knew all too well. That excitement he felt whenever he did something risky — everyone felt it, it was a normal thing. When action was necessary, even dangerous action, that was what men did, they stood tall and marched side by side, but they hummed with energy, too, enjoying that thrill of fear. Then, when the threat was over, they went back to their desks or stables or fields, quite contented. As Gil would be, one day. Surely he would.

The Northumberland constables were to arrive at the house at noon. Half an hour before, Gil led his brothers and Merton through the gate from Watersmeet into the grounds of High Berenholme. There was plenty of shrubbery to hide them from the house, but at that hour of the day, there was a real risk that a member of the household would be walking that way. They were lucky, however, and saw no one as they made their way to the main gates of the house, where the lodge was situated.

The lodgekeeper was a retired estate gardener who lived in the lodge with his wife. It was not an arduous position, for the gates stood wide open all day. There was no sign of the couple as Gil and his band stealthily approached. The lodge and gates were out of sight of the house, but the village lay just beyond the gates, and any undue noise might attract attention from passers-by. Carrbridge and Monty went round to the front door, to knock and be admitted openly that way, while the rest of the group crept in through the back door.

Both the lodgekeeper and his wife went to the front door, so when Gil lifted the latch and entered the warm kitchen, the fire gently smoking beneath a kettle, the room was empty. They silently filed in, and Merton softly closed the door again. Voices drifted down the passageway from the front of the house, a low murmur at first, then louder. Eventually, there were footsteps, the inner door opened and the astonished faces of the lodgekeeper and his wife appeared.

"What the devil is going on?" the lodgekeeper said. "What are you all doing here? What do you want of us?"

"Nothing at all," Gil said. "Only the use of your cottage for a few hours. We are engaged in an important mission for the constables from York, who will be along shortly. You are providing a great service to His Majesty's law and the safety of the good people of Yorkshire by aiding us."

"Oh," the lodgekeeper said, round-eyed. "Well, if it's for His Majesty…"

His wife was less easily subdued. "Who *are* ye, anyway? Honest folk don't sneak into other folk's homes like this, pretending to be a vicar, too. It's not right."

"I am the Marquess of Carrbridge," Carrbridge said in his loftiest manner. "These are my brothers — Lord Gilbert, Lord

Humphrey, Lord Augustus, Lord Reginald. Mr Merton is my secretary. You have already met Lord Montague, who truly is a clergyman. He is parson at Kirby Grosswick."

Monty beamed at her, as she looked from one to the other, still not entirely convinced. "The Marquess of Carrbridge?"

"Look, here is my card," Carrbridge said. "And here is my watch, you see, engraved with my name. *'Francis Marford, Earl of Deveron'* That was before I became marquess, of course." He dangled it on its chain.

"How typical of you still to have your watch, brother," Gil said.

"Well, naturally! Do you mean that you no longer have yours?"

"Lost it at faro long since," Gil said.

"Well, really, Gil! Is nothing sacred to you? Your own watch, engraved with your name, given to you by Mama with her own hands, and you offered it in a wager?"

"Several times, actually."

"He is not alone," Humphrey said. "I won mine back a few times, but Wareham disappeared with it in the end. He always was a scoundrel."

"Well, of all the—!" Carrbridge began, but the lodgekeeper's wife burst out laughing.

"Aye, ye be brothers, sure enough. Harold, fetch the gentlemen some ale. Sit ye down, milords, and make yeselves at home. I'll just fetch the apple pie through from the pantry." She surreptitiously tucked Carrbridge's card away in a fold of her apron, as if worried that he might claim it back again.

"What an excellent woman you are, madam," Gil said.

She dimpled at him, and bobbed a curtsy. "Call me Fanny, milord, please do."

After that it was easy enough. The York constables arrived not long after, in time to see the two Northumberland constables pass by in a plain carriage on their way to the house. Then, in small numbers, the various grooms and gardeners, who settled in the small byre at the back of the lodge, whispering together. Last of all, Gen arrived with a large portmanteau.

"What are you doing here?" Gil hissed. "This might be dangerous! I do not want you anywhere near Sharp."

"Don't worry, I shall stay well out of sight, but I can help if anyone is injured."

"Let us hope it does not come to that," Monty said worriedly.

"Now we are equipped for every eventuality," Humphrey said cheerfully. "Lady Gil for the bloody noses, and Monty for the last rites."

Gil and Gus laughed, but Monty looked horrified. "You do not think—? No, surely not! It will not come to that... will it?"

"I think he may be teasing you, Lord Montague," Genista said.

"Oh, very likely. Humphrey never takes anything seriously. But you really must call me Monty. Everybody does."

She blushed, as she always did at kindness, as if she never expected anyone to be kind to her. Gil smiled, his heart overflowing with love for his gentle wife.

"Thank you... but it seems disrespectful to the son of a marquess."

Monty shook his head. "But you are family now, Lady Gil, so you need not stand on ceremony." His eyes twinkled and he whispered conspiratorially, "Especially if you have inherited your father's disdain for the nobility. He called me Mr Marford, you know, and he talked of Gil as Captain Marford. Quite a character, your father."

"I beg your pardon, I—"

"Oh, no, no, no! I did not mean to make you uncomfortable. He is an eccentric, and we have a few of those in our own family. We also have our share of the sort of people your father despises — rich, idle wastrels, who spend their lives in selfishness and indolence, creating nothing nor engaged in useful occupation. Those are the besetting sins of my class."

"Every class has its own besetting sins," she said quietly. "Those of my class are envy and greed and ambition and a horrid sort of two-faced insincerity, where wickedness is kept quiet so that a man might go smiling to church on Sundays. I believe I prefer your class, Lord Montague, for although many are indolent and pursue only pleasure, a rich man has the power to do great good. Look at Lord Carrbridge, who is having a hospital built to serve the poor. What greater charity could there be?"

"But that is part of the responsibility laid on us," Monty said. "We have been given great wealth and power, but we are expected to rule with wisdom and compassion. That is the point of the expensive education we undertake. We have not been given freedom from the need to plough and harvest and grind our own flour in order to play faro. Carrbridge is a magistrate who dispenses justice. He sits in the House of Lords, and helps to run the country. He might advise the King or the Royal Princes, or speak for the country in foreign courts. It has taken him a few years but he is finally taking up the mantle of his responsibilities."

"I have never felt worthy of the position," Carrbridge said, overhearing. "I was so young when I came into my honours — just twenty-one, far too young. And I am not the cleverest of us, or the most worthy, or the bravest. Why should it be me? Why not Harriet, for that matter? Nothing would have defeated her. She would have made a wonderful marquess, if only she had been a man."

"And if she had been older than you," Gil said, laughing.

"Oh, very true," Carrbridge said, laughing. "But I have finally come to accept my destiny, Lady Gil. I am a marquess, and I cannot have all the advantages without accepting the duties as well. I want to do some good in the world, if I can, within my limited capabilities. And if ever I am unsure what to do, I have five brothers who will all give me the benefit of their opinion."

"Five brothers and a sister," Genista said. "Do not forget Lady Harriet." Carrbridge bowed to acknowledge the point.

Gil raised her hand to his lips and gently kissed it. "Now *this* is the lady I remember from Lavender Cottage, who was not afraid to speak her mind. Welcome back!"

She laughed, and, as he had known she would, turned bright red.

"There is a carriage coming," Humphrey said. "The constables are coming back."

The room fell silent, as the sound of carriage wheels crunching over the gravel drew nearer. Was it possible that they had managed to arrest Sharp and Mrs Ballard? Gil and Carrbridge moved to a window overlooking the drive. The carriage drew near, they had a clear view through the window of the constable inside, he shook his head. Then the carriage rolled out of the gates and away through the village.

"How long will it be before they try to escape, do you think?" Carrbridge said.

Gil considered. "It is past noon now, and unless they have another house very near by, they will need to stay at an inn overnight. They will not dare to delay long. Two hours, maybe three. Money and a few clothes is all they will need initially."

Carrbridge nodded.

"So now we wait."

28: A Confrontation

After a while, the lodgekeeper was sent out to close the gates. Gil was reluctant to entrust the task to him, in case he decided to abandon his wife and run away to raise the alarm, but the couple seemed to have accepted the idea that it was a secret mission for the King. Sending anyone else would have been a greater risk, since the gates were clearly visible from the village. But the lodgekeeper did his job, returning with a conspiratorial grin, and not asking any of the awkward questions that Gil had expected.

Then they waited.

After an hour, two women came to the closed gates on the village side and peered through the bars. "Fanny? Harold? Is everything all right?" they called. But no one answered and after a while they went away again.

Then, an hour or so later, a woman came and tried to push the gates open. They were barred on the inside, so it was impossible, but she rattled and pushed and pulled. "Pa? Are ye in there? Ma? Anyone home? It's Lucy. What's goin' on?"

The lodgekeeper's wife looked at Carrbridge, but he shook his head and raised a finger to his lips.

"Ma, answer me! Pa! Open t'gates!"

It seemed an age before she gave up and went away again. Gil released his breath gustily. "Have you any more children who might come looking for you?" he said to the lodgekeeper.

"Not in t'village, no. A niece in t'kitchens o' t'big house, tha's all. Not her day off, so she won't come by."

But others in the household could and did come by. Not five minutes after Lucy had finally gone away, two women, rather drably dressed, strolled down the drive from the house, and stopped dead at the sight of the closed gates.

"Miss Haversmith, governess to the young ladies, and Miss Platt, lady's maid to Mrs Richard," whispered the lodgekeeper's wife. "They have friends they visit in the village."

Gil cursed.

"Harold, go out there and get them inside the lodge."

"How? What do I say to them?"

"Anything you like, but get them out of sight without any screaming. Tell them Fanny is ill — that will do it."

But it did not. One of the women argued vehemently, pointing first at the lodge and then at the gates and then, worryingly, back towards the house. When she set off determinedly in that direction, it was time to act.

"Gus, Humphrey, grab her and get a hand over her mouth. Reggie, Carrbridge, get the other one."

"We have a house full of constables," Reggie grumbled.

"Not our jurisdiction," one of the constables said. "We're only here to make the arrests. The rest of it's up to you."

"What will *I* do?" Monty said.

Gil grinned. "Pray for us, brother. And look after Lady Gil."

Had he thought about it, Gil would have supposed that two rather slender young ladies would not be any match for five well-grown men, but he would have been quite wrong. Those two ladies put up such a spirited defence, and the Marford brothers were so wary of injuring them, that Gil was forced to wave a pistol at them to enforce their compliance.

Just as they were half-dragging and half-carrying the two towards the lodge, a mob of men armed with knives and pitchforks appeared on the far side of the gates.

"Oy! What's goin' on!" someone shouted. "What you doin' to them ladies? Right, lads, over t'gate. Let's get 'em!"

And at that precise moment, a stylish travelling carriage bowled down the drive from the house. The coachman saw the confusion and pulled up the horses well short of the gate. The carriage door opened, a face peered out and then, almost before the carriage had stopped moving, two figures leapt to the ground and ran off in separate directions.

Gil swore. *"Everyone outside!"* he yelled. "Quick, get after them!"

Mrs Ballard was a lady of more than fifty, who had been stout before imprisonment had weakened her, and had not walked further than the twenty steps to her carriage for years. She was soon caught and brought, struggling mightily, back to the lodge. Sharp was fitter, but even so, he would undoubtedly have been caught in time, with Gus's long legs in hot pursuit. However, some of the mob beyond the gates had managed to climb over and open the gates from the inside. Seeing the opportunity for escape, Sharp veered back and headed straight for the open gates and freedom.

Gil, not able to run like the others, watched it all unfold. The drive in front of the gates was now a boiling mass of humanity, angry villagers mixed with his own troops, with fights breaking out here and there, the constables shouting unheeded orders and two screaming women. And Sharp was headed straight for the chaos, and perfectly capable of slipping through the milling crowds to freedom. With the pistols still in his hands, Gil pointed one into the air and fired.

The noise echoed violently. The women screamed once more and fell silent. The fights stopped, heads turned, frightened eyes looked in Gil's direction.

"Stand!" he yelled in his most commanding voice. "Everyone stand still! You there, and you — get those two ladies to safety in the lodge. Constables, hold that man!" And he pointed at Sharp, who had stopped running but was edging towards the gates.

As the constables closed in on him, Sharp backed against the lodge's garden wall, dropped the bag he had over one shoulder and pulled out two pistols.

"Keep away!" he yelled. "I will shoot the first man to approach."

They kept away. The mob, Gil's troops and even the constables backed slowly away. Only Gil and his brothers, and Mrs Ballard, still held firmly by Reggie and Humphrey, remained within range.

"You cannot escape, Sharp," Gil said. "Not this time."

"Constables!" Carrbridge called out. "I identify this man as Ambrose Sharp, my former land agent, who has defrauded me of a great deal of money. Arrest him at once!"

One of the constables, braver than the others took a step forward. "You'd best put t'weapons down and come wi' me, Mr Sharp."

"Never!" he cried.

"At least we have this one," Gus said, pointing at Mrs Ballard. "Humphrey, hand her over to the constables."

"No!" Mrs Ballard screamed. "I won't go back to prison, I won't!" She struggled violently, but she was held fast. "Ambrose! Ambrose, you promised me!"

Sharp looked around at the assembled crowd. Between the villagers, Gil's little army, the constables and the Marfords, there were at least fifty men surrounding them. He nodded once. Then he raised one pistol, and fired straight at his wife. She crumpled and lay still.

With a wild laugh, Sharp raised the other pistol to his temple.

"Do not let it end like this, Sharp," Carrbridge said, taking a step forward. "You had much better surrender. At least then you could make your peace with God."

"God? Pah!" He looked around at the assembled Marfords. "You're the ones who think you're God!"

"Do not shoot yourself," Carrbridge said, moving nearer. "Please."

Sharp straightened himself. "As you command, *my lord.*"

He lowered the pistol, and then pointed it directly at Carrbridge.

Gil had no time to think, no time to position the pistol in his other hand, no time to aim with precision. He fired directly at Sharp and prayed. The report echoed in his head. He thought he heard a scream. Then everything went dark.

~~~~~

Genista gave a little yelp when she heard the first shot fired. Monty was at the window, watching.

"Gil fired into the air," he said.

"I didn't know he had a gun with him," she said anxiously.
~~~~~

"We all brought pistols," Monty said. "He was the only one sensible enough to carry them with him when he went outside." He waved an arm ruefully at several boxes sitting on the kitchen table. "They are not much use in here."

"I wondered what was in the boxes," she said. "Still, better here than shooting at people."

Monty smiled at her. "Perhaps, but a pistol is a powerful threat, even without being fired."

The riotous noise outside died away, and, into the silence, Gil's voice sounded very authoritative. "Stand! Everyone stand still!"

More talking, with long pauses. Then the door burst open and two women almost fell into the room. One was crying, but the other was red-faced with anger.

"This is the most appalling—" She looked around, seeing only Monty in his clergyman's attire, the lodgekeeper and his wife with anxious faces, and Genista. "Oh."

"Are you injured?" Genista said quietly.

"I don't think so. We have been manhandled, rather, but... whatever is going on, Fanny?"

"Secret mission for t'King," she said promptly. "Would you like some ale, Miss Haversmith? Miss Platt? Do sit down, and have some cake."

And then, just as they were getting comfortable, another shot, shouts, then an ominous silence. More shots, and a scream. Then yelling.

"Someone is down, but I cannot see who," Monty said. Then, urgently, as she moved towards the door, "Do not go outside until you are sent for, Lady Gil, not with firearms in use."

"No, I shan't," she said, standing uncertainly, holding her bag of medical equipment.

More yelling, and feet running around on the gravel. She waited, head bowed, dreading what she might find out there. How many shots had there been? Two — no, three, after Gil had fired into the air. Three shots, perhaps three men dead. And there had been fighting before that. But no more shots had been fired, and thank God the other pistols had remained safely in their boxes.

The door burst open once more. Humphrey, grinning. "All over," he said. "It is safe to come out now."

"Is anyone hurt?" Genista asked fearfully.

"Sharp needs Monty's care rather than yours, but you might be able to save his wife for the hangman's noose."

"No one else?"

"A few bloody noses, nothing worse."

She released her breath, relief washing through her so fast that she almost laughed. Gil was safe! They were all safe, apart from Sharp and perhaps his wife.

Genista followed Humphrey outside. There were crowds of people everywhere, standing in groups talking animatedly or ambling around or just watching, with more appearing from the village every moment. She looked around for Gil, but couldn't see him anywhere in the scores of people milling about.

"Where is Gil?" she whispered to Humphrey.

"No idea where he went. We will find him for you in a moment. Here is your patient."

He led her into a small crowd gathered at a respectful distance around the fallen woman. Her gown and pelisse were dark, and it was not, at first glance, possible to see any blood. Only when Genista knelt beside the woman could she see the spreading stain on one side of her stomach, the liquid glistening.

Reggie was kneeling beside her, holding her hand, murmuring encouragement. "Ah, here is Lady Gil to sort you out. You will be as right as a trivet in no time."

The woman moaned a little.

"Reggie, go and find Gil, will you?" Humphrey said. "Lady Gil is concerned about him."

Reggie disappeared in a crunch of gravel, and Genista bent over her patient. It was but the work of moments to determine that there was only a single bullet wound through her side. If she could stem the bleeding, then with luck the woman would survive.

She pulled scissors from her bag to cut the clothing away from the wound, then she placed pads of cloth over the wound.

"Don't you dare!"

Genista looked up from her work in surprise. The woman was fully alert and glaring at her. "I beg your pardon?"

"Don't you dare fix me up! They'll only hang me anyway, so what's the point?" For a moment, she clenched her jaw in pain, eyes closed. But after a moment, she recovered. "And I *won't* go back to prison, I won't! It's evil in there. Have pity on me, please." A gasp, and a low moan, but with astonishing willpower, she overcame the pain to speak again. "Ambrose is gone, and there's nothing left now. Let me go. Please... have mercy..." She finished on a hiss of pain.

Genista stared at her, then at Humphrey. He gazed back at her, understanding in his eyes. "If you do not need me, Genista, I shall go and see what is keeping Gil," he said.

And then she was alone with the shot woman, the watchful crowd a little distance away. No one to see precisely what she did. No one to know whether she tried to save her or not, whether she did everything in her power to stem the bleeding, or whether perhaps she held the pad in slightly the wrong place, or failed to press hard enough. After all, she had never dealt with so serious an injury before, so no one could blame her if her efforts were to no avail. And perhaps the woman would have died anyway, no matter the exertion, or the skill of the physician.

Whatever the case, the blood continued to flow and flow, and gently, silently, the woman's life trickled away with it. Genista had seen death before many times, but never violent death, like this, a woman who had been perfectly well not a few moments ago, and now lay motionless in a pool of her own blood. Just an hour or two ago, she had been drinking tea in her own drawing room, with nothing more to trouble her than the dishes to order for dinner and whether to wear a blue gown or a green. The constables had come and shaken her little world, but even then, it was not irrevocable. There was still a chance of escape. She had escaped more than once already — from a menial life at High Berenholme all those years ago, and then from her mill town in the north, and more recently she had contrived to escape from prison. But this time, there had been no escape, and her blood seeped unresisting into the gravel of the drive. With the first shower of rain, it would be washed away and it would be almost as if she had never been. But Genista would remember her.

Just as she stood up, Reggie returned.

"Ah, you could not save her then," he said. "Pity."

"Pity, yes, indeed. Did you find Gil?"

"I did not." His face creased in puzzlement. He turned to his brother, who came tearing up to them. "Humphrey, have you found Gil?"

"No, I hoped *you* had. He seems to have vanished. Where was he standing last?"

"Beside that big bush... oh! I see a boot."

The three of them raced over to the bush and Humphrey furiously pulled branches back to reveal Gil's motionless form. Genista uttered a squeak of alarm, but she could see at once by his colour and his steady breathing that his life was not in danger.

"Silly boy has got himself shot again," Humphrey said, with a grin, clearly seeing the same positive signs. "At least it is the *other* leg this time. He will have a limp on both sides now."

"Really, Humphrey!" Genista said crossly. "You are too frivolous, when two people have died this day. He looks well enough, but why is he unconscious from a leg wound?"

"Must have hit his head as he fell and knocked himself out cold. I beg your pardon, Lady Gil. My levity is just relief, I suppose. Matters could have gone much, much worse."

She couldn't argue with that. They had been very fortunate. "Would you be so good as to lift Gil out of there so that I may tend to him, if you please."

Together, Humphrey and Reggie gently lifted her husband's unconscious form.

~~~~~

Gil woke to brilliant sunshine. He was warm and comfortable in a soft bed. Above him, the velvet bed hangings were blood red where the sun caught them, and near black in the shadowed hollows. Nearby, someone was humming. He smiled and turned his head. There she was, her hair lit up into a thousand shades of gold and copper and amber and rich burgundy.

As soon as he moved, her head lifted. She set down her sewing and stood up, bending over him to feel his forehead with the back of her hand.

"My angel," he murmured.
~~~~~

That made her laugh. "You don't feel hot, but you must be fevered to talk such nonsense. Are you thirsty?"

"A little." She lifted him up and helped him to sip from a glass.

"Do you remember what happened?" He shook his head. "I'm afraid to say that you were rather a hero again. You managed to shoot Mr Sharp quite through the heart, which everyone agrees was an impossible shot from that distance and angle, and thereby prevented him from killing Lord Carrbridge. Unfortunately, Mr Sharp's shot bounced off the wall somehow—"

"Ricocheted," he said.

"Yes, that. Anyway, it hit you in the leg. The *other* leg. But don't worry, it was the most glancing of injuries, and you will be as right as rain in a week or two, so long as you rest it."

"And if I do not?" he said, suddenly terrified.

"You will, because your brothers have sworn to sit on your head if you even think about walking about on it just yet. They are very protective of you, you know. Humphrey has gone off to have a special wheeled chair made for you."

He pulled a face. "Must I? That is a hideous prospect."

"You must, because it's the only way I'll allow you to attend Humphrey's grand opening night."

"The gaming house! Oh, famous! I must be at that. Shall I try to break the bank on the first night?" Then he saw her face. "Well, maybe not. But I must be there, and I shall have to play high, you know. My own brother, after all."

"I suppose he won't make you pay if you lose money to him, will he?" she said.

"Hmm, that is not quite how it works. A gentleman must pay his gaming debts, as a matter of honour."

"Even to your own brother?"

"Even so."

"Oh."

"Have no fear, I shall be very circumspect." But he was aware of a tremor of apprehension, all the same. Would he be able to play a little and then draw back? So many times he had gone on, getting deeper and deeper into trouble. What if the madness took him again?

29: A Long Night

Humphrey's gaming house was rather a splendid place, very well positioned in the centre of York, with a reputable inn just round the corner for the benefit of patrons from the country. The ground floor was given over to a cloakroom, office, kitchen and supper room.

On the floor above, four rooms had all their interconnecting doors thrown open to make a capacious gaming room, with tables for every kind of play. Two floors above that held bedrooms for family and guests. Humphrey had appointed a cousin, Julius Whittleton, as his office manager, whose pleasant manner and ingratiating ways had already wheedled numerous subscriptions from the wealthy merchants, burghers and financiers of York.

Gil could not remember when he had last played properly. At Bella's house, he supposed, but even that was tame compared to a real gaming house. There was not the same thrill in playing against old friends, for one knew them too well, knew exactly how they would play and how deep they would go. Besides, they mostly played cards, and although Gil had some skill there — he could not be Humphrey's brother and not learn a few tricks — he favoured dice. Now that was a game for a man of strong nerves. Luck, not skill — that was true gambling. A run of luck with the ivories was an incomparable experience.

Gen and Davy between them got him dressed, an awkward business, since he was not allowed to put any weight on the newly injured leg, and the leg with the old injury was not yet capable of holding him aloft.

Then Davy left and Gen swiftly dressed herself. She had made the lack of accommodation for the servants her reason for leaving Holland behind, but he guessed she was still uncomfortable with a maid. She had a new gown for the occasion, pale blue silk with dark blue trimmings, which suited her admirably. All she wore in her hair was a silver circlet, with one long ringlet falling to her shoulder and the delicate cameo he had given her around her neck.

"You look magnificent," he said, and meant it. She blushed, of course. How he loved to see her blush.

They sat down sixteen to dinner — the six Marford brothers and their wives, Merton and his wife, Julius Whittleton and Uncle Lucius, who had arrived uninvited.

"Damned if I intend to miss all the fun," he said cheerfully. "Think of the convenience of our own gaming house in York. If the supper is half decent, I may never need to go to London at all."

"It will be more than half decent, I assure you," Humphrey said indignantly.

At nine o'clock precisely, Humphrey opened the front door to find some twenty gentlemen and several ladies already waiting outside. Within an hour, the place was as full as it could hold, and every table had play going on.

Gil wandered about at first, with Davy pushing his wheeled chair and Gen by his side, rather wide-eyed at the sums being bandied about.

"Is it always like this?" she said. "So much money?"

"Usually. Do you want to play?"

"Oh no! I couldn't. I don't even like to watch so much money wagered on the turn of a card or the throw of a die."

"Everyone plays what they can afford to lose," he said, although uneasily aware that it was not always true. Many lost everything they had at the tables. His own father had not lost everything, but he had both won and lost vast sums of money, houses, estates, horses… and an earl's daughter, once.

"Why do they do it?" she said. "What is the pleasure? I should be sick with worry to risk such sums."

"It is the excitement," Gil said. "Losing is not much fun but winning — and winning a fortune — the feeling is magnificent, like nothing on earth."

"But then at the next play, it may be lost again," she said. "It is ephemeral."

"All amusement is ephemeral," he said, only half attending. "Look, there is a place free at the hazard table. I shall play for a while, I think."

"Don't forget you promised to take me in to supper," she said.

"Of course." But his mind was already turning to the game, as the familiar frisson of excitement coursed through his veins. He emptied his purse onto the table, introduced himself to the other players, rolled the dice through his fingers for luck and cleared his mind of every extraneous thought.

The dice were with him that night. It was odd how some nights were like that, and almost every throw went the right way. Even when he was not the caster, his bets somehow worked out right. He bet modest amounts, nothing wild, and gradually the piles of coins in front of him grew. One by one the other players dropped out until only one remained, a florid-faced man with the whiff of trade about him.

"Just the two of us, milord," he said. "Shall we make things a little more interesting?"

"As you wish," Gil said languidly. He could see the glitter of excitement in the other man's eyes, the desire to play deep. The more money at stake, the more interesting the game — that was a principle he understood well. He called for a refill of his wine glass, and leaned back in his chair. It did not do to show one's excitement.

They played three games. Gil lost every one. A third of his winnings gone already. But that was abnormal play. He had had such a run of luck that evening that the next game must be his, surely. He could not fail. Should he make things even more interesting, and wager everything on the next throw? Humphrey would certainly take his vowels if he lost it all.

He was vaguely aware of the swirl of a silken gown at his shoulder, a thread of perfume and a small hand on his arm.

"I'm going to the supper room now, Gil," his wife said, leaning down to kiss him on the cheek. So soft, so sweet-smelling. Then she whispered in his ear and was gone.

His concentration was broken. Frowning, he played a smaller amount than he had intended.

"Oh, you disappoint me, milord," said the man with the red face.

Gil paused. He had meant to bet high, in fact, to put everything on the table, and perhaps that was just what he should do. He reached for the rest of his coins—

Haddlewick.

That was what she had said. He paused, hand hovering over the coins, pondering. Where had he heard that before? It meant something but—

His wife. Gen, his beloved. They had agreed that if he went crazy again, she would remind him of Haddlewick. He withdrew his hand.

"Cast, if you please, sir."

Gil won that game, and the next and then, feeling that honour was satisfied, he scooped his winnings into his purse, and bade his opponent farewell.

"Leaving so soon, milord? I'm sorry for it."

"I daresay we shall meet again," Gil said, smiling at him. "I certainly hope so, for then you may have your revenge on me."

"Look forward to it, milord, look forward to it."

"Davy, take me down to the supper room."

She was sitting, ramrod-straight on a chair, eating and drinking nothing. As soon as she caught sight of him, her face lit up with happiness. She jumped up and ran across to him, kneeling beside his chair, and whispering in agitation, so as not to attract attention.

"Please don't be angry! But I thought… and you had that look in your eye… but Humphrey said he could not interfere, it would be humiliating to have anyone try to persuade you to stop. I'm so sorry, but I was so worried and I don't want you to go wild and leave me behind, for I couldn't bear it!"

He smiled, his love for her so overwhelming that he thought he would burst. "Thank you, my love," was all he could manage to say.

She burst into anguished tears.

"Here," he said, pushing his purse into her hand. "You may count my winnings for me."

They found a corner of the supper table that was unoccupied, and she tipped the contents of the purse onto the cloth. After some considerable time, she said, round eyed, "Two thousand two hundred and forty seven pounds."

"Now count out five hundred pounds."

Obediently she did so, piling the coins and notes up neatly. He swept them up and stuffed them into a pocket. Then the rest of the coins went back into the purse. He took her hand, turned it palm up and placed the purse into it.

"There. That is for you. I have taken back the monkey I started with, but you may have my winnings, all of them. That way I will not be tempted to gamble them away."

She stared at him. "But what shall I do with this?"

"Whatever you want. Spend it, put it in the bank, turn it into diamonds, buy whatever takes your fancy."

"But it's a fortune — enough to buy a house!"

"Then buy a house, if that pleases you."

"Are you serious?"

"Completely. If I have it, then sooner or later I shall sit down at one or other of these tables and lose it all, and probably a great deal more besides. I remember Haddlewick, my love. Never let me forget Haddlewick and all the things I said and felt there."

"Oh..." she breathed. "It worked."

He smiled and kissed her fingers very gently. "It worked."

"If you truly mean it, then I should like to buy a little house for Di, for they live with his family, all squashed into the old farmhouse. It is not comfortable for them. She should have been a baroness, and lived in a grand house, and spent part of each year in London, and she would have loved all that, unlike me. Instead, she's a farmer's wife and although she's happy enough, I'd like to make her life a little easier."

"Then so you shall, my darling. We had better go down to Canterbury soon, then, before you become too constrained by this baby of ours. We shall visit Di and the rest of your family, including your father, for you will wish to assure yourself of the welfare of Marmaduke the pig, I know. We can put everything in train for a house for Di, and then we shall find ourselves a cosy little house in Sagborough where we may be happy for the rest of our lives. How does that sound?"

"It sounds... wonderful," she breathed.

"Then that is settled," he said contentedly. "What a lucky man I am, my darling Gen, to have fallen insensible on your doorstep all those weeks ago."

~~~~~

It was five in the morning and the sun was already up when the last players rolled out of the front door, in various states of happiness or gloom, soberness or inebriation. The ladies had long since gone to bed, and even the servants had vanished, the remaining detritus of the night left to the housemaids. In his office, Julius Whittleton was counting up the night's takings. The six Marford brothers and Merton settled down at one end of the supper table for a celebratory brandy.

"That went better than I had anticipated," Humphrey said. "No one broke the bank, lost their entire fortune or called anyone out. There was not even a fight."

"How dreadfully dull," Gil said. "You will have to do better in future, Humphrey."

"How much did you win, in the end?" Humphrey asked, looking searchingly at him.

"A couple of thousand."

They murmured their approval of this satisfying sum. "I thought you were about to plunge," Humphrey said. "You had that look in your eye. But Lady Gil said something to you, and you settled down."
~~~~~

"I have a reason to settle down, now," Gil said, smugly. "A wife I adore, *and* a child to look forward to."

And that led to a great deal of brotherly backslapping and the drinking of toasts to the health of Gil, Lady Gil and the coming baby Gil.

"It is astonishing how far we have all come in just a year," Monty said. "In January last year, Carrbridge was in the suds and we all had to make sacrifices to help out. It seemed as though we were in for many lean and difficult years. Now, the Marford fortune has been restored and we are all married and blissfully happy. Whoever would have thought it?"

"So much has worked out well," Carrbridge said. "I am sorry Sharp and his wife died, but at least that business is behind us now."

"And the Ben Gartmore affair, too," Gus said. "Gil did well, there, in ferreting out the truth."

"But I still do not understand it," Humphrey said. "Why did Sharp and Annie Gartmore pretend to marry as Father and Amelia Gartmore?"

"I may have an explanation for that," Monty said diffidently. "I have read through all the letters Father wrote to Amelia Gartmore, and almost all of them are just trivial news — balls, routs, hunts, visitors to Drummoor, that sort of thing. But there was this one..." He drew a paper from an inner pocket. Carrbridge has seen it, but the rest of you have not, I think."

"Read it out loud," Carrbridge said.

Merton rose to his feet. "My lord, this is family business. I will withdraw."

"Nonsense," Carrbridge said. "Merton... Daniel. You are as much a part of this family as any of us. Sit down."

"Thank you, Carrbridge. You are very good." His voice was not quite steady. He bowed deeply to Carrbridge and resumed his seat.

Monty read from the letter.

'My dearest wife, something of a disturbing nature has occurred. You will remember Ambrose Sharp, who was so sweet on Annie? I have discovered that he has established her at some mill town I won from a friend, and lets her run the place as she pleases. When I remonstrated with him, he said I must not interfere, for he had evidence that you and I had married and that Ben was my legal heir, and if I acted against him or Annie, he would use that evidence to cause trouble. I can only imagine that he has kept the special licence I obtained for us, and believes that would be sufficient to cause doubt to be cast upon my marriage to Adela. He swears that he is acting in my interests and protecting my assets, and I trust him enough to let him be. He is an excellent agent for my father, and it would be awkward to explain all this to the family. He will not betray you, and expose you to the censure of the world. Sometimes, my darling, I wish we had truly married and that Ben was indeed my heir. We could have found a way, surely, for you to live the quiet life you crave, even if the responsibilities of the marquessate eventually fall to me. But that ship has sailed. You are happy in your seclusion, and I am content to do my duty. Adela is a good wife to me, and Francis is the most delightful child. Yes, I am content. But sometimes there is a wildness in me that cannot be assuaged, and then I must do something foolish or burst. I have this terrible fear that I have left a part of me — the best part, my heart, my goodness, my soul — with you, my darling, so that only the wicked part of me remains. Truly I do not want this burden that will be placed upon me. If only my great-uncle had lived just a few more weeks, and then we would have been married and we would have had adapt to the new circumstances together, as all married couples must. But regret is useless. You are happy, and that is all that matters, and I will respect

your wishes and leave you and Ben to live in obscurity, no matter what happens. Do write soon, my love. I have not heard from you for three weeks now, and your last letter was so brief. Are you ill? Or Ben? Do relieve me of this anxiety, and write soon. Your loving husband, Charles.'

They sat in silence for some time, pondering the words of the eighth Marquess of Carrbridge, long dead, his voice echoing from thirty years ago.

Carrbridge sighed and shifted in his chair. "He dreaded the responsibility too."

"He had wild moments just as I do," Gil said wonderingly.

"He knew about Sharp all along," Reggie said indignantly. "Not the full extent of it, perhaps, but he knew he was up to no good."

"Sharp held on to that special licence all these years," Gus said. "It was there to keep Father in line, if ever he fell out with Sharp, and when we started closing down his thievery, he set out to wreak vengenace on the whole family."

"How amusing he must have thought it," Humphrey said. "Such a joke, that he had evidence that could have destroyed us."

"Thank God it did not," Monty said. "Or, better still, thank Gil. Our hero."

The others murmured their agreement.

"But this is also further proof, if any were needed, that there was no marriage to Amelia Gartmore," Merton said. "And the reason why — your father became the likely heir to the title, and she could not face the prospect of a public life."

"She would have adapted to it, as Lady Gil is managing to do," Gil said quietly. "Each one of us must live the life we are given as best we can, for running away and hiding and turning to wildness is no answer."

"Speaking of running away," Merton said, "I have had a letter from Mr Bridlington. He regrets that he must resign his position as chaplain with immediate effect, Carrbridge. He has gone to London, and we may guess what draws him there."

"Not Bella Dryton?" Gil said, trying not to laugh. "I wish him good fortune there, for I do not think she will look twice at him in London. Poor man! Does he not realise she was merely amusing herself because she was bored and no better entertainment offered? Lord, but you are unlucky with chaplains, Carrbridge. First poor Penicuik, and now Bridlington."

"I do wish someone would explain exactly what happened to Mr Penicuik," Merton said. "All I ever hear is that it was too dreadful for words, and that it is never spoken of."

Gil burst out laughing. "Have you been wondering all this time? But it is a very tragic story." He laughed again. "Penicuik went out one day for a walk. Finding himself in need of a little... um, self-comfort, he settled down behind the creamery, well-hidden, as he thought, by a pile of butter churns. But he became a little too vigorous and dislodged one of the churns, which fell on him, knocking him insensible, with his manly parts all exposed. And it so happened..." He stopped, laughing too hard to continue.

"Gil, really," Carrbridge said reprovingly. "Although it *is* rather funny. Unfortunately, the field contained a pig which wandered over to investigate, and finding... finding... oh Lord!" He stopped, laughing too.

"Oh no!" Merton breathed.

"Finding a large and tender comestible," Gus went on, grinning, "it proceeded to... well, pigs will eat anything."

"Oh no!" Merton chortled with glee. "It did not!"

"It did!" they chorused. And then they were all laughing.

"Poor Mr Penicuik!" Merton said, with feeling. "But he was all right... otherwise?"

"Perfectly," Gus said. "I found him wandering about in some distress, as you might imagine, but he would not see the physician, and he swore me to secrecy. Although it is too good a tale not to be shared between brothers."

"He left soon afterwards," Monty said. "Poor man."

"Who left?" Julius Whittleton had entered the room unnoticed.

"Penicuik, who was chaplain and secretary at Drummoor some years ago."

"I remember that," Julius said. "It was very abrupt. Whatever happened to make him leave so suddenly like that?"

Merton spoke out without hesitation. "An event too dreadful for words. It is never mentioned." He shivered. "Poor Mr Penicuik!"

"Oh well, if it is a great secret," Julius said huffily. "There, Humphrey. Your takings for the night." He put a paper down on the table.

Humphrey whistled. "So much! This is going to be more profitable that I had supposed."

"So long as no one breaks the bank tomorrow," Gil said.

"Even so, this has been a very good night."

"Better than you yet know," said a quiet female voice.

"Gen!" Gil said, pushing his chair away from the table. "I thought you had gone to bed long since."

"I had, but I was summoned by Lady Humphrey."

Humphrey went white as chalk. "What happened? Is she all right? Oh... the baby? Why did nobody tell me?"

"Lady Humphrey didn't want to spoil your evening," Genista said. "She insisted you should not be told. Everything went perfectly well, but you may be sure I'd have sent for you straight away if there had been the least concern. You may go up now and admire your daughter."

"A daughter." A beatific smile spread across his face. "But Hortensia? She is well?"

"Perfectly. She wants to see you, so don't keep her waiting."

Still grinning, he raced out of the room, and his footsteps could be heard thundering up the stairs.

"Well now," Gil said, smiling. "That is the perfect end to a perfect night."

And they all agreed that it was.

Thanks for reading!

If you have enjoyed reading this book, please consider writing a short review. You can find out the latest news and sign up for the mailing list at my website: http://marykingswood.co.uk/

This is the end of the *Sons of the Marquess* series — I hope you've enjoyed reading about the Marford brothers as much as I've enjoyed writing their stories and giving them their happy ever afters! Their lives are changing, but they will always be close, and I'm sure they'll be in and out of each other's houses and meeting up at Drummoor for the children to get to know their cousins. And I've no doubt that some of them will pop up in other stories in the future.

While it's sad to say goodbye to favourite characters, there's the joy of discovering a whole new family embarking on life-changing events. My next series features five young ladies whose father leaves them destitute when he dies. The eldest, Rosamund, is already married and safe — you can read her story in the series prequel, *The Betrothed,* a free gift to all my mailing list subscribers. Her younger sisters are not so fortunate, so they have to slip a few rungs on society's ladder and find employment. And each of them encounters a murder mystery in her new job (but don't worry, the romance will still be centre stage)!

The series is called *The Sisters of Woodside Mysteries.* Book 1 of the series is *The Governess*, and you can read a sneak preview of Chapter 1 after the acknowledgements.

A note on historical accuracy - and an apology!: I have endeavoured to stay true to the spirit of Regency times, and have avoided taking too many liberties or imposing modern sensibilities on my characters. The book is not one of historical record, but I've tried to make it reasonably accurate. However, I'm not perfect! If you spot a historical error, I'd very much appreciate knowing about it so that I can correct it and learn from it. Thank you!

One area where I have taken some liberties is geographical. In *The Daughters of Allamont Hall,* I squeezed the mythical county of Brinshire into a non-existent space between Staffordshire and Shropshire. In *Sons of the Marquess*, however, Drummoor is firmly set in the (very real) county of Yorkshire, the West Riding to be precise, and not too far away from York itself. I haven't attempted to place it precisely, to give myself the freedom to add estates and towns and villages of my own invention. In the interests of such creation, several very real towns have been wiped off the map. To the good people of Yorkshire, I apologise.

About Sons of the Marquess: *when the ninth Marquess of Carrbridge finds himself short of funds, his five younger brothers have to make a choice: take up a career to support their lavish lifestyle or marry an heiress. But love has a strange way of appearing when it's least expected...*

Book 0: The Earl of Deveron (a novella, free to mailing list subscribers)

Book 1: Lord Reginald

Book 2: Lord Humphrey

About the author

I write traditional Regency romances under the pen name Mary Kingswood, and epic fantasy as Pauline M Ross. I live in the beautiful Highlands of Scotland with my husband. I like chocolate, whisky, my Kindle, massed pipe bands, long leisurely lunches, chocolate, going places in my campervan, eating pizza in Italy, summer nights that never get dark, wood fires in winter, chocolate, the view from the study window looking out over the Moray Firth and the Black Isle to the mountains beyond. And chocolate. I dislike driving on motorways, cooking, shopping, hospitals.

Acknowledgements

Thanks go to:

My mother, who first introduced me to the wonderful world of Jane Austen.

Shayne Rutherford of Darkmoon Graphics for the cover design.

My beta reader: Mary Burnett

Last, but definitely not least, my first reader: Amy Ross.

Sneak preview of The Governess: Chapter 1: The Will

'To Mrs Price, Miss Winterton, Miss Margaret Winterton, Miss Frances Winterton. My greetings to you, and sincere condolences on the sad demise of your esteemed father. If convenient to you, I shall do myself the honour of waiting upon you at noon tomorrow for the purpose of conveying to you the material contents of the last will and testament of your late lamented parent. Yours in deepest sorrow, Horatio Plumphett of Plumphett, Plumphett, Witherspoon and Plumphett, Brinchester, Brinshire.'

JANUARY

Annabelle huddled in her favourite chair in the morning room, too numb even to cry. In the matching chair on the opposite side of the fireplace, Lucy sobbed noisily. Margaret had taken her usual place at the worktable, but for once her hands were still. She stared into space, white-faced and wide-eyed with shock. Beside her, tears poured silently down Fanny's face.

Annabelle could hardly take it in. Whatever was to become of them? Their ignominy could not long be concealed from the world. *'Have you heard about the Winterton sisters of Woodside?'* their acquaintance would say. *'Dreadful, quite dreadful.'* And indeed it was dreadful. She had no idea what they were to do.

Out in the hall, a murmur of voices as the solicitor was shown out. Poor Mr Plumphett! The reading of a will was always a doleful business, but he must seldom have had such bad news to impart. His usual urbane voice was high with distress. "I am so sorry, so very sorry," he had said, over and over. Perhaps he was still saying it, even as he was ushered out of the house and into his gig.

Doors opened and closed, the gig rattled away down the drive and in the hall, more murmured voices. Then Rosamund and Robin came into the room, their faces grave. At least Rosamund was safe, and that was a mercy. She had been wife these five years to Mr Robin Dalton, heir to Lord Westerlea of Westerlea Park, and could not be harmed by the scandal. One sister, at least, uninjured by the catastrophe.

But four sisters remained at Woodside, with no brother or husband to shelter them from the disaster.

"Lucy, do stop weeping," Rosamund said. "Tears never helped anything."

"But we are destitute!" Lucy cried. "Whatever are we to do! Thrown out of our own home! It is unbearable, and I will *not* go to the workhouse, I will *not!*"

"It will never come to that," Robin Dalton said firmly. "No one is throwing you out of Woodside. It is yours, after all, left to you all equally by your father, so you may stay here as long as you wish, until you have decided how to proceed."

"What option do we have?" Annabelle said. "The house must be sold to pay the debts Papa left. Then we shall be homeless and penniless."

"You will have a home with us for as long as you want," Robin said. "Penniless does not mean friendless."

Annabelle softened at once. She had not much liked Robin when Rosamund had first married him. He was something of a dandy, who spent more time before his pier glass than was proper for a man, and far too grand for country girl Rosamund. But Annabelle had warmed to him when she had seen how happy he made his wife, and how solicitous of her comfort. And now he would take her sisters under his wing, too.

"You are all goodness, Robin," Annabelle said, "but we cannot possibly impose on you. You could not squeeze us into Holly Lodge, and we cannot inflict ourselves on Lord Westerlea. Nor would your mama want us in London."

"Then a small cottage in the village," he said. "With a couple of servants and your own good sense, you might live comfortably enough at very little expense."

"You have your own family to think of," Annabelle said.

"My wife's sisters are my family, too," he said mildly. "Besides, it is Rosamund's dowry which contributed to your father's ruinous financial state. We wondered greatly at the time where he had contrived to find thirty thousand pounds, but if I had known he had been obliged to mortgage the house to pay such a sum, I should never have agreed to it. Just because Mr Winterton promised it years ago, when he was better off, does not mean he was obliged to pay it when his circumstances had changed."

"And *why* did they change?" Lucy cried. "We were once very well off, and Papa bought Mama expensive jewellery every year for her birthday. Oh... is that ours, or part of the estate? Perhaps we will have something to live on after all."

The sisters brightened visibly at the thought.

"No, all the good pieces have gone," Annabelle said. "There are only a few trinkets left. Would those be ours, Robin?"

"Mr Plumphett will need to advise on that point," Robin said. "He is also to let us have a full reckoning of all your father's assets and debts, and which of the latter may still need to be paid, somehow. The mortgage, perhaps, but not his gaming debts, I suspect. Which were considerable, from what I have heard. I do not think we need to look further for an explanation of how the estate came to be so encumbered."

"If Jeremy had lived—" Annabelle began tentatively.

"It would have made no difference," Robin said quietly. "Your father's affair with the dice began many years ago, long before your poor brother lost his life."

"But what are we to *do?"* Fanny cried, with a sob.

"Nothing at all, yet," Robin said crisply, "except to dry your tears, Fanny, and Lucy, too, and wait for Mr Plumphett to report his findings to us. Then we may begin to consider how to move forward. And you must come for dinner again today."

"Yes, of course," Rosamund said.

"You have been so kind to us, sister, brother," Annabelle said. "However, I believe it would be best for us to return to our usual routine, at least for as long as we can. Who knows what the future may bring? So let us enjoy Woodside while we can."

Rosamund hugged each of her sisters in turn, and then she and Robin departed for the short walk to Holly Lodge.

"Well, if we are to dine here, I had better go and speak to Mrs Thompson," Annabelle said.

She found Havelock, the housekeeper, loitering in the passageway outside the kitchen.

"There now, Miss Annabelle, that's the worst over," she said.

If only that were true! Annabelle looked about her with new eyes, seeing, as if for the first time, the worn carpet, the faded paintwork, the chip taken out of the wooden panelling when the footman had dropped a whole tray of glasses. A footman... how many years was it since they had had a footman? Ten at least. The signs of increasing poverty had been clear for a long time, for those with eyes to see. But Annabelle had been beguiled by the comforting familiarity of her home. She loved its mellow stone, its odd wings of different ages and styles, its dusty, seldom-used corners and the passageways and stairs so well-known that she could find her way about blindfold. Her home.

She had been born at Woodside, they all had. Rosamund first, then Andrew who had died in infancy, then Annabelle, Lucy, Margaret and Fanny. Then poor Jeremy, sent away to sea at the age of twelve, to be made into a man worthy to inherit Woodside. But the sea had taken him from them on his first voyage, and there had been no more children after him, none that survived. Jeremy... the boy with the laughing eyes and the hair that always flopped across his forehead, no matter what he did to it. He would have been seventeen now, if he had lived. Almost a man. This mess would have been his responsibility, if he had lived.

This would never do! She must not get maudlin. What had happened had happened, and they must make the best of it.

"We shall be dining here this afternoon, Havelock," Annabelle said.

"Very good, Miss. Shall I give the orders to Mrs Thompson? You will not wish to be bothered with domestic matters today."

"Thank you, Havelock. She will know what to prepare. I cannot... cannot think about food at the moment."

"That's very natural, Miss, with the master only just buried and hearing the will, and all. But forgive me if I'm speaking out of turn, Miss, but... you look... I mean to say, it wasn't bad news, was it? The master didn't leave Woodside away from his own daughters?"

Annabelle gave a wry laugh. "Oh no, he did not do *that*. He left Woodside to us, equally, and he very generously left us all his debts, too. Tell me Havelock, have the servants been paid this quarter?"

The housekeeper shifted uncomfortably. "Well... no, Miss, not for a couple of years now, but it don't matter. Most of us have a bit put by, and we had a roof over our heads, and food on the table. We understood how it was."

Which was more than Annabelle had. No, that was not true. She had known perfectly well that there was less money than there had been, but she had assumed that Papa's income was being diverted to the gaming tables, leaving little for candles and coal. She had not suspected that the house was mortgaged. Rosamund had helped Papa with his accounts at one time, but whenever Annabelle had offered to do the same, he had bitten her head off, so she had never suspected the true state of affairs. They must have been living beyond their means for years.

She went back into the morning room. Lucy was alone there, still curled up in a miserable ball in the same chair. Annabelle took her usual seat on the other side of the fireplace.

"Where are Margaret and Fanny?"

"Probably in the attic, rearranging the furniture in the baby house."

Annabelle wished she had a comfort of that sort to turn to. Her books were her usual refuge, but today even that enticement held no charm for her.

"Fanny, at least, will be safe from poverty," Lucy said. "Mr Hawes will offer for her at last, and will whisk her away to Kellingborough. But as for the rest of us… you still pine for your lost love, I am a widow at two and twenty, and Margaret is too shy even to look at a man. I do not know what is to become of us," she ended tearfully.

"Now, do not start crying again, dearest," Annabelle said. "Rosamund is a little… *sharp*, sometimes, but she is quite right — crying never made anything better. As to what is to become of us, we have only three choices… to find a husband, to live on the charity of our relations or to find employment. The first two do not appeal to me, so I shall find myself a post as a governess."

Lucy swung her legs round to plant them squarely on the floor. "No!" she cried, leaning forward in her anxiety. "You must not, Belle, truly you must not! The role of a governess is of all things the most disagreeable, neither family nor servant. I do not remember ours, but I know that the Claremonts' Miss Lackey ate all her meals in her room, like a leper. *Most* disagreeable."

Annabelle laughed. "That was because she was young and pretty and made sheep's eyes at John and Rupert… *and* at Mr Claremont, and so Mrs Claremont banished her, and she was too proud to eat with the servants. I should not be so proud, I assure you. No, it will suit me very well to be a governess, Lucy, so do not repine upon it."

~~~~~

For a fortnight, they continued almost as if nothing had happened. Callers came to offer their condolences, letter after letter arrived expressing sorrow to varying degrees, and the sisters sat in their
~~~~~

morning room each day sewing handkerchiefs and trimming bonnets almost as if their lives had not come unceremoniously to an end. Only the quantity of black crepe reminded them. But several times Mr Plumphett's gig creaked up the drive, and once the handsome tilbury of Mr Martin from Martin's Bank in Brinchester, and each visit reduced Annabelle's spirits a little more. There was no money in the bank, no investments secure in the three percents, there were debts everywhere, some astoundingly large, and half the tenant farms had been sold off. The remaining holdings were worth no more than two or three hundred pounds a year.

Something needed to be done. The sisters met in their father's book room, together with Robin and Rosamund, to discuss their plight.

"We cannot survive on so little money," Annabelle said, looking at the reckoning Robin had made of their financial situation. "It would be a good income if we had no other obligations, but these debts... Yet some need not be met? That seems unlucky for the debtee."

"Some debts are written off when the debtor dies," Robin said. "Some, however, are not and therein lies the problem. If you were to sell the house and remaining estate holdings, you might just clear all obligations of that nature. It would only be possible to stay on here on such a low income if one of you were to marry a man of substance."

Annabelle tried not to look at Fanny, but she herself spoke up. "I do not have any expectations from Mr Hawes, if that is what you were thinking," she said, her chin rising defiantly. "He has not come near me since Papa died, and I must presume that any... any *regard* he might once have felt towards me has been extinguished." Tears sparkled on her lashes, but she held her head high.

"You are very brave, dearest," Annabelle said, and Margaret hugged her sister fiercely.

"I fear you may be correct," Rosamund said gently. "Lord Westerlea met Mr Hawes a few days ago at a card party. He felt Mr Hawes was avoiding him, rather, but when he approached him directly, Mr Hawes asked very politely after Robin and Aunt Mary, but made no mention at all of you."

"Which gives me a very poor opinion of him," Robin said sharply. "That is not the behaviour of a gentleman."

"Oh, but I cannot blame him for withdrawing," Fanny said, two spots of colour in her cheeks. "I daresay he cannot afford to marry without a dowry, and after all, there was no engagement between us. He had never spoken. I do not blame him in the least."

"So, your hero is proved to be no more than a mortal man, swayed by money like every other," Rosamund said impatiently. "Annabelle, Lucy, do you have any rich, lovelorn swains hidden away?"

Annabelle smiled, but shook her head.

"If I had ever been the type to attract rich, lovelorn swains," Lucy said, "I should never have taken poor Walter. Who marries a man of almost four score years except in desperation?" But she smiled as she spoke. "Dear Walter! Such a sweet man. I shall never find another like him."

"Then it seems that Woodside must be sold," Robin said sadly. "If you will give me the authority, I will engage to find an agent to manage the sale, and will myself undertake to settle with the tradesmen and pay the servants here."

"You are too good, Robin," Lucy said. "I do not know what we should have done without you." The others murmured their agreement.

"It is unfortunate that I do not have access to the income that will be mine one day," he said. "I could then have—"

Annabelle reached across to squeeze his arm. "Even if you had, it would not be prudent. The income to support us in such a house is gone. It must be sold and that is an end to it. So we must look to what we shall do next. We have few relatives close enough for us to apply for aid, and none at all on Papa's side, but Mama's family has been helpful. Aunt Letty and Aunt Pru can offer a home to one of us. Aunt Letty has recently suffered some ill-health and is almost bed-bound, and Aunt Pru writes that they would welcome a companion who could provide some company so that Aunt Pru is not tied to the sick room. They live very secluded, so perhaps that would suit Margaret. Do you think you could manage that, dear?"

Margaret nodded, but her face was pale.

"Mama's only brother, Uncle Arthur, writes that he has twelve children now, poor man, so his house is quite full up. However, his sister-in-law is unwell and in need of someone to chaperon her two step-daughters about. He suggests that Lucy might be acceptable — a respectable young widow and so forth."

"Oh, yes!" Lucy said. "I should love to, although... I am in mourning. Would it be quite seemly? To attend balls?"

"Your mourning period for your husband has passed," Rosamund said. "For Papa, there is no reason not to go about after the first month or so. You will not dance, of course, but you may certainly act as chaperon. Do you not agree, Robin? I have seen widows even in deep mourning at entertainments in London, although nothing of a frivolous nature."

"Oh, certainly," Robin said. "For a husband, it could not be thought of, but for your father it is not necessary to keep secluded."

Lucy smiled happily. "Then I should be very glad to do it."

"Excellent," Annabelle. "So that leaves Fanny and me."

"As it happens, I might have some possibilities for you," Robin said, with just a hint of smugness. "Aunt Mary wrote to her friend Lady Harriet Hay, do you remember her? Lord Carrbridge's sister. Lady Harriet supports a charitable endeavour for women with no family to support them. They make fashionable gowns for ladies of lesser means, those not handy enough with a needle to make their own. She employs a number of women as seamstresses, and would like someone of a more elevated background to talk to the customers."

"It sounds charming," Rosamund added. "The mamas bring their daughters to buy something special for an important ball, or to be married in."

"Oh, how romantic!" Fanny breathed.

"And you are so nimble with a needle, too," Rosamund said. "It would suit you admirably."

"Well, then," Annabelle said, with a sudden tremor. "It remains only for me to seek a post as a governess." After all the discussion and wondering and hoping and fearing, finally her family would be split asunder.

"Are you quite determined on such a course, sister?" Rosamund said. "I cannot bear to think of you in such a position. Governesses are hated by everyone — their employers, their charges, the servants. It will be miserable for you."

Annabelle was so tempted to answer with the stark truth. *I am miserable everywhere, so it hardly matters.* Instead, she said firmly, "My mind is made up, and I am well suited for the role, you must admit."

"Indeed, but... Well, no matter. If it does not work out, you may return to us and we will find room for you. For any of you, if you find your posts uncongenial. But if you are set on this, Annabelle, then there is a possibility. I asked Lady Carrbridge if she could help. Do you remember her? You will have met her in town."

"I remember her," Annabelle said. "I doubt she remembers me."

"Well, she meets a great many people, it is true. Here, read her letter."

She passed across a sheet of paper covered in neat script. After the usual salutations, Annabelle read, *'There is an old friend of Lord Carrbridge's who might be in need of a governess. His wife died last year, leaving him with three young daughters to raise. The poor man is distraught and hardly knows what he is about, so he has not yet thought what he should do for them. Lord C has written to enquire of him if he would like a recommendation for a governess, but we have not yet heard from him. I will let you know if we hear word from him. In the meantime, do tell me a little more about your sister, so that I may know how best to describe her accomplishments. Constance Carrbridge.'*

"This came just today," Robin said, holding out another sheet.

'So happy to tell you that Allan would be delighted to offer Miss W a post as governess. It had been on his mind that he should do something about the matter, but had not the least idea how to go about it. If she is all that you say, I am sure she will do very well there. His mother is in residence, so there will be not the least impropriety. He lives at Charslby, near Kenford in Cheshire, and is a very pleasant, amiable man. All the Skeltons are charming. I know his sisters quite well, and they are delightful. I am sure Miss W will be very happy there. Constance Carrbridge.'

Happy. Annabelle could not imagine being happy ever again, but she was content to be unhappy at Charlsby. Robin wrote to accept Mr Skelton's offer, and to Charlsby she was to go to begin her life as a governess.

END OF SAMPLE CHAPTER OF *The Governess*

Printed in Great Britain
by Amazon

66148147R00213